Lana Eklund

Kira Salak has won the PEN Award for journalism and appeared five times in *Best American Travel Writing*. She is a contributing editor for *National Geographic Adventure* magazine and was the first woman to traverse Papua New Guinea. Her nonfiction account of that trip, *Four Corners*, was a *New York Times* Notable Travel Book of 2001. Her fiction has appeared in *Best New American Voices* and other publications. *The White Mary* is her first novel. She lives in Montana.

www.kirasalak.com

The

WHITE
MARY

The

WHITE
MARY

A NOVEL

KIRA SALAK

PICADOR

———

HENRY HOLT AND COMPANY
NEW YORK

In loving memory of
Marc Salak
1969–2005
(remember to wait for me)

www.picadorusa.com

Picador® is a U.S. registered trademark and is used by
Henry Holt and Company under license from Pan Books Limited.

For information on Picador
Reading Group Guides, please contact Picador.
E-mail: readinggroupguides@picadorusa.com

Designed by Meryl Sussman Levavi

Library of Congress Cataloging-in-Publication Data

Salak, Kira, 1971–
The white Mary / Kira Salak.—1st Picador ed.
p. cm.
ISBN 978-0-312-42904-1
1. Women journalists—Fiction. 2. War correspondents—Fiction. 3. Missing
persons—Investigation—Fiction. 4. Jungle survival—Fiction. 5. Papua New
Guinea—Fiction. I. Title.
PS3619.A4255W48 2009
813'.6—dc22
2009017274

First published in the United States by Henry Holt and Company

First Picador Edition: September 2009

10 9 8 7 6 5 4 3 2 1

He who is near me is near the fire.

—Jesus, Gnostic gospels

Part One

MARIKA

The black waters of Elobi Creek show no sign of a current. It is another dead waterway, Marika tells herself, one that will breed only mosquitoes and crocodiles. Another waterway that somehow reflects—in the darkness of the water, in its stillness—all of her failings. These waters, this breathless heat, seem to be waiting for a response from her, a call to action. But she has no answers. And if she's to be honest with herself, she never had any. Things will unravel. They will fall apart.

If she is to be honest with herself—and the pain from self-honesty, but the duty of it, too—she must admit that this time she seems to have started something that is beyond her ability to stop. It is as if the dominoes of her life have begun to fall, and she can only watch each moment disappearing in the futile fractions of a second. She is still looking for her ghost. Nearly three months spent in Papua New Guinea, and no sign of him. Does Robert Lewis know she has given up everything to find him? More to the point, would he care? She ought to go home. Go back. Call this for what it is: a failure.

Beauty intrudes upon her. Flocks of red and green parrots. Butterflies of blue and gold dancing over the black waters. Crowned pigeons with their regal headdresses of gray plumage. She would like to *know* this beauty, not just see it. In the same way, walking down a city street, she might gaze at the featureless crowds and catch sight of a face that awakens something vital in her. A longing, perhaps. A burst of compassion. She looks at the thick, ripe jungle around her: squat sago palms nesting beside the riverbanks; ancient trees rising toward darkening clouds. It should not be so hard, she tells herself, to know this beauty.

Thomas, the lanky young man driving their dugout canoe, stops the outboard motor. The intense heat never seems to bother him, his green T-shirt saturated, his exposed black skin glistening from sweat. He picks up his bow and a bamboo arrow ending in four prongs, and aims at a crowned pigeon. Releasing the arrow, he watches it cascade into the rain forest, just missing the bird. As the pigeon flees for the sky, Thomas speaks sharply in a tribal language, putting down the bow and starting up the outboard motor. The jungle didn't seem to notice. The butterflies continue whirling. The parrots chatter. A white cockatoo .fluffs out its feathers and relaxes them. As the sun disappears behind a large gray cloud, Marika yanks down her hat's brim, staring into the tangled greenery around her. She wants a sign. She would like to know that all the events of her life have conspired to bring her to this exact instant in time, with nothing—none of it—being a mistake.

But this world of Papua New Guinea won't tell her anything. It will just burn her white skin a deeper red. It will suck all the remaining moisture from her, stinging her, biting her, keeping her from sound sleep. The jungle rises thick on either side of the narrowing waterway, interconnecting overhead as if she were entering the bowels of a giant green serpent. Miraculously—or so it seems to her—she actually arrives somewhere at the end of each day, alive.

And closer, she hopes, to Robert Lewis.

The sun becomes shrouded by gray clouds. Their canoe passes some reeds, and the screeches of grasshoppers ring in Marika's ears. She sits with her hips wedged between the narrow sides of the vessel, her feet resting in an inch of muddy water in the bottom of the hull. Her toes show the last traces of red nail polish she applied months ago, back when she still lived with Seb.

During her worst, most unattractive times, she often imagines he can see her—like when she's squatting on muddy riverbanks brushing her teeth, or smearing bloody mosquitoes from her face. What would he think of her now? Her skin sunburned and sweat soaked, her nose peeling, her T-shirt filthy and torn. Surely his worst suspicions about this trip would be confirmed.

Marika pulls her hat's brim even lower. Rain falls, the heavy, cold drops shocking her skin. But rain is always welcome over sunlight, allowing her the rare chance to cool off. She never stops sweating otherwise, not even during the night. This world is sticky and sultry without respite.

Thomas stands behind her, manning the outboard of the canoe. The prow of the boat is carved in the shape of a crocodile head, and Marika likes to imagine him riding the very creature of creation. The locals believe that the earth was once completely covered with water. Then in boredom, or perhaps arrogance, a giant crocodile dived down to the bottom of the sea and returned with mud on its back—thus the world was formed. As Creator, the crocodile is the most feared animal in these parts. It is the king of the gods in a land where locals believe that every plant and animal, every stream and stone, contains spirits requiring near-constant propitiation. Even the missionaries' religions compete with the crocodile. Once, when beginning her search for Lewis, Marika saw a carving in a spirit house of Jesus himself riding on a crocodile's back.

"Missus," Thomas says. The canoe stops moving and butts against reeds. She looks back, seeing him pointing to a narrow corridor between a cluster of mangroves. "Tobo," he says.

"How far to his village?" she asks.

"Not far."

But Thomas doesn't move. A hornbill with a giant yellow beak flies above the jungle canopy, its wings making a sound like an approaching chopper. Marika knows choppers don't come this far into the jungle, though. Virtually nothing does. The malarial swamps plague any attempts at civilization. Mostly hunters pass through, their crude lean-tos appearing beside the creek every few miles. The more deadly it is for humans, the more rich the game. Wild pigs. Giant cassowary birds. The docile, helpless cuscus, a marsupial that can be plucked from the trees. To live out here, you'd have to be half crazy. Which is why she thinks she can find Lewis in such a place.

Thomas doesn't want to continue. He complains about what she paid him. Three hundred dollars isn't enough. He wants three hundred more. They're going to see Tobo, after all, and Tobo can use sorcery to curse him. He doesn't think the white woman knows the danger they could be in. Probably, they've already passed through several areas that Tobo has bewitched. Thomas touches the cross around his neck, wondering, as he has for many years, just how powerful the Jesus spirit is. The missionaries told him that Jesus is a king, a *bigman* among all big men, but Thomas has long had his doubts.

"Four hundred *kina*, Missus," he says. "I will take you there for four hundred more."

Once they'd left the outpost on the Sepik River for the interior, floating through the empty expanses of jungle, Marika expected to be asked for more money. It has happened to her all over the world. Thomas, missionary schooled and English speaking, understands this game and plays it well. She takes out the equivalent of two hundred dollars in *kina* bills. She puts it in his palm and turns back around.

"*Four* hundred, Missus," he says.

She just studies the chipped nail polish on her toes. The sun, catching a break between clouds, momentarily lights up a patch of black water beside her. Thomas has noticed that this white woman doesn't talk very much, and he assumes it's because she's angry with him. The white people always seem to be getting angry with him, though everyone knows that trip prices change.

Thomas sighs and yanks the outboard from the water, not wanting the blades to catch on any roots. Picking up his paddle, he propels the canoe through the narrow channel between the mangroves. The route hasn't been cut back recently, mangrove branches arcing before them. Marika constantly ducks to avoid being struck, while Thomas chops at the bushes with his machete, leaves and small branches raining upon her.

Hours pass in this way. To Marika, the mangroves seem never-ending. Thomas stops periodically to bail water from the canoe and to recaulk cracks in the hull with balls of river clay. Marika can see nothing but the maze of bushes around her and the dark, anvil-like clouds in the north, heralding rain. As the channel widens into a small lagoon, she sits up, squinting into the half-light of approaching dusk. She sees a tiny village opposite them. A few huts sit on the edge of the lagoon, a cooking fire blazing beneath one of them. Several upright tree trunks, painted red and cut to different heights, line the shore like totem poles. Each is carved in the shape of a creature—not human, but not quite animal—and decorated with large tufts of cassowary feathers.

"Tobo lives there," Thomas says, pointing at the huts. "That is Anasi village."

"What are those posts for?" she asks.

"Posts, Missus?"

"Those carvings?"

Thomas squints at them. "It's witchcraft," he says, dismissing them with a wave of his hand. "Tobo is not a Christian."

"But what are they *for*?" she asks again.

Thomas laughs at her ignorance. "They are protection from demons, Missus," he says.

Marika knows the Anasi witch doctor is famous for his "powers." According to several missionaries she talked to, he's in great demand in the villages of the Sepik River region. His "powers" don't interest her, though; rather, Tobo travels widely and is said to have visited many of the villages in the interior. If anyone would know about Robert Lewis, Tobo might, so she's spent the past two weeks trying to reach him. Two weeks of traveling waterways so low from drought that fallen trees and limbs littered the route for miles. She and Thomas have used up entire afternoons chopping through the branches or pulling the heavy dugout canoe over them. It was day after day of such tedious travel in the undying heat, cutting, portaging, paddling through swamps, only to return each night to her tent reeking heavily of mildew and sweat.

Being in Papua New Guinea for nearly three months has begun to take its toll on Marika. It's been three months of enduring extreme humidity and heat. Of being protein-deprived, eating the tasteless, starchy food that villagers survive on. During that time, she's been spreading word up and down the Sepik River that she wants news of a white man named Robert Lewis. But news—if there is any—comes slowly in PNG and can take months to arrive. There are no phones, nothing but word-of-mouth to travel the vast distances. Little information has come but for a few dubious reports of white men seen in different villages, all of whom turned out to be missionaries. Lewis, though, is far from being a missionary. And the person who wrote about Lewis being alive in PNG—an elderly American pastor named John Wade who'd lived on the Fly River—died nearly half a year ago. No one else in the missionary outposts knows anything further, and Marika contacted every one of those outposts.

Marika puts on her long-sleeved shirt and covers all exposed skin with repellent, as the mosquitoes will soon be out in droves. They aren't lethargic in PNG. They dive for her skin like kamikazes, biting the instant after landing. She hates nothing as much as the mosquitoes, which force her to wear pants and a long-sleeved shirt at dusk, though such covering makes the heat virtually unbearable. She has noticed that PNG requires constant surrender and submission, the entire country designed to humble— even humiliate—her.

She hears the dull beatings of a wooden *garamut* drum. Some men and old women leave their huts to stand onshore, peering at her and Thomas in the rising darkness. The women wear only woven bark skirts. Some of the men wear ratty shorts and have smears of ochre paint on their cheeks. Each holds a bow and backward-barbed arrows—the sort used for human warfare. The missionaries like to insist that the tribes have all been tamed by Christianity, that cannibalism has ended, but Marika doesn't believe it. In a small, out-of-the-way village, she's glimpsed smoky skulls lying beside spirit effigies.

Marika doesn't expect the men to shoot their arrows. Her arrival, a blond-haired white woman in a dugout canoe, is surely more bizarre than threatening. The old women—clutching staffs, their breasts hanging flat against their chests—are an astounding sight; people in these parts almost never live past forty. Younger women crouch behind a nearby hut, watching her arrival with terrified eyes. Thomas stops paddling just before shore, and he speaks sharply to the Anasi men in Pidgin. She's learned enough of the language by now to understand that he's telling them that a *wait meri,* literally a "white mary," a white woman, is here to see Tobo. The men lower their bows. A boy runs into a nearby hut, and after a few minutes a new man emerges.

Marika sees his eyes first, which remain wholly fixed on her. She knows from his fierce presence that he must be Tobo, the famous witch doctor, long before Thomas confirms it. The man is covered in red ochre, his face painted to look like a skull, his white eyes glowing in the dusk light. Around his neck rests a half moon *kina* shell, the mother-of-pearl gleaming in the departing light. Large hoop earrings made from cassowary quills hang from his distended earlobes and graze the tops of his shoulders, a single bird claw jutting from a hole in each nostril. He wears a breechclout of long, rubbery *tanket* leaves, which swishes as he walks on flat, heavily calloused feet. Tobo strides to shore, an arresting certitude in each step, and stands there silently, arms crossed. He looks intently at Marika, as if expecting her.

Thomas refuses to paddle closer.

"Thomas," Marika says impatiently, "take me to shore."

"Tobo has great powers," he warns.

"You told me that already, back in Ambunti."

"Yes, I know. But . . ." He fingers the cross around his neck, noticing that Tobo is now grinning and mimicking him. "*Eh!* Look at him!"

"Just take me to shore," Marika says. "Let's go."

Thomas sighs and makes a quick sweep with the paddle. The canoe shoots forward, the carved crocodile head ramming against the muddy bank. Marika rises and tries to balance herself in the unwieldy craft. She carefully tosses her backpack onto the ground. Getting a foot anchored, she leaps to shore, Thomas following reluctantly. Tobo eyes her all the while. His stare reminds her of the look a priest gave her once, when she was visiting a cathedral in Peru. There is the same intense, dignified aloofness. The quiet piety. The red ochre skull painted on his face disconcerts her, but only mildly. She has met many "sorcerers" like him, mostly in West Africa, in places like Benin and Mali, and she doesn't really believe in what they do. Her interest in animism has been mostly sentimental. She finds it colorful, titillating.

Compared to someone like Tobo, Marika imagines herself as hopelessly ordinary. No distinguishing features but for her job, which brings—or, at any rate, *brought*—her speaking gigs of all sorts around the United States, usually at journalism schools. After her series of magazine cover stories came out on the civil war in Liberia, winning several prestigious awards, she acquired a surprising amount of media attention and, more to her discomfort, fame. Hers was often the only name that came to mind when people thought of female war reporters. She'd been everywhere the boys had been, and then some. The usual dangerous places—the Somalias and Bosnias—but some uniquely awful places, too. Sierra Leone. Angola. Chechnya.

Women, Marika has come to understand, still aren't supposed to wander alone in places like Liberia or Papua New Guinea—though doing so feels no more extraordinary to her than what an auto mechanic or an accountant does. It's what she does because she's competent at it. She has an unusually high threshold for fear. She's willing and able to travel to uncomfortable, inhospitable places to get her stories. In her view, it's the only thing she's ever been good at: facing the unpleasant.

As she stands on the mud bank of another forgotten corner of the world, Tobo stares at her with his oddly priestlike eyes, ready to condemn and absolve her in the same moment. Marika bows to him—a habit she picked up in the Far East and never got rid of—and hoists her backpack to one shoulder. Should she shake his hand? How does one greet witch doctors in this newest corner of the world?

Tobo considers the white mary. He can easily read a person's energy, and hers is unusual and complex. This one, he feels certain, has a relationship with darkness. In his opinion, most white people do. The whiter their skin, the more they seem to attract unwholesome spirits; they're like bright flames that attract moths during the night. But she's unique in that she has great will. She came here to see him, and that's no small feat. It is nearly two weeks by motorized boat to his village from the nearest settlement on the Sepik River, and at least three weeks by paddling. Only one other white person—the Jesus Man, John Wade—has ever come to his Anasi village to see him. She must have powerful light spirits assisting and guarding her.

Tobo wonders if she will bring trouble with her, as he already has enough of his own. He has never met a people who invite such trouble into their lives as the white people. There was Reverend Richard over on Green River, a Jesus Man whom he met years ago. The man had bright red hair and an even redder nose. Tobo visited him because he was told that the white man was a witch doctor like him, though a Christian one, and that he gave away things if you went to see him. It was true, too. Reverend Richard gave him a clock and taught him how to use it, though it stopped working a long time ago. Now, it is always 8:41. The gods choose to give the white men many fantastic things, though they do not seem better than Tobo's Anasi people. Reverend Richard did not have any powers that Tobo could detect, yet he was a rich man. He had a large house with a noisy machine that kept the rooms cold, and an object that took away his and his wife's *pispis* when they pushed a button. It wasn't fair that the gods gave such things only to the white men, so Tobo took some of the wife's American money and some of the reverend's socks from the clothesline, putting them into his *billum* bag as he left. He still has the objects, though they've been useless to him.

Marika holds out her hand. The Anasi witch doctor holds out his. They shake—to the horror of Thomas, who stands several feet away. Marika walks with Tobo toward his hut, noting that he seems cordial enough, skull face or no.

It is a disturbing feature of Papua New Guinea, she thinks, the way night falls so quickly, the way sunsets barely have time to declare their beauty. She smells the heavy wood smoke of cooking fires as she approaches Tobo's hut, which is raised high on stilts. Six pig carcasses, cut into quarters, hang from the support beams below, each section smoking over a separate fire. Drops of blood have left grotesque designs on the hard-packed earth. The pig heads are impaled on sticks decorated with palm leaves and spotted cuscus fur. A large wooden bowl holds the animals' blood, and Tobo casually dips his thumb into it, bringing his finger to his lips as if tasting cake batter.

Thomas gapes, his eyes wide and unblinking. "Tobo is preparing a payback," he tells Marika. He wonders if she knows the danger they're currently in. He is sure there are heavy spells all over Anasi village associated with the payback, and probably even Jesus can't help them here.

Marika glances at the pig heads on the sticks. She sees the animals' tongues hanging out the sides of their mouths, sees the dull, pasty look of eyes that have been stripped of life. It's gruesome, but she's witnessed worse. Like quartered human beings. People's heads on sticks.

"Payback," Tobo says to her, pointing around him and smiling cryptically.

Marika is intrigued by the idea of "payback." She knows it's the New Guinea way, and understands the custom as a way of undoing all the crimes, mistakes, accidents that life brings. In such a remote, traditional part of the country, she has yet to meet a person who doesn't believe that their troubles are caused by sorcery or by someone's "humbug" nature. In this sense, a person can always be found to blame for whatever happens, and justice achieved from a simple exchange of material goods—be it money or pigs. A payback is local and immediate, precluding distant rules or courts. But if a man refuses to make a payback, he will have to live by the feud, always in danger, along with family members or friends, of being attacked or killed. Marika knows that retaliation—usually violent—is a normal occurrence in these parts.

She figures Tobo did something egregious, to account for the large number of pigs killed for the payback exchange. His six slaughtered animals are surely worth a great deal.

"What has he done?" she asks Thomas.

He shrugs, fingering his cross. Turning to Tobo, he asks her question in Pidgin, the lingua franca from colonial days when the Australians needed a way of communicating with PNG's hundreds of tribes. Though Pidgin has become a language in its own right, with its own grammar and vocabulary, Marika has easily picked it up because of its similarity to English. Now she can understand some of what the Anasi man says. Something about killing a man.

"Missus," Thomas says, "it is very bad. Tobo is a humbug man, and he has caused many problems. It is very dangerous to be in this village with him."

Thomas explains that a young man from Baku, a village several days distant from Anasi, met up with the witch doctor while hunting. According to a witness, the Baku man accused Tobo of sickening his family's pigs and causing one to die. When Tobo denied doing this, the young man came after him with his machete; Tobo picked up his own knife in retaliation and killed the man. Tobo maintains that the death was an unfortunate accident—he had been defending himself. But accident or not, the man's family demanded a payback. That was a year ago, and as

Tobo still hasn't delivered any kind of compensation, several Baku men are threatening to come to Anasi village to kill him or a member of his family. Hoping to keep the peace, Tobo finally slaughtered six of his pigs to give the Baku men.

Tobo eyes Marika in silence. He sees that this news is disturbing the white woman. He feels her fear energy. He speaks to Thomas for a long moment.

"Tobo tells me," Thomas says, "that the dead man's heart was bad. It was his time to go. Tobo says he did nothing wrong, but he will offer the Baku people six pigs so they won't bother him anymore."

What Tobo didn't mention to Thomas was that the dead man's spirit had cursed him. It started with the death of his sister. She died from a snakebite beneath his hut, though he had never seen a snake there in his forty years of life. Such an unlikely death, one so close to his own home, was a sign. A warning. He hadn't delivered a payback, and the *dewel bilong man i dai*, the dead man's spirit, was coming to exact vengeance.

In Tobo's view, the dead man's spirit is unusually cruel. Knowing it isn't strong enough to harm Tobo directly, it instead goes after those related to him who are weakest. Three weeks after Tobo's sister died from snakebite, his young nephew caught a sickness that saw him vomiting and bleeding when he went *pekpek*. Tobo performed all the spells he knew, and made many difficult vows to the spirits in exchange for the boy's healing. In spite of this, the child lived for only three days, writhing in pain the whole time before finally dying in the night.

It was then that Tobo realized what he must do. He must gather what valuables he had—the pigs—and give them to the Baku tribe as payback. Hopefully, then, the dead man's spirit would release him from any further claims. After sending word to the Baku people to come collect the pigs, Tobo launched a three-day-long ceremony, entreating the man's spirit to release his family from further revenge. He can't say whether the man's spirit finds the payback agreeable, though. Every spirit is different. Many are cruel and spiteful and almost impossible to please.

Tobo dips his finger in the pigs' blood again and licks it. The flames of one of the cooking fires light up his eyes. He stares at the white woman, an enigmatic smile lingering on his lips.

"*Wanem nem bilong yu?*" he asks her in Pidgin. He wants to know her name.

"Marika Vecera," she says.

"*Ma-ree-ka Va-cha-ra,*" he repeats. He stares at her unabashedly. His fingertips run over the smooth edge of the bowl containing the pigs' blood. "Why do you come here, *Ma-ree-ka?*" he asks in Pidgin.

"I'm looking for someone," she says.

Mosquitoes hover around his face, but he doesn't seem to notice them. "*Mi save husat yu bin lukim*—I know who you're looking for," he says. "Rob-ur Lu-ees."

He runs the pig blood across his lips with a fingertip, flaring his nostrils. His dark eyes study her, his oily face paint shimmering in the firelight.

Marika feels a shot of excitement.

"Rob-ur Lu-ees," Tobo says again. "Yes?"

Marika pulls Thomas aside. "How does he know?"

"He knows everything," Thomas says. "That is why people come to him. The spirits tell him everything."

Marika sighs, frustrated. She was looking for a reasonable answer. "How do you know about Robert Lewis?" she asks Tobo in Pidgin.

"The people in Sumi village said you are looking for him," he replies.

Marika glares at Thomas. "Spirits didn't tell him anything."

"*Em i Amerikan,*" Tobo adds. "He is an American."

"Have you met Lewis?" she asks him.

"No," he says. "I never met him. But I heard about him. I know where he lives. By Walwasi Mountain."

"Lewis is *alive,* then?"

"Maybe he is alive. Maybe he is dead." Tobo shrugs. He could ask the spirits for more information, but he is tired, and he has other work to do tonight. His newest, youngest wife will not get large with child.

"Could I visit him?" the white mary asks him.

Tobo purses his lips. It was more than a year ago when he first heard about this man. He stares at one of the fires. When he sees Lewis in it, he looks back at Marika. He explains that Lewis—if he is still alive—lives in a village below Walwasi Mountain, far in the interior. It would take a long time to reach him. A very long time, as the distance can only be traveled on foot, through the jungle. Tobo leans closer to her. The mountains around Walwasi, he explains, are high and sharp like the teeth of a *masalai,* a demon, and Lewis lives right in the midst of them.

He forms his hands in the shape of jaws, clamping them together. Thomas takes a step back from him, doing a quick dance as he slaps mosquitoes on his arms and legs.

"He knows where Lewis is," Marika says to Thomas.

He shrugs, dancing from the mosquitoes. "I think he is telling lies to you."

"Rob-ur Lu-ees," Tobo says, looking at her. He pretends to push up a pair of glasses and to write on a piece of paper.

She realizes what he's doing. Tobo is imitating Lewis, who wore glasses, who was a journalist—a writer.

"*Yes?*" Tobo asks her, eyes gleaming.

She peers more closely at him, considering the unlikely possibility that this man knows more about Lewis than anyone else she's met so far.

"How do you know these things about Lewis?" she asks Tobo in rough Pidgin.

He tells her that, during his travels, he met a humbug man from the Solomon Islands, staying in Green River village. This man had a very nice object from the white men: you held it to your eyes, and it made faraway things come close to you. Tobo asked this young man how he came across such a prize, and he was told that a white man had given it to him for guiding him far into the jungle. The boy told Tobo about their trip: how he and a local tracker had been paid to take the white man to a very distant village. They traveled up Tumbi River, then entered the jungle. The white man had been a strange companion. He didn't like to talk much, and he didn't seem to listen when they spoke to him. He had a beard and wore eyeglasses, and was strong like no other white man the boy had seen—though he couldn't walk well, so they had to help him a lot. They traveled for a long way through the jungle, to a village below Walwasi Mountain, and the boy became a rich man after being paid for the trip.

Marika listens raptly to Tobo's Pidgin, followed by Thomas's English translation. She reaches into her daypack and pulls out a small pad, jotting down notes, transfixed to have heard the name Tumbi River. It is the *exact* river mentioned by the old missionary, John Wade, in his letter. And then there is Tobo's physical description of Lewis, which, though not specific, still matches—a lone, bearded man with glasses. It strikes her as uncanny.

"Do you know how to get to Walwasi—to that place where you think Lewis is?" Marika asks Tobo.

"Of course," he says. "I went near there once when I was a young man. But that was a long time ago."

"Can you take me there?" she asks him immediately.

The Anasi man laughs, and Thomas joins him.

"You are a white woman," Tobo says apologetically. "You cannot go to this place. You will die."

Without another word, Tobo walks over to the notched log ladder and climbs up to his hut. Marika puts her backpack on and follows. She will again ask the Anasi man if he will guide her. Or she will ask if there is someone else who can. She'll pay a lot of money. She'll pay nearly everything she has.

When she enters Tobo's hut followed closely by Thomas, the Anasi man is already sitting cross-legged in a corner, swaying back and forth, brushing away mosquitoes from his body with a boar's-hair whisk. He starts chanting the same phrase rapidly in a tribal language—a magical mantra, Marika supposes—in a sharp, high-pitched voice. Almost like a woman's voice. Marika looks around her. The hut is sparsely furnished. A few sleeping pallets of woven grass lie on the palm bark floorboards. The air is full of the thick gray smoke of burning coconut hulls, to keep the mosquitoes away. When Marika shines her flashlight on Tobo, she sees that he's sitting in front of an altar covered with several wooden figures and bowls of red bird-of-paradise feathers and yellow hornbill beaks. A young woman—probably a wife—approaches them and tells them where they can sleep, passing each of her guests a banana leaf holding balls of dusty white, sago palm pith. As Marika sits down and picks up one to eat, she notices that Thomas refuses to touch any.

"I can feel Tobo bewitching me," Thomas whispers to her. He scowls at the Anasi man at the far end of the room, absently slapping at a cockroach crawling over his foot.

Marika coughs from the thick smoke in the hut. She stands, removing her tent from her backpack and setting it up. Thomas follows suit, tying his own gauze mosquito net to the overhead rafters. Marika feels tired again. Profoundly tired, after the excitement of finally meeting someone who claims to know where Lewis is. Could it be true, that Lewis is actually alive? By asking herself this question, she becomes aware of all her hidden doubts. Doubts she didn't dare acknowledge until now.

Marika gets into her tent, which smells more strongly of mildew than ever before. Still, it's a luxury to be in a hut, beneath a roof that will keep out the rain. Not using a rain fly will mean a cooler night's sleep. She won't think about Lewis or the news she's gotten. She won't try to make sense of it yet. Tomorrow, she tells herself, she'll mobilize. She'll find a guide to take her to Lewis's village.

A rooster's piercing morning call startles Marika awake. Outside, she sees the first gray suggestion of dawn. Beside the bird's call, there is another sound. A louder sound. Groggy from sleep, she vaguely recognizes it as a kind of roaring. *Thomas. Their canoe. The outboard motor.*

Marika sits up, panicking, and fumbles for the zipper of her tent. Squeezing out, she runs for the doorway of the hut. On the far end of the lagoon, she sees Thomas's flashlight beam moving feverishly over the surface of the water.

The stars gaze fiercely down at Marika. She shines her own flashlight into the lingering night. As its beam hits the jungle, an animal's red eyes glare back at her.

It's too late. Thomas is gone. Marika knows she's stuck in Tobo's village.

She goes back inside her tent. It is that time of night, just before dawn, when the world seems to lie between birth and death, and she understands the magnitude of what she's done. She is in a hut in the middle of a New Guinea jungle, alone, at the mercy of a witch doctor, having already spent nearly three months searching futilely for a man who's supposed to be dead. Though Marika knows she should be concerned, she's convinced, on a certain deep level, that all setbacks are actually challenges. That the world is always trying to test her and send her home in defeat. She won't let it have that victory.

Tobo is up. As he lights a fire in the hut, she can hear his faint incantations.

Marika reminds herself that she could probably find someone in the village to return her to the Sepik River, if necessary. Once there, it would be relatively easy to find a canoe or a boat to take her to an outpost with an airstrip. She hasn't gone too far. She can still change her mind, turn back.

Sleep overpowers her. Tobo's fire flickers and fades. Marika lies down and stares at the thin walls of her tent. In her mind, she sees Seb again. His gentle brown eyes. His strong hand, reaching out, as it always did, to touch her cheek.

"I'm still going to look for Lewis," she tells him out loud. Like a warning.

She's certain she has gotten her first break, her first lead.

It is a strange curiosity about life, Marika has often mused, how, the moment she no longer looks for something, or wants it, it comes to her. Sebastian Gilman arrived in her life at a time when she didn't need a man or a relationship. She'd been having great success, had felt at the height of her career and powers, and wanted no one or nothing beyond that.

At least, that was what she told herself.

She wouldn't have predicted someone like Seb, either. To the casual observer, they seemed to have little in common. She spent her time reporting on the world's wars; he was busy getting a doctorate in psychology. When she first met him, Marika didn't even have much respect for psychology. She thought it smacked of self-indulgence, self-pity—which were like swear words in her own universe. Though she hadn't had anything close to an easy childhood, it'd always seemed the height of bad taste to mention that to people. And anyway, she'd dealt with it, gotten past it, made something of her life despite the odds against her. Now, as a successful adult, she categorically refused to dwell on what was behind her.

Seb's overly romantic, earnest nature would make up for what Marika lacked in awe or melodrama. He believed in universal infallibility: everything happened for a reason. When he saw her for the first time, giving a lecture at Boston University's School of Journalism, he knew he was meant to meet her. He would even tell her later that he'd felt completely "drawn" to her.

Seb came into Marika's life at a time when she'd landed a record number of cover stories for the *New York Herald Magazine*. She'd been invited to BU's journalism school to give a talk about her magazine work, and Seb had come early to get a front-row seat. One of his clinical focuses was trauma studies. For his dissertation, he'd been researching the effects of post-traumatic stress disorder on prison guards and police officers, and he was curious how PTSD applied to other, similarly dangerous professions like Marika's.

It was the first lecture he'd seen by a woman journalist. Already, he'd attended several presentations by male war reporters, fascinated by how they formed identities around risk taking and near-death escapes. Unlike combat soldiers, these journalists had jobs that required them to watch—or, sometimes, morally deconstruct—the violence they saw, while forbidden to interfere. By all accounts, it was disturbing, dangerous work; most had colleagues who had been injured or killed. Yet, they kept going back for more, ignoring all natural impulses for self-preservation. At many of their lectures, Seb had been the only person in the audience to ask about motivation. What was the attraction of their job? How were they able to keep doing it, given the risks? Their answers tended to sound canned: they spoke of "a duty to tell people's stories," of the "importance of being the world's witness." Their explanations wouldn't get personal, though, perhaps because they regarded introspection as a sign of weakness.

On that day when Marika was giving her talk, she'd often noticed Seb sitting in the front row, listening intently. He had dark, sincere-looking eyes. His brown hair was swept back, gray coloring his temples. He appeared to be in his early to midforties, and she assumed he was a journalism professor. Or a journalist himself, though she didn't recognize him. He wore an expensive black suit, a folded wool overcoat and leather briefcase on the floor before him. To Marika, he looked unusually professional. Bookish. Intellectual. But most of all, safe.

She'd been discussing one of her latest magazine stories dealing with northern Uganda's Lord's Resistance Army, a rebel group which kidnapped children, forcing them to become sex slaves or soldiers, and to commit atrocities against the local population. After reading from her article, she took questions from the audience. People wanted to know more about what was being done to stop the conflict, or how the U.S. government or the United Nations might help. Audience members began to debate each other about the proper role of U.S. foreign policy, and Marika listened in silence. Seb stayed out of it, too. In his view, most people seemed unable to discuss politics without falling into anger and self-righteousness. And then they got ugly. Above all else, Seb didn't like to see people getting ugly.

At last, bored by the verbal sparring, he raised his hand. Marika called on him immediately.

"What's your next project?" he asked her pleasantly, with his strong Boston accent.

"I plan to go to the former Zaire," she said. "They call it Congo now."

"What will you do there?"

"I want to cover the genocide in the east."

"It sounds dangerous," he said.

"Maybe."

He leaned forward and looked straight at her. "Do you ever worry about dying?" he asked.

She considered his artless expression before answering. "I wouldn't say I 'worry' about it. I mean, I know it could happen at any time. I don't have an illusion that I'm immune to it or anything. But I don't let it bother me. If I die, I die. Everyone's going to die sometime."

Just then, someone broke in: "Don't you think it's selfish, risking your life when you do these trips?"

Everyone turned to look at the speaker, an old man sitting in the back of the room.

"How is it selfish?" Marika asked him.

"It's selfish to your family, for one thing."

"I don't have a family," she said.

"I just think it's extremely selfish to go risking your life, without caring how it would affect anyone if you died."

"Would *you* care if I died?" Laughs erupted from the audience, but Marika looked completely serious. She leveled her eyes on the man.

"Well, I can tell you, God would care."

Marika shrugged. "When he starts to care," she said, "let me know. I'll want the scoop."

There were guffaws and exclamations from the audience. Seb sat back, grinning and studying her with even greater interest.

The man might have saved himself the embarrassment. Marika strongly believed in her job, and she didn't devote much care to what other people thought of her. She kept her skin thick by directing her focus outward, on the world. She would do her job, and do it with as much integrity as she could, and none of the rest mattered. While growing up in Communist Czechoslovakia, in Prague, she'd had a schoolteacher who loved using the Russian idiom *A kak vcegda*. As always; so it goes. It had become Marika's response to just about everything in life. *A kak vcegda*. She was not one to give away her power.

The audience waited in awkward silence, until a man raised his hand with a new question: "What's been your scariest experience?"

Marika got this question nearly every time she gave a lecture, but she never found it easy to answer. How could she rate her frightening experiences, anyway? As the bloodiest? The luckiest? Yes, it was true: many times, she'd come close to getting killed; many times, she'd been fortunate to make it home alive.

She'd finally chosen one experience as her official Scariest Moment and stuck to it at every lecture.

"Liberia was really bad," she told the man. "I was there, off and on, for two years, covering the war."

"What happened?" he asked.

She had her short answer ready: "I was caught in a village that was attacked by rebel soldiers. I had to flee for my life—they were killing everyone on sight—and I almost didn't escape. Let's just say I'm lucky to be alive."

Seb recalled her article about the massacre. It'd been a hard story to read. She had described, in unflinching detail, the slaughter going on around her. He could easily surmise how close she'd come to death.

Marika immediately took the next question, from a young female student: "Do you find it hard to be a woman and do what you do?"

Here was another question that she got, in one form or another, at every lecture. She gave the usual answer, which she'd repeated so many times that it probably sounded rote. No, she didn't find it hard to be a woman and do her job. In fact, sometimes it worked to her advantage. Men in foreign cultures might not expect much out of women; or, conversely, they might go out of their way to assist and protect her. In particular, male officials tended not to see her as a threat.

But the truth—if Marika had been in the mood to reveal it—was that she paid no attention to her gender, whatsoever, and was always fascinated when other people did.

The rest of the question period ran without incident. Marika lingered after the presentation ended, speaking to a crowd of journalism students, and—though it embarrassed her—autographing copies of her magazine articles. When everyone left, and she was heading toward the door, Seb approached her.

"Ms. Vecera . . . ," he said.

She would always remember that greeting for its unusual politeness.

"Yeah?" She looked at him.

Up close, Seb saw that she had dark blue eyes and a somewhat guarded expression. The blatant femininity of her appearance pleasantly surprised him: the knee-length skirt and tight blouse, buttoned down just enough to offer occasional glimpses of cleavage. She had long, strawberry blond hair, a shapely figure, and, above all else, an arresting face. He searched for the right adjective for her expression: *dignified, regal, self-assured. Strength and beauty*, he thought. It was not the kind of obvious beauty that one saw in fashion magazines or on movie stars. Marika's beauty was subtle and paradoxical, a combination of the sharp, strong lines of her Slavic cheekbones and the well-concealed vulnerability in her dark eyes. Like the sole chink in an otherwise impenetrable coat of armor, her eyes seemed to speak of barely suppressed pain or longing. Whatever it was, Seb was riveted. He wanted to know much more than she'd been willing to tell the crowd.

"That was an interesting Q and A," he said to her. "That one man who called you 'selfish'—he was getting pretty worked up."

Marika shrugged and smiled. "Never a dull moment."

"I'm Sebastian Gilman—Seb." They shook hands. "I've been reading your stuff for years, and I'm a big fan. I'm always on the lookout for your articles."

"Thanks." She remembered Seb from the front row, remembered his peaceful presence and the personal nature of his questions.

He ran a hand quickly through his dark brown hair. "I know this is probably a long shot, but I'd love to take you out to dinner and hear more about your experiences. I'm really fascinated by what you do."

"You're a journalist?"

"No. Actually, I'm a doctoral student in psychology."

"Oh."

She didn't usually accept such invitations; they just came too frequently. She'd have spent half her life going out to eat if she hadn't started saying no. As it was, people only tended to approach her when they wanted something from her. A job. A contact or recommendation. An evaluation of their writing.

(She'd been handed entire book manuscripts.) It was a relief to finally meet someone who wasn't in her line of work, who didn't seem to have any hidden, self-serving agenda other than sincere interest in getting to know her as a person. It was refreshing.

There was something comforting about Seb, too. In part, it had to do with his self-assured stride as he'd walked toward her, as if nothing could topple his confidence. And during her presentation, she'd found herself repeatedly seeking out his supportive stare. Even now, whenever her eyes found his, she was drawn to his kind smile, rapt expression, interest.

"So when you go to journalism lectures," she said to him, "do you always ask the speakers out to dinner?"

A grin erupted on his face. "Actually, you're the first person I've ever asked. I'll be direct with you. I find you a very smart, attractive woman. And obviously, you're really accomplished. I couldn't pass up the opportunity."

She blushed. "Well, you're blunt."

"I always have been. Life's too short for bullshit." He stared frankly at her. "So do you ever go out to dinner with complete strangers?"

"Not usually."

"Could I persuade you to make an exception tonight? I know a really excellent restaurant, and of course it'd be my treat. How long will you be in Boston?"

"I live in Boston," she said.

He laughed. "That makes it easier."

She glanced behind her. "I have to go out with some j-school professors and their students tonight."

"How about tomorrow night?"

She gazed into his eyes. Saw the sincerity and attraction. "Okay," she heard herself say.

"Great."

But she agreed to meet him in a café instead; it would be easier to extract herself from the situation, if necessary. They chose a place and time. When Seb passed her his card, she considered giving him her own number and decided against it. She didn't know anything about him. It was too soon. She shook his hand again—he had a strong, firm handshake—and felt his fingers lingering in hers. Her body shivered.

Slipping on his overcoat, Sebastian Gilman gave her another of his generous smiles and left.

Later, Marika would have trouble explaining just what had struck her about Seb on that night they met at the café. She'd taken the subway to Harvard Square in Cambridge, was climbing the steps from the station, when she saw Seb rising from a nearby bench and waving at her. She'd stopped. Stared at him. There was something more than the look in his eyes in that instant—the welcoming joy in them. Something more than the way he confidently walked toward her. Seb offered an all-consuming peace that gave Marika a sudden, uncanny feeling of homecoming. She had never believed in love at first sight—and she definitely didn't entertain it then—but still, when she looked at Seb it was with an odd feeling of recognition, as if she already knew him. Or should have.

This was Seb. Somehow. She could believe their meeting was no accident, which thrilled her with the possibilities. She had longings within her that, though carefully concealed, nonetheless ran deep, and she wasn't such a cynic that she would deny them utterly. The longings told her that, in Seb, there was a chance for—and dare she even say the word, dare she even speak with such flagrantly romantic lack of inhibition—*rapture.*

Seb walked her to the café, opening the door to let her inside. He took off her coat, guided her to their table, pulled out her chair, and sat down only once she had. Marika found his chivalrous manners pleasantly novel; her male journalist friends had long forgotten or rejected the art.

Seb ordered them a pot of green tea to start, and he sat back to gaze warmly at her. He noticed everything about her. Her low-cut black top and jeans. Her reddish blond hair curled about her shoulders. The beauty of her face, hidden behind nervous smiles. When Marika forgot herself, relaxing into each moment, those awkward smiles would suddenly transform, brightening her whole face. And then she was something else entirely—a real knockout—though Seb was sure she had no idea. Most people, he'd discovered, hadn't even begun to suspect their real beauty. But Seb showed respect to others by truly seeing them. People's subtle qualities of character impressed themselves upon his intellect like notes in a symphony. He wanted to know everyone's music. Hear each poignant beat.

Intense, Marika would remark to herself about Seb almost immediately—an adjective she'd never stop applying to him. She would later learn that he didn't see the world in the same way as most; which is to say, he saw far too much of it. Everywhere, people's joys and woundings gaped at him, and he could barely contain his awe before the offerings of humanity.

"Thanks for meeting me," he said to Marika, touching her hand across the table.

She gave him a wary smile and fiddled with her napkin, her eyes finally meeting his. Shrewd eyes, Seb noticed, that would see everything about him. That could match him.

"No problem," she said.

It had been a long time since Marika last dated. She'd done three magazine stories back-to-back—first in Rwanda, then in Iran and Sri Lanka—and she'd barely had time to look at a man for the past year and a half. (Unless Max Sanders counted. But Sanders wasn't the same thing. Sanders was *never* the same thing.) It felt good to be in an attractive man's gaze again.

"So did I underdress?" she asked Seb teasingly, noticing his dark gray suit and expensive, blue silk shirt. Designed-to-impress clothes—he might have just gotten out of a job interview—but overkill for a Harvard Square café.

"I had to moderate," he explained, grinning and running his hand through his hair. "Our department had a symposium."

"What about?"

"Psychopharmacology."

"Oh." She shook her head, uncomprehending.

Seb smiled. "I wouldn't want to bore you with the details. And believe me, they *would* bore you." He loosened his tie and pulled it off. Undoing the top buttons of his shirt, he sat back, sighing. "It's been one of those days. All I wanted to do was finally see you again."

She crossed her legs, studying him: the ease with which he looked at her, his undeniable good looks, his strong hands resting on the tabletop.

Seb reached into his briefcase and pulled out a magazine— one that contained her most recent piece about Iran, just arrived on newsstands.

"I loved your article," he said, slapping the magazine on the table. "Just loved it."

She blushed. "Thanks."

"Sounds like you had a few run-ins with the secret police, huh?"

"Just a few."

"More like some major run-ins."

"Well," she said, "fortunately, I made it to Saudi Arabia."

He wanted to hear more, so Marika told him about it. She'd been doing a story on Afghani opium running along Iran's far eastern border, and had chartered a small plane to fly her over the desert, when the Iranian secret police made up their minds she was an American spy. Marika, learning from her translator that they were on their way to arrest her, left her bags behind in the hotel and fled to the Tehran airport, just catching the next flight to Riyadh. Had she not escaped, it would have surely been a very serious, very awful situation—one well beyond the scope of her imagination.

Once Marika got home safely from trips like that, once her articles finally came out months later, her greatest nightmares often took on morbid humor—became tales of cop-and-robber games in which no one ever got caught or hurt. It was how she coped with what happened to her, how she adjusted to the excruciating what-ifs: by presenting it as comical.

Seb, riveted by what she'd just told him, had completely neglected his cup of tea and was leaning toward her across the table. While Marika saw his interest, and appreciated it, all she'd done was relate a fairly typical work experience: being called a spy, entanglements with local police, fleeing a country. None of it would have impressed her journalist colleagues beyond a few raucous laughs.

"Have you always done foreign reporting?" Seb asked her.

"Yeah. Since I was twenty. I'd fund my own trips and bring back stories, trying to sell them to magazines. It took me years to break in, though."

"You mean you'd go off to war zones by yourself?"

"Yeah. There'd be problems in Angola or some other place, and I'd go there."

"By *yourself*?"

She saw his disbelief and laughed. "I needed to prove myself. How else was I going to do it? I was this young writer and a woman. Nobody knew who the hell I was. Nobody cared. In my business, you've got writers falling from the trees. No magazine editors are going to send you somewhere if they've never heard of you. When I was an undergrad, I'd work extra jobs to save up money; then, in the summer, I'd go to central Africa or someplace like that to get article experiences."

"You didn't want to do something safe back home, huh?"

"No." She smiled. "I always wanted to be like Robert Lewis."

"The journalist?" Seb asked.

She nodded. But to Marika, Lewis was far more than a journalist. He was probably the most famous writer and foreign correspondent of his generation. Winner of the Pulitzer Prize in journalism. Author of *Cold Summer*—a masterpiece and international best seller—about the war in the former Yugoslavia.

Perhaps more important, though, he was someone who had devoted his life to relating the plights of those suffering most in the world.

"I once saw Lewis being interviewed on TV," Seb said. "I remember him saying that he didn't listen to anyone—that it was the secret of his success. My ex-girlfriend heard that and thought he sounded completely arrogant."

Marika laughed. That was Lewis. Classic Lewis. Irreverent. Destined to offend.

"Have you ever met him?" Seb asked.

"Nearly. He was about ten rows away from me at a Rachmaninoff concert in New York."

"I figured you would have known him personally, given your line of work."

"No. Actually, he's pretty reclusive. He doesn't even give interviews anymore."

Seb poured some tea into her cup, handing it to her. They glanced at the snack menu, ordering breadsticks.

Marika glanced at the gray hairs over Seb's temples.

"How old are you?" she asked him bluntly.

"Forty-four."

"You ever been married?"

He smiled and put down his cup of tea. "Actually, I was engaged a year ago."

"How close did you get to the wedding?"

"We were six months away," he said, "but then we realized we weren't compatible and broke everything off."

"Did you break it off, or did she?"

Seb seemed delighted by the frankness of her question. "She broke it off. She was cheating on me."

"Ouch."

"Yeah. Just last month she married the other guy." He leaned back in his seat, his smile lingering. "How about you, Marika? What's your story?"

"There isn't one at the moment. I travel a lot, so it's been hard for me to meet men." She wondered if it sounded like an excuse.

"Well, you're still young," Seb said. "How old are you? Thirty?"

"Thirty-two."

What Marika didn't tell Seb was that, in addition to meeting few men willing to put up with her long absences and dangerous assignments, she'd never been the kind of person to enter into a second-rate relationship out of need. Her independence meant too much to her. It was the source of her pride and strength. She told herself that she didn't *need* a man in her life, though she might want one. She didn't *need* a love relationship in her life, though she might desire it. For many years, she only took lovers, avoiding the problem (for to Marika, it was a problem) of getting too attached to someone in a relationship. Of liking someone too much.

Someone like Seb, for example. His very presence, his attractiveness, made her feel oddly out of control, as if she'd drunk too much and couldn't trust herself to behave properly. It unsettled her.

Thankfully, though, Seb changed the subject, asking her questions about how she'd gotten into her line of work. Marika gave him the abbreviated version: how, seven years earlier, when she was going to graduate school in journalism at Northwestern, a magazine editor found her essay in a "slush pile" of unsolicited manuscripts and called her, saying he wanted to publish it. For Marika, it had been a terrifying moment of destiny at work. Overnight, her life had changed completely. The magazine sent her on assignments around the world, and soon she broke into other, more celebrated magazines, winning the confidence of important editors and making scores of contacts. In a matter of a few years, she'd gone from wannabe obscurity to the height of a demanding career. It'd been dizzying and exciting—and exhausting. As millions of people were now reading what she wrote, and as she believed she could make a positive difference in the world, dedication and impeccability meant everything. She'd never had to work harder in her life, nor, ironically, prove herself more.

"Is there a lot of competition in your business?" Seb asked her.

Marika picked up one of their newly arrived breadsticks, wondering how to answer; she didn't want to sound cynical. "There can be," she admitted. "In the beginning, when I was just starting out, I kept noticing all the backstabbing and jealousy. There'd be people who seemed to be praying for everyone else to fail."

"There's a word in Sanskrit," Seb said. "*Mudita*. There's no equivalent word in English, but basically it means, 'sincere rejoicing for another's good fortune and success.'"

Marika gazed at him.

"Buddhists consider *mudita* a 'God-like' state." Seb was staring intensely at her now, and he spread his arms out across the table. "It's supposed to be the single hardest thing for a person to feel for another. Even harder than feeling compassion for an enemy."

"Really?" Marika laughed, intrigued.

"Whenever I can," Seb said, "I practice *mudita*. I do it for everyone. For people I know, for complete strangers. And you know what I've found?"

She shook her head.

"When I'm feeling sincerely glad for others, I'm also feeling it for myself. It comes right back."

Marika had heard how passionate his voice had gotten, saw how intently he was looking at her now. It occurred to her that this *mudita* might be the ineffable quality she'd felt from Seb from the very beginning—the overwhelming sense that he'd sincerely wished her well. That he wished *everyone* well.

Seb was so different from most of her dates. With those other men, the conversations almost never rose above uninspired small talk, but Seb didn't seem to say anything unless it truly mattered to him. And he seemed to ask the same from whomever he was with—that they be authentic with him, show a glimpse of their souls.

"So did you always want to be a psychologist?" Marika asked, even more curious about him.

"No." He poured them both some tea. "It took me thirty-five years before I finally figured out what I wanted to do with my life."

"That seems pretty common. I know so many people who change careers around that age."

Seb laughed. "Well, in my case there wasn't a career to change. There was no career whatsoever."

"Oh?"

"You could say I had a lot of motivation problems when I was younger. I had some *serious* motivation problems." He took a playful sip from his tea, pretending it was a cocktail. "My parents didn't know what they were going to do with me. They were at their wit's end. Everyone was. But then—and I thank God Almighty—I did a complete one-eighty. I turned my life around."

"What happened?"

He grinned at her and cleared his throat. "Rehab happened."

"For alcoholism?"

He nodded. "And for blow. For cocaine."

"Oh."

"I really got a lot of bang for my buck at rehab. I haven't had a drink for ten years, six months, and . . . eighteen days."

Marika didn't know what to say.

Seb stared candidly at her. "Do you find it shocking?"

"Not shocking, just surprising. You just seem really together. There's this ease about you. This goodness. I don't know how to explain it."

"I think I know what you mean." He bit into a breadstick.

But Marika wanted to find the right word. "You have this *certainty* about you. Like you know nothing can touch you."

"That's very flattering," he said, "but I have my blind spots like everyone else. And they really hooked me when I was younger."

Marika reached for her cup, studying him again. "Did you have to hit rock bottom—or is that question too personal?"

"Not at all." He gazed at her with that pleasant intensity of his. "Just so you know, you can ask me whatever you want."

He cleared his throat.

"Yeah," he continued, "I definitely hit rock bottom. There was this one night when I snorted enough to kill a horse, and I got into a fight at some guy's house. The last thing I remember is him hitting me hard, right in the jaw. I woke up in an alley in South Boston, naked—I mean, all my clothes were gone. My wallet was stolen. And just for the hell of it, someone had decided to beat the shit out of me. A couple of my ribs were broken. My arm was broken. I couldn't even move. And then I started having seizures. I probably would have died if some guy hadn't been driving by and seen me."

"Jesus!" Marika was, literally, on the edge of her seat.

Seb gave her a quick wink to say: *But everything's all right now.*

"So I completely overdosed and nearly died," he said matter-of-factly. "I had to stay in the hospital for a while; then I checked myself into rehab for nine months. And you know what? I've never relapsed. Not once."

"That's great." She could feel *mudita* for him.

"Which isn't to say I don't get tempted. Addictions are weird like that. They're always lurking in the shadows, trying to get you to fuck up just once. That's all it takes. *One* fuckup. Then they've got you."

"Thank God I've never been addicted to anything," Marika said.

Seb looked pointedly at her. "I've never met anyone who hasn't had an addiction. To food. To sex. To Coca-Cola. You name it."

"To danger," she said, letting loose a quick smile.

Seb leaned forward across the table. "So what's the attraction there?"

"You mean, my job?"

"Yeah. Your job. The nature of it."

"I wouldn't say there's an 'attraction.' I just like the . . . urgency of it."

"What do you mean?"

"Well, nothing's trivial about what I do. I'm always dealing with life-and-death issues. I try to experience what the local people are going through. I try to climb into the trenches with them—which can get dangerous. Nothing's petty."

"Does life otherwise feel petty?" Seb asked.

Marika paused, stared at him. "A lot of the time," she admitted.

He took a long sip from his cup. Noticing that her awkward smile had returned, he reached out to touch her hand. "Your job sounds tough," he said.

She just glanced at him.

"You know, I find you really amazing," he said. "And brave."

Blushing, she slid her hand from his and reached for a piece of bread.

Seb politely sat back. "And you have an interesting name. Marika Vecera."

"It's Czech."

"Are your parents first generation?"

"No. I came to the U.S. when I was nine. I defected with my mother."

"So you were *born* in Czechoslovakia?" He looked impressed.

"Yeah."

"How'd you get out?"

"We snuck through a train tunnel, into Austria."

"And then you emigrated to the U.S.?"

She nodded.

"I don't hear an accent."

"No. My mother taught me American English when I was little, and she was always correcting my accent. She's a linguist—*was* a linguist. At Charles University in Prague."

"During the lecture, you said you didn't have any family."

"I don't. I mean, not really. It's hard to explain."

Seb looked at her quizzically.

"My mother moved back to Prague in the early nineties, after communism collapsed," Marika said. "She's got family there. And my father's dead."

"Oh, I'm sorry."

"Well, I didn't really know him. He died when I was six."

"So you don't see your mother anymore?"

"We talk on the phone every once in a while," she said hesitantly. "But my mother is . . ." She tapped her head. "She's mentally ill."

"Does she have a diagnosis?" Seb asked. "If you don't mind my asking?"

Marika paused. Normally she wouldn't say anything further about it, but she found herself trusting Seb.

"Schizophrenia," she said at last.

"That's pretty serious."

Marika shrugged, not wanting to make a big deal out of it. "When I was growing up, my mother would get into these moods. She'd just stop taking care of herself, you know? I mean, she'd let her teeth fall out. Or she'd disappear for days. That sort of thing."

Seb nodded gravely.

"And she had a million bizarre theories about the most outrageous things. Like spacemen working covertly for the government. Pretty outrageous stuff."

"That must have been tough," Seb said.

Marika shrugged again. "When she got really bad, I'd go live with my American cousins; my aunt and uncle became my legal guardians. Then I got this scholarship to go to boarding school. So, basically, I've been away from home and on my own since I was thirteen."

"And now you're writing articles and going to places like Iran." Seb fingered the magazine on the table.

"When I was young," Marika said, "I had my life completely mapped out: I was going to get into a good journalism graduate program, write for the *New York Herald Magazine,* and then meet Robert Lewis. In that order."

"And you've done it all—except meeting Lewis."

She laughed. "There's still time."

"I'll have to get one of his books," Seb said. "I'm ashamed to admit I haven't read any of his stuff."

"I really recommend *Cold Summer,*" she said. "He's an amazing writer. He has this incredible eye for irony. It breaks my heart. Lewis is the reason why I went into journalism. He's got to be one of the most important people alive today."

"I'll take your word for it."

"He *is,*" she insisted. "He definitely is." Her expression had turned so serious that Seb was intrigued. "Lewis is one of the only people writing about what's really happening in the world. He doesn't care if his articles are too long, or if they wouldn't bring in advertising revenue; he just gives editors what he thinks is important. He *cares* like no one else."

Seb nodded intently, taking a sip of tea.

Marika smiled suddenly, almost apologetically. "Better not get me started on Lewis," she said.

The first time Marika had ever heard about Robert Lewis was when she was thirteen. She was in a courthouse in the western suburbs of Chicago, waiting for her aunt Ivona and uncle Frank to fill out some paperwork. They were to become her legal guardians—which was necessary for enrolling her in boarding school in Minnesota, using the scholarship she'd just won.

Even at the time, Marika understood the significance of the day. She knew that it meant she would be losing her mother. Not completely—not as she'd lost her father. But close enough. Her mother, hospitalized in a psychiatric unit, had been deemed "mentally unsound" and "detrimental" to Marika's well-being, unable to take care of her anymore.

By that time, Marika didn't even like talking about her mother. There had been too many interviews by court staff. Too many questions from Uncle Frank and her American cousins and teachers. How often had she been forced to describe, in detail, her mother's incriminating behaviors? The sudden, inexplicable absences. The swings into despair. The endless crying about her husband's death and her forced exile in the United States. Everyone always asked about the suicide attempts, of which there had been several, none ever done very earnestly—as if she'd barely been able to summon the energy for genuine escape. Usually, she'd swallowed some of her antipsychotic drugs or sleeping pills. Marika had found her most of those times—had even learned to check up on her during the night or before going to school. Pills, Marika had learned, were a lousy way to do it. Just too much vomiting and never any solid results. Perhaps her mother had realized this too, using a knife for her latest attempt. But this, too, had been done halfheartedly, sloppily, without design. All she'd wanted to do, she told Marika afterward, was join her husband, Petr. All she'd wanted was that elusive thing called "release."

Marika didn't find her mother after the knife attempt—her aunt Ivona did—but it was enough to make Marika have to pack her bags and move back into Ivona's house for the summer. That was when she was twelve. Already, by that time, Marika hated living with her cousins, noisy American teenage girls with whom she seemed to have nothing in common. Marika had always been quiet, self-possessed, the weight of her past giving her the unsettling air of someone much older. Her cousins didn't know what to do with her, and Marika spent most of her time alone in their basement, mastering the language of her adopted country, becoming a straight-A student.

By the time Marika found herself sitting in the courthouse waiting area, she knew her mother was leaving her life for good, and there was nothing she could do about it. The news didn't come as a shock; rather, the years seemed to have been slowly building to that point. She would be tossed out into the world again, forced to fend for herself. She remembers flipping through the magazines in the waiting room when she came across Robert Lewis's article about Czech dissidents in the *New York Herald Magazine*.

Lewis might have been writing about her own father as he described his experiences with a Czech novelist in Prague, who'd risked everything to distribute anticommunist literature in defiance of the Soviet occupation. Learning that the man's life was in imminent danger, Lewis smuggled him out of Czechoslovakia to West Germany. He'd put himself at serious risk, though he'd undoubtedly saved the man from a grim prison sentence or death. To Marika, it had seemed like true heroism. In a world that felt entirely out of control, and overflowing with heartbreak, here was someone—Robert S. Lewis—who wouldn't let the darkness win.

Marika tore out the article and kept it. At boarding school during the freezing Minnesota winters, she liked to reread it, glancing at a small photo of Lewis she'd pinned to her wall. She'd study his broad nose and angular jaw. His long brown hair and beard. His intense blue eyes that challenged the camera. Whenever she looked at him, she had a feeling that he would know her better than she knew herself. That in the sharp wrinkles at the corner of each eye, in the furrowed brow and deep stare, he had already taken an accurate measure of her life and *understood*.

Marika opens her eyes to the heat and humidity of New Guinea. For a moment she forgets where she is. She studies the slanting walls of her tent. She hears the loud droning of jungle insects. Her dreams had taken her elsewhere, to worlds she can only remember in passing reflections. She recalls lying on a grassy plain, of the sort she saw in central Africa. In Congo. Seb was there, but when she called out to him he just walked by without recognizing her.

Marika is covered in sweat, her clothes entirely soaked. She accidentally left the top of her tent unzipped, and engorged red mosquito bites cover her body like a series of reprimands: do not underestimate this world. The sun is high overhead; it must be late morning. She sits up and takes her weekly tablet of malaria prophylactic, finishing the last of her bottled water. She will have to get potable water from somewhere. She will have to wash what few clothes she has: a couple T-shirts, underwear, a pair of pants. She will need to find ways to curb the rising anxiety in her. She'll need a Plan.

Thomas's departure early this morning has left a heavy, sickening feeling in her gut, like a hangover. She knows she must find a new guide, someone willing to take her to Walwasi Mountain and the village that Tobo spoke of last night, where Robert Lewis is supposed to be. She won't give up until she finds someone.

Marika suddenly thinks about Seb, wonders

what he's doing now. The time difference is extreme—a day and a half lost when coming to PNG from Boston. She has no idea what time it is back home, and glances at a clock hanging on the wall of Tobo's hut: 8:41. But the hands don't move. Time is frozen here.

Marika hears the rooting of hens beneath the hut, their chicks making sharp, staccato calls. The loud screeching of grasshoppers won't cease until dusk, and it already leaves an unnerving ringing in her ears. She wipes sweat from her forehead, gingerly touching the swollen mosquito bites on her face. Today is another day of nearly unbearable heat and humidity. Another day she takes personally, like a punishment.

She gets out of her tent and looks around the hut. An ear of corn, the kernels burned a glossy black from having been baked in cinders, lies on a banana leaf near her tent; Tobo's wife must have left it for her. She blows away the ashes and eats greedily. It's completely tasteless like most of the New Guinea fare she's had. If she's lucky, she'll be able to buy river catfish from someone and get some valuable protein.

Neither Tobo nor his young wife are here. She sees only a girl, no older than six, sitting in a corner and knotting tree bark cord into netting for a *billum* bag.

"Hello," Marika says to the girl in Pidgin.

The girl bows her head shyly and glances away. As Marika steps closer, the girl's eyes widen in fear. She drops the bark cord and runs for the doorway, disappearing.

Marika feels the floor shake as Tobo walks into the hut. All his body paint is gone, though he sports long cassowary talons from the top of each nostril. Two women in woven bark skirts follow him in. The younger one can't be older than fourteen, her hair cut close to her head, her bare black breasts small and perfectly rounded. Both women carry banana leaves full of baked sago pith, looking like powdery white balls of clay, setting them on the floor in front of Marika's tent. The women gaze at the white mary unabashedly, pointing at her hair and commenting to each other until Tobo sharply reprimands them.

"My wives," he says to Marika in Pidgin, pointing to the women. "They made a meal for you."

"*Tenkyu,*" Marika says to them, but they look at her curiously, only understanding the Anasi language.

Tobo sits cross-legged near Marika and studies her. He gestures to her to take the first serving. She picks up a sago ball, biting off a piece, and winces at the dry, chalky taste.

Tobo chuckles deeply. "It is not white people food," he says to her in Pidgin.

"No."

His wives watch her incessantly, whispering and giggling to each other like schoolgirls.

Marika puts down the sago and turns to Tobo, eager to broach the subject of Lewis with him again. "I will pay you a lot of money," she tells him, "if you will guide me to the village where Lewis lives."

Tobo purses his lips and says nothing, picking up some sago for himself. Marika wonders if he understood her, but suddenly he says, "Woman, you must listen to me. It is too far and difficult for you. If you go, you will die."

"Then I'll die," she says, looking him in the eyes. "But I still want to go."

Tobo is certain now that she's bewitched. He thinks she is touched by something very dark and formidable that he has never confronted before, some sort of demon that she brought with her from America that would like to destroy her. If he took her, and if she died in the jungle because of this demon, it could create many problems for him. What if other white men came looking for her body? What if they accused him of putting sorcery on her and killing her? It could mean more paybacks, and great trouble for him. He doesn't know how much a white man's payback would be, but he's sure it's much more than he could ever afford. He has yet to meet a white person who isn't rich.

"I'll pay you a lot of money," the white mary says again.

Tobo merely shrugs. "I have pigs here. And many good taro plants. And wives. What more do I need?"

"You can use it to buy things."

Paper money has never been of any use to Tobo. He's received it a few times for his sorcery services but has always found it worthless compared to pigs. If he travels to a town— which means weeks of hard travel to reach the Sepik River—he could use it there, but he's never liked going to the trouble of such a journey. He knows that other people, like the Baku rascals demanding payback from him, want the paper money more than anything. They buy alcohol with it and then act like fools for days. He's sure the Baku men would be happy to have her money, but that would mean he'd have to guide her over steep mountains and through raging rivers. If he were going on such a trip by himself, it could take about thirty days. But if he were guiding a weak white mary, it could easily take twice as long.

"No," Tobo says to Marika, "I can't take you."

In Tobo's mind, nothing more needs to be said. He hopes the white mary will stop bothering him about it now. Silently, he eats his fill of the sago, his wives waiting obediently nearby. When he finishes, he burps and gets up, gesturing to them to partake of what's left.

But the white mary is persistent, like a begging dog. "Is there someone else in the village I can pay to guide me to Lewis?" she asks him as he leaves the hut.

"No," he says. "I am the only one who knows the way."

Tobo blows sago dust from his hands. He has too much on his mind to be listening to this woman any longer. The Baku men will be coming soon to collect their payback. All he can spare are six pigs, and he hopes this number will suffice. He shouldn't have to pay them anything, as he was only defending himself, but he has his wives and children to think of, as well as other relatives in Anasi village. If he doesn't give those Baku rascals the pigs, they will probably kill him or one of his family members, and then there will be a feud. And his people would lose the fight, because there are many more Baku than his own Anasi.

Of course Tobo has thought about putting black magic on the Baku people. This he could do, and quite easily, but he knows it would not be a smart choice. Lesser sorcerers would consider such a thing, but only because they are fools who don't know the true nature of demons. In this world, every act comes back to a man. When a sorcerer opens the spirit door and invites demons into the human realm to poison someone, he will poison his own body at the same time. And so it is always advisable to take darkness out of a person, but not to put it in.

Which explains why Tobo is not a wealthy sorcerer. Wealthy sorcerers have many more pigs and wives because they will just as soon poison a man as cure him. Most people will pay handsomely just for the chance to create mischief in the world.

Tobo sees the white mary looking at him with frustration. He doesn't know what she's going to do now, because her guide is gone and she doesn't have a man to look after her. He would ask his son-in-law to put her in a canoe and take her downriver, except that everyone in the village must wait for the Baku men to come and collect their payback. The Baku are rascals of the first order and not to be trusted. Tobo needs as many fighting men here as possible, in case of problems. Maybe, Tobo considers, the Baku rascals would take this white mary with them when they leave. He wouldn't trust them with a member of his own family, but this woman is none of his business and can do as she pleases. As it is, she is clearly bewitched, her spirit always leaving her body, giving her the long stares. It would be better for the health of the village if she left.

Marika sees Tobo studying her. She sighs, wondering what she should do now. She can't go forward in her journey, and she can't go back. She glances at Tobo's clock: always 8:41.

❧

Marika wakes to the sound of voices. Men's voices. An argument. She has been stranded in Anasi village for nearly a week, no one able or willing to take her back downriver. She has considered borrowing the village's only canoe and leaving by herself, but she knows she'd get lost. She and Thomas traveled many streams and rivers to get here, crossing swamps and even portaging through patches of jungle. She'd never be able to remember the route on her own.

The other day, she traded a cigarette lighter and a ballpoint pen to Tobo's youngest wife, Bina, in exchange for meals. She's still been unable to get any protein, just the usual, tasteless stock: white, heart-shaped taro tubers, sago palm pith, burned corn. She has started taking two sleeping pills every morning as soon as the rooster calls awaken her, sending her back into her dreams until afternoon. The Anasi people don't bother her, whether she sleeps or not. She could be alive or dead in her tent, and she's sure no one would notice.

Marika puts her sandals on, ties back her hair, and grabs her daypack. She leaves the hut, climbing down the notched log ladder to the ground, seeing no one in the village or in the nearby gardens. A couple of scrawny dogs sniff around the old blood trails from the slaughtered pigs, trotting off toward the jungle as she approaches.

"Where is everyone?" Marika asks out loud. She hears voices again, this time loud and distinct. There's clearly an argument going on. She heads toward the sound, crossing through a patch of jungle and appearing on the shore of the lagoon. Farther down the bank she sees Tobo, covered from head to foot in red paint. All the inhabitants of Anasi village stand behind him, facing down eight men who wear grimy shorts and T-shirts, and who carry machetes. The smoked pig carcasses lie onshore near a couple of dugout canoes. Marika assumes this is the long-awaited payback. These men must be from Baku village, here to claim compensation.

Tobo stands sternly, his face composed. He holds on to a bow and arrows. The bow's ends are carved into miniature crocodile heads, the bamboo arrows sporting reversed barbed points. The two tribes stare belligerently at each other, a Baku man gesticulating at the pig carcasses.

Marika has a bad feeling about the scene and instinctively backs up toward the village, but a Baku man sees her and points. Everyone turns and gapes at her, as if she were an exotic zoo animal. Tobo gestures impatiently for her to come over. As Marika approaches cautiously, a few young Anasi children cry at the sight of her and flee into the nearby jungle.

"*Husat?*" one of the Baku men asks Tobo, astonished.

"*Wait meri, tasol,*" Tobo replies. "She came last week. I don't know why she stays here. Maybe you can take her with you."

"Hello-how-are-you," the Baku man says to her in rough English, a smirk on his face.

Marika says nothing. She doesn't like the man. He has a knife scar across half his face. His eyes are shifty.

"She is bewitched," Tobo says. "Just forget about her."

The discussion resumes, and it soon reverts to an argument, Tobo trying to get the Baku men to accept the pigs for payback. He puts a section of pig carcass into one of their canoes, only to have it tossed back onto the ground. Dogs race up to lick the meat, becoming so feverish from the taste of it that the Baku men aggressively kick and chase them into the jungle. The Baku mediator, chief of the tribe, tells Tobo that he will confer privately with Sal, the brother of the man who was killed, to discuss the acceptability of the payback. As they step aside, Sal glowers at Marika with wild, bloodshot eyes.

Marika knows that six pigs *is* a large payback; brides are often sold for just a couple of animals. Pigs are unusually valuable in PNG. She has seen ones that were fed and treated better than

women, staying in the family hut during the night. But the matter with Tobo is outside Marika's sphere of comprehension. How
many pigs could possibly make up for the death of a man?

Several minutes go by, while Tobo and his Anasi brethren
stare down the Baku men. Finally, Sal comes striding back,
yelling at Tobo and violently waving his machete. The man's
message is clear: the payback is unacceptable. Sal's friend, the one
with the scar across his face, approaches Tobo boldly, ready to cut
him down. The Baku chief races to restrain the man, convincing
him to lower his weapon. Tobo and his friends raise their own
machetes, and for a long moment the two parties glare at each
other. Marika fears the start of a bloody fight.

Tobo knows he can spare no more pigs. He tells the Baku men
they've already taken nearly all he has, and as he's not a rich man,
his payback of six pigs ought to be sufficient. He explains how the
dead man had been drunk and started the fight—and had Tobo
not defended himself, *he* would have been the one killed. Which
the Baku chief can verify with witnesses who saw the fight.

The chief shrugs. "I have told this to Sal," he tells Tobo. "But
he doesn't listen. He wants more from you."

"I can't give more," he says.

Sal strides off to one of the canoes and gets inside. "*Mi kom-
bak sun.* I will be back soon," he says ominously.

Marika walks through the crowd and steps forward. "I'll give
you money for more pigs," she tells Tobo in Pidgin, "if you guide
me to Lewis."

Tobo looks at her, stunned. "No," he says immediately. "I
cannot do this."

"Lewis?" The Baku chief looks at her. "Who is this?"

"I'm looking for a white man named Lewis," she says. "Tobo
knows where he is."

The two men converse in rapid Pidgin, and the chief starts
laughing heartily. "He is telling lies to you, Missus. There is no
white man in that place. Tobo is a witch doctor, and he can make
great magic. He tells you lies and makes you believe them."

The Baku men nod their heads.

"I think Tobo told me the truth," Marika says soberly, crossing her arms.

"Missus, he is a humbug man," the chief says. "This place he talks about—no white men go there. It is too far. Planes can't land. How do you think a white man can get there?"

"By foot," Marika says. "Through the jungle."

The Baku chief laughs even louder. Marika ignores him and opens her backpack, removing several thousand dollars in Papua New Guinean *kina* bills. Sal immediately gets out of the canoe, entranced by the sight of so much money. With such money, he would instantly be a rich man and could have any wife of his choice.

"I'll pay for the pigs that Tobo needs," Marika says to the Baku chief. "I'll give him nine thousand *kina*." It is the equivalent of nearly eight thousand dollars—an exorbitant amount in a country where the average person is lucky to make seven hundred dollars a year. She wants to impress them, present an offer they can't refuse.

As the crowd grows quiet, Tobo shakes his head. "No," he says, an angry tone in his voice. "I cannot do this. If we go, you will die."

"Fine," she says. "Then I'll pay you twice as much." She takes out several more wads of money—nearly all she has.

Everyone in the crowd stares at the money. It's more than they have ever seen. There is complete silence. Disbelief. Sal eyes the money, mouth agape.

"Eighteen thousand *kina*," she says to Tobo. "You can buy a lot of pigs and settle the payback."

Sal steps forward. "I accept this money on behalf of my dead brother's spirit," he says to Tobo.

Tobo looks at the bills in her hands, at the colorful bird-of-paradise drawings on them. When the white mary first came to his village, he was sure the gods sent her for a reason. Now, he knows what it is: she is to give him the means to fulfill his payback. Probably, to the crowd, she must seem like good fortune, but Tobo doesn't agree and can only assume a trickster god is at work. Still, he knows if he doesn't use this money to settle the payback, Sal will return to Anasi village to cause him trouble again, and of course the dead man's spirit will continue to curse his family. Only by fulfilling the terms of the payback—by taking the woman to Walwasi—will he end the curse, which will require making a pact with the spirit of the dead man. That is always a very disagreeable thing to do. He doesn't like making agreements with such spirits. They're too vengeful. Too demanding. If something happens and Tobo fails to get her to Walwasi, he knows there could be grave consequences. At the very least, demons might decide to curse his family for generations.

Tobo regards the money, pursing his lips.

"If you accept this money for the payback," the Baku chief says to Tobo, "you must guide her. That is the agreement."

Tobo nods, gazing grimly at the jungle. "Lewis is far from here. Very far."

Marika nods.

His fingertips run down the smooth black wood of his bow. He wants her to know that Lewis, if he is alive, lives deep in the interior. It will take at least a month to get there. Probably longer. He picks up a stick and carves a circle in the mud bank to mark where she is: Anasi village. Far, far to the left of it, he draws another circle: Walwasi Mountain. This he surrounds with the narrow, jagged lines of mountain ranges.

"The journey will be too difficult for you." The Anasi man looks off at the lagoon. At the reflections of clouds on the black water. It never fails to astound him—what the gods ask him to do. All fierceness leaves his expression, replaced with sorrow. "And probably Lewis is dead now. If he is dead, you will waste a long journey."

"I don't care," she says, feeling irreconcilably committed. "I still want to go."

Tobo reflects for a moment, taking the money from her. He

removes nearly half of the bills and hands them back to her. "You have given me too much," he says. "If this man takes it all for the payback, he will be greedy."

Sal protests, but the Baku chief advises him to be quiet.

"So you *will* take me to Lewis?" Marika asks Tobo.

He nods reluctantly. "I will try. But if you die, your ghost must not bother me." Tobo turns to the crowd. "If she dies," he says to them, "I don't want her ghost to bother me. I want everyone to hear this."

The chief nods and takes the money from Tobo. He gives it to Sal, who strides away with it, eyes wide in amazement.

"This woman has given you a lot of money," the chief says to Tobo. "She needs a guarantee that you will guide her." The other Baku men angrily voice their assent. "I don't want you to steal her money and leave her in the jungle to die."

Tobo puckers his lips. Yes—he knows it is a reasonable request. If he is to be an honorable man, he must give her some kind of guarantee to complete the agreement.

Marika looks from one man to the other, having caught only traces of what they said.

"We are asking Tobo for a guarantee to help you," the Baku chief explains to her in slow Pidgin.

"What kind of guarantee?" she asks.

He motions to Tobo, who has begun chanting. The Baku men take several steps back, terrified of sorcery, as Tobo beckons Marika to him. Cautiously, she comes forward.

"Look at the ground!" Tobo orders her.

Fear cuts through her. Tobo has to force her head down, and Marika expects to feel the blade of his machete against her skin. But Tobo only takes off the necklace he's wearing and puts it around her own neck. He stops his chanting and says something in Anasi, tapping Marika several times on the top of her head. Turning to the Baku chief, he explains that he's given the white mary his mourning necklace. This is to be his guarantee.

To everyone in the crowd, it is an unspeakably taboo act, and they look at each other in horror. They know that such a necklace is worn only when a loved one dies. It cannot be removed until it falls off on its own—at which time the soul passes to the next world and the mourning period ends. But to remove it before it naturally falls off?

Anxious whispers erupt from the crowd. Children clutch their mothers' legs, whining.

"Here is my guarantee!" Tobo announces to the crowd. "I am giving this white mary my mourning necklace."

It is a powerful pledge that impresses the entire crowd. Everyone gapes as Marika stands with the soul of Tobo's dead sister hanging as collateral around her neck, a few people running away. Marika fingers the necklace: a small, oval piece of wood covered with a woven bark netting. The wood feels light around her neck, the rough bark cord scratching her skin.

"You must not take it off," the Baku chief warns Marika. "You are responsible for the soul of Tobo's sister now. It is a great responsibility."

"What would happen if I did take it off?" she asks.

He looks shocked that she would even ask such a thing. "The woman's soul will stay in this world! She will be born again as a human."

Marika doesn't understand. "Is that bad?"

The Baku man just stares at her. "Missus, this world is not the Good Place!"

Tobo breaks in, impatiently. "When we have done bad things," he explains to Marika, as if instructing a child, "our spirit is born into this world, so the gods can show us what we did wrong." He motions to the jungle, the sky, the black waters. "But it is much better not to come here."

The crowd murmurs their agreement as Marika fingers the mourning necklace.

"So is everything settled?" Tobo asks the Baku men.

The chief nods.

"We will leave immediately," Tobo says to Marika. He shoos away the Baku men as if they were pesky dogs. "You have no more business here. Go now."

They load the pig carcasses into the canoes. Without further word, they start paddling across the lagoon. Tobo watches them, his expression serious. As soon as they disappear into the mangroves, he turns to Marika.

"Pack your things," he tells her. "Bring only what you can carry on your back. We will travel by canoe for ten days. After that, we must walk through the jungle for a very long time. The walking will be hard. It is best to bring only important things with you, and things that are not too heavy. Meet me here with your bag."

Tobo heads back to the village. Marika watches him go, stunned. It happened too quickly—the money changing hands, the agreement to find Lewis.

"*Yumi go!*" Tobo yells to her over his shoulder.

The reality of what she's about to do hits her: she's just given away a huge sum of money to try to find a man who probably doesn't exist. But she reminds herself that there are always pangs of doubt and fear when she's about to embark on a difficult trip. The only way to overcome them is to be utterly steadfast.

"*Yumi go!*" Tobo insists.

She runs back to his hut, climbing up the notched log ladder. She stuffs her things into her backpack and dismantles her tent, pausing long enough to gaze out a window of the hut. There is the familiar spread of water and jungle on the opposite shore of the lagoon, the betel nut palms bowing solemnly in the afternoon breeze.

Tobo's young wife comes over and gives Marika a knotted bark *billum* bag full of dried sago balls, nodding, her eyes seeming to say, *Be strong*.

Marika thanks her. She straps on her backpack and heads to Tobo's canoe.

The sorcerer arrives without a word, carrying his own *billum*. He secures Marika's backpack in the middle of the boat, and she climbs in front. She's never experienced such a small dugout canoe before; it feels like balancing on a tightrope. The fragile vessel nearly tips over as she sits on her knees, her machete in clear view on her lap. She doesn't know if she can trust Tobo. She doesn't know anything anymore.

Tobo's two wives and three children stand onshore to see him off. He gives them instructions in Anasi and turns to some nearby men to do the same. Everyone still looks bewildered, staring incredulously at Marika as Tobo speaks to them. Abruptly finishing his speech, Tobo climbs into the canoe and stands in back—the man's position. Marika accepts the woman's place: kneeling in the front bow. Unceremoniously, Tobo dips a long-handled paddle into the water, and they shove off.

The slightest movement causes the canoe to bob hazardously, and Marika tries to remain as still as possible, the people of Anasi offering her a flurry of hand waves and good-byes. She reminds herself that, from this point forward, there can be no room for fear.

CHAPTER FOUR

Marika is surprised by how often she thinks about Seb. It can't just be boredom, she decides. Not just the tedious days spent paddling a canoe with Tobo in the relentless New Guinea heat. Seb returns to her memory as a light might pierce beneath a drawn shade, seizing her attention, demanding acknowledgment.

She never did tell Seb the real reason why it took her a week to call him back after their first date. She'd told a white lie instead—that she'd gone on a sudden business trip. In truth, she'd been debating whether she should get involved with him. Not that she hadn't liked him. Not that there hadn't been sparks. Rather, *because* she'd liked him so much, *because* of all the sparks, she'd delayed. She hadn't trusted anything that seemed too good to be true. That was the heart of it.

And she still doesn't. She glances behind her at Tobo. The Anasi man stands solemnly in the back of the canoe, returning her stare as he paddles.

❧

Marika remembers how she finally did call Seb back. They went all the way to New Hampshire, to the White Mountains, for their second date. It was mid-November, and cold, but she was excited just to be with him. He was the most genuine person she'd ever come across, whereas most people seemed forever one step away from showing their true selves. In Seb's unfettered honesty and kindness, Marika saw a different kind of world. A better world.

They drove high into the mountains, looking for a trail that would offer a good view of the surrounding hills. The path they chose wound through a forest of sugar maples, frost outlining the shapes of fallen leaves and giving the calm, silent impression of a world frozen in time. Marika walked closely beside Seb—as closely as she could without touching. Then, as they climbed up a hillside, his hand reached out casually, innocently, and took hold of hers.

It felt like an ecstasy. The warmth of his fingers around hers. The newness of his presence. At times, she was sure she'd never need anything else but the pleasure of having him next to her. And the good part was that they didn't really know each other yet. They could still be anything to each other.

Marika told him about her travels. At first she spoke of what she thought might interest him. The reporting. Working with photographers. But as she relaxed, she spoke of other things. Private things. The way the Sahara ran like a sea of golden sand toward the distant cliffs of Chad. The pirates' cemetery she'd seen off the coast of Madagascar, being washed by the waves.

"One tombstone read, PASSANTS PRIEZ POUR LUI," she said.

"What does that mean?" Seb asked. "French isn't one of my languages."

"'Passersby pray for him.' There was something touching about it. I never imagined a pirate would end up asking for anyone's prayers."

Marika told Seb that some things, even the most unexpectedly sad things, would astound her with their grace.

Seb listened intently as she spoke, squeezing her hand, brushing her hair from her cheek whenever the wind tousled it. When he talked of himself, it was to tell her more about his Ph.D. work or to answer her questions about his family. How his brother Chris was head chef in an upscale Boston restaurant, his sister Jenny an art history professor at Stanford. Or how his father—now retired—had been one of the world's top cardiovascular surgeons.

Marika was fascinated by Seb's stories of his wealthy, close-knit upbringing; they were as exotic to her as her own life must have seemed to him. Having never experienced much of a family environment, and having no contact with relatives, Marika invariably felt rootless, like an orphan, convinced she had no one to rely on but herself.

They passed through a thick stretch of forest, the sun blocked out, the trees surrounding them like stoic sentries.

"You told me at dinner that you didn't start any kind of career until you were thirty-five," she said to Seb.

"That's right. Actually, I was going to Harvard Law School, but I dropped out."

Marika looked at him, surprised. "You dropped out of Harvard Law?"

"Yeah."

"Why?"

"I was having too much fun getting high."

She stared at him.

"I got a lot of money from my grandfather," he explained, "and for years I just blew it all on drugs. Toward the end, I was spending nearly four hundred dollars a day on cocaine."

He scratched his nose, waiting for Marika's reaction.

"Well," she said, smiling, "I guess you can't become the next pope."

He laughed. "I guess not." But he stopped and faced her, his eyes running soberly over her face. "Most women get a little freaked out when I talk about that."

"It'd take a lot more than that to freak me out," she said. "Do you have any more deep, dark secrets I should know about?"

"No." Seb smiled. "That's it."

Marika drew her hand across her forehead in mock relief.

"How about you?" He nudged her.

"What? Secrets?" Her eyes followed the trail before them. "I've just had the usual, run-of-the-mill angst. Actually, my life has been pretty straightforward."

"Straightforward?" Seb glanced incredulously at her, reaching out to smooth her hair back. "I'd still love to hear about it."

"I want to hear more about *your* life," Marika said quickly.

"Like what?"

"Did your brother or sister have drug problems, too?"

"God, no," Seb said. "None whatsoever."

"So you were the only one?"

"Yeah. I was the official black sheep." He sat down on a nearby rock and pulled up the collar of his coat, looking at her with those guileless eyes of his. "My parents didn't know I'd dropped out of Harvard until six months after the fact. They didn't know I was a drug addict until a year later, when I ODed for the first time."

"That must have surprised them."

Seb chuckled. "That'd be an understatement. It's so poignant— parents try to do the best they can, but they really can't control how their kids turn out. When you bring a child into the world, it's almost like there's an unspoken agreement that you have to turn them over to the fates."

He retreated into his thoughts for a moment.

"That's why I don't think I'd want to have children," Marika said. "It'd be heartbreaking if something bad happened to them."

"But that would be assuming that life is all about suffering. Or that suffering is bad, somehow. Or wrong. But really, it's not."

Seb's face got serious. Reflective. He was still caught in his thoughts.

"Most of the time, we're our own worst enemies," he added. "In my case, I'd convinced myself that my parents never really loved me. But the worse things got for me, the more they stood behind me and tried to help. When I finally had that episode I told you about—when I hit rock bottom—I realized it wasn't my parents who didn't love me. It was *myself*."

Seb glanced at her, and she saw a flash of sorrow in his eyes.

"That must have been a big realization," Marika said, sitting beside him, close to him.

His fingers touched her back, and he lightly caressed.

"It was. It was huge. And that realization saved my life. It allowed me to get sober. It gave me permission to reclaim my life. And now, all I want to do is help people who are in the same situation. All I want to do is help them realize that they can save themselves, too."

The forest stood silently around them. A cold wind cut across their faces, freezing rain falling. Marika zipped her coat beneath her chin, trying—futilely—to imagine Seb as he'd been when he was younger, spiraling out of control. Full of self-hatred. Now, he was in Boston University's Ph.D. program in clinical psychology. She'd looked it up; it was one of the most prestigious programs in the country. Of six hundred applicants a year, only ten were admitted.

"It's uncanny," Seb told her. "The worst things in life usually turn out to be the greatest gifts—if you can just wait long enough to discover that."

To Marika, it sounded like a nice platitude. She supposed she could always make the argument that her father's death had led to her later successes. It had prompted her and her mother to defect from Czechoslovakia and emigrate to the United States, where Marika got a master's degree, moved to Boston, and broke into journalism. Perhaps, everything considered, her father's death had led to something good—though she thought the price was still much too high.

They got up and walked again, following the crest of a ridge. Around them lay undulating hills of leafless maple and scraggy pine. The rain was picking up.

"It's freezing," Seb said. "We should go back, huh?"

"Yeah. Probably."

As they turned around, Marika gazed down the ridge they'd just hiked, seeing their trail far below. They would have to backtrack down the many switchbacks. She saw a pine tree a few feet from the edge of the cliff. Without a thought, she leaped onto one of its branches and started climbing down the trunk.

"Let's go this way," she said to Seb. "It'll be a lot faster."

He stood above her, on the top of the ridge, looking at her with complete surprise.

"Did you just jump onto that tree?"

She nodded, smiling.

"I'm not going to do that." He laughed.

"But it's easy."

"Easy for *you*."

"You just get on that branch there." She pointed to it, but Seb wasn't moving. He stood with his hands in his coat pockets, grinning and shaking his head. "Sorry to be a wuss, but it's kind of dangerous. I'm going to walk down."

Marika climbed back up. As she was about to leap back onto the cliff top, Seb held out his hands, adamantly shaking his head.

"Don't! I don't want you to get hurt. I'll meet you down there."

She was confused. Getting on the tree had seemed so natural. She would have done it in a second, had she been alone. She feared Seb would think she was trying to show off. "I'm sorry," she said to him.

"No problem." He smiled. "I just haven't had a lot of practice jumping onto trees, so I'd better not start now. I'll meet you down there, okay?"

"Well . . . okay."

Certain she'd screwed up their nice time, Marika climbed down carefully, not wanting to get sap on her clothes.

It would take Seb nearly twenty minutes to catch up with her. When he appeared at last, Marika was sitting on a boulder under a rocky overhang, clutching herself in the cold. The rain had just turned to snow, and Seb looked soaked.

"Hey, there," he said.

"Seb—I'm sorry," she told him. "It was just an impulse. I wasn't thinking."

He laughed and shrugged. "Don't worry about it. You know, I don't think I've ever met a woman like you before."

She shivered and pulled her coat tighter around her.

"Come here. You're freezing." He reached his arm around her and drew her against him. "Let me give you my scarf."

"Thanks."

Seb lifted her hair and draped the scarf around her neck. As he tied it, Marika studied his face. The dark stubble that had begun to sprout on his cheeks and chin. His hazel eyes—brown, with flecks of green. His lips, slightly parted.

Seb suddenly caught her staring at him, and there was a long pause between them. Marika's heart pounded as he leaned forward to kiss her.

For a few minutes, she let herself drown in the sensations. The press of his lips against hers. His hand reaching beneath her coat and circling her waist. Finally, she pulled back.

"Sorry," she said, "I need to take things slow."

Seb smiled awkwardly, stepping away. "No problem."

"I just . . . I don't want to rush anything."

"Don't even worry about it." He let his arm fall from her, trying to smile as if nothing had happened. He cleared his throat. "Shall we go?"

"Okay."

They got up. As they started walking, Marika slowly slipped her hand into his.

Seb took it slow with Marika after that, wanting to respect her boundaries, waiting until she felt ready to go further. All the while, they saw each other more often. They'd go running together along the esplanade, or would meet for lunch in the Public Gardens on a bench by the swan pond. Marika usually tried to arrive early for these meetings so she could watch Seb approach from a distance. On warmer days, she knew he'd be wearing his beat-up brown corduroy jacket and sunglasses, carrying a briefcase, and when she spied him each time, it was as if a rush of wind had caught her off guard. Her skin tingled; her cheeks felt hot. She could not hold back a smile.

Seb would sit down next to her and put his arm around her shoulder. She liked to lean her head against him. Or hold his hand. All those things she'd always seen other couples do. All the things she had largely denied herself for years by choosing not to get seriously involved with anyone. It never stopped feeling like a privilege, being touched by another.

How was it, she wondered, that the mere sight of a person could fill her with such joy? Though she didn't dare admit it to Seb, she wanted to be with him all the time. Yet, she thought it sensible to take things slowly, limiting the number of times she saw him, not having sex with him too soon. Surely, she told herself, she was only experiencing that early infatuation most relationships went through. That month or two of heady bliss that would inevitably succumb to reality and painful truths. But as one month passed, and then another, Marika discovered that things were only getting better between them, and her feelings for Seb were growing.

One evening in late January, after they'd been together for nearly three months, Marika showed Seb her apartment for the first time. They were going out to dinner, but she needed to take a shower and change her clothes, and he'd asked to come over and wait. The truth was that he wanted to have a conversation with her about where things stood between them.

As Marika showered, Seb walked around her apartment. She always preferred going to his place—a large condo in Cambridge, overlooking the Charles River—remarking how "quiet" it was there. Now he understood why: her small studio was less than half a block from the Massachusetts General Hospital subway stop. Every fifteen to twenty minutes the room rattled belligerently from passing trains, and the noise from downtown traffic was deafening.

Seb noticed her bed: a single mattress on the floor beneath a window, blankets and pillows lying in a pile. *Very Bohemian,* he was thinking, reminding himself with a laugh that she *was* Bohemian, from Bohemia, in what was now the Czech Republic. Still, her place gave off the appearance of scarcity, of poverty, and it puzzled him; he knew she could have much better for herself, though for whatever reason she had decided against it.

On an entire wall she'd stuck up scores of objects—photos, magazine cuttings, drawings, and the like—creating a kind of large, cryptic montage. Curious, he walked over and searched for a place to enter. There were snapshots of an Asian girl smiling shyly at the camera. Shredded Tibetan prayer flags. A black-and-white photo of a newborn baby sleeping peacefully. Affixed over the entire scene were pieces of a broken mirror, arranged to give the appearance of having just shattered upon the wall.

Seb sat down at Marika's desk to marvel over the chaotic, eclectic mass of symbols and images that, he knew, meant something to her, unconsciously represented her. He studied a postcard of the St. Vitus cathedral in Prague. Beneath it was a scribbled quote from Rilke: "Perhaps everything terrible is, in its deepest being, something helpless that wants help from us."

Seb got up. Marika had kept all this hidden from him—the enigmatic images pasted to her wall. The mysterious hopes and fears they contained. If only he could understand it all, learn the language of her soul. He noticed that her furniture consisted mostly of random-colored milk crates acting as makeshift shelves and tables. It was the home of someone who wasn't often home. A place that looked transitory, half-used. There were a lot of books, though—all American and British literary classics from the nineteenth and twentieth centuries—the only contemporary titles by Robert Lewis.

Seb sat down on Marika's sofa to wait. He was realizing how

little he knew about her, and wondered whether this was, on her part, deliberate. A copy of T. S. Eliot's *The Wasteland and Other Poems* sat on her coffee table, and he leafed through it until she emerged from the bathroom. She was dressed smartly for dinner in a black sweater and gray slacks. Her long, reddish blond hair lay in curls about her shoulders.

"You look nice," Seb said, his eyes taking her in.

She walked slowly toward him. "Thanks."

He put his arms up on the sofa, his eyes still fixed on her body. On the sway of her hips.

"So you're not big on furniture, huh?" he asked, grinning.

"No. It's too much trouble carrying it up here. And then I'd have to keep taking the stuff with me when I moved."

"Are you planning on moving?"

"I don't know." She smiled. "Maybe."

She sat beside Seb, and he could smell her perfume. He ran his fingertips across her cheek, needing to touch her.

"I was wondering if we could talk before dinner?" he asked.

She saw the sudden seriousness in his expression. "Sure. What's up?"

"Well, you know, we've been seeing each other for over two months now, and we haven't gotten intimate yet—sexually."

"Oh." She crossed her legs. "Yeah."

"I'm just wondering if you're attracted to me in that way. I'd like to know where you stand."

He took her hand in his, and she could see the longing in his eyes. As he sat closer to her, putting his hand on her thigh, she felt warm chills rushing through her.

"So what's up?" he asked. "*Do* you find me attractive?"

She smiled. They both knew the answer already. But Seb needed to hear her say it.

"I've never been so attracted to anyone in my life," Marika said frankly, glancing at him. "And I don't just mean physically . . . It's everything about you."

He now had such affection in his eyes that for a moment she couldn't speak.

"You know something?" he said. "You know why I've been going really slow with you? Because I didn't want to do a single thing that might make you think I didn't respect and value you as a person—which hasn't been easy, just for the record. I've practically had to tie my hands behind my back since I first met you."

Marika laughed, blushing.

"This may sound strange," she said, "but I'm just not used to being with someone I like so much. I keep thinking the bubble's going to break or something."

"Or it could get even better," Seb said. "Have you ever thought of that?"

She had thought of that. But it had only increased her anxiety. The better it got with Seb, the higher the stakes seemed to get.

"Look," he said, "I'm going to put everything on the table, all right? This is what I'm looking for. First of all, I'd love to have you as my girlfriend, okay? I'm looking for a commitment. And, yes." He smiled awkwardly at her. "What can I say? I'm a guy. I'd really love to have sex with you. I'd love to experience that with you."

She stared at his fingers as they caressed her thigh.

"So what do you think about all that?" he asked.

She was silent for a moment. "Well, you should know that I travel a lot."

"Yeah," he said. "I know."

"And I don't usually go to friendly places," she added.

He nodded gravely.

"Then, when I *am* here, I can get really obsessed with my work. *Really* obsessed."

"So are you saying you're not interested in a commitment?"

"No, I'm not saying that." She tried to focus. "I'm just saying I can't make you any promises about what's going to happen between us."

Seb smiled, relieved. "You know, no one can make any

promises about anything. All we can do is take it one day at a time. But I just need to know you're at least willing to give it a shot. Because I'm not looking for anything superficial, you know? That's not where I'm at in my life, so I want to make sure we're on the same page."

She felt her heart beating hard.

Seb moved closer to her, looking into her eyes. "Marika," he said softly, "will you trust me?"

As she turned away from the intensity of his stare, he put his hand on her cheek.

"Will you?"

She glanced at him. Nodded.

"We'll just do it one day at a time," he said. "All right?"

"Yeah."

He pressed his lips against her neck, inhaling the scent of her. "Is this okay?" he whispered. "Can I touch you?"

When she nodded again, his fingers traveled beneath her sweater and up her waist, finding her breasts.

She ran her own hands beneath his shirt. Unzipping his jeans, she reached a hand inside and watched his body shudder. It struck her as one of the most beautiful things she'd ever seen— the way she could, merely through her touch, bring such ecstasy to another. She kissed Seb, stroked him, listening to his gasps.

He took her in his arms. Gently, he laid her on the floor beneath him and straddled her. Shedding his shirt and jeans, he lifted off her top. As his eyes took in the sight of her, he started moving his fingertips over her body.

"You're so beautiful," he whispered. "Do you know that?"

She gazed shyly at him, and Seb took her in his arms and held her. Kissing her, he slowly unhooked her bra. Slipping off her pants and underwear, he laid her naked before him, his hand gliding between her legs.

She reached a hand between his own legs, but he stopped her.

"I want this to be for you," he insisted.

She was about to protest when he began moving his lips down her thighs. Intense jolts of pleasure overwhelmed her. It was more than any man had done for her before. Such sensations. At last, she stopped him and pulled him toward her, wanting to feel him inside of her.

Seb fished in his coat pocket for a condom, putting it on. But he looked directly into her eyes, pausing long enough to ask, "Are you sure?"

She could barely talk, barely breathe for the feel of his hands on her.

When she nodded, he drew her legs apart. He wanted everything slow, deliberate for their first time, and he looked at her with each movement, his breaths hushed. He wanted to hear her respond when he entered. He wanted to know that she felt him and wanted him. His hair swung down, brushing her face. His eyes held hers. It wasn't until the very end that she closed her own eyes, breathing, urging, forgetting the world as they fell to stillness.

Only a couple of days later, Marika left for Africa. The Democratic Republic of Congo. She'd gotten a magazine assignment to cover the war and genocide there, and she didn't know how long she'd be gone. Maybe three weeks, or four—if all went well. She told Seb not to worry about her. She'd be fine. She'd be back.

Last night, Marika had shaken the hand of a dead man. Pierre. The Congolese kid she'd hired as a translator. Someone found him early this morning by the side of the road, shot in the head, robbed, stripped of his clothes. Strange how the mind worked—all she could think about was what a poor translator he'd been, how little English he knew, how heavy his accent was. She'd let him go to find another, better guy, tipping him fifty dollars. That was yesterday. And then, today, the dogs had found him.

There were some things she would never understand about Bodo: why the blue morning glories still climbed the bullet-pitted cement walls and opened their flowers to the sun; how the UN soldiers from Uruguay could flirt with her after she'd just walked down a street full of corpses; why rain animated the refugees in shock, when nothing else could.

The gunfire had settled to a pop here and there, like kids lighting off firecrackers on the Fourth of July. Throughout Bodo, the child soldiers, bored but armed with AK-47s, were searching for havoc to create. The drugs they took eradicated fear and buried emotions, perhaps permanently. Bodo was not a place to find conscience or compassion. Or mercy.

Marika decided to leave the priest's compound to look around. A service had started in the small brick chapel opposite her room, the singing of hymns sounding almost vulgar after the night's firefights and mortar blasts. The gatekeeper of the compound, slumped in a chair beneath an overhanging acacia, watched her approach, his hands clasped tightly in his lap.

"*Ça va?*" she asked him.

He shrugged but otherwise didn't move.

"I'd like to leave," she said in French.

He appeared to ponder this for a moment, looking at the bolt to the gate. Wearily, he rose. Producing his keys from a pocket, he unlocked it and opened it to a crack, peering out. With sudden animation, he beckoned her to leave. Marika caught a flash of a smirk on his face that said many things at once, but most strongly this: "Go, Journalist, see what my world is like." She dashed through, and he immediately closed the gate behind her, relocking it.

Bodo was like any central African town of moderate size. A main strip. Unpaved in this case. Or, perhaps, paved once a very long time ago when the country was called Zaire, but reduced now to mud and potholes. The stucco on brick buildings flaked off like nail polish as soon as bullets started flying. There were few trees anywhere, as trees represented charcoal for cooking, which represented money. Vehicles groaned with the labors of low gear as they maneuvered down bad roads, distance measured not by kilometers but by minutes and hours, by how long it takes to get from one place to another. From the UN compound to the airport: twenty minutes, barring rain, barring a new rebel takeover attempt, barring corpses blocking the street. Corpses were the worst. Someone must be found to remove them, even though snipers could be hiding anywhere.

Today Marika saw gaps that were once filled with something: a building, perhaps, or a tree, or a vehicle. Sometimes she'd just see the gap itself, and she couldn't remember what had been there before. There were just holes now, empty spaces. How bizarre—she didn't notice the familiar stuff, only what was missing.

Today, Bodo was misleadingly calm. She stopped at the

corner of a bullet-gutted wall. The smell of rotting flesh assailed her, a heavy, dense scent that consumed her senses. Bodies lined the street in all manner of positions, limbs bent under torsos, legs splayed. Many had been stripped of clothing. She looked around for Pierre. She probably wouldn't recognize him if she saw him. The sun's heat bloated and disfigured bodies, inflating them to twice their normal size, giving them the black, surreal appearance of monsters. She remembered how, when she'd asked Pierre about his parents, he'd started to cry. He said they'd been shot before his eyes, and he'd escaped to the priests' compound, finding employment by doing odd jobs for them. She'd reached out and touched his hand as he told her about these things, but that was a mistake; allow yourself to care about anything in such a place, and the heartache will destroy you.

What Marika hated to admit to herself was that she felt at home in such places. The danger gave her an increased sense of purpose. Her life—the great senselessness of it, the mystery of it that she had never understood—found direction in a place like Bodo. She felt absolute, unequivocal confidence that there, finally, was a place that wanted her and could use her. She had only one issue to face at all times: living or dying. Everything else fell into the realm of the meaningless. She had no past or future. She could be anyone at any moment. She found constant reasons for fear: it might be her last hour, her last day. She found constant reasons for gratitude: the world had kept her alive for yet another night. She felt only two things in any given moment: terror or gratitude. And that was enough. Only thirty-two years old, Marika felt as if she were living an entire lifetime with each day that passed.

The UN, with its pathetic contingent of soldiers stationed in town as "peacekeepers," seemed to care little about the place. They weren't mandated to protect anyone but themselves, and could only gaze at the violence, not allowed to stop it. Every day a new flood of victims poured into the refugee camps and makeshift hospitals: women with their arms chopped off, babies shot, old men nearly decapitated. It was unimaginable, ingenious cruelty. People left alive, but without any limbs. Women raped with machetes. Eyes gouged out. Children forced to eat the flesh of their parents. And on and on. She had seen it all. For the past few days it had been an endless stream of the worst, most inconceivable acts of inhumanity paraded in front of her. Then something had happened: she saw, but she no longer saw. Her eyes perceived and collected sights, but her mind no longer tried to make sense of them. It just stored them away somewhere—in the twitch in her gut, perhaps, or in her headaches. She had a large mental album full of such memories that, she knew, would return in her dreams, but only when she was back home again, thinking she was safe, secure, and, God forbid, fortunate.

Was it possible to see such things and be the same afterward? To live that "normal" life? She didn't know. A few of the UN soldiers—"the weak ones," a commander had described them to her—had gone insane and were sent home. But their "insanity" had struck her as the sanest possible response in such a place. The specter of *not* going insane was enough to haunt her.

Marika stopped. She was approaching a group of Hema *kodogo*, child soldiers, standing on the road nearby. Aged thirteen or fourteen, they were older than most. Each carried an AK-47 strapped over a shoulder. One larger kid held a prized M-60 in both hands, ammo belt draped around his neck like a poor imitation of Rambo. The country was raising an entire generation that knew only killing, raping, looting. An entire nation of psychopaths.

Above her, birds began singing loudly and obscenely in the silence. What would it take, this time, for her to feel again? Marika sprinted back to the priests' compound.

✑

Bodo's only restaurant, the Okapi, was a dingy place with an open air patio sporting white plastic lawn chairs and bullet holes in the cement walls. Marika could find only two explanations for its continued existence: first, because it was across the street from the UN headquarters; second, because it gave free meals and beer to whichever rebel group happened to be in control of the town on a given day. Curiously, while no one in Bodo had drinking water to sell, this restaurant had an unending supply of Primus, the Congolese national beer, and cigarettes.

Marika joined the only other journalists who had gotten into town: four men sitting at a table on the patio. They were all in their late twenties or early thirties, all unmarried. She'd met three of them before and had learned that the new guy, Chris, worked for a paper in New York. All were prodigious drinkers and chain-smokers. Their eyes revealed a hearty nonchalance, a certain formidable immunity to suffering. Unlike Marika, they worked for newspapers; most of them lived in Kenya or South Africa, spending their days flying from one African war zone to another. Somalia this week, Liberia the next. Sudan. Sierra Leone. Angola. The wars had become background noise. They had seen it all; it was nearly impossible to impress them with stories.

"Marika Vecera," greeted Craig, a photojournalist. "Would you like a beer?"

"Yeah, why not," she said.

He offered her one of the four bottles that sat in front of him on the table, opening it for her with his Swiss Army knife. Craig was always a pleasure to run into; he was a blond-haired, blue-eyed giant from South Carolina, with a melodious twang and an incongruously shy smile, who pulled out one of the flimsy, bullet-torn plastic chairs for her. The Okapi had once again run out of food, so they were filling their stomachs on Primus.

Marika sipped her beer, listening to the newest stories from the others; Bodo had just changed rebel hands for the third time in the past two weeks, the Hema seizing back control from the Lendu.

"Did ya'll see the corpses all over the streets?" Craig was saying. "Ducks were eating them."

"Ducks?" said Simon, an Irish reporter. He was a frail-looking, red-haired, bespectacled man, one of the craziest risk takers Marika had ever met. "You mean *dogs*."

"No," Craig said. "I mean *ducks*. Baby ducks were eating the corpses."

"I thought ducks were vegetarians," she said seriously.

There were laughs all around.

"I got some good shots of it," Craig said. "Un-fucking-believable."

Which led to the familiar laments from the two photographers at the table about the "squeamish" Western market refusing to publish such photos. Simon resuggested the obvious: sell them to the Asian market. The Asians would publish anything, the more gruesome, the better.

"When Rob Lewis was here last year," said Michael, a journalist from D.C., the oldest—at age thirty-five—and surliest of their group, "he said he saw a kid wearing a necklace of human hands. I shit you not."

"I've seen that," Simon said.

Marika sat up. "Robert Lewis was here?"

"The man, himself."

It would have been appropriate if she had met Lewis for the first time in a hell-on-earth like Bodo, Congo.

"What's he like?" she asked.

Michael picked off a piece of tobacco from his tongue and flicked it to the ground, eyeing a passing group of Hema soldiers. "I liked him. He didn't talk much, but he was a huge drinker. And the guy's smart as hell. It's almost like he can read your mind."

Craig nodded in agreement. "The guy's brilliant."

"I met him once in San Salvador, about three years ago," Michael said. "He just suddenly shows up in the hotel lobby. No one else with him. He tells me he's 'checking out the country.'"

"You never know where he's going to show up," said Chris, who was otherwise ignoring their conversation and going over his notes.

"He doesn't have to show up anywhere," Michael said. "His books made him a multimillionaire. That's what I said to him when he was here in Bodo. I said, 'Why are you still coming to shit holes like this?' "

A skinny, mute Congolese boy in torn clothing appeared from the dark bowels of the restaurant to take further beer requests. Knowing the beer could run out at any time, the journalists ordered ten bottles for the table. The boy dashed off. He returned shortly with a box full of warm Primus bottles, placing them on the table furtively: Hema officers were coming down the street. But too late. They saw the journalists—saw the beer—and came trotting over.

"Shit," Michael whispered, slumping in his seat. "Another welcome committee."

Marika slid her backpack far under the table. The soldiers, already drunk or stoned, waved their AK-47s at the journalists' faces.

"We are your friends!" the head officer said. He was one of the tallest human beings she had ever seen. Easily seven feet. Perhaps because she was the only woman among the journalists, he offered her his sweaty, sticky hand to shake first. Marika shook it limply, glancing into his eyes: they were a dark morass, beyond communion. She took a long sip of beer, wondering what prevented him, or any of the soldiers, from killing the whole table of them. Craig's expensive digital camera sat on his lap: a prize that was surely worth more than the combined value of all their lives.

"I am *kodogo* captain!" the giant of a man announced, waving his rifle in the air. He gripped the top of her chair. His breath smelled acrid, of decay. "I will kill Lendu! I will kill them all! Man, woman, child! Journalists, are you scared of me? I will kill you, too! Ha!"

Marika and Craig gazed at each other across the table as the soldier started a drunken dance. She had never been able to look so easily—so willingly—into someone else's eyes. But this wasn't romance; it was comfort. The comfort of being seen by another in a place where most people became anonymous, their humanity stripped from them. Where they, themselves, were in fear of losing it, too.

The silent boy brought out new beers for the soldiers. They grabbed them eagerly, saluting the journalists.

"I will kill you, journalists!" the Hema officer said. "Ha! Are you scared?!"

Marika took another swig of beer—a long swig—and allowed herself the slightest gesture of contempt toward the soldiers: she narrowed her eyes at them. Craig was still looking directly at her from across the table, and she sought his stare again.

The soldiers became bored with the journalists and stumbled off into the night. When there was no more sound of them, Marika got up from the table and headed into the darkness to find somewhere safe to take a piss. "If I'm not back in five minutes," she said to the others, "send out a search party."

"We'll send the UN," Craig said. Their table erupted into laughter.

The next day Stefan flew in on a Ukrainian cargo plane. He was the German freelance photographer she was assigned to work with, and at noon she found him in a room in the priests' compound, his door open. He sat on the bed, a cigarette hanging from the side of his mouth, cleaning his camera lenses. She and Stefan had worked together on five assignments before this one. Marika liked him, perhaps because she knew nothing about him. It was the secret of how they got along in a business where collaborating writers and photographers often hated each other. As Stefan didn't enjoy talking, and as she usually preferred listening, there was never any cause for disagreement between them.

"Knock, knock," she said to him. "It's Marika."

"Yes," he mumbled, waving in her general direction.

"How was the flight over here?"

"Long and boring. I came from Kinshasa. It was a big pain in my ass."

"Try going through Rwanda next time. From Goma."

He shrugged.

"It's faster," she added.

"If you go that way, you have to pay too many bribes." He blew gently at a lens.

What she knew about Stefan came mostly from his eyes: from the way they moved, from what they noticed and deemed important, from what they overlooked. Award-winning machines of observation, his eyes needed to see what other people couldn't; they needed to capture the ineffable, tell stories and histories. He preferred working in black-and-white, with a fifty-year-old Leica. Critics often called his work "raw" and "haunting." But there was something more, something nameless about Stefan that Marika especially admired. Something to do with the ease of his shrugs. With the way she'd never caught his cigarette shaking between his fingers.

"There's nothing going on today," she told him. "Just some people taking potshots. There were a lot of bodies on the streets yesterday, but I think they've removed most of them."

He nodded absently.

"Look—I'm going to leave town tomorrow," she said. "I want to visit one of the goldfields."

Stefan saw her for the first time, looking up and brushing back long, greasy brown hair. "And how are you going to do this?" But he was curious rather than disapproving.

"The priests will let me rent one of their old trucks. It's really expensive—they could buy a new one with what they're asking for—but I've got enough money. I just need to find some gas."

He stared at her for a couple of seconds, taking a long drag from his cigarette. Lying back on the bed, he exhaled sharply. "Try to buy petrol from the Yugoslavian," he said. He meant Yuri, the UN officer they'd befriended the last time they were assigned to cover Bodo.

"Is he still in town?" she asked.

Stefan nodded.

"Well, I thought I'd try the black market, instead. It's cheaper."

"Try the Yugoslavian," he said immediately. "Fuck the black market. You don't know what they put in that petrol." He opened a bottle of Primus and took a long sip.

She waited, staring at a framed portrait above Stefan's bed of a Congolese bishop wearing a red satin skullcap. The man had a drawn expression, angry eyes.

When Stefan said nothing further, she asked, "Are you going to go with me?"

"Of course."

"It'll be dangerous."

He rolled his eyes. "Yes, I know this."

"If I could get to the Kolo Muto fields, that would be even better. Foreign politicians actually line their pockets with profits from that place. We're talking about real-deal blood money."

Stefan shrugged. She'd forgotten that these things did not surprise or interest him, and were to be expected in a world gone mad.

He wore, as always, and without exception, a black T-shirt and jeans. Neutral colors that, he claimed, wouldn't raise eyebrows among authorities. In a few days, the unattended stubble darkening his chin would erupt into a full-blown beard.

"Once we leave town, we'll need to find some Lendu soldiers to take us to the goldfields," Marika told him. "It could work, if we're lucky, and if the price is right."

Stefan considered this, stroking his chin. "Or they could simply rob us or kill us, and say to hell with taking us there." He smiled wryly.

"But I have a letter," she said. "From a Lendu commander."

He was silent, evaluating her with his eyes.

"It's signed and dated. It's supposed to be the real thing," she added.

"I think this scheme is crazy," he said at last. "But I have been involved in crazier schemes."

"You don't have to go," she said.

"I am a grown man, yes? I can make my own decisions."

"Well, just so you know, I'm leaving tomorrow as soon as I get gas. If that doesn't happen before ten a.m., then the plan is scrapped until the next day. It'd be suicide to be caught outside town after dark."

"Of course," Stefan said, dropping his cigarette butt to the floor.

✑

"Do you think it's advisable for a magazine to send you here alone?" Yuri, the Yugoslavian, asked Marika. They sat in the Okapi drinking beer. It was nine in the morning, and the gas he'd promised he could get for her had been "on its way" for nearly two hours.

She shrugged at his question. "It was my choice."

"They have eyes, you know," he said, pointing at the nearby Hema rebel soldiers standing in the street. "They see that you're alone. They watch what you do. They want to capture a journalist. Particularly a woman. Do you know what they do to women?"

"Yes."

"I've seen what they do to women. It's unbelievable. Horrendous."

He tapped his cigarette several times before raising it to his lips. They sat on the patio, watching child soldiers trying out a stolen motorcycle on the road. One boy, having never ridden, or perhaps just too stoned for adequate control, sailed over a pothole in the street and did a dramatic backflip onto the muddy road. His comrades laughed uproariously.

The Yugoslavian cleared his throat and took a swig of beer. He was a tall, strong-looking Serb with dark blond hair and sharp cheekbones. He reminded Marika of old black-and-white photos of her Czech grandfather: piercing eyes, rectangular face, strong jaw. All morning she'd been trying to say something to break his stoicism, to get him to smile. Nothing worked. Not even speaking to him in Czech, which was close enough to his own native language to breed familiarity between them. He began to tell her how he joined the UN to avoid having to choose sides during the Bosnian War. So, while his countrymen killed each other, he was stationed in Congo's capital, Kinshasa, watching the Congolese doing the same to themselves.

"Kinshasa was not so bad," he said absently. "We had a swimming pool."

They watched the Hema soldiers picking up the boy who had crashed the motorcycle: he was unconscious, his arm twisted at an unusual angle just below the shoulder.

Yuri sipped his beer, tapped his cigarette. Toyota Hilux trucks roared by full of stolen property, soldiers sitting in back, shouting and waving their rifles. These looting rounds, a familiar and noisy spectacle, became a source of anxiety only when the vehicles decided to stop just outside the restaurant.

"If one of those soldiers came in here and tried to do something to me," she said to Yuri, "could any of the UN soldiers intervene?"

"Yes, but they would be breaking the mandate."

"Which means they wouldn't?"

He gave her a disapproving stare. "I cannot discuss this, you know."

"Which means you probably wouldn't intervene?" she asked him.

He tapped his cigarette aggressively. "I'm not authorized to answer that," he said. "You must direct your question to our public relations officer."

Just then, the gas arrived.

Marika drove the priest's ancient, rattling truck out of Bodo, Stefan taking streams of photos through the window. The view outside: green, deforested hills on one side, the dark mass of jungle on

the other, with a trickle of refugees walking cautiously along both
sides of the road. Marika and Stefan drove past the airport, which
was protected by the last of the UN outposts. White armored per-
sonnel carriers, or APCs, sat beside trenches, Uruguayan peace-
keeping soldiers in light blue helmets waving at Marika. The rebel
fighters knew that these men were off-limits. They knew that if they
didn't touch anything UN-related, or, God forbid, hurt one of the
soldiers, they could go on killing and looting indefinitely.

After the airport, there was no more semblance of safety—
however real or imagined—from the UN. As the Lendu ruled the
countryside, Marika's safety depended on enlisting the help of a
high-ranking rebel officer in the field. Her letter, the key to their
survival, had come from a man in one of the displaced person
camps who claimed to be a Lendu colonel. He had looked different from the other refugees. Well fed. Arrogant in a situation that
reduced most to begging and humility. He'd even signed his
name in a garish flurry of curlicues—the signature typical of
African petty warlords. He'd claimed his letter would gain her
access to anything she needed—in particular, officers whose assistance might be invaluable. In exchange, of course, he would
expect a generous *cadeau*, or gift, when Marika returned.

"Your colonel," Stefan was saying to Marika, sitting back in
his seat and bracing himself as the truck dipped into a deep pothole, "did you trust him?"

"I don't know. You can't trust anyone out here," she said.

"Can I see the letter?"

She handed it to him, and he skimmed it.

"It is a very impressive letter," he yelled over the groaning of
the engine, "but most of them are impressive. It may work, but it
could also get us killed."

Marika stopped the truck, the UN flag over the airport still
visible behind them. "Last chance," she said. "I can take you
back. I have my own camera. I can always take some shots if I end
up getting anywhere."

Stefan laughed. "I am in this truck, yes? Don't worry about me."

She wondered, as she had during past assignments with him, if he felt the need to protect her because she was a woman. She'd heard that he had a number of girlfriends in various countries, yet he'd always maintained a strict hands-off policy with her. He did not open doors for her, did not help her in or out of vehicles, did not offer her a hand with anything. Perhaps, she speculated, this was his way of paying her professional respect.

Thoughts of Seb suddenly forced their way into Marika's mind, though she always forbade herself to think about home— and anything good she may have left there—when she was on assignment. The memories of Seb were hard to banish, though. She could still feel the lightness of his fingers on her body, could still feel his lips against her skin.

She quickly turned to Stefan.

"Robert Lewis was here a few weeks ago," she told him, slamming on the brakes and thrusting the truck into first gear.

He nodded. "I heard this."

"I bet even he wouldn't try what we're doing right now."

Stefan pondered this for a moment. "He has done much worse," he concluded.

Marika saw only a handful of people as they drove: women in sarongs and ripped T-shirts carrying bundles of firewood on their heads, older men digging up roots from a sallow field, children holding up single potatoes for sale, their entire pile barely enough to complete a grown man's meal. As they started passing through grassy fields seemingly empty of all life, Marika had the growing feeling that she was being watched. By whom or from where, she couldn't say, but she was sure of it. She had put a PRESS sign on the front and back of the truck, just in case, and a white flag on the antenna, but in a game without any rules, it wasn't reasonable to expect a bunch of drugged-up child soldiers to play fair.

In the distance: a Lendu checkpoint. At least, she inferred it was Lendu, as the soldiers wore stiff new camouflage uniforms— gifts from the Ugandan army. Tires lay in the road, piled four high, on top of which sat some young men with AK-47s.

Marika didn't know if they'd try to shoot her before she reached them. She wasn't sure if she should stop early, or advance slowly, or give any number of signs or signals to make known her intention. Every checkpoint had entirely different rules.

She stopped the truck. "What do you think?" she asked Stefan.

He was out the window again, taking photos of the soldiers at the checkpoint. "Keep going," he insisted.

As Marika began driving forward, a couple of young soldiers crept in front of the roadblock. Abruptly, they raised their rifles and aimed. She slammed on the brakes, Stefan nearly falling to the ground. Marika expected to be shot right there, but the soldiers broke into surprised grins when they noticed that she was a white woman. They waved her toward the checkpoint, and as she approached it slowly, one of them stepped in front of her vehicle and ordered her to stop.

Marika greeted the teenage kid through her open window. "We're journalists," she explained to him in French.

But Marika and Stefan might have been movie stars by how their presence mesmerized the boy. He called his friends over, and several skinny kids soon crowded around the truck, clutching their rifles.

"Where are you going?" they asked Marika with excited eyes.

Stefan sat on the window frame and began taking pictures of the soldiers. He didn't notice an older man striding out of a nearby shack, who grabbed the camera around his neck and nearly pulled him from the vehicle.

"No photos!" the soldier raged. "No photos!" His eyes were bloodshot and jaundiced, and he held a beat-up AK-47 in his hand, spare cartridges tied crudely to the stock with strips of inner tube. Letting go of the camera, the man pressed his rifle barrel against the side of Stefan's head. "No photos!"

"Okay! Okay!" Stefan held up his hands. "No photos!"

"We're journalists!" Marika kept telling him.

Slowly, Stefan reached in a pocket and took out some cigarettes, offering them to the man. "*Cadeau,*" he said. "A gift for you. Take them."

The man lowered his rifle and took the cigarettes, putting one between his lips. Stefan lit it for him, then pulled out a cigarette for himself.

Marika called over one of the young soldiers, a boy no older than thirteen. "We'd like to see the officer in charge," she said to him. "Go find him for us."

The kid ran off down the road. Minutes later, someone appeared in the distance, walking swiftly toward them. In his wake were several armed men—perhaps bodyguards.

"Our savior," Stefan said drolly, watching the approaching man and inhaling sharply on his cigarette.

Marika could tell that this was obviously someone in command. He wore sunglasses, had an erect, imperious gait. Looking paunchy in his trim new uniform and black boots, he carried a holstered handgun, his bodyguards gripping new AK-47s with smooth wooden stocks. Marika sighed, steeling herself. Here was someone—she knew—to be reckoned with.

"That is Colonel Katembo," a soldier told her.

Katembo looked to be in his late twenties—already too old for this children's war. Marika forced out a smile as he walked up to the truck, but it had no effect on his hardened expression. His eyes were dark, empty.

"We're journalists," she said to him in French. "I'm Marika Vecera. This is Stefan Muller."

Katembo examined them stoically, lips pursed. "Passports," he demanded.

Neither she nor Stefan had thought it a good idea to bring their passports. They pulled out press cards instead, and Marika unfolded the letter from the Lendu colonel.

Luckily for her, Katembo could read. He regarded their

paperwork with strict concentration, his finger running over the bleeding red stamp on the letter.

"I was told that we would have your cooperation to travel in the countryside," Marika explained, deciding she wouldn't mention anything about the goldfields. At least, not yet. "We'd like an escort." Then she said the magic words: "Of course, we'll pay."

"What is it you want to see?" he asked with a suspicious tone in his voice.

"We'd like to visit some Lendu villages, see what the Hema have done to them."

"I can already tell you," Katembo replied without emotion. "Those cockroaches have butchered our men, women, and children. They have burned our villages to the ground. There is nothing left to see."

Of course, she knew that Katembo and his people were doing the same to the Hema; most of the women and children with severed limbs, whom she'd seen in Bodo, had been Hema. It was nearly impossible to know who had started the whole conflict, or when it had started, or why. Some said the troubles began with the Belgian colonists, back in the nineteenth century—which sounded entirely plausible to Marika, though she suspected that all wars were just natural, diabolical expressions of the human soul.

Katembo led them to a thatched hut and ordered them to sit on a wooden bench inside. They obeyed, a couple of soldiers standing guard nearby. The colonel headed back the way he had come, strolling purposefully down the dirt road with their press cards and letter in hand.

"We wait," Stefan said, leaning back against the thatch wall. He stuck all of his camera equipment carefully under the bench before closing his eyes.

Marika's mind ran over everything that had happened so far. Things looked remotely promising. Of course, if they couldn't get past this checkpoint with an escort, they'd head right back to

Bodo. It would be sheer lunacy to drive deeper into the country-side alone.

❧

A soldier called out to Marika: Colonel Katembo was returning.

She and Stefan had been waiting in the hut for over two hours. Now it was well past noon, and the loss of critical daylight was concerning her. Even if Katembo did give them permission to continue, she knew they'd have to return to Bodo and attempt the trip on another day.

"Stefan," she whispered, waking him. "Katembo's coming back."

As he sat up, crossing his arms, a soldier burst inside the hut and pressed a rifle barrel against her head. Katembo soon followed, eyes ablaze.

"Who gave you this letter?" he demanded of Marika.

Adrenaline cut through her. She told him the name of the man back in Bodo.

"Lie!" he said. He turned to Stefan. "Who gave you this letter?"

As Stefan repeated the name Marika had already given, the colonel slapped him across the face.

"You're both liars," he said. "Are you spies for the Hema, for the CIA?"

Katembo's bodyguards pushed them out of the hut and over to the truck. They were held at gunpoint as the soldiers rifled through their possessions, tossing them in a pile on the dusty road. One of the men seized the camera around Stefan's neck.

"Colonel," Marika said as calmly as she could, "we're journalists. You have our press cards—"

"You're both liars and spies."

"We're *journalists*. Look at our press cards—"

Katembo smacked her across the face, and her lip struck her teeth. She tasted blood, felt stinging aftershocks of pain.

"Don't say anything else to them," Stefan told her, a soldier backhanding him across the face for talking.

Katembo yelled something in a tribal language, and several young soldiers raced to remove some tires from the roadblock. Another soldier jumped into the driver's seat of the truck. He started it, grinding the gears several times before getting it in first. Katembo ordered Marika and Stefan to get in back, and threw their things in behind them. The truck passed through the checkpoint and stopped half a mile down the road, in front of a pockmarked building half reduced to rubble. A soldier told them to get out of the truck and go inside. As they entered, Marika smelled the strong stench of urine. Stefan paused, his eyes evaluating the scene: an ancient desk sitting at one end of the room, garbage strewn about, mildewed walls covered with flaking white paint and torn posters of young, scantily clad Congolese women advertising Primus beer. As he studied the rubble at the far end of the room, and the single fluorescent light hanging from the ceiling, its bulb shattered, Marika saw a quick wave of anguish break across his face.

"Sit down," a soldier said to them, pointing to the floor.

"First you must bring in our things," Stefan demanded.

The soldier just trained his rifle on him. "Sit!"

They sat. More soldiers entered, all the naive excitement they'd displayed upon meeting Marika and Stefan having vanished. Their young faces looked stiff, frozen, unreachable. She and Stefan waited in silence. Fear edged up Marika's body, making her hands shake.

"They're playing a game with us," Stefan whispered. "When they get bored, we can give them money and they'll let us go."

But she had heard an uncharacteristic hesitancy in his voice.

"How much money did you bring with you?" he asked her.

"About two thousand dollars," she whispered.

She was wearing what looked like a normal leather belt. Inside, however, folded up, were a dozen new one-hundred-dollar bills. She'd put more down her socks and in a secret pocket on the inside of her pants. In her backpack, which the soldiers now possessed, were only a few decoy bills.

"Good," Stefan said. "We will bribe them."

They heard footsteps outside. Soldiers parted from the doorway, and Katembo burst inside with a bevy of armed guards. Immediately, his soldiers seized Stefan and dragged him to his feet. Marika got up too, but they shoved her back down.

"Where's he going?" she demanded.

"You are staying here!" Katembo ordered.

"I'm not leaving her," Stefan said.

Katembo just ignored him.

"Look," Stefan told him, "the UN soldiers know we're here. If we don't return soon, they'll come looking for us."

"To hell with your UN soldiers," Katembo said. "They're as useless as women."

As Stefan was being escorted from the building, his eyes found Marika's, and she saw fear in them—fear for *her*, she realized. For what the soldiers might do to her in his absence.

She stood up again. "I'm going with him," she said.

A soldier tried to push her down, but she punched him in the chest. Enraged, he struck at her face. As she ducked away, the man drew his knife.

Stefan swore at the top of his voice—a deep, otherworldly shout that caused everyone to freeze. For a moment, the room sat in heavy silence.

Katembo ordered the soldier to put away his knife. He walked casually up to Marika and pulled out his gun. "You will not talk anymore," he said to her. Abruptly, he struck her on the temple with the pistol butt. There was blackness, and she collapsed to the ground.

Marika opened her eyes. She lay on the filthy cement floor of the building, her head throbbing. Stefan was gone, and a group of soldiers stood at the other end of the room, staring at her with smirks on their faces. She crawled against the wall. Blood traveled down her temple and fell onto her shirt, but she didn't dare reach up to feel how bad the wound was. Fighting off dizziness, she strained to hear any sound from Stefan, her imagination going wild with thoughts of what they were doing to him. Nothing felt more excruciating than her inability to help him.

The sun was dipping toward the western horizon. An hour passed. Another hour. Marika sat huddling against the cold cement wall. Mosquitoes entered the building, buzzing near her ears, hovering restlessly around her. Occasionally, the sound of gunfire cut through the predusk air. She kept thinking of Stefan and glanced at the expressions of the soldiers across the room, but their faces revealed nothing.

When the sun was an orange sliver on the horizon, she heard people approaching the building. A dark silhouette filled the doorway. Stefan! He limped inside, his body lightly quivering. Bruises and dried blood covered his arms. His face, raw and swelled from having been beaten, was almost unrecognizable.

A soldier pushed him down beside her.

"They kept asking me the same questions," he told her immediately, his words slurred. "They wanted to know where we got that letter. They wanted to know who wrote it. They said they don't believe we're journalists. That kind of bullshit. Then they shot bullets around my head. I can't hear out of this ear."

Across the room, the young soldiers lounged against the wall, talking absently to each other. Their rifles lay across their laps, the barrels pointed at Marika and Stefan. One of the boys kept staring at her as a cat might patiently watch a bird before pouncing.

Stefan shook his head. "You can't reason with these people. The only thing that interests them is money. We must bribe them to let us go back to Bodo." His voice got softer, was barely a whisper. He spoke close to Marika's ear. "I am so sorry to say this, but I think they want to kill us. I think I heard Katembo say that he's waiting to get the order."

Marika pressed her hand against her forehead, taking quick breaths. She saw Seb in her mind. His kind eyes. His smile. She just wished she could hold him one more time. Could he some-how know, somehow *sense*, what was happening to her now—and be sending his love?

"Listen," Stefan said, "we must try to bribe someone. It's our only option now."

"Who should we bribe?" she asked.

He stared at the soldiers across the room. "Maybe one of them. Or maybe Katembo would be better."

The room was sinking into darkness with the coming night. One of the boys lit a couple of candles, affixing them to the desk-top. In distant Bodo, Marika heard a succession of deep booms as the mortar fire began. She contemplated the soldiers before her, trying to decide who would be best to approach. There was the kid with the red bandanna around his neck. He couldn't have been older than thirteen and seemed shy and withdrawn. He'd even seemed to understand their French. Yes, he would be good to try. She would call him over.

But just then, Katembo entered the building. Scowling at her and Stefan, he walked to the lit desk. In his hand were their press cards—and the letter that might cost them their lives.

"*Bon soir,*" he said to them with mock politeness.

As he leaned close to one of the candles, reading their letter again, Marika studied the features of his face. The wide nose, sharply angled cheeks, bloodshot eyes. The smirk rising from a corner of his mouth.

"Do you know what I did to the last spy I caught?" Katembo said to them. "I put a rope around his neck and tied him to a truck. Then I put a rope around his feet and tied him to another truck, ripping him in half."

"If you let us go back to Bodo," Stefan said, "we'll pay you."

Katembo looked at him and laughed. "You will pay me?"

"Take out the money," Stefan whispered to Marika.

She didn't want to do it. She didn't think Katembo was the person to deal with. But Stefan nudged her, so she pulled out the bills from the secret pocket in her pants.

"It's five hundred dollars," she said to Stefan.

"Here's five hundred dollars," Stefan announced to Katembo in French. "We'll give you more when we get back to Bodo."

"Bring me the money," Katembo said to Marika.

She glanced at Stefan before getting up. Reluctantly, she walked over and held out the bills. Her hand was shaking—surely Katembo noticed. She reiterated to him that she and Stefan were journalists. She told him where they'd been sent for assignments, by which publications. She even told him that they'd met the president of Uganda, a great friend of the Lendu.

But Katembo wasn't listening. He was studying her body unabashedly.

"Get to your knees," he ordered her, pointing to the spot beside him. "*Mets-toi à genoux!*"

Marika's hands were shaking uncontrollably now. "No," she said. Outside, she heard the close sound of gunfire, but this didn't faze Katembo.

"I ordered you to get down."

"No."

Astonished by her reply, Katembo motioned to a couple of soldiers nearby, telling them to force her to the ground. They stepped forward, grinning.

"Do you know who I am?" Katembo asked Marika.

She nodded.

"No, I don't think you know who I am. I am commander here. You will listen to me. Lie down!"

Stefan suddenly yelled out, swearing at him.

Katembo spoke calmly to one of the soldiers. The boy strode across the room and shoved his rifle barrel into Stefan's mouth. The German looked at Marika with the sullen, dead-eyed expression of someone who expected to be killed at any moment.

Mortar blasts landed in the nearby hills. Katembo quickly put out the candles, just as the building started shaking. Something sharp sliced into Marika's arm. Further blasts rattled the ground, causing plaster and dust to fall upon her. As Katembo ducked for cover, Marika ran back to Stefan. The soldiers crowded to a nearby window, their rifles at the ready. Marika lay low on the floor, hearing the panicking boys calling to each other. A shell landed closer than ever, and more dust rained down.

The metallic stinging of bullets peppered the corrugated iron roof of the building. Probably, Marika reasoned, the arriving Hema soldiers were just beginning their assault. She pressed herself against the cold concrete floor. With each volley of gunfire, she waited for a bullet to find her. To end her nightmare. Several blasts went off nearby. The sound of gunfire intensified. Some of the soldiers ran from the building and shot into the darkness. Others took up a position near one of the windows. Marika eyed the window closest to her, noticing that no one was there. Instinct took over: she would climb out and run.

"I'm going through the window," she told Stefan over the deafening noise of the gunfight. "Come on!"

Another blast shook the building. Before he could reply, she was crawling out and jumping to the ground. To her relief, he followed. They sidled up against the building, machine-gun fire spraying across the nearby road. Marika saw several dark figures coming toward her. Tugging at Stefan's arm, she sprinted to a clump of bushes. The moon hadn't risen yet, and the darkness of the countryside soon enveloped them. Knowing that Bodo was only a few miles to the south, she waited until she no longer saw anyone in that direction, and ran. Stefan tried to follow but lagged from his injuries. She had to slow down, encourage him, urge him forward.

After they'd put about half a mile between them and the building, they sat behind a bush to rest. Marika could still see the checkpoint in the distance, at the epicenter of what looked to be a fierce firefight. She could make out a large crowd of soldiers surging toward it from the hills.

"We're still too close," she whispered to Stefan.

He nodded. They got up again and trotted through some more fields. Hearing Stefan's labored breathing behind her, Marika again slowed her pace. As they reached the top of a small hill, he collapsed in the tall grass, gasping. Gunfire echoed from various spots in the countryside. Flames swept down a neighboring field, devouring the grass in a chain of fire. Marika could see the distant fires of the UN refugee camps and knew they were approaching the outskirts of Bodo. Not far to safety. But more Hema fighters streamed out of town and raced toward the checkpoint, rifles firing. She and Stefan lay low, trying not to move. An hour passed. Another hour. Soldiers kept trickling out of town. At one point, fighters traveled so close to Marika that she could smell their cigarettes.

At last the sound of gunfire subsided. A new day was announcing itself with the merest hint of light in the east. Marika had never paid much attention to the sun rising. Had never watched darkness give way to dawn. On that morning, though, as she prayed for her life in eastern Congo, the sunrise seemed to come too slowly—too cruelly—convincing her that it would never arrive at all. But finally: bloodred rays erupted over the earth, illuminating the grassy hills.

In the near distance, Marika now saw the UN's white, tank-like APCs. She helped Stefan up, and they made their slow, cautious way to the airport.

CHAPTER SIX

As Marika's plane landed in Boston, she stared through the window at the glare of rain on the tarmac of Logan Airport. Boston looked the same. Only colder now. Wetter. The city locked in February's hibernation.

She struggled to sit up. Everything seemed to take too long. The plane's slow crawl to the gate. The interminable wait before the door would open. As soon as the seatbelt sign went off, passengers swarmed into the aisle, bodies moving and jockeying around her as if rushing a breadline. She stayed in her seat. She would stay in it as long as possible. Turning away from everyone, she pulled out one of her minibottles of whiskey, taking a surreptitious swig.

Just two days earlier, she'd been in Congo. She'd said good-bye to Stefan at the UN compound, knowing from his dull, bewildered eyes and vacant expression that he would never be the same. She flew out of Bodo as soon as she could, in a Cessna bound for Rwanda's capital, Kigali. From there, waiting a few hours on standby, she got a flight to Brussels. How bizarre, leaving a part of the world where passengers actually clap as their plane takes off, as if they'd all been launching a great escape. To Marika, it had felt more like a betrayal. She'd spent her life visiting wars and massacres, but unlike the people caught in them, she never had to stay. What had she ever done to earn such egregious favor?

On the plane ride home, her appetite gone, she'd helped herself to several minibottles of Johnny Walker in lieu of meals. Her injured arm wouldn't allow her to sleep. The pain was too sharp, too incessant, even with all the ibuprofen she'd taken. At the UN compound, she'd rinsed off some of the blood and dirt only to discover a deep puncture wound cutting into her bicep. She could see fatty tissue and muscle, but as there hadn't been much bleeding she'd just slathered her arm with Betadine ointment and slapped on a couple of jumbo-sized Band-Aids. The doctors hadn't been able to help her; they'd been too busy treating all the cholera cases, all the machete wounds and severed limbs, and there was a Cessna leaving for Rwanda's capital in an hour. She'd barely enough time to retrieve her backpack from the priests' compound and buy herself a seat.

Once in Europe, Marika called the magazine to tell her editor what had happened. But he knew already—Stefan had contacted him. Pulling some strings, he got her on the first flight back to the States. Guilty, he even flew her home business class; it was a first for the magazine, spending that kind of money on her. Her editor didn't like to hear about, or deal with, writers' messes. Most of Marika's closest calls never ended up appearing in print. She had to constantly anesthetize her past, the ugliest growths separated and surgically removed. There was the Official Truth of her experiences abroad, and then there were the closer, more private truths.

As passengers started leaving the plane, Marika willed herself to stand. She felt feverish and couldn't move her injured arm for the pain, pus leaking through the bandages. She asked a flight attendant to pull down her overhead bag and put its strap on her shoulder, and when she finally did get off—when she finally set foot on American soil at last—she felt like a prisoner paroled by mistake.

She stood for several long moments in the airport, inhaling the fresh sea air of Boston, looking around her in a daze. As the indifferent crowds swept past her, a sudden fear took hold, telling her that she hadn't really escaped Congo at all—that Boston was actually the dream.

She would not remember falling. She would not remember collapsing and hitting her head on the floor of the arrivals hall.

☙

Seb's voice.

"Marika—can you hear me?"

"Seb?"

Someone lightly shook her shoulder, and she opened her eyes. She found herself in a hospital bed. Seb was sitting beside her, looking straight at her.

"Hey, there," he said, tears of relief in his eyes.

She could only stare at him. Breathe in the safety of his presence.

He took her hand. "How do you feel?"

She glanced at everything around her. All the nondescript features of the room. The generic cleanliness. The IV tube sticking out of her arm. "How did I get here?"

"You fainted in the airport," he said, scooting his chair closer to her.

"I did?" She tried to remember. She could vaguely recall getting off the plane.

"You were unconscious for a while, so they had to call an ambulance."

She looked at him, confused. "How did you know about it?"

"The airline had my name as your emergency contact."

"Oh." She'd forgotten about that. Usually her emergency contact was an editor. Someone neutral from work. Yet the one time she'd used Seb as her contact, he was the person the airline called. It seemed too coincidental to be a coincidence.

Seb cleared his throat. "The doctor said you probably fainted from dehydration—you had a high fever. You also hit your head when you fell, but they checked it out and didn't find any internal injuries. That's the good news. But the wound on your arm was pretty infected."

"It was?" She looked at the bandage around her biceps.

"Yeah. The doctor said it was really dirty inside, so they had to clean it out and remove the dead tissue. It's not stitched up yet. I guess it has to drain."

"Oh."

"But he said it should heal well."

"That's good."

Seb cleared his throat again. "The doctor said there was an exit wound, so he was thinking you may have been shot."

Marika didn't say anything.

"Were you?" Seb asked, his voice strained.

"I don't know. There was a lot of noise. I was just trying to get out of there."

"Out of where?"

"A building." She touched her head. "God—I've got a huge headache."

Seb grabbed an ice pack from a nearby table, handing it to her. "Use this."

She suddenly noticed his teary eyes, drawn brow, anguished expression. She'd never seen anyone looking so concerned for her.

"Seb, I'm all right." She attempted to smile. "I'm okay."

He sighed, squeezing her hand. "You really matter to me, you know? I could have lost you."

She didn't know what to say. She wasn't someone who easily handled the sight of other people's tears—especially if they were for her. Tears seemed to *require* something from her. And she felt too wiped out and battered to know how to respond.

Seb reached out to touch her cheek, but she flinched away.

"Sorry," he said, pulling back his hand and studying her with renewed distress.

"I'm a little edgy," she said, forcing a smile. "This happens sometimes, right after I get back. But it'll go away."

She pressed her fingers to her forehead, the headache pounding.

"Marika, what happened to you?" Seb asked gently. "You

have a bruise on your face." He pointed out the spot on her cheek. "Did someone hit you?"

She felt her temple instead. It was throbbing—from where she'd fallen down in the airport. But no. She remembered Colonel Katembo. How he'd struck her with his gun.

"Marika, what happened?" Seb asked again.

"There were these rebel soldiers holding me and Stefan," she said. "And then there was a firefight."

She stared at her bandaged arm. It occurred to her, for the first time since she awoke, that it was giving her pain. And her IV bag, she noticed, was empty, her own blood inching its way up the tube.

"Who's Stefan?" Seb asked.

"The photographer." She tried to sit up. They'd put her in one of those awful hospital gowns that barely covered her legs. "I don't have to stay here, do I?"

"For a little while."

"Do you know how long?"

"I don't know. I'll ask." But Seb didn't move.

"That ambulance is going to cost me a fortune," she said. "My health insurance is a joke."

"Marika," Seb said slowly, gently, "why were soldiers holding you?"

She rubbed her eyes and looked at him. "They thought we were spies," she said.

She saw concern sweep across his face.

"Places like that," she added quickly, "they think *every*body's a spy. It gives them an excuse to rob you or kill you or whatever."

Seb's intense eyes were trained on her. "*Were* they trying to rob or kill you?"

She could still hear Katembo's grainy-sounding French: "*Mets-toi à genoux!*"

She felt a shot of rage. Glaring at her blood in the IV tube, she nearly ripped the whole thing out of her arm. But caught herself. And sighed. And shrugged. Sitting back, she gave Seb her full attention finally.

"In those places," she told him matter-of-factly, "they're always trying to rob and kill you."

Marika spent another day in the hospital, the doctor wanting to make sure no complications arose. When none did, and when she insisted on leaving, he stitched up her arm and sent her on her way. Seb urged her to go to his place; he didn't want her to be alone after everything that had happened to her. Marika didn't bother protesting; she was too exhausted. As it was, the antibiotics and painkillers had numbed her into a state of complete indifference.

Seb owned a condo on the tenth—and highest—floor of a building that overlooked the Charles River in Cambridge. The first thing Marika had always noticed about the place was its giant living room window showing a completely unadulterated view of the Boston skyline. She'd seen his condo a few times in the weeks they'd been dating, but for some reason it looked new to her now. Completely unfamiliar. Had it always been so elegant, so palatial? She gazed at the high ceilings and gleaming hardwood floors, at the bloodred Persian carpets and framed black-and-white photographs lining the walls. There were shots of birds breaking toward sunlight. Shots of an old man with a creased face and warm smile. The place struck her as being unusually full of light, the sun gleaming through many windows.

"Welcome back," Seb said gently, guiding her inside.

She wanted desperately to take a shower, so he led her to the bathroom and started the water for her. Getting her a towel and one of his clean T-shirts, he even tried to help her undress until she sent him away. She needed to be alone. She pulled her clothes off, looking at the bruises on her face and body; she must have gotten some of them while escaping from that building near Bodo. She felt profoundly tired all of a sudden and didn't have the courage to look herself in the eyes. Careful not to get her bandaged arm wet, she stepped into the shower, the dirt of Congo disappearing unceremoniously down the drain.

She had barely left the bathroom, when Seb came over and tried helping her to his large leather couch. It was more concern than she was used to, or willing to tolerate, having just spent weeks in a central African war zone taking care of herself. All she wanted now—and she didn't think she was asking too much—was for the world and everyone in it to just leave her alone for a while.

"I'm *all right*," she said to Seb testily, shaking him off. "I'm fine."

"Sorry," he mumbled.

She lay down on his sofa, hugging her legs against her. Seb hesitated, then offered her a pillow. As she took it, she noticed that it had his smell on it. Seb's unique, musky scent, which was part cologne, part something intangible. She had always loved the smell of him. It gave her chills.

As she put the pillow beneath her head, it brushed the bump on her temple, and she let up a cry, wincing.

"Are you hurt there?" Seb asked.

"I'm hurt everywhere," she whispered.

He kneeled down before her, and she felt his lips brush against her cheek. "Can I look?" he asked.

"Yeah"

Delicately, he parted the hair over the knot and examined it. "Is this from the fall in the airport?"

"No."

"From Africa?"

She nodded.

Intense worry filled his expression. He was about to speak, but she closed her eyes. "I'm really tired," she said.

He gently moved her hair back. "You rest now, okay?" He kissed her on the head, breathing her in. Then he said it: "I love you."

❧

She awoke in the middle of night. For an excruciating moment she didn't remember where she was, and panic overtook her. She glanced around her until the familiar sights entered her consciousness: the skyline of Boston, the Charles River, the living room window. She was in Seb's place, of course. On his couch. He'd wrapped her in his cashmere blanket, and now she drew it tightly around her. She heard the sound of breathing and looked down to see him sleeping on the floor below her. She studied him for a long time. The gentle rising and falling of his chest as he slept. The way his hands were clasped beneath his chin. She noticed that he was still wearing his clothes from the previous day.

Slowly, she reached down and touched his hand.

He woke with a start and looked at her. "Hey," he said. "How you doing?"

"Better."

He yawned and stretched, sitting up. "Can I get you something? The doctor wanted you to drink lots of fluids."

"Maybe some water?"

"Sure." He glanced at his watch. It was half past three. "You sleeping okay?"

"Not so well. It's probably the jet lag."

Seb got up and went to the kitchen. She watched the light go on. Listened to the sound of the faucet running.

"You want any ice?" he asked her.

"No, thanks." She was trying to grapple with such a drastic change of realities. In a matter of days, she'd gone from a Congolese jungle to Seb's Cambridge apartment, listening to him rifling through the kitchen.

She pulled the edge of the blanket over her chin. Almost magically, Seb appeared next to her again.

"Here's your water." He handed her the glass.

"Thanks." She put it to her lips—but paused before drinking, for fear the water would be contaminated. It was the Congolese reality, trying to reassert itself. Like living in double exposure.

"How's the pain?" Seb asked. "Do you need any medicine?"

"It's all right. I don't want to get doped up again."

"Yeah, but if it's hurting you—"

"It's okay."

Seb gave her a long look before going to light some candles, putting them on the coffee table nearby. The flames' reflections flickered against the large glass window, as if Boston itself were alight.

"So you're not sleeping well?" he asked.

"Not really. I'm sorry I woke you. I'm sure you have work or classes tomorrow."

"Don't even worry about it." He sat cross-legged before her. "I told everyone I'm not going to be in for the rest of the week. I don't want you to be alone right now."

She felt a flash of anxiety, wondering what the price would be for his concern. She didn't know him that well, after all. They'd only been dating a couple of months.

"Seb, I'm okay. You can go to work. You must have important stuff going on."

"It's not as important as you." He studied her for a moment, then tentatively put his hand on her cheek, over the bruise. "Can I ask what happened to you?"

Here it was. The price she would have to pay. Marika found herself squirming. She knew she'd just have to get used to it all, like learning a new religion.

"When you go through something difficult," Seb said, choosing his words carefully, "some kind of really tough event, it's a good idea to talk about it while it's still fresh in your mind."

"But there's nothing to talk about." She ran her hand along the bandage on her arm, and ever-so-slightly raised a corner of adhesive with her fingernail. "It's over."

"Do you find it hard to talk about?"

"*No*. There's just nothing to talk about. I had a scrape with some soldiers, but I'm fine now."

She saw worry filling Seb's expression. "Can I ask you one thing?" he said.

She shrugged, studying the glass of water.

"Those soldiers . . . did they do anything to you?"

"Like what?" She looked at him.

"You know . . . did they try to rape you?"

She sighed and gazed out the window.

"You'd tell me, wouldn't you?" he asked.

She saw the building outside of Bodo again. The candle on the desk. Stefan with the gun in his mouth.

"No," she said finally, "they didn't 'do anything' to me." But her voice had cracked, betrayed her.

"Marika—"

"They *wanted* to," she said quietly. "They were going to. But I got away."

"Jesus . . . ," Seb said.

She crossed her arms.

"Were those soldiers the ones who hit you?" he asked.

She said nothing, her silence answering his question.

Tears filled Seb's eyes. He reached out to hold her, but Marika pulled back, frightened and embarrassed by his concern. He got to his knees. Slowly leaning forward, he kissed her on the forehead, his lips lingering there. She would always remember the encompassing presence of him in that instant. How she'd trembled from his touch. But most of all, she would remember the way he'd kissed her. It had been like a priest's kiss—a kiss of absolution, of unbounded love.

She didn't want the moment to end. Tears rolled down her cheek. "Goddamn it," she said, wiping them away.

Seb's hand touched her face. "You're safe now," he told her.

"Nowhere's safe," she said angrily. "No place on earth."

"No," Seb whispered, "here you're safe."

She hugged her legs against her and stared out the window at the dark skyscrapers. "I can't do this right now," she suddenly said.

"Do what?" Seb gazed at her, uncomprehending.

"*This.* This playacting." She swiped at more tears.

"I don't understand."

"*This.* All of it." She gestured around her, at the high ceilings, the photographs on the walls. She could still smell the stench of urine in that building outside of Bodo. *"This!"* She tossed down Seb's blanket, putting her glass on the floor. "I need to be alone for a while."

"Marika—"

"No place is safe!" she said to Seb, glaring at him.

For a fleeting second, she thought she might actually try to hit him, hurt him. Tears flooded down her face, onto his blanket, and she tried vainly to wipe them off.

"Marika," Seb said soothingly, "it's okay." He was still on his knees, facing her. "Hey, it's okay."

"I'm sorry—I can't fucking do this," she said to him. "I'm too much of a mess right now."

"It's okay," he said.

He put his hand on hers, but she yanked it away.

"I *can't* do this."

"You don't have to," Seb said.

She got up, wiping her nose. "I have to go back to my place. I just need to be alone for a while. I'm sorry. It's nothing personal. I just need to be alone."

"Okay. Let me help you." He paused to collect his thoughts. "Why don't I call you a taxi, all right?" He got up, looked around in the darkness. "Where's your bag?"

"I don't know," she said.

"Let me find your bag." But he stopped, stared at her. "Marika, I want you to know I'm here for you. Don't think you're alone with this, okay? If you need *any*thing, just give me a call—day or night, it doesn't matter. All right?"

She nodded. "Okay."

As she stepped away from the sofa, she knocked over her glass. Water rushed onto Seb's Persian carpet, across his hardwood floor.

"Fuck!" She shouted it with such rage, such violence, that Seb was momentarily stunned. "I have to leave," she said.

For the next two weeks, Boston slowly ingratiated itself to Marika: tourists in trolleys, swan boats, crumbling tombstones with their carved, winged skulls. She ate in fast-food joints a couple of times a day for no other reason than that she could. She walked through the Common late at night because all fear had left her. One morning, she found herself on the observation deck of a skyscraper, staring down on a world that could be contained in a single glance. And she slept. A lot. Only red wine and sleep could silence her mind. If thoughts arose about how close she'd come to being raped or killed in Congo—*when* they arose—she told them to solicit at another doorstep.

She still didn't want to see Seb. She just wanted to forget her time in Africa, and it had seemed like Seb's whole modus operandi was to make her remember. Not to mention, her post-trip edginess was getting worse. She'd never taken so long to readjust after one of her trips, and she could only blame him; he'd kept trying to open doors he had no business approaching. Shortly after leaving his place, she'd let him know that she'd be busy writing her article and wouldn't be contacting anyone until it was finished. But, now that she was done, she didn't want to call Seb. She told herself she just wasn't ready yet.

Instead, Marika decided to find Max Sanders.

She took a long bath, carefully put on makeup, picked out something special to wear: tight, revealing clothes that felt oddly exotic on her. Though the bruises on her face had nearly disappeared, and her arm was healing well (she'd taken out the stitches

herself, saving the cost of a doctor's visit), she didn't feel particu-
larly beautiful or attractive—she didn't feel much of anything.
She went looking for Sanders at his regular haunt in the Beacon
Hill Pub and saw him and two other men at a table in the back.
Ties loosened. Legs splayed. They were watching a baseball game
on the overhead television.

"Vecera!" Sanders called from across the room.

Theirs was a business of using last names. There was a certain
team spirit behind it, and a strange affection. Sanders waited until
the batter struck out, then leaped from his chair and walked over
to her, giving her a hug and peck on both cheeks. He always
appeared enormously happy to see her.

It'd been over four months since she'd last slept with Sanders.
She never got attached to him, nor he to her. It was always about
sex—or something akin to sex. It was always about something
raw and primeval, and patently without significance. This did not
seem, on the face of it, an egregious thing to Marika. For her, it
was enough to go through the motions of intimacy without anything being expected in return. No deep talks. No revelations.
Sanders was much too self-absorbed for that sort of thing, and
she, much too disinterested.

Sanders was deputy editor at *New England Life,* and he and
Marika ended up at a lot of the same parties, had a lot of the same
friends. He would readily admit to anyone that he respected her
work—he thought Marika Vecera was one of the best freelance
writers out there—and though she wouldn't write for *NEL*
because she thought it was "frivolous," he didn't take offense.
Max Sanders was someone who admired dedication wherever he
found it, and he had never met anyone more hardworking and
ambitious than she.

"How goes it?" Sanders asked her.

"All right," she said. "I just got back from Africa."

"They don't pay you enough for that. How about I make you
a senior editor at *New England Life?* Six figures." He picked up

his drink. As he excused himself from his friends, they looked at him knowingly.

Sanders guided Marika over to a booth. She had known him, off and on, for six years. Always as friends. Sometimes as lovers. Nearly forty-seven, he kept all relations with women "open," brandishing his bachelorhood like a badge. He often spoke, with a blend of curiosity and contempt, of commitment, marriage, and—that most objectionable subject of all—children. He was invariably well coiffed, with his short brown hair carefully combed back. Smelling heavily of fine cologne, wearing expensive shirts and Italian leather shoes, he was a walking *Esquire* ad.

Marika sat down next to him, and he turned to face her. Whether he'd had a few drinks or not, his dark eyes always ran fearlessly over her face and body, taking her in like a photographer considering his next shot.

"You smell really good," he said.

"Thanks."

He spread an arm out behind her, encapsulating her in his gaze. A part of her loved the aggressive sexual energy about him, how he liked to make all the moves and got straight to business. It was what she needed now—to relinquish control. Seb would have been totally the opposite. Slower, much more attentive.

"So where have you been this time?" Sanders asked.

"Congo."

He whistled under his breath. "Was it pretty hairy?"

"Yeah."

He ran a finger over the top of her arm. "Welcome back. Can I get you a drink?"

"Whatever you're having."

He whistled to the waitress, giving a sharp wave of his hand. "Two more," he called out, pointing to his drink. His eyes settled on her again. "Congo, huh? So you're still pushing your luck."

She shrugged.

The drinks came, double shots of Jack Daniels, and he

toasted her: "To your safe return." They clinked glasses, and she finished her whiskey in one long gulp.

"So what are you working on now?" Sanders asked, putting his hand on her thigh.

"Not much. These trips have been taking a lot out of me."

Sanders, surprised by her disclosure, looked her over again. He noticed the bandage around her arm, sticking from the sleeve of her shirt. "What happened?" he asked.

"I hurt my arm."

"How?"

She shrugged again, saying nothing.

His hand momentarily lifted from her thigh, only to return again shyly, his fingers lightly pressing.

"Jesus—is it *serious*?" he asked.

"No. It's okay."

"Ever think of doing a story in the States?"

"No," she said.

"I could get you a job at the magazine. Cement you to a desk."

"No, thanks."

He raised his glass for another toast: "To your death wish," he said, chuckling.

She paused, thinking about his words. Sighing, she clinked his glass. "To my death wish. Can we get out of here?"

The taxi dropped them off at his place, a large brownstone apartment in the upscale part of Beacon Hill. Sanders let her in, and as soon as the door closed behind them he gave her a long kiss. Her body quaked. She felt his hands reaching under her shirt, his cold fingers gliding over her back. Touch—how she missed it! Sometimes it was just enough to know that, in a city of several million people, she was one of the blessed who wasn't alone that night.

Sanders' cold fingers ran across her belly, causing her to lurch.

"Are you sure everything's okay?" he asked her, removing her coat and hanging it in the closet.

"Yeah." She kicked off her shoes.

"You're a dark forest, Vecera."

She didn't care what she was. She began taking off her shirt.

"Hey, wait!" he said. "Let me do that."

He moved toward her confidently, without hesitation. Pulling her against him, he unbuttoned her shirt and tossed it to the floor. His fingers found the zipper of her jeans, and he tugged them down along with her panties. Marika reminded herself that Sanders was fast. Too fast. He could probably be persuaded to slow down if she said something, but she knew it wouldn't make any difference. He would never be like Seb.

As Sanders expertly reached behind her back and unlatched her bra, Marika remembered how he once told her that he brought home a new woman every week. He laid her down on the sofa beneath him, his eyes drinking in the sight of her naked body. Casually, his hand searched between her legs.

"How's that feel?" he asked.

When she didn't say anything, he licked his thumb and pushed it inside of her. She arched her back, closing her eyes, and he pushed deeper. Soon, his lips found her breasts. His face flush, he stopped to unbutton his shirt and take it off. Removing his pants and boxers, he put his hands on her waist and pulled her body against his.

Marika surrendered completely now, letting him put her hands wherever he wanted them. Sanders reached for a condom in a nearby drawer, putting it on and spreading her legs. He fondled her for a few moments before guiding himself into her with a loud groan. He moved carefully, slowing whenever there was a threat of quick orgasm, speeding up when the impulse to with-hold became too great.

"You're so tight," he moaned, pushing and prodding inside of her.

She hated when he said things like that. She felt like a whore.

It wasn't long before Sanders climaxed. He lay still, his penis resting inside of her. "God," he whispered, his heart beating swiftly against her chest.

She looked out his window, at the lights of the city. A heavy sorrow descended upon her, and she turned away from him.

"You all right?" he cooed.

She didn't answer. In the apartment opposite, she saw a couple of people inside. Two men—or perhaps a man and a woman.

Sanders pulled off the used condom and sat up. He gave her a quick kiss on the cheek, pulling a strand of hair from her face. "You're a dark forest."

"Can you hold me for a minute?" she heard herself say.

"What's wrong?"

"Nothing. Can you just hold me?"

He looked surprised, chastened. "Sure." He moved beside her, putting his arm around her. He kept looking at her. "What's wrong?"

When she didn't say anything, his hand slid to her breast and he absently stroked her nipple. She glanced at the sight of his fingers sprawled across her chest. Thick, clean fingers. Neatly clipped fingernails.

She saw Congo again. The building outside of Bodo. Colonel Katembo shouting, *"Mets-toi à genoux!"*

Marika was sure, now, that these thoughts were Seb's fault. She would have gotten rid of the memories long time ago, had it not been for him.

She felt new rage toward Seb. Complete fury—only to suddenly remember the kiss he'd given her. The one on her forehead. No one had ever kissed her like that before. In that instant, Seb had cared more about her than she'd actually cared about herself. The idea astounded Marika, and she could only lie in silence, absorbing its truth. Unexpected love and gratitude flooded through her, drawing tears, filling her with wonder.

Sanders didn't notice. He had his hand on her breast, was watching the couple across the street turning out their lights.

Marika quickly got up.

"I'm going home," she told him.

Marika was leaving Max Sanders's place when she noticed the newspaper lying on the sidewalk. She froze as she scanned the headline: JOURNALIST ROBERT LEWIS, DEAD AT 52. Grabbing it, she stood in the dim light of a streetlamp to read it better. It was true: Robert Lewis—*the* Robert Lewis—was dead. In Malaysia. Suicide.

Marika had to put the paper down. She smelled Sanders's cologne in her hair, on her clothes, and the odor repulsed her. She walked swiftly down Beacon Hill, the heels of her shoes rapping harshly against the cobblestones. She didn't know where she was going. She just needed to walk, to keep walking. She passed through the streets of the Back Bay, watching her shadow stretch beneath each passing streetlamp. She found herself going in the direction of the Charles River. Coming upon the Mass General freeway, she dashed across it to the riverside esplanade, where the dark waters of the Charles loomed before her.

She knew she didn't belong there. It was too dangerous on a Friday night. She could almost feel the insanity in the air, crouching in the shadows of park benches, loitering behind guano-streaked statues. ROBERT LEWIS DEAD AT 52. BY SUICIDE.

Marika walked to a dock and stood by the river. Across the water, the lights of Cambridge gleamed coldly through her tears. She was feeling a million things she couldn't name. A million untold yearnings. She wanted to understand why a man like Lewis—so brilliant, so successful—hadn't been able to find enough good in the world to sustain him. Why had he let all the tragedy win?

It was then that Marika decided to write a book about him.

Yes. A biography about Lewis's life—and death. A book that, ultimately, would try to explain how he could have been driven to kill himself.

Marika could still remember the first and only time she'd ever seen Robert Lewis. It had been strictly from afar, at a concert in New York City. She was visiting the city on a business trip, and her editor friends had invited her to a concert at Lincoln Center: a famous Russian pianist was playing Sergey Rachmaninoff, one of Marika's favorite composers. It hadn't been long after they took their seats that her friends pointed behind them. Just a few rows away, to the right. *Robert Lewis is here. Look!* It was a real movie star sighting. Robert Lewis, in the flesh, with a beautiful blonde next to him, clutching his arm. Marika might have just heard that her own father was paying her a visit from the grave. She could barely contain her excitement as she glanced behind her, yet she didn't want to gape like all the other people. Lewis deserved respect and privacy, like anyone. She forced herself to face front, though part of her wanted to keep looking at him, pretending she was the woman beside him, pretending she could actually speak to Lewis and he would answer her.

It was during Rachmaninoff's Concerto No. 2, Opus 18, during the start of the *adagio sostenuto*—the briefest of interludes that never failed to sear Marika with anguish—that she turned in her seat and glanced surreptitiously behind her. Lewis's head was raised. His eyes were fixed on the ceiling of the auditorium—only they seemed to gaze through it, transfixed by the longing of the chords. His hands had become the music, reaching, rising, grasping for his own moment of mercy, of grace, his whole being urging the crescendo. It came far too soon: the despairing breakthrough of notes, the plaintive transcendence. Lewis's eyes were wet with tears, and he sat as a prisoner to the notes. Shyly, secretly, Marika watched him through the rest of the performance, unable to get that image of him out of her head. It had looked like Lewis was facing his own death.

Tobo hears unusual sounds.

Tobo hears unusual sounds. A gliding through reeds. Heavy steps on branches. He looks out from his lean-to, seeing nothing but the gray hints of dawn straining through a rainy sky. A crash now. Something tears away the palm fronds covering his shelter. He hears men's voices and jumps to his feet, grabbing his machete. Someone knocks him to the ground, and he loses his weapon in the darkness. A flashlight turns on, and Tobo sees a man looking inside the white mary's tent. Another man stands nearby: Sal, the Baku rascal who collected payback from him in Anasi village over a week ago.

Someone strikes Tobo on the back of his head, and he falls forward. He feels the cutting pain of the blow. Feels his face hit the muddy ground. Someone strikes him again, and for a brief moment there's blackness.

The sudden shock of rainwater on Marika's shins causes her to awaken. She hears men's voices. When she turns on her flashlight, she sees a knife slitting through her tent. Outside, a man holding a machete is kneeling down and peering in at her. She can barely breathe. She remains silent, motionless, staring back at the intruder. His one eye looks shrunken, and a long knife scar, running from forehead to chin, clips his eyelid. His expression is manic-looking, insane.

She realizes she's seen this face before. Back in Tobo's village. He was the man who wanted to hack Tobo to death on the shore of the lagoon. She waits, not moving. The rain intensifies, creating a heavy patter on the jungle foliage. The crazy man continues cutting open her tent, and sticks his head inside. He sees her backpack by her feet and rummages through it, pulling out a brush, toothpaste. He fingers a pair of panties and looks at her.

She draws her legs in against her, waiting.

"I no can hurt you," he says, smiling.

She doesn't say anything. She grabs her machete, holding it before her.

"Miss," he says in his rough English, "I no can hurt you." But the smile is gone, and he looks soberly at her weapon.

She wonders what he means. Does he want to "hurt" her but for some reason can't? The noise of the rain lessens, and the night insects start up their sharp calls. She hears Tobo now. He's talking to someone. Marika strains to make out what they're saying in Pidgin, but can't.

"Out. You come, Miss." The crazy man reaches for her, and she kicks at him, holding up her machete. The man yanks his head out of the tent, and it shakes and collapses around her as he hacks it to pieces with his knife.

"You come out!" he yells. "Now, come out!"

She hears Tobo's voice speaking to her in Pidgin: "*Ma-ree-ka, yu kam!* Marika, come out!"

In a panic, she untangles herself from the scraps of tent fabric and gets to her feet, throwing her daypack—with her money, passport—beneath some brush. She recognizes two other Baku men: Sal, the one who came to Anasi village for the payback, and his skinny friend. She sees Tobo sitting Indian-style by the remains of their fire, his hands tied behind him. She is about to speak, but Tobo fervently shakes his head.

The skinny man holds a flashlight beam on her, looking at her and her machete, unsure what to do. Sal walks over, carrying Tobo's *billum* bag. He dumps out the contents onto the ground:

sago balls, fish hooks and twine, a flashlight, a small wooden effigy of a man. He takes everything but the wooden figure, leaving it untouched for fear of sorcery.

The crazy man drags Marika's backpack to his canoe, dropping it inside. He goes back to her tent but can't figure out how to dismantle it. At last, furious, he takes his machete to it. He hacks the frame until it's worthless and flings it into the river. He goes to Tobo's canoe and takes everything out—a supply of yams and taro tubers, a bow and arrows—and puts the objects into his own canoe. Sal walks over, and the two men flip Tobo's canoe, chopping a hole in the hull with an ax.

"Why do you do this?" Tobo demands, trying to get to his feet.

The crazy man walks over and pushes Tobo back to the ground.

"I gave you enough for payback!" Tobo says to Sal. "Now why do you do this?"

Sal ignores him, creating a large hole in the hull. He pushes the vessel into the middle of the river and watches it sink.

Tobo speaks ominously to the men in his Anasi language until they come over and kick him into silence. Tobo merely glares, knowing he could easily put black magic on them. The dark spirits love it when a person calls on their services. They are the ones responsible for all the evil in the universe, and they now speak to Tobo in his thoughts, demanding that he seek revenge. But he knows that if he curses another, he curses himself at the same time; it is the law of things, and there are no exceptions. He must keep reminding himself of this, because the urge is great to call on the most formidable dark spirits he knows and to ask them to place a curse on these men. It would be a heavy curse. Probably, Tobo could cause the men and their families to quickly die.

Just the thought of all the dark spirits in the world, waiting for humbug men to call on them, gives Tobo a shudder as he sits in the rain before the three men. All he knows is that if these men were to kill him, his spirit would haunt them and their families for generations. They would have no peace. Perhaps they know this, too, because they don't seem brave enough to harm him further.

But he's scared for the white mary. He wonders if these Baku rascals will harm her or try to take her womanhood. There is nothing he could do for her if they get such thoughts in their heads. He knows that this entire situation, this misfortune, is because he killed that man. It was the worst mistake of his life, and now—once again—he must suffer for it.

He watches as the crazy man walks up to the white mary with a machete. "Hello, Miss," the man says to her.

Marika feels nothing now. She's alert but detached, as if watching herself from far away, having stepped out of her body. She knows she should be scared, but there is only numbness. Part of her hopes that God or Whomever or Whatever will just get this nightmare over with, one way or the other. With her eyes, she tries to tell these men she's not scared of them. She has looked death in the face—her own and others'. She knows, when it comes to people who are irrational and crazy, that you don't want to show them you're scared. Then it just makes everything worse.

The crazy man grabs her hair and pulls her head up. "You no have scared," he says to her.

She just looks at him. At the deep scar. The excited, enraged eyes. She feels nothing.

"Give me bush knife." He reaches for her machete.

"No." She holds it out of reach behind her back.

"Missus, give him the bush knife," Tobo says to her. "These are dangerous men."

"No," she says.

Sal shouts and calls all the men over. He's standing at the edge of the jungle, jubilantly holding up Marika's daypack. He announces that he's found the rest of her money, as well as her passport. He pulls out wads of Papua New Guinean *kina* bills and several thousand U.S. dollars, and the other men crowd around to look. Sal stuffs her passport and money—all she has left in this world—into Tobo's *billum* bag, putting it into their canoe. It is the end of things for her now. What can she do, with no money, no passport, nothing but the clothes on her back? The world will take every last thing from her. It will strip her bare, leave her with nothing.

So be it, then. She makes a decision not to care. She will relinquish complete control to the Universe.

Tobo looks anguished as the men sift through the stolen goods in their canoe. He knows it would be unwise to say anything to them. They are an edgy and unpredictable people, prone to violence—which is how he got into his predicament in the first place. He gazes to the east. The dawn is growing through thick gray clouds. A single white crane cries out and breaks for the sky, and Tobo follows its flight until it disappears behind nearby trees. The rain has nearly stopped, and the morning mist hangs heavily above the jungle.

As the men finish going through the things they've taken, Marika watches the crazy man striding toward her with his machete raised. She runs to the river's edge, but, unable to go farther, can only turn to face him.

"Give me bush knife," he says to her.

"No."

"Give it!"

"*No!*"

She has barely spoken before the man, enraged, takes a swing with his machete. She ducks, and the knife nicks her in the neck. She feels a sharp pinch, a warm surge of blood. Her heart pounds wildly, and she drops her knife into the water.

The man stares in awe at Marika's neck, at the blood traveling down her shoulder.

"Look what you have done!" Tobo yells at him. "Her United States is powerful! Their police will hunt you!"

"I no can hurt you," he says to her. "No dead."

"You and your family will be hunted like dogs," Tobo says, furious.

Sal looks anxiously at Marika's injury. Panicking, he tells his Baku friends to get into the canoe. Moments later, the three men paddle away. When they reach the other side of the river, Marika sees the crazy man stand up and shout threateningly at Tobo. But the canoe soon disappears into the early morning haze.

Tobo examines the white mary from a short distance away.

"You should not be alive," he says to her.

She stands where she is, lightly shaking. Had she not ducked, she knows she'd be dead right now. But something inside her chose to live. Something inside her always chooses to live, no matter what happens to her. She stares at the river—it is the Tumbi, along which the old missionary John Wade claimed to have seen Robert Lewis. Marika imagines Lewis stepping out of the jungle now, staring at her predicament and laughing.

"Come untie me," Tobo says to her impatiently.

He must repeat his request several times before she hears him. She walks over and unties the rope around his wrists. He stands up, feeling the bump on the back of his head. His body hurts from the kicks he received, but not too badly. He shakes his head, staring at the river and allowing himself a rare moment of self-pity. He's convinced that more bad luck is visiting him. Some men's spirits seek unusual vengeance. It is hard to satiate them, especially if they don't like the payback that has been given. Tobo wonders, sadly, if he will ever be able to pay enough. Or if the price will always be too high. Already, he has lost his sister, his nephew, and most of what he owns. And now this woman with him, whom he barely knows, was robbed and almost killed. He shakes his head again.

"The Baku are rascals," he says solemnly to Marika, gazing at the opposite shore of the river. "They told me I did not give enough for payback. But they lie. They saw the money you had in Anasi village, and they wanted to rob you."

The blood feels warm on Marika's skin. She wipes at it and is surprised by how much red covers her hand. She reaches above the strap of her tank top and gently touches the cut. It's a couple of inches long, slicing into the flesh where her shoulder meets her neck. Fortunately, though, it doesn't feel deep.

Tobo marvels at the white mary. She really should have been

killed, and the fact that she lived unsettles him. He walks up to her and makes a bizarre sign over her before sitting her on the ground.

"You bleed," he says, pointing to her shoulder.

"It's not bad," she says.

Tobo examines the cut more closely. "Yes, bad!"

He picks up a piece of tent fabric and soaks it in the river. Coming back, he awkwardly wipes the blood away from her wound.

"*Nogut, nogut,*" he keeps repeating. "Bad, bad." He presses a couple of fingers against the cut to stop the blood, mumbling an incantation in the Anasi language.

Marika holds the fabric against her cut and walks over to their cooking fire. Seeing that it's still smoking, she throws on some palm bark and stokes the cinders with a stick. As a flame leaps up, she retrieves a piece of aluminum tent pole from the river and puts it into the fire. She waits, watching the morning sun breaking through clouds.

"So what do we do now?" she asks Tobo.

He sighs angrily. "We go to Krit village." He hadn't been planning to go there. He wanted to take the canoe beyond the village, to where there might be signs of an old trail leading into the interior—the one Lewis might have taken. "Krit village is a bad place to go." He shakes his head. "But we have nothing now. If we don't go, you could die."

Tobo expects that, once they reach the safety of Krit village, the white mary will forget her crazy trip and ask him to take her back to Anasi village. It is bad enough that they have been robbed of everything and his canoe was sunk. It took him two months to hollow out the log for that canoe, to say nothing of the time it took to carve it. Now he will have to make another, and it is long, hard work in the hot sun.

Marika squats by the flames. She removes the fabric from her shoulder, nimbly feeling the length and extent of the wound. Pulling the tent pole from the fire, she quickly applies the hot metal to her cut. There is the sharp smell of burning flesh. Tobo rushes over to stop her, but she's already done and is throwing the tent pole to the ground.

"There," she says, taking a long breath from the pain.

"*Eh?* What do you do to yourself?!"

"I can't be bleeding all over," she tells him in English, getting up.

Tobo stares at her and tsks, making a sign of protection over himself. Turning to the camp, he looks around for anything the men might have left behind. Happily, he sees the white mary's machete in the water and easily retrieves it. It is all they have, but it means they can survive in the jungle. The clouds briefly part overhead, and the waters shimmer in the early morning sunlight.

Marika feels marooned on their tiny sliver of shore. She slides a hand up her arm, smearing several mosquitoes bloated with her blood.

Tobo points at the jungle. "Krit village is this way." But he shakes his head. "*Nogut ples,*" he says, spitting. "Bad place."

Without further word, he raises the machete and starts chopping a path into the jungle.

Tobo figures they are one or two days' walk from Krit village, if they go straight through the jungle. He doesn't expect to meet up with anyone else going there, as the Krit people are the Ones Followed by Death. No one visits them but the white missionaries, and they do it only because they don't know any better. Everything the Krit people touches, dies. Their children constantly fall sick. The giant *pukpuks* in the swamps catch them in their jaws and carry them away. He has never seen a people so befallen with misfortune. He will have to call on great protection for himself before he enters their village.

Marika has traveled through jungles for magazine assignments in Borneo, in the Amazon—but not like this. Not without solid ground or trails. This lowland jungle is really a swamp, resting in several feet of water. She moves as if navigating a creature's wet innards, the trees dwarfing her, vines spiraling like great intestines.

It is slow going having to cut their own path. But Tobo is a natural with the machete, chopping assertively through vines and brush, passing effortlessly between trees. Marika must travel barefoot, as Tobo does, her hiking boots stolen by the Baku men. Sago palms litter the forest floor, the undersides of their fronds lined with inch-long thorns that hide in the water like miniature booby traps. Marika regularly screams out as her feet get punctured, and she has to keep stopping to pull out the thorns. Tobo doesn't wait for her, nor does he seem to get any thorns in his own feet. She thinks there must be a magic spell around him, or that he knows a secret way to negotiate the jungle that he still refuses to teach her.

Tobo would be amused by the white mary if he weren't impatient to find the Krit people. The woman knows nothing about traveling in jungle, of course. She does everything wrong. He, himself, rarely steps on thorns because he skirts patches of water by stepping on tree roots and vegetation. This takes knowledge and dexterity that she doesn't possess. She flounders through the brackish water like an old woman. She is so slow that he fears they may not be able to reach Krit village before dark, in which case she will have an unpleasant time trying to sleep in the swamp. And of course, she stops so often that she attracts leeches. The way to avoid them is to go swiftly through water, but instead she stops to pull them off her body, which only attracts more. Tobo expects that they'll soon be covering her.

Toward midday the sharp-thorned sago palms gradually disappear, but the water gets deeper. At times, Marika must wade through it up to her neck. She knows nothing about this land. If there are any dangerous creatures hiding in the water, she is at their mercy. She tries to calm herself by recalling that the island of New Guinea has no dangerous mammals like leopards or hippos, only to remember that it has some of the deadliest snake species on earth. Snakes that, according to the locals, chase after you. And of course there are the *pukpuks*—the crocodiles.

Tobo seems unfazed by such dangers, nearly running through the brackish pools with his machete held aloft. Marika wonders how long she will be traveling like this. All the way to Lewis's village? She already knows she can't do this kind of swamp travel for many more days, let alone weeks. Equally distressing is that she doesn't recognize what she sees. She can't name most of the plants or animals, and doesn't know what she can safely touch. Even the noises are new, birds making strange calls as they flee before her approach.

Marika's foot suddenly catches between some roots, and as she tries to free herself, her other foot gets sucked farther into the swamp mud. She lets out a cry, but Tobo is already so far ahead that she fears he can't hear her. She struggles to pull herself out, but only sinks in deeper. Grabbing onto a nearby tree trunk, she yells more loudly for Tobo. But he doesn't appear. She looks around her. At the canopy overhead. At the dim jungle, the sunlight blocked by foliage. There is such indifference in this jungle. Glancing down, she sees several leeches on her stomach just above her pants waistband, engorged to the size of little sausages, their black bodies contrasting sharply with the whiteness of her skin. She rips them off in a frenzy, blood trails streaming down her belly.

She hears a rustling behind her that gets louder. Panicking, she tries to turn around. All at once, Tobo appears in front of her. He stares at her solemnly, shaking his head.

"*Nogut*," he says, pointing to the leech bites and blood. He performs a sign of protection over himself before reaching beneath her arms and pulling her free from the mud. "You must go faster," he says. "We are a long way from Krit village."

"I need water," she says to him, her water bottle and purification tablets stolen along with everything else.

Tobo reaches down and cups some swamp water in his hand,

drinking it. "Water," he says. But she won't dare do the same. She has gotten dysentery on too many of her trips. Amoebic dysentery is the worst—feels like someone is ripping her guts out.

"Will we cross a river today?" she asks.

"No rivers. Drink this water." Again, he reaches down and takes a drink.

Black inchworms drop onto her from the nearby foliage— more leeches. She flicks them off, feeling their fat little bodies on her legs, her back. She searches her body, ripping them off wherever she finds them, until Tobo stops her, tsking.

"When they are finished drinking, they will fall off," he says. "Do not pull them!"

He leaves abruptly, chopping a new path into the jungle. Marika reluctantly follows. As she travels, she reaches under her tank top, finding several moist bodies attached to her breasts. Enraged, she tears them off, her tank top becoming saturated with bloodstains. She wishes she were able to negotiate this new world as Tobo can. She tries to keep up with him, to imitate his movements. He seems to have no fear of dangerous creatures lurking in dark pools or foliage. He simply plunges through the water, even though it's up to his neck and rampant with leeches. As far as Marika can tell, there are two rules to be learned and mastered in this jungle: speed and confidence.

It's a mystery to her, too, how Tobo knows where to go. There are no trails to follow. He chops and plunges through the undergrowth with what could only be blind instinct. Marika pushes on, desperate to follow his example. *Learning,* she tells herself. She is learning to ignore the cuts and leech wounds, the aching of her punctured feet and injured neck. She becomes aware of another rule of jungle travel: ignore the pain. It has become her most valuable lesson.

Several hours later, approaching sunset, Marika sees patches of big-leafed taro plants invading the jungle at intervals. The forest soon thins out, giving way to groves of banana and papaya trees intermingled with long cassava vines curling up sticks. She figures they must be approaching Krit village, though she can't see it yet. For once, she ignores her exhaustion and thirst, and forces herself to keep up with Tobo at a near jog, grateful to have reached some kind of civilization.

They wade through a final, muddy stretch of swampland and emerge into a small clearing. Tobo stops at the edge of the water, speaking an incantation in his Anasi language and making elaborate signs with his hands: before him stands Krit village. The dark energy over the village is so strong that Tobo would never think of setting foot in it unprotected. He says a protective prayer for the white mary, who will surely need more help than he. Already, he can hear the angry voices of demons taunting him from nearby trees.

A few decrepit huts stand on the edge of a large black lagoon. A yellow dog barks incessantly at Marika as she approaches, its raw, abscessed teats dragging in the dirt. Nearby, a scrawny black rooster keeps tossing a corn husk, pecking at it when it lands. Aside from these animals, she sees no other signs of life.

They make their way closer. The dog sidesteps and whines, running off. The jungle has already started taking back its holdings, green shoots prying through the hard-packed earth under the huts and curling up the stilt legs. The sagging houses, made of palm bark and thatch, reek of mold and urine. Marika sees a little girl with a distended belly relieving herself under one of the huts. Flies buzz over piles of feces scattered about the village, and a fetid stench wafts to her on the breeze.

"They are bewitched and touched by death," Tobo says to her. He points under one of the huts, to a pile of disturbed earth. "There is the mother, daughter, son. All dead."

"You mean they bury their dead under the huts?"

Marika sees more piles of disturbed earth beneath the huts. She thinks she can smell rot.

The little girl watches them absently beneath the hut. Tobo

lets out a yell and waits. No one. He yells again, louder, and this time a muffled call answers him. He remembers visiting these people in the past, at their previous village, when they invited him, needing a sorcerer. That was many years ago, but even then they were followed by death and there was little he could do for them.

The dog barks again. Two men appear from the jungle at the opposite end of the village; one carries a bow and arrows, the other, a cassowary carcass. The large, ostrichlike bird, with a knob on its bill and gray feathers so narrow and fine that they resemble fur, hangs lifelessly from the man's shoulders. Tobo says nothing but waits patiently for the men to walk over. Several women materialize from nearby fields and stare at Marika, other people leaving their hiding places in the huts.

Tobo raises his hands and makes a sign of protection as the Krit hunters—a teenager and older man—arrive. To Marika, they look pasty, moldy, their skin peeling away. *Grili* covers every square inch of their bodies, the ringworm fungus peeling in ever-widening circles and swirls, covering them with festering sores.

The men gape unabashedly at Marika, at her tank top covered with blood and the leech wounds dotting her body. Tobo tells them about the Baku men who attacked his camp, and they listen in awe, staring at Marika all the while. When Tobo makes a chop with his machete and points to Marika's neck, the men's eyes widen. They step closer to her, exclaiming at the wound.

Marika's attention stays on the older man, his flaking, *grili*-covered skin pulled taut over large arm muscles. His belly swells over a pair of faded red shorts, his distended navel a couple of inches long and protruding from his body like an additional appendage.

Tobo turns to Marika. "Aren," he says, introducing the man.

Aren strides up to Marika. "Hello-how-are-you," he says, in unexpected English. He drops the heavy cassowary from his shoulders and reaches out to shake her hand. "Missionary teach me *liklik* English," he says.

She nods. The *grili* on his hand feels rough and leprous.

The teenager also comes forward to shake her hand. "Why are you alive?" he asks her in Pidgin.

"Why am I alive?"

"He wants to know why you were not killed today," Tobo says, pointing to her wound.

She sighs, feeling completely exhausted. "*Mi no save.* I don't know," she tells the boy.

Aren reaches forward and plucks a couple of hairs from her head, rolling them into a ball between his palms. "For good luck," he says, putting them into a small pouch he wears around his neck.

An incredible yelping begins. They turn to see the rooster on the yellow dog's head, its outspread wings flapping violently as it pecks at the animal's face. The Krit men watch, amused, as the dog's face becomes bloody. Aren casually picks up a rock and aims a decisive shot at the bird, hitting it in the head. As the rooster falls to the ground, the dog runs into the jungle.

Marika doesn't want to move, to become engaged in this rotting, lost place. But Tobo waves his hand at her and gestures for her to follow Aren into the nearest hut.

"We move this village three time," Aren tells Marika as he hoists the cassowary to his shoulder and climbs the hut's log ladder. "Three time. But *nogut*. Every time child die. Old people die. Is hard for find animals to eat. Today good luck. I kill *dispela* bird. Please, you eat with us, okay?"

"Thank you," she says, eager for the protein. "Do you have some water I can drink?"

Aren snaps an order to his wife. The woman, sitting in a corner of the hut, comes shyly forward with a bamboo cup. She wears a T-shirt covered with holes, a thin *laplap* wrapped about her narrow waist. The ringworm covering her body has invaded her scalp, her hair gone in patches. Marika doesn't know if the water in the cup is safe to drink, but tired and dizzy from dehydration, she doesn't care anymore. She takes the cup and swallows its contents, giving it back to Aren's wife.

The woman spreads out a reed mat, and Marika lies down on it. She gazes at her new surroundings, her shoulder wound stinging. The cut could be getting infected, but she has no medicine. Nothing. She's completely at the mercy of the world and can only wonder what it will do with her next.

Marika wakes to the chirping of night insects, sweat covering her, mosquitoes biting her face. She slaps at them and sits up, her body aching with fatigue, the soles of her feet throbbing in pain. Tobo kneels by a cooking fire in the middle of the hut, red paint covering his face. He glances at her casually as he uses Aren's machete to carve a bow from a long piece of wood.

Aren's wife busily cuts up the cassowary carcass by the fire. She wipes her hands on the dirty *laplap* around her waist, smearing the skirt with gore. Her daughter plays with the dead bird's head; it is the same little girl Marika saw under the hut earlier. Like everyone else, the child is covered with ringworm, her hair growing in patches around rings of fungus.

Marika slaps at more mosquitoes, her body tingling and itching with bites. Tobo, annoyed with her noise, gestures for her to come close to the fire and its smoke. Reluctantly, Marika agrees, though the heat feels nearly unbearable. Aren's wife eyes her curiously as she cuts out the bird's innards with the tip of a machete and deposits them onto a banana leaf beside her. Her daughter, bored with the bird's head, fingers the intestines instead.

The floor shakes. Aren walks in and sits beside the fire. He observes Marika with interest, his forefinger massaging the tip of his distended navel. She looks unlike any white woman he has ever seen, and he has seen three in his life. This woman has yellow hair and a bloody shirt. She looks very dirty and tired, and she doesn't say much. Worse, she doesn't seem to have any gifts to give him. The other missionaries always brought gifts.

"Do you have Bible book?" Aren asks Marika in Pidgin.

She glances at him. "A Bible?"

"I want one," he says.

"I don't have anything," she says. "The Baku men stole all my things."

"*Eh?*" Aren looks to Tobo.

"This white mary is not a missionary," Tobo explains.

"What is she?" he asks, alarmed.

"I don't know." Tobo shrugs. "She is bewitched. But don't worry; she can't hurt you."

Marika purses her lips in irritation at Tobo's description. "I'm looking for a white man," she says to Aren. "His name is Robert Lewis. He's a very important man."

"Is he a *pater*?" Aren asks.

"No, he's not a priest. He's not any kind of missionary."

"Then what is he?"

Marika doesn't know how to explain. And anyway, she feels like he's missing the point. They all are. "He's a very, *very* important man," she tells Aren in English. "I have to find him."

"Maybe he is lost in the jungle?" Which, to Aren, seems perfectly reasonable. He has observed that white men never know where they're going, and they're always getting lost. He, himself, has guided two missionary men through the jungle, and it took them twice as many days to reach their destination.

Marika vigorously shakes her head. "Tobo thinks he lives in a village called Walwasi," she continues in Pidgin.

"Is this man your husband?" Aren asks.

She scratches at the mosquito bites on her ankle. "No."

Aren, uncomprehending, looks to Tobo for assistance, but the Anasi man remains silent. Aren puzzles over the lost white man as he watches his wife place cassowary meat into a dented aluminum pot.

"The man I'm looking for is an American," Marika says to Aren in English. "He is tall and has a beard."

"A 'beard'?"

"*Mausgras,*" she says in Pidgin. "Mouth grass. And glasses. Have you seen him?"

Aren thinks for a moment. "Three men came here before the rains last year," he says. "But they were missionary men."

"Did you see any white men before those missionaries?"

"No."

Marika asks his wife if she's seen someone looking like Lewis, but the woman doesn't understand Pidgin. Aren translates the question into the Krit language, and the woman gives a one-word reply: "No."

Marika shrugs and gives up. Sweat rolls down her back and chest, stinging her leech bites. She asks for water, and Aren's wife brings over a wooden bowl and ladle.

"I will tell my wife to ask the people in this village about the white man," Aren says to Marika.

He gives her the order, and she abruptly leaves with her daughter. As the bird boils in the pot, Aren gives Tobo news of the village since he last visited. Tobo had successfully cured his son, but his daughter still died. Aren is certain that dark magic was placed on the Krit people by a humbug witch doctor, and now it follows them everywhere, even when they move their village.

Tobo listens silently, carving his bow. He knows that Aren wants him to perform spells for the village to try to protect it, but Tobo suspects the Krit people are doomed. He wishes people like the Baku rascals would be doomed instead, as the Krit never hurt anyone and have always been helpful to him. Tobo has noticed that the gods often select good people to punish instead of bad ones. He thinks the gods just get tired sometimes and forget who the bad ones are. After all, there are a lot of people to keep track of.

Aren's wife returns with an old woman, who wears an

oversized, threadbare T-shirt as a dress, and talks quickly to her husband.

"This old woman's name is Raza," Aren says to Marika. "She lived at the other Krit village. She remembers a white man who came there. Just one man. This was a long time ago."

Marika stares at her with surprise and sits up. "Does she remember his name?"

He translates, and Raza looks down shyly, speaking barely above a whisper.

"No. She doesn't know his name, but he had hair on his face and *aiglas*."

Marika makes circles around her eyes. "Glasses?"

Raza nods. She speaks softly to Aren.

"She tells me," Aren says, "that this white man came to her village in a canoe, with two guides. They only stayed one night, to buy meat."

"Where did they go?"

Aren translates, and Raza shakes her head.

"She doesn't know."

"Was this white man an American?" Marika asks. "From the U.S.A.?"

The question is translated, and Raza shrugs.

"Was he a missionary?"

Again Raza shrugs, mumbling something.

"This white man gave her grandson a magic thing," Aren translates.

"A 'magic thing'?" Marika looks to Tobo, but he busily carves his bow. "What is it?"

"She doesn't know what it is. It is a magic thing. I have never seen it. She says she is scared of it."

"Did the white man say anything to her?" Marika asks.

Aren translates and listens to the response. "No," he says.

Marika is intrigued—but before she has a chance to ask Raza anything, the old woman leaves the hut. Aren's wife dishes out the cassowary meat onto banana leaves, dropping the innards into the pot. Aren offers Marika one of the large drumsticks, and she thanks him warmly, eager for the protein. The meat is almost too tough to chew, but she could devour the bone itself, she's so hungry. As they eat, the hut shakes again. Raza reappears, out of breath, with a boy carrying something wrapped in a dirty cloth.

"This is my grandson," Raza says to Aren. "He will tell you about the white man."

The boy looks bashfully at everyone until Raza prods him with a finger. Meekly, he sits down by the fire, his thin arms clutched against his chest. Only when Raza reprimands him does he recount his story.

Wait man bin kam long . . .

> *The white man came to our village in a small canoe. We didn't know the guides with him, and they wouldn't tell us the white man's name. They wanted permission to stay in our village for the night, so they could buy meat. The white man looked sick and had a strange walk, so our* bigman *allowed it, but we didn't like him. The man was far away in the eyes and wouldn't speak to us.*
>
> *The guides said they were taking the white man over the mountains to the land near the Walwasi tribe. We had never gone that far away or heard of those people. The mountains they spoke about are very high and sharp, and no Krit people have ever crossed them. But the guides said they were going there, and so no one asked about it again.*
>
> *In the middle of the night, the white man left our hut and went into the jungle with his torch. I feared sorcery, so I followed. But the white man only went to the jungle to* pispis, *and when he was done and returning to the village, he saw me. He wanted me to come to him. But I was scared and wouldn't go. Then he took something out of his bag. He wanted to give it to me. When I wouldn't take it, he put it*

on the ground and went back to the hut. The thing had an
odd light in it, and I was scared of it. But finally I went and
took it.

His hands shaking, the boy holds out the object wrapped in
the dirty cloth. Aren's wife stops stirring the boiling cassowary
innards to watch. Tobo, full of sudden interest, walks around the
fire to stand by the boy's side.

"Here is the magic thing," Raza says.

The boy unfolds the material. A round, shiny object emerges.
It catches the light of the fire and glows brilliantly. Marika sees
that it's a gold coin of some sort. She asks to look at it, and the
boy nervously hands it over.

She kneels by the fire to read the inscription: THE MOST DIS-
TINGUISHED AND MERITORIOUS PUBLIC SERVICE . . . She scrapes off
the clay caked onto its surface and sees a picture of a printing
press. Turning it over, she can make out a profile of Benjamin
Franklin. Marika realizes she's holding a Pulitzer Prize gold
medal. The date on it goes back to 1982—a time when Lewis
would have been working for the *New York Herald.* The newspaper had received the award because of his exclusive reporting on
El Salvador—reporting which had nearly cost him his life: he'd
been kidnapped by antigovernment guerrillas near their strong-
hold of Morazán and badly beaten. Lewis, miraculously, had managed to talk his way out of the crisis, and the *Herald* made an
unprecedented gesture of appreciation by giving him the medal.

Marika looks at everyone, unable to speak. If the medal
belongs to Lewis—and who else would it belong to?—it is the
first tangible evidence that he didn't die in Malaysia. That he may
actually be alive in New Guinea, of all places. But more than anything, finding this medal means that she may have actually found
Lewis's trail at long last.

Marika gives the medal back to the boy. THE MOST DISTIN-
GUISHED AND MERITORIOUS PUBLIC SERVICE RENDERED. She looks

behind her, at the darkness standing before the entranceway of the hut. No stars yet, nothing to diffuse the blackness of night.

"Lewis . . . ," she whispers.

She closes her eyes for a moment. Tears of relief, or perhaps sorrow, sting her sunburned cheeks. The heat from the fire would like to bake her alive.

"Lewis was *here*," she says, glancing at Tobo.

She stares out of the hut again, into the blackness.

Tobo feels disappointment and dejection. Her eyes have that long, bewitched look now, and he knows what she's going to say next.

"I need to find Lewis," she tells him.

In Boston, early that spring, Marika went ahead with her plans to write a biography about Robert Lewis and gathered background information for a book proposal. She sent e-mails to editors, journalists, and writers who had known Lewis, asking for impressions of him, but to judge from their replies, no one could agree about his virtues or vices. Marika quickly learned that Lewis had been as widely disliked as respected, having lost many old friends and gaining few new ones. His suicide had struck his handful of loyal supporters as completely surprising—even "unaccountable."

Marika knew it would be a major undertaking, writing the book. Lewis's life had spanned continents, and he'd gone through periods of the most puzzling metamorphoses. From the rebellious kid on a rural Missouri farm to a stringer for foreign news bureaus; from a high-profile, award-winning writer to a cynical recluse. He was, in a word, complex. But even as her project would explore the many whys of Lewis's life—those inevitable contradictions and intricacies of character—Marika didn't think she could ever know who he truly was. Beyond the facts of his life, her biography could only stand as inspired guesswork.

But she vowed it would be impeccable guesswork. An honoring of a great man's life.

Marika felt that writing such a book was what she was always meant to do. Lewis couldn't be forgotten. He had given a voice to people's plights, had spoken of their loss—and her own. Beneath all anger, jealousy, grief, it seemed to Marika that people just need someone to acknowledge their pain. When she was thirteen, sitting in the courthouse reading Lewis's work for the first time, he'd somehow met her where she'd felt most alone. He had done far more than comforted her in that moment; he had filled her with hope.

Marika's research for the book proposal took more than three months. She needed, above all else, to secure the cooperation of the people who had been closest to Lewis. His friends were the easiest to reach; her magazine editor seemed to know everyone in New York and connected her with many of Lewis's old colleagues, as well as his ex-wife, Margaret "Maggy" Howe. Lewis had met Maggy in 1968, when he was twenty-one and going to college in New York. They hadn't known each other long before he got her pregnant, and in 1969 she gave birth to their only son, Daniel. That same year, Lewis married her. The marriage had been a disaster and lasted just three years; for the rest of his life Lewis would refer to it as the reason why he chose to remain a bachelor. Yet, fate had also been on his side; it had been Maggy's parents, pulling some strings, who got him his first newspaper job.

Marika could only marvel at how quickly Lewis had risen in the ranks to become one of the country's most celebrated journalists. When she'd read his piece on Czech dissidents, he was already in his mid-thirties and the *New York Herald Magazine*'s hottest writer, doing an unprecedented eight cover stories in a single year. The other big magazines all wanted Lewis to write for them, and he was offered lucrative contracts, and regularly appeared on television news shows. (*People* magazine even named him one of the "sexiest bachelors alive.") It was inevitable that he'd turn to book writing. He churned out five books about his experiences abroad, each becoming a huge best seller, offering readers the powerful, haunting writing that would become a Robert Lewis trademark. When Lewis reached his forties, at the same time that Marika was studying journalism in college, he was not just one of the most famous nonfiction writers in the country but also one of the richest.

As Lewis reached the zenith of his career, enjoying renown as a war reporter and best-selling writer, Marika noticed that he'd come into his own at last, sure of his talents and no longer wasting energy seeking confirmation from the world. He began producing articles with clear political and philosophical agendas, inviting not only more attention and celebrity, but also strong disdain. His list of enemies became huge. Literary critics denounced him as "arrogant" and "flippant"; TV personalities censured him for outspoken remarks made on their shows. Lewis's personal life mirrored the public backlash. His many ill-fated romances involved public shouting matches and ex-girlfriend tell-alls that made him a popular target of the tabloids. Lewis would describe this time in his life, infamously, as "getting rat-fucked by fame."

While conducting her research, Marika was shown a letter Lewis wrote during the period, and its sensitivity had surprised her. "Have you noticed all the people busy hating me?" he wrote. "I think it's because they know, on a certain level, that they've settled for mediocrity in their lives. So they have to find some poor son of a bitch, someone who actually worked like hell and *made* something of his life, to judge and drag down. And I know it shouldn't bother me (I can hear you now!), but these people aren't as harmless as you might think. These are people who worship the destruction of others. There's no way to guard against them, because they're everywhere, cringing under the rafters, plotting endless moments of revenge to make up for their petty, unfulfilled lives. They would be laughable, if they weren't so dangerous—like a bunch of wounded dogs making a last stand."

After his son's death, however, Lewis's vitriol vanished altogether. He left the public stage, and his appearances on television ceased. He gave only a handful of interviews and was otherwise a recluse in his home in the Hamptons. When he did go on magazine assignments, it was irregularly, though he spent a lot of time in the former Yugoslavia during its war—the experiences of which would lead to his best and most celebrated book, *Cold Summer.* Part memoir, part war reportage, Lewis wrote about his odyssey through Bosnia and Serbia in the wake of his son's death. The comparisons between his grief over his son, and the grief he felt for the deaths of so many innocents in the war, made for a poignant account that won over many critics. The book was Lewis's most candid work; he, who had so often been called "contemptible," now appeared completely humbled by his son's tragedy.

Marika, trying to learn more about the death of Lewis's son, found that his immediate family members were nearly impossible to track down. For one thing, both of Lewis's parents were dead. His mother had been killed in a car accident when he was eight— a fact which had obviously scarred Lewis and altered his entire outlook on life. "I knew—*really* knew—that I could die at any moment," he'd told an interviewer about the incident. "And I knew everyone *else* could die. But for years, what I found incredible was the number of people who actually went through their lives never knowing what it was like to lose someone. For the longest time, I called them 'lambs.' They just didn't understand death. They thought it was like a bad breakup or something. They never seemed to realize that their innocence was going to shatter someday, and they'd have to learn the truth of things. But I, personally, had no more illusions. Which was a blessing for me and the work that I did, because few things could shock me anymore. Death sobers you up like nothing else."

Lewis's father had died about twenty years after his mother, and so Marika's best bet for researching his youth lay with his only sibling, Elizabeth Lewis Nichols. Beth, a married mother of two, still lived in rural Clyne, Missouri, with her husband. Marika had paid an Internet service to track down the woman's contact information, only to discover that her latest phone number had been disconnected. She did get an address, though, and sent several letters, but Beth never replied. It hadn't daunted Marika. She decided, if a publisher ultimately made her an offer on the book proposal, she would visit Lewis's sister and appeal to her in person.

And then the offer came. A big offer, which gave Marika enough of an income to stop her magazine work and focus on book writing. She would regard that period of her life as unusually charmed, as if the planets had aligned in the most auspicious of ways, just for her.

∽

Marika's personal life had felt just as propitious: she'd gone back to Seb.

She'd taken a taxi to his condo in Cambridge the very morning after she'd left with Sanders. It'd been far too early when she went, around 5 a.m., but guilt had overwhelmed her. She hadn't seen Seb for two weeks, and she'd been fighting the fear that he'd forgotten her and had moved on. Whenever such doubts arose, Marika would recall the last time Seb had kissed her, and all the love she'd felt from him. What she'd needed more than anything was to experience that love again. That safety. That *mudita*-like peace that had held her in his thrall over the many months of their dating, reminding her that no matter what she experienced, no matter what her failings, she was never far from grace.

When she rang the bell to his place in those dim, predawn hours on a Saturday morning, Seb was still in bed. He anxiously raced to the door in boxers and T-shirt, a day's worth of dark stubble on his chin, hardly able to believe that Marika was standing there. Tears in her eyes, she threw her arms around him, and it was more vulnerability than Seb had ever seen from her. He could only cradle her against him, trying to understand the reason for her visit.

"Are you all right?" he asked. "Did something happen?"

"I just missed you," she said. "I've really missed you."

Seb ended up making her a nice breakfast, and they talked about what was happening in their lives. Marika told him about her plans to write a Lewis biography, describing all the research she'd be doing for the book proposal, and Seb couldn't have been happier with the news. Not only would she have to put her dangerous magazine work on hold, but she'd be revamping her life in Boston—with him, he hoped, as a major part of it. After they ate, Marika surprised him by climbing into his bed. As he joined her, lying behind her and wrapping his arms around her, she decided she'd try out his love, let it fill her for a while. Already, the memories of Congo seemed to be fading.

But Marika really wanted to make things up to Seb, and suggested they travel somewhere over his upcoming spring break. Somewhere special, where they could get to know each other better. The idea had come out of her mouth spontaneously, surprising even herself. Seb was the first man to whom she'd ever made such an offer—the first man with whom she'd ever felt such a deep connection. Of course, he readily agreed. In fact, his childhood home on Martha's Vineyard had a cozy guesthouse by the ocean where they could stay. He thought it would be the perfect place for them to enjoy some private time.

Seb's parents lived in a restored colonial home on several acres of wooded property overlooking the ocean at Vineyard Sound. When Marika saw the house for the first time, she'd called it "huge," to which Seb casually replied, "Plenty of houses around here are bigger." It was the first time Marika realized just how much money his family had. Seb didn't usually bring up his parents' wealth, though she knew he couldn't have paid for an expensive Cambridge condo with the modest stipend he received from his doctoral work.

Seb's father had been away in Germany, but his mother, Virginia, was at home, and Seb wanted her to meet his girlfriend. He wanted to show off Marika; she'd just won a big award for an article on Zimbabwe that investigated how land reform policies were sending the country spiraling into bloodshed. Seb had shown his parents that article, as well as her other ones, and they'd begun to marvel over his girlfriend and her extraordinary life. When would they get to meet her?

Just as Seb and Marika parked in front of the house, Virginia rushed out the front door to greet them, taking Marika into her arms with such enthusiasm and affection that they might have known each other their entire lives.

"Well, you must be Marika!" she said graciously, kissing her on both cheeks. "I've heard *so* much about you."

Virginia was seventy-two, but she looked ten years younger. It wasn't so much her youthful appearance—the dyed blond hair and smooth complexion—as her incredible vitality, her exuberance. Marika felt immediately at ease in her presence and could only marvel over the effect it would have on a person to grow up around such love and attention, while never having to worry about money. Ironically, though, none of it had saved Seb from the problems he would face later. All the drugs. The addictions.

The three of them had dinner together, then Seb took Marika to the guesthouse by the ocean, wanting her for himself. Marika was grateful for the chance to finally be alone with him, too, no longer on display. It was nearly dusk, and the setting sun was striking the sea with brilliant orange light. Having grown up in the Midwest, Marika had always found oceans a novelty, and she sat on the shore to enjoy the beauty.

As night approached, it grew cold. Seb started a bonfire for them, wrapping Marika in a wool blanket. Disappearing into the house, he soon returned with an enormous bouquet of white lilies.

"For you," he said to her, laying them in her arms.

Marika felt her cheeks getting hot. "What's the occasion?"

"*You're* the occasion."

The sweet smell of the flowers overwhelmed her. She buried her nose in them. "Thanks," she said shyly. "I love lilies."

"You mentioned that once," Seb said, pleased with himself for remembering.

He sat beside her, and Marika held him so tightly that he

glanced at her in sudden concern. But she was just happy. Too happy. It was a rare moment for her, and she was trying to hang on to it for as long as she could.

The fire blazed. The ocean's waves reached toward them. Seb leaned over and gave her a long kiss.

"So what did you think of my mom?" he asked, stroking her hair.

"She seems really nice," Marika said.

"My father wants to meet you, too. Too bad he's in Europe."

Marika gazed into the fire. "I wonder what my mother would think if she could see us now," she mused out loud.

"What do you mean?"

Marika smiled wryly. "She was always telling me I'd never get hooked up with a man."

Seb laughed. "That's supportive."

"She was always saying things like that—she couldn't help it." Marika ran her finger over one of the lily's delicate white petals. "In my mother's universe, everything was always going wrong. The sky was always falling. Especially after my father died."

"You know, you don't really talk much about your parents."

"There's not a lot to say."

Seb smiled. "Somehow, I find that hard to believe." He drew her closer to him. "Will you tell me about them?"

Marika sat in silence for a long moment. She felt like she was about to give an introductory lecture for a Marika Vecera 101 class. So much history. So much to unearth and explain. It wearied her. She decided to tell Seb about her father. At first she gave the short version: when she was six, how her father, Petr Vecera, a Czech writer, was arrested for "spying" against the Communist government and executed.

Seb, of course, wanted to hear more.

So Marika told him what else she knew. How her father's subversive behavior ran in the family: her grandfather—Petr's father—had been taken away in the 1950s and executed as a member of "British imperialist circles," a "traitor" to the Communist Party.

Petr's siblings were subsequently blacklisted by the Communist government, which would explain why Marika and her parents ended up living in one of the poorest areas of Prague, and why Petr, a brilliant man, had never been allowed to enter any Czech university. But though he could only get menial factory work to support the family, he'd been unrelentingly self-educated, reading as many Western political and philosophical books as he could get his hands on.

Petr met Marika's mother, Svetlana, in the back-alley German class she was teaching. Before the onset of her mental illness, Svetlana had an eidetic memory and had always been unusually gifted at learning foreign languages, holding advanced degrees in linguistics. Petr took private lessons with her, and they soon fell in love. What Svetlana didn't know at the time was that her husband-to-be was learning languages like German in order to oppose the Communist government and its *tajná policie,* secret police. When the Soviet Union invaded Czechoslovakia on August 21, 1968, he made his first contribution to the resistance movement by running one of the secret Prague TV studios scattered about the city, broadcasting anti-Soviet messages. In hilarious disguises, and in different languages, Petr gave the world the real news about the occupation.

It wasn't long before the Russians seized control of the transmitter on Cukrak Mountain, ending the broadcasts. Petr then turned to publishing his *samizdat,* clandestine writing in defiance of the occupation. He became what the Communist regime called a "subversive writer." His stories and essays, and later a novel, appeared around Czechoslovakia in shoddy-looking folders with a publication run of eleven or twelve copies—the maximum number of legible copies that could be typed at once with carbon paper. He used a smuggled West German typewriter whose typeface and owner's name weren't on file with the secret police; to Petr's dismay, the Communists thought of nearly everything. Petr saw himself playing a high-stakes game with them of "who's smarter," never balking at the enormous risks he took. Marika had always deeply admired her father's courage. Later, Robert Lewis would remind her of him.

It seemed only a matter of time before Petr was caught—which happened early one summer day; her father simply never came home. Svetlana learned that he'd been arrested and executed for spying. She, herself, was taken away by government people for questioning, and Marika ended up spending several weeks with relatives. When her mother finally returned—haunted, speechless—Marika realized that her own life would never be the same. Her father was gone, and her mother's mental illness was already starting to manifest.

With Petr dead, Marika's mother badly wanted to defect, but it would take years to arrange and afford. In the meantime, Svetlana could only get work as a cleaning woman, and they barely survived. Then one morning when Marika was nine, her mother came into her room and told her they were going for a ride. Marika took nothing except her school bag, assuming they'd be back home by nightfall. But they never returned. There was a long train ride to Bratislava. A bus ride to České Budějovice, near the Austrian border. Then a late-night drive by car into a forest, where they met a man who guided them through a train tunnel to Austria. Once safely in the West, they soon emigrated to the United States.

As Marika got older, she suspected that her father had been secretly involved with the CIA. She'd inferred it from some of her mother's remarks about Petr's "help" for the U.S. government, and about how "easy" their emigration to the States had been. Even back in Prague, they'd always had enough money to get by, though her father's meager earnings should have left them in poverty.

Although safely in her adopted country, Svetlana couldn't leave Czechoslovakia in her mind. She had loved Petr deeply, completely, and would never get over his death. Marika's mother started to forbid her to talk about him; Petr Vecera might not have existed. Grief, to Marika, had become a secret weight, an oppression that she wasn't supposed to acknowledge. Privately, she sometimes found herself crying—not just for her father but for the *idea* of him, for all he could have brought to her life, had he lived.

The moment she found herself excited or happy about something, she'd feel that weight. As if all happiness were a betrayal.

ↂ

Marika cleared her throat. "So that's the whole story about my father," she told Seb.

"That must have been awful," he said.

She shrugged. "Poor me, right?"

"Hey—don't minimize it."

She told him how her mother never made a big deal out of her—or anyone's—suffering. When Marika was young and feeling upset, her mother would always say something like, "What? Do you think you're supposed to be happy? Look at all those people living in the slums of Calcutta—do you think *they're* happy? You're really going to have to toughen up."

"Growing up with my mother taught me that no one is ever going to come save me," Marika told Seb, watching the flames of the fire tugging in the wind. "I got it. I knew I was on my own and had to take care of myself. I knew that even if there *is* a God, he isn't going to help. It's sink or swim."

"What if you're wrong about that assumption? About God?"

She turned to look at him. "Well, where's God in places like Africa, while all those wars are going on? He's sure as hell not helping."

"But then there are plenty of things that seem like miracles," Seb said. "Like a peaceful western Europe after thousands of years of bloodshed. Or a program like Alcoholics Anonymous, and what it's done for people, how it's saved lives. There are so many examples like that."

"Well," Marika said, "then I guess God is pretty selective about who he chooses to help."

She stared at the dark waves. The fire was burning low, and the cold air began to chill her through the blanket.

"You know, you've never really told me if you believe in God," Seb said to her.

"It's complicated. I grew up with communism. The government closed down all the churches, and they taught us in school that God didn't exist. But my mother was really religious, and so she raised me to at least believe there could be more. But with my father getting killed, and after all I've seen in the world, I let those beliefs go. They seemed naive."

Seb said nothing. They watched the waves creeping toward them, leaving a film of foam in their wake. A single white seagull marched across the sand, barely avoiding the incoming swells.

"What if God had nothing to do with the ugly, awful things you've seen?" he asked her gently.

"What do you mean?"

"What if he allowed people to create all that pain and struggle, so they'd have to learn how to get beyond it?"

She sighed, getting angry with him. "Then that would *really* be learning the hard way."

"I agree. It would be. But people are stubborn. Look at all the people in the world who would rather *die* than admit they might be wrong about something."

She sighed again, chucking a handful of pebbles into the waves.

Seb looked kindly at her, squeezing her hand. "What I've learned is that everything in life—and I mean, even the *worst* of it—can be turned into grace. I discovered this when I was overcoming my addictions. The test is—for even one moment in our lives—not to strike back at something, no matter how bad it gets. Think Martin Luther King and the nonviolent protests. When you're faced with the temptation to get angry or upset and to hit back—you just *don't* do it. You let the temptation roll over you and not touch you. The idea is not to add to the collective pain."

"Okay. So we allow people to hurt us, and just let it 'roll over us'?" Marika shook her head.

"No. You protect yourself. If you're going for a drive, you put on your seatbelt. If you're smart, you don't walk through the Boston Common at night. But the point is, when it comes down to those moments in life that you can't control—when you're faced with something that's really tough and you want to strike back—*that's* when you refuse to respond out of fear or anger. You don't go hurting someone. You don't take revenge. You don't go running to drugs or alcohol. You don't *add* to it all, and by not doing so, you make the world a better place."

"Easier said than done," Marika said.

"Of course! But it's the key to freedom."

"Freedom from what?"

"From hatred and wars. From unhappiness, addictions, depression—you name it. It all starts within ourselves."

Marika looked away from him and gazed out at the ocean. Clouds were gathering overhead, and it was getting cold. Too cold. They needed more wood for the fire, at the very least.

"I think it's just a lot more complicated than you've described," she said.

"It doesn't have to be complicated." She could hear the passion, the utter conviction, in Seb's voice. "Unless you *believe* it has to be complicated. Unless you're addicted to struggle."

She resented his goodness in that moment. Resented *him*. Or, rather, resented whatever it was he was getting at. Seb, perhaps sensing this, put his hand over hers. He ran his fingers across her cheek.

"Life doesn't have to be about struggle," he whispered, kissing her.

Feeling the warmth of him, the softness of his breath against her skin, all her frustration left. She could only stare into his eyes, wondering where he got his power from. His strength. Times like now, it dazzled her.

"What?" he asked.

She couldn't stop looking at him. "I love you," she said. It came out boldly, like an announcement, and there could be no taking it back.

CHAPTER NINE

Missouri in late August was a green, steaming place, its thick, junglelike forests droning with cicadas. Marika drove her rental car over the Missouri River into the middle of the state, past rolling hay pastures and limestone cliffs once traversed—signs told her—by Lewis and Clark. It was a whole other world from Boston. Quiet. Bucolic. With neither the busy drama of the eastern cities nor the majestic emptiness of Wyoming or Montana. Here in this transitional place, in this unsettling ambivalence that had seen Missouri as a slave state in the Union, Lewis had grown up. On a farm, with a few horses and several acres for growing hay. He rarely talked about his childhood in interviews. Rarely had a word to write about his life prior to his New York days. Marika could imagine, driving off the highway and up a lonely gravel road into the throbbing heat and green hills of Clyne, that this place would repel someone with Lewis's restless ambitions. One of the things she knew for sure: Lewis had abandoned his Missouri home when he was just seventeen.

Lewis's big sister, Beth, lived at the end of a rural road, in a small white farmhouse built around the turn of the century. It was the Lewis family home, though NICHOLS was now painted in blue letters on the mailbox. A couple of giant oaks shaded a freshly cut front lawn, but the house was otherwise surrounded by open sky and fields of green soybeans. Marika noticed that the barn, twice as large as the house, had been newly whitewashed, its entranceway decorated with blue paint that exactly matched the mailbox. Rainbow-colored wind socks, tied to clotheslines, whipped in the breeze. An old covered wagon, missing a wheel, its hitches rusted, sat as decoration near the road. Marika searched in vain for a sign that Robert Lewis had grown up here, for an indication that one of the greatest journalists and writers of the twentieth century had called this place home.

She pulled into the driveway and got out of the car. An overweight black lab sat up on its haunches on the front stoop of the house, its red tongue drooping from its mouth. It watched her for a few moments, barked dutifully, and lay down again. Marika took a minute to center herself. It would be crucial to gain Beth's trust and cooperation on the book, yet she had no specific plan for winning her over. With many would-be interviewees, even sincerity and good intentions weren't enough. Understandably, people often expected to be stung by journalists. Marika had been interviewed plenty of times herself, and she knew what it was like to be ridiculed, stereotyped, condemned in print. She'd had her words taken so out of context that she'd barely recognized them, the profiles revealing more about the state of the writer's heart than her own.

Marika walked up to the screen door of the house. (There were still parts of the world, she mused, where people artlessly left their front doors open to complete strangers.) The black lab gazed up at her, panting benignly, and she stepped over it to see if she could see anyone inside. Noticing a large, red-headed man in the back of the room, she called out a hello.

"Just a sec'," he yelled over his shoulder.

The man soon appeared at the door. He had a sunburned face, was dressed in paint-splattered coveralls and a yellow Mizzou Tigers T-shirt. He smiled amiably at her, rubbing the stubble on his chin.

"I'm Marika Vecera," she said to him. "I contacted Beth a few months ago. I'm writing a biography about her brother's life, and I was wondering if I could talk to her for just a minute?"

The man's smile faded. "Well, I don't know if she'll want to talk to you. She doesn't like talking to journalists."

"Well, if I could just tell her a bit about my book. I've always really admired her brother—"

"Yeah, we all did."

"He was a *huge* inspiration to me, personally."

"Yeah. Well, look, I'll go ask her, and we'll see what she says. I can't promise anything, though. Hate to send you right back to wherever you came from—"

"Boston."

"Boston. Home of the Red Sox. They could be doing better this season."

Marika knew nothing about it, but she nodded politely.

"I'll let Beth know you're here. But she never did like all those media folks bothering her with their cameras and whatnot."

"I don't blame her," Marika said.

"Those people need a lesson in common decency. Let one of their loved ones die and see how they like having a camera stuck in their face."

Marika felt a rush of shame. She was little better than the others, coming uninvited to Beth's doorstep.

"Anyway, I'll go talk to her and see if she'll see you," he said. He disappeared from the screen door.

Marika waited, staring at the big black dog with its lolling tongue. The animal looked back, panting as if to a metronome beat. As Marika knelt down to pet its head, its wagging tail started loudly whacking the stoop. She listened for any hint of conversation coming from inside the house. At last, hearing a cough, she rose to see Beth's husband returning—alone.

"I spoke to Beth," he said. "I told her who you are. 'Marika,' right? What is that? Russian?"

"Slavic. Czech."

"Oh. Well, so she says she'll see you, but she's in the shower right now. You'll have to wait."

His answer had taken her by surprise. "Thanks so much."

"I'm Tom, by the way. I'm her husband." He tried to open the screen door to shake her hand, but the dog was in the way. "Jake! Move out of the way! Let the lady in."

The dog got up slowly and stepped aside.

"Thinks he owns the place."

Marika smiled, shaking Tom's hand and walking into the house. It smelled richly of fried steak and washing detergent. Tom directed her to the living room, mostly furnished with faux antiques. A wardrobe. A rolltop desk. Shoe molds with ducks painted on them, sitting atop a mantel. Incongruously, there was an old, pricey Persian carpet spanning most of the room. A Qashqai tribal rug—Marika recognized the designs from her travels in Iran.

"Was this Rob's?" she asked of the carpet.

"That's right." Tom looked impressed with her observation. "Beth got it after he died."

As Marika sat on the sofa, letting her eyes wander, it was easy to tell which things in the old, creaking farmhouse had once belonged to Lewis. The monkey-skull ornament—a Borneo longhouse charm—hanging on the wall beside a bouquet of silk daisies. The centuries-old Dogon granary door from Mali, its carved facade now providing hidey-holes for plush toy rabbits. The Tibetan *tangka* painting of the Buddhist savior Maitreya, competing with a framed "Footprints in the Sand" poster.

An all-white cat, tail up like a flagpole, meandered carefully along the far side of the room, ducking beneath a couple of hard-backed Quaker chairs and emerging at Marika's feet.

"That's Shiroi, but we just call her 'Roy,'" Tom said with a chuckle. "You're an old lady, ain't ya?" He leaned down and scratched the animal's head with his thick, calloused fingers.

"Interesting name."

"Means 'white' in Japanese. That was Rob's cat, when he lived out in New York."

Robert Lewis's cat. Marika reached down and petted it, and the animal erupted into purring. It looked up at her with startling green eyes, its face wizened and wise-looking.

"By the way, excuse my appearance." Tom gestured to his paint-covered overalls. "We've been working on the barn all day. Want anything to drink? We've got some Pepsi. Beer."

"Water'd be great," she said.

"Water it is." He walked into the kitchen and turned on the faucet, filling a glass.

"Did you see Rob a lot?" she asked him, as he returned.

"Oh, off and on. A couple times a year. It was hard getting him out here—though he did come back from some war in Liberia for our wedding. All the guests kept wanting to hear his war stories. They completely forgot me and Beth were getting married!" Tom hooted. "Rob was already famous by then. That must have been— oh, fifteen years ago. He was always off doing God's work."

Tom handed her the glass of water and sat down on a nearby armchair.

"Yeah," Tom mused, "Rob had one of those lives."

"What did you think of him personally?" Marika asked.

Tom cast her an astute glance, suspecting a trick question. "Oh, he was all right. What little I knew about him. He was kind of intense, though. Whenever he looked at you, it was like someone had turned the floodlights on. But now my parents couldn't *stand* him." He hooted again.

"Why not?"

"Oh, he had a temper. He wouldn't shake my dad's hand when he found out he worked for Gulf Western Oil. Said the company was causing natives in Ecuador to kill each other." Tom looked over his shoulder to see if Beth was in earshot. Then, in a quieter voice, "Dad thought Rob Lewis was holier-than-thou."

"Did you think so?"

Tom sat up, watching the white cat rub against his leg. "Well, Rob was an idealist. He called it like he saw it, and people don't like being called on things. People like to pretend everything's pretty."

Marika saw a blond-haired woman coming down the hall. Tom heard her and looked over his shoulder.

"Here's Beth," he said with relief.

Marika stood up as Beth entered the room. She looked to be in her mid-fifties. Her face was as long and chiseled as Lewis's was—had been—but her expression held none of her brother's trademark intensity. Her blue eyes, when they settled warily on Marika, just looked exhausted.

Beth studied Marika. She'd been approached by dozens of journalists since Rob's death, and in the beginning, not knowing any better, she'd indulged them, thinking she was keeping Rob's memory alive. She'd sat before their cameras, shell-shocked and distraught, giving interviews mere weeks after Rob's suicide. She still regretted doing that. All they did was ask her questions about Rob's "dangerous life," and if it had become "too much for him." Of course the Malaysian government released Rob's suicide note to the press without asking the family first. The American media obsessed over it and rebroadcast it for weeks, savoring the line: "When you find this note, I will already be dead." Reporters kept wanting to know why Rob had killed himself. They loved to throw out theories and call in the usual talking heads. Was it the death of his son? The violence he had seen all over the world? His depression? As if Beth knew why. As if anyone could know.

Were those even the appropriate questions? It didn't matter why he had died; it mattered that he had *lived*. Beth was determined not to let Rob be defined by his death.

She stared at the young woman in her living room. Marika Vecera. It meant nothing that Rob had "inspired" this girl to pursue a life of journalism. Those were words, and Beth didn't like or trust words. She was someone for whom actions counted more than anything. What mattered to her, above all else, was what Marika would ultimately write about her brother's life. Would she give Rob—whose body had never been found—the proper burial he deserved? A literary burial, with honor? Because Rob had not been perfect, and he had not always been kind, and he had not always been good. Death brings out the starkest of truths about people—reveals all the ugliness along with the goodness. Would Marika understand this? Would she see it in Rob and forgive him for it? Or would he become, as he had so often been portrayed in the media in the months since his death, a kind of blighted malcontent who had chosen to "abandon the world"?

Beth finally spoke. "Your writing," she said, "reminds me of my brother's."

So Beth had researched her, Marika realized. Which meant that Beth had gotten her letters—and may have taken them seriously.

"I'm sorry about being so forward like this—"

"No, you're not sorry." Beth had a trace of a smile on her face. She sat down on the couch and gestured for Marika to sit back down. "I know how you journalists work. My brother was one of them. When you want something, nothing'll stop you. Here you are, all the way in Clyne, Missouri, because you can't take no for an answer."

Marika looked away, guilty. "Well, I didn't know for sure if you'd gotten my letters."

"I did."

"I came here because I was hoping I could talk to you about it face-to-face. I have only the best intentions for this project."

"Really? How so?"

Marika reiterated what she'd already put in her letters: how the biography was meant to honor Lewis as the greatest writer and reporter of the twentieth century. It would describe the many ways he'd championed the world's dispossessed, giving them a voice and drawing attention to their plights.

Beth listened patiently until Marika was finished.

"You know," she said, "you're not the first person who's

approached me wanting to write a biography about Rob. But you're definitely the youngest. How old are you? Thirty?"

"Thirty-three."

"Thirty-three. So young. What could you know about what my brother went through? Have you ever lost anyone?" Beth asked this last question as if she were already sure the answer was no.

"My father was killed," Marika said. "And my mother never got over it, so it was like I lost her too."

Seeing that she'd gotten Beth's and Tom's attention, she told them about her father's arrest and execution, and her mother's descent into mental illness.

Beth listened intently, her eyes softening.

"Your brother's life inspired me to try to make some good come out of my father's death and all the tragedy in the world," Marika said. "Maybe that sounds quaint, but it's true."

"Rob used to say the same kind of thing after his son, Daniel, died," Beth told her. "He said he'd dedicate his work to him."

Daniel had been the one subject that Lewis refused to talk about in interviews; evidently, his son's death had been far too sacred a subject to be tossed to the "sharks"—as Lewis had called the news media. The "petty," "self-serving," "heartless" sharks. Lewis, an oft-reluctant member of it, himself, had always been eager to point out its vagaries and vindictiveness.

"What really happened to his son?" Marika said. "If you don't mind my asking?"

"Daniel wanted to follow in Rob's footsteps," Tom interjected. "Only Daniel didn't like writing very much. He didn't have the talent for it. But he had a huge heart, and he wanted to do good. Even as a boy, he used to get all worried when he'd see those starving kids on TV. He'd keep asking us to help them. Remember that, Beth?"

"I do," she said.

"So Daniel ended up going into aid work. He did the Peace Corps in . . . where was it? . . . I can never remember the name of that place."

"Burkina Faso."

"Yeah. Then he stayed in Africa and, I guess it was in 1992, he worked for some NGO in Mozambique, when the war was letting up. And then one day he went out in his truck and never came back. Rebel soldiers shot him."

"They did find his body, though," Beth added. "That was how they knew what happened to him."

"Of course Rob and Maggy were devastated," Tom said. "We all were. But it just shattered Rob. I mean, I don't think you ever get over the loss of a child. Daniel was only twenty-four—he'd barely tasted life. How do you ever deal with something like that?"

"You just do," Beth said solemnly. "Somehow, you deal." She absently petted Lewis's cat beneath the table. "At least Rob didn't hole up—I mean, not for very long, anyway. Of course, he was badly depressed . . . worse than I'd ever seen him. But he still didn't quit his job or give up on everything. Instead, it's like the opposite happened. He focused on his work more than ever. He wrote his two most successful books a few years after Daniel died."

Marika nodded. She'd learned as much from her research. Robert Lewis had achieved his greatest fame in the years after the tragedy.

"What's that line from that movie?" Tom asked. " 'Whatever doesn't kill us makes us stronger'? That's Rob. Indestructible."

"That *was* Rob," Beth said, her eyes moist.

There was silence in the room. Lewis's cat slept beneath the table. The Tibetan painting of Maitreya, the Buddhist saint prophesied to save the world from suffering, caught Marika's eye from across the room.

Beth cleared her throat. "People will tell you all sorts of things about Rob and his life, and they'll want you to believe it all. But nothing's ever as simple as it seems. A lot of people were jealous of his success. They'd find any reason to discredit him. Rob used to think the most dangerous people in this world are people who are jealous."

"They think there's only one piece of the pie," Marika offered.

"Right. When they don't seem to realize there are a million pieces out there waiting for them, if they only bothered to look." Beth gazed wistfully across the room. "The only way you can envy what someone else has is if you're sure you can never have it for yourself."

Marika nodded politely.

"Which is why I always used to feel sorry for Rob's enemies," Beth said.

Marika could see that there was a lot of Robert Lewis in Beth. Or, perhaps, it was the other way around—that Lewis's older sister had helped shape him into who he was. Marika didn't know if Beth would help her, but at this point she wasn't as concerned. Her mind was too caught up in the story about Daniel and with questions about Lewis and his death.

"I don't know if you'll want to tell me more about Rob," Marika said to Beth, "but I want you to know that I'll show you a copy of my book before it goes to print, so you can weigh in. That's my promise to you."

Beth was surprised by Marika's pledge. She knew that Rob would've never shown anyone—not even *her*—his articles before they went to press.

"Why don't you help her out?" Tom said. "She seems all right to me. I think she'll do a good job." He winked at Marika and got up. "I've got to take a shower and get this paint off."

Beth turned to Marika, sighing. "All right, I'll help. But come back on Monday. My son's got a game tonight."

Marika ended up changing her plane ticket and spending an entire week in Missouri, heading out each day to Beth's house to interview her. Beth was true to her word. A homemaker, she put off doing work around the farm to talk to Marika. She told her about her brother's life, from his childhood days in Clyne to his decision to leave home at seventeen. To Marika, Robert Lewis seemed proof that people are fated to have certain paths in life.

He had spent his youth helping his father harvest hay and raise cattle, and it was assumed that he would eventually take over work at the family farm. Rob grew up without a mother, so it was hard to say whether his life would have been different with a maternal influence; as it was, his father never remarried and fell heavily into drink. Rob ended up having to do most of the farmwork, which, in Beth's opinion, turned him against it. The day after he graduated from high school, he left Missouri for good, heading to New York. His father never forgave him for leaving. As the farm began to fail, Beth and her first husband were invited to move in and take over the work.

Rob never did return to Missouri as long as his father was alive. They remained estranged for years. Their father was, according to Beth, a "hard drunk," and he lived the last of his days in an apartment over the family garage, drinking away the nights. Then the inevitable: while driving drunk one evening, he flipped his truck on the highway and was killed. To Beth's surprise, Rob showed up for the funeral. To her even greater surprise, he cried long and bitterly for days afterward. It was the first time Beth had realized that her brother actually cared deeply for their father, and he mourned the relationship that had been lost.

"Rob was gentle, if you got to know him," Beth insisted. "He had a good heart."

Marika hadn't come to associate the word *gentle* with Robert Lewis. His colleagues often spoke of his formidable, violent temper. Get a couple of drinks in him, and no one was safe from his wrath—it was as if the entire world was out to get him; he saw injustice everywhere and could not bring himself to trust even his closest friends. Those same friends all claimed he was witty and erudite when sober, and the truest of gentlemen—at least, when he wasn't caught in one of his trademark depressions.

Ultimately, Lewis's friends would speak of a love and loyalty from him that was deeply unshakable. Yet, Lewis expected impeccability from people; betray him even once, and you could never hope to redeem yourself. Marika reconciled Lewis's striking polarities of character by remembering one of the lines from his first book: "I am worse than a hypocrite," he wrote of himself, "because I know my faults, yet I persuade myself that they are necessary somehow, that without them I would be lost in banality, in the curse of normalcy. To understand the suffering of another, we must know what it is to suffer within ourselves, always rediscovering the truth of our ignobility, vanity, foolishness—our thousandfold mistakes."

Uncovering the "real" Robert Lewis brought Beth and Marika together, like allies fighting for a common cause. Beth wanted Rob to be remembered properly, respectfully, and she found in Marika someone who had nothing but the utmost admiration for her brother—admiration which may have bordered on infatuation. Marika's knowledge of Rob's life, and her dedication to the biography, were unparalleled. In particular, Marika had been to many of the same conflicts in the world that her brother had—which mattered to Beth, who was sure no one could even begin to understand someone with Rob's complexity unless they had the same sorts of experiences.

One afternoon, Marika finally asked the question that Beth had been expecting all along: "Would you tell me about Rob's suicide?"

For Beth, this meant going back to an excruciating place in her past, where no body had been found, where no real closure had been granted. She had never been able to bury her brother. One day he was alive, the next dead, and the world went on with its trivialities, its obsessions, as if nothing had happened. Perhaps that was the worst of it, Beth had often thought. The great indifference of life. The fact that the world didn't stop for even a minute to bow its head in compassion, to offer its condolences.

"Well," she said finally, "you probably already know that Rob died off the east coast of Malaysia."

"Near Tioman Island," Marika said.

"Yeah. That's the last place he was seen alive."

Beth explained how her brother had paid a local man a hefty two thousand dollars to borrow his dinghy and outboard for the day. When he didn't return by nightfall, the police launched a search for him. The next morning, locals found the empty boat with a note inside in Rob's handwriting, indicating that he'd drowned himself. An identical note was later found among Rob's belongings in the bungalow where he'd been staying, and so Malaysian officials called off the search, pronouncing him dead by suicide. Still, Beth hired dive crews to look for Rob's body—it was believed that he'd weighted himself before going over-board—but their efforts proved futile. It was impossible to know how far Rob had traveled by boat, or where he'd jumped in. As Rob was a high-profile American, and as his death had received extensive news coverage in the States, people had pressured the U.S. Embassy to conduct its own search to rule out foul play. But after a couple of weeks, having conducted many fruitless inter-views on Tioman with local Malaysians, embassy officials closed Robert Lewis's case and issued the death certificate.

The suicide note, which had been spread all over the Inter-net, had been brief and disturbingly matter-of-fact. Marika had easily obtained a copy:

> *My name is Robert S. Lewis. I'm an American citizen.*
> *When you find this note, I will already be dead. I have*
> *drowned myself. Please know that this decision was my choice*
> *only. I ask you to inform my sister, Elizabeth Lewis Nichols.*
> *She is now the legal recipient of all my possessions and finan-*
> *cial holdings.*

"And they were sure there wasn't foul play?" Marika asked Beth.

"Yeah, they were sure. I mean, Rob had transferred all his assets to me right before he died. And then, I got the other note."

"There was another note?" This was news to Marika. No one had ever reported it.

"It was just for me. Rob was always a private man. He didn't like people knowing about his personal life."

Without another word, Beth got up and left the room, returning with a large box. She opened it and rifled through the contents, removing a piece of yellow notebook paper preserved in a clear plastic sheet.

"This is the letter," she said. "It's in his handwriting. I've only shown it to a couple of people from the State Department, who were working on his case. Rob sent it to me from Malaysia, the day before . . ."

Her voice cracked. She looked at Marika, and after a moment of hesitation, gave her the letter. In flighty scrawl, it read:

Dear Beth,

I need to write to you, so maybe you'll understand what I'm about to do. My thoughts haven't allowed me to sleep. They keep me awake at all hours now, running over everything in my life I should have said or done differently. Worse, they keep showing me Daniel's face— emasculating me, eviscerating me—reminding me how I was supposed to have protected him from harm, and didn't. The world will not stop punishing me for that.

I want to tell you about Jicin. (So much of my life I've never written about. All the things that really mattered— Daniel, you—I never shared with the world. I was supposed to be someone else. Someone called Robert Lewis. He was "famous." A prize winner. But I don't recognize that person anymore. If I met him on the street, I wouldn't like him. He would seem stale to me, and ordinary, and vain. He would seem, above all else, *too earnest*. I try to imagine a place for myself without any earnestness, where people have forgotten what they know. God save us from people who claim to have all the answers.) I must tell you about Jicin. I had taken a stopover in Prague before my flight to the Caucasus and Chechnya. Secretly, I knew there was a fair chance that I could die in Chechnya—it was the riskiest story I'd done in years—so I wanted to take some time to myself before the trip. I took a bus out to the countryside, and I got off at a place called Jicin for no particular reason that I can remember. There was a trail passing some fields. I took it, and it followed a stream a ways; everything was quiet and mossy-smelling, as if I were in a jungle. Then I saw a field up ahead, on a hillside. It was a field of long, green grass with stark, haunting, periwinkle-colored flowers; here and there, a single red poppy rose like a beacon. Beside this field was a spread of browning wheat. Can you picture it? Verdant green on one side; crackling, dying brown on the other. I walked the line between them, up the green hill, and I saw on a nearby crag the broken ramparts of a small castle overlooking the countryside. Suddenly, I stopped. And how to explain this to you? There it *was*, Beth. *There*, all around me. All I needed in that moment to be happy. I knelt down, and probably you won't understand this, but I started to weep. I asked the world—begged the world— to tell me how I could keep such beauty. How to keep it?

There was no answer. The clouds shifted above. A drizzle hit me, and then sunlight crept out tentatively again. White butterflies twirled beside the wheat field, and a red poppy shook at the top of the green hill. *How to keep it?* I wept like a madman, with everything I had. I wept for the past few years of my life. (That I could tell you, or anyone, about the loneliness.) I wept for Daniel's death. I wept for everything I had ever wanted out of life and hadn't been able to find. But I wept for the grace and grandeur of things too, for all I've been allowed. And I've been allowed a great deal in exchange for, or perhaps in spite of, the years of pain.

Of course, I didn't want to leave that hillside, but I had to. The last bus was coming in an hour, to take me back to Prague. And you think all sorts of things in moments like that—how to explain? All hope rests tangibly around you, and nothing in the world could hurt you. You *believe* in moments like that. You *know* in such moments. The world wants you, but more important, *you* want *it*. And this was what my hike in Jicin was like. Pure belief. Pure faith.

Of course, I soon lost that feeling. And now I'm certain I'll never find it again. For years, I tried to get it back, but my life only felt more broken and lost. And then fate came around, and my life collapsed, and I was left standing in the flames, shaking, unable to sleep, tormented by a need to be at peace. Do you know, all this time I haven't been able to get that hike in Jicin out of my head? If only it were possible to hold on to such states of grace.

When you hear about my death, you won't understand the reason for it. I don't think anyone will. You must know what it is to be me, having lived a lifetime in my shoes. Maybe you won't want to forgive me, but you must. You *must*. If there *is* any salvation in this world, it can only come through forgiveness. We must learn to see in each other the scared children we all are. The needy children. The lost children. Still, know that I'm the worst of hypocrites, because I haven't been able to forgive. I'm not sure you can forgive some things. (If only I didn't still believe in God; perhaps only an atheist knows real peace.)

But you mustn't be like me. You must forgive. You, who are so much greater a spirit in compassion, empathy, faith. You must be the light in the world—if there is any light left.

> Dear Beth. Forgive me. I love you.
>
> Robert

Marika fingered the letter. Beth sat in silence, tears running down her cheeks.

"My God," Marika uttered, Lewis's last words a weight upon her heart.

"That's what my brother was like," Beth said, pointing at the letter. "Beneath it all, that's how he was."

She took Marika's hand and squeezed it.

"What do you think happened to him?" Marika asked.

Beth shook her head. "Maybe he finally saw too much. You know, when he was young, if he saw a June beetle on its back, he'd have to stop to turn it over. After he killed his first deer with Dad, he came back crying about it. Of course Dad called him weak and tried to shame him, but Rob said he'd never go hunting again. And you know what? He never did."

Marika felt overwhelmed with questions. There were many other people—reporters, combat soldiers, aid workers—who had seen the same sorts of things that Lewis had. Worse, probably. Yet, they had survived, managed to cope. What would Seb have to say? Had Lewis reached his breaking point after a lifetime of "suppressing" and "compartmentalizing" his experiences? Had he, as Beth suggested, finally "seen too much"?

It sounded too simple, somehow. *Fate came around, and my life collapsed* . . . With Lewis, nothing was ever simple.

"What was his last assignment before he went to Malaysia?" Marika asked Beth.

"Something in Indonesia. I remember him mentioning East Timor."

Marika thought for a second. "But he never published anything about East Timor."

"No. I don't think it was an official kind of thing. He never even made it back from Southeast Asia." Beth stood up and handed Marika the box of letters. "You can go through these if you want. They're from friends and whatnot. They're mostly condolence letters, so I don't know if they'll be of any use to you, but I'll let you take them to your hotel tonight. Just promise you'll bring them back in the morning."

That night, in her hotel room, Marika went through the letters in the box. There were endless condolence cards from friends and colleagues, readers and fans. She jotted down any useful addresses or information, in case she needed to follow up. Late in the night, when she was almost finished going through the contents, she pulled out a letter that was wholly unlike the others—a letter from Pastor John Wade of Birmingham, Alabama. It was post-marked only a month earlier—about six months after Lewis's death—and it had been sent to his book publisher, who'd then forwarded it to Beth.

> To the Family of Robert Lewis:
>
> First of all, I would like to offer you my condolences at this difficult time. I have been debating whether I ought to write to you, and my conscience finally compelled me. I have no intention to bring you any further grief, only to offer you the following information, should you wish to pursue it.
>
> Let me introduce myself. I am a pastor for the New Life Church, and I have spent the greater part of my life as a missionary in Papua New Guinea. I have just retired from that work due to health concerns, and I'm now back in the States. Approximately five months ago, while engaged in evangelical work in remoter regions of the country, I

came across an unlikely occurrence: a white man with a
beard and glasses, who bore an exact resemblance to
Robert Lewis, the writer and journalist. I should preface
this by saying that I am an avid fan of Mr. Lewis's books. I
often looked at the author photos, and I occasionally
caught Mr. Lewis on the news. As far as I am concerned,
the man I saw in PNG was undoubtedly him.

Now I know how unlikely this seems, and should it be
true, it would obviously raise all manner of questions.
Please know that the last thing I would ever want to do is
cause you pain by suggesting that Mr. Lewis is, in fact,
still alive. Yet, I feel I would be remiss if I did not at least
inform you of my discovery. I saw the man in question
camped along Tumbi River, which is a remote tributary of
the Sepik River (the country's main waterway). When I
approached and spoke to him, he wouldn't answer me
and went immediately into his tent. He looked disheveled
and did not appear to be in his full senses. I went to the
two local men who were with him, asking for the man's
name, but they claimed not to know it. Further inquiries
in the villages along the river proved fruitless. At that
point, I went on with my business and left. That was the
last I saw of him.

I would be glad to assist you in any way I can, should you
wish to look further into this matter. Unfortunately,
Papua New Guinea is not an easy place to launch any
investigation due to the lack of roads or infrastructure,
but there are ways of getting the word out via the missionary network. Please don't hesitate to contact me if
you have any questions, or if I could be of help to you in
the future.

Yours most sincerely,
Pastor John Wade

Marika felt a stirring within her. She read the letter a second time. A third time. It was such a bizarre claim—and, as Wade himself had said, so unlikely. But the pastor seemed a man of integrity, and he'd gone to the trouble of writing and getting the letter to Beth. While Marika tried to dismiss the matter as one of mistaken identity, she still found herself carefully taking down Wade's address—*just in case,* she told herself.

The next morning, when she returned the box to Beth, she pulled out Wade's letter. "Did you do anything about this?" she asked.

Beth took the envelope and glanced at it. "Oh," she said acidly. "*That* letter."

Tom, eating breakfast in the kitchen, overheard her.

"Is that the letter from that crazy pastor?" he called.

"Yes," Beth murmured.

"Did you ever look into it?" Marika prodded.

"What? My brother, alive in New Guinea?" Beth laughed coldly. "Rob is dead. You saw the note he sent me." Beth crumpled up Wade's letter and walked over to the kitchen garbage can, throwing it in.

"Rob and Elvis got a house there in New Guinea, huh, Beth?" Tom chuckled, getting up and putting his arm around her.

"There are a lot of crazy people out there," Beth said to Marika. "I've learned that much since Rob died. This other man sent me a bunch of newspaper articles about Rob that'd he'd been saving for years. His whole theory was that the CIA killed him. It was supposed to be some kind of cover-up."

Tom hooted and squeezed his wife's arm. "I remember *those* letters."

"Unbelievable," Beth said, rolling her eyes.

Marika wasn't surprised. When she'd worked at a newspaper years ago, one of her jobs had been to go through reader mail sent to the editors. She remembered a lot of it: the bizarre manifestos, conspiracy theories, rants. Still, Wade hadn't seemed crazy to her. Not on paper, at least.

A few hours later, as Marika ended her last interview with Beth, the woman handed her an envelope.

"For you," she said. "It was probably the last thing Rob ever wrote. I've been thinking about it, and I've decided it's okay for you to put it in your book."

Marika opened the envelope. Inside was a copy of the Jicin letter.

Tobo studies Marika as they sit in a hut in Krit village. The white mary remains just out of reach of the sunlight slanting through the window, fingering the *billum* bag that Aren's wife gave her as a gift. Her red-blond hair rests in tangles about her head, making her look like a witch. Her pants legs are pulled up, showing white calves covered with puncture wounds and scratches—she hasn't even bothered to wash the cuts. Angrily, Tobo points at her legs, handing her one of Aren's water gourds and a piece of old T-shirt as a rag.

"Go outside!" he scolds her in Pidgin. "You must wash yourself."

Marika looks at him, wondering why he's getting so upset. "I'll go wash in a minute," she tells him in English.

"You are getting your blood in this hut. You will poison these Krit people!"

Marika had forgotten about the issue of "poison" in these parts. She gets up and limps across the hut. As Aren watches her go, his wife clucks her tongue.

"Where did you find that white woman?" he asks Tobo in Pidgin.

The Anasi man glances at Marika as she disappears down the notched log ladder. "I saw her in one of my dreams, and then she came to my village the next day. The gods brought her. I had no choice."

"*Eh?* I am not surprised."

Marika walks into the bright sunlight, wincing. A scrawny dog barks at her several times, trailing after her as she makes her way to the black waters of the lagoon. Naked children, their skin covered in ringworm peels, hide behind hut posts and stare at her wide-eyed. Marika got hardly any sleep last night due to the droves of mosquitoes, and the world appears foglike, insubstantial.

She maneuvers carefully down a slippery clay path to the foot of the lagoon, her feet letting out cries of pain. She has sago thorns imbedded in her soles, and no way to get them out. Farther down, a Krit woman squats onshore, washing cooking pots. An infant is tied to her back with a piece of sarong, and the child studies Marika with its dark brown eyes.

Marika leans over the dark water. Her reflection appears indistinct, quivering from a slight breeze. White cumulus clouds seem to float across the oily water, across the surface of her face. She dips a hand into her reflection, scattering it.

The Krit woman is watching her unabashedly. Marika ignores her and sits down on the muddy ground, inspecting her legs. She uses the rag Tobo gave her to wipe off the mud on her feet, exposing a large thorn in her big toe. Ignoring the pain, she tries gouging it out with her fingernail.

"*Eh!*"

Marika looks up to see the Krit woman standing over her. The woman is shaking her head and clucking her tongue. She squats down and grabs the rag, dipping it in the swamp water. With tremendous care, she thoroughly washes Marika's feet. Removing a fishhook from the *laplap* around her waist, the woman patiently examines Marika's soles for thorns, her fingers deftly using the tip of the hook to remove each one.

A number of small children slowly approach the two women. Whispering and gesticulating, they dare each other to touch Marika's hair. One brave child finally does—only to run off into the jungle, screaming in mock terror.

As the Krit woman works, she gently scolds Marika in her

tribal language, as if berating a small child. Marika says nothing, just notices how perfectly the oily black swamp water reflects the clouds and betel nut palms.

"*Ai!*" the woman exclaims, staring at a large thorn in the heel of Marika's foot. Clucking her tongue, she looks Marika in the eyes and says something that can only mean: "Doesn't this hurt?"

Marika shrugs. "Lots of things hurt," she says to her in English.

The woman yanks her *laplap* out of the way and leans forward so her nose is nearly touching Marika's foot. Carefully, with full concentration, she extracts the thorn. The crowd of children gathers closer, watching with excited whispers. Marika can feel the heat from their little bodies all around her. Can smell the smoke of cooking fires on their skin.

The woman's baby studies Marika, reaching out a chubby hand to grab her hair. The woman laughs and pulls the baby's hand back, the crowd of children giggling. One boy forces open the baby's fist to remove a strand of Marika's hair, running off with it in triumph, the other children chasing after him and begging to see. Marika studies the dark brown eyes of the infant. She sees such light in them. Such peace. She wonders how he perceives the world—as an incomprehensible mass of form and color and sound? As a place without worry or threat? He is in that blessed place of not-knowing. Maybe that's the place Lewis was trying to describe in his suicide letter? A place where, for a single instant, the weight of the world was lifted from his shoulders and he felt the staggering grace of peace.

Ah, thinks Marika. To have even a taste of that.

The Krit woman manages to remove the thorn at last and wipes away some blood with the wet rag. Standing, she glances down with a smile of triumph, pinning the fishhook to Marika's tank top as a gift. Before Marika can even thank her, she heads back to the village. The crowd of children runs after her, looking over their shoulders at the white mary.

Marika wades into the lagoon, her feet sinking into the muddy ooze of the bottom. As she washes herself, she submerges her head. It feels cold, fantastic. It is the first thing that has felt good in a very long time. She remains submerged for as long as she can stand it, then erupts into the blinding white sunlight. About to dunk herself again, she stops, fear slicing through her. *What about crocodiles?* She scrambles out of the lagoon, onto the slippery shore, and scans the water. There will always be something, she knows. Something lurking beneath the surface, waiting for the very moment when she starts enjoying herself.

She lies on the muddy shore, sunlight stinging her eyes. Birds let out calls from the jungle, and a single green parrot flits overhead, looking down at her. Today, she'll be leaving again. She has nothing but the clothes on her back and a few things the Krit people gave her. There will be weeks of travel, and Tobo doesn't even think she'll make it. The Anasi man is convinced she will die.

Marika lets loose a smile. Tobo obviously doesn't know her yet. She'll just have to live, to prove him wrong.

She gazes off at the jungle to the west. Somewhere out there is a village that supposedly holds Robert Lewis. And she is determined to find him.

Tobo and Marika stand on the edge of the black lagoon, beside a shabby, leaking dugout canoe. The entire population of Krit village waits silently to watch them go. Marika waves good-bye to the woman who gave her the fishhook, and she waves back, her baby staring with solemn eyes.

Marika is relieved; there will be no jungle travel today. She will have another day to rest her legs, as Tobo thinks it best to go through the swamps, covering as much distance as possible by boat before heading inland. Once they enter the jungle, he told her, the trip won't be easy; there won't be any trails. The rivers and mountains will guide them, though there will be weeks of hiking and climbing before they reach Walwasi Mountain.

Aren helped provision Tobo and Marika as best he could. Mostly sago palm balls and smoked cassowary meat, wrapped in banana leaves and placed in a *billum* bag. He also gave Tobo some fire-making implements, water-filled gourds, and walnut-sized betel nuts to chew. Less willingly, he parted with an old canoe, Tobo assuring him he'd pay back the favor when he returned.

Aren's wife gave Marika one of her most valuable possessions: a plastic water bottle that the missionaries had left in the village. She doesn't know what will happen to the white mary, but she suspects the woman will die just like her friend Lewis probably did. She wishes there was more she could do for her.

Tobo stands in the back of the canoe, holding his paddle. Marika kneels in front, the precarious craft nearly tipping. The Krit villagers watch ominously as Aren runs over, handing Marika a plank to use as a seat. She has barely thanked him before Tobo quickly paddles away, anxious to be rid of the cursed village. The canoe veers left and right from his powerful strokes, its bow cutting through the heavy black water. White cranes laugh at their approach, kicking themselves into the air and spreading wide white wings. In a few minutes, Krit village is gone.

As soon as he's out of eyeshot of the village, Tobo grabs the *billum* bag Aren gave him and tosses all the food into the lagoon.

"Those people are touched by death," he explains to Marika, making a sign over the water with his fingers.

"But what are we going to eat?" she exclaims, furious.

"I will catch us something."

Without a word, Tobo continues paddling. Marika sighs, grabbing her own paddle, the sun glaring down at her. She wears only a tank top and knows she'll be badly sunburned before long. Picking up some of the clay that Tobo stored in the canoe for caulking up holes, she smears it on her face and over her exposed skin. It's the best she can do.

They make good progress. Toward midday, distant mountains of jungle rise sharply from the lowland swamps looking like the teeth of one of Tobo's *masalai,* or demons. When Marika first arrived in Papua New Guinea and saw an airline office's map, this part of the country appeared as a big gray void. Gray must have meant uninhabited, unknown. Even back in the United States, she hadn't been able to find any good maps of PNG's interior. It's a place that, as far as the Western world is concerned, doesn't seem to exist. Which satisfies Marika. PNG keeps its secrets.

Their canoe leaks continuously. Marika keeps bailing it with a coconut shell, stuffing balls of clay into the many holes. The clay, poor caulking, soon becomes waterlogged and loosens. It serves better on her skin as sunblock, though without a hat she still crumples in the heat.

By the end of the day, as Tobo stops the canoe by some dry land and hauls it up for the night, Marika can barely lift herself out, the sun having sapped all strength from her. He notices this—notices everything about the unusual white woman—and wonders how long she will last.

Marika sits onshore with her water bottle between her legs. She'd been saving the water inside, sipping from one of the gourds instead, and now she unscrews the cap to take a long drink. But the contents smell sharply of kerosene, and Marika spits out the water, wiping her lips several times.

Tobo eyes her curiously.

"Petrol," she explains to him, pointing at the bottle.

He just stares at her. At the dried clay on her face and arms. At her yellow hair that gets more tangled by the day.

She pours the contents onto the ground. Refilling the bottle with swamp water, she shakes it furiously, trying to clean it out. Tobo sits cross-legged now, machete in his lap, entirely absorbed in the spectacle of her repeatedly emptying and refilling the bottle. Whenever the mourning necklace gets in her way, she flips it over her shoulder, glancing guiltily at him.

"*Ma-ree-ka*," he says, trying out her name on his tongue. He reaches into his *billum* bag and pulls out some betel nuts, coral lime powder, and mustard stalks. Using his teeth, he breaks open the coconut-like hull of one of the nuts, pushing the kernel into the back of his mouth. Dipping a mustard stalk into the powder, he bites off its end and chews vigorously, sending a projectile of bloodred spit onto the ground.

"Can I drink this water?" she asks Tobo, pointing to the swampy water around them.

The Anasi man finds it an odd question. She might be asking if she can sit on the ground. Of course she can drink the water. He shrugs at her.

Marika pauses, not knowing what Tobo's shrug means. Finally, she just dips the bottle into the black water and fills it. Sitting back, she uses her fishhook to pick out a sliver from her calf.

"Where is your husband?" Tobo asks her, chewing and spitting.

It is a question he's been wondering about since she first appeared in his village. White men, he has noticed, are usually married, but only to one wife at a time. Which makes no sense to Tobo. Who is a man supposed to lie with when his wife is heavy with child or sick? Or during her blood time? Two wives, at the very least, are necessary, though more than four can be costly. He, himself, has a very young wife and an older one, his third wife having died while trying to push out her baby. Tobo often tells his youngest wife to meet him in the yam garden for *puspus*, but she never gets big with child. He thinks it is the gods' way of joking with him. They know how risky it is for a man to touch a woman, let alone get her *bokis* fluids on him after lying with her. Were it not for all the protection Tobo puts around his body, he would surely be poisoned by now. He has often wondered if the fluids from a white mary *bokis* are equally dangerous. Or even more so. It is a question that none of the white Jesus Men would answer for him.

Marika glances at Tobo, alarmed by his question. In some

countries, when a man asks her if she's married, it means he's trying to flirt with her. But Tobo has no prurient look in his expression, just curiosity.

She thinks about Seb. His bright brown eyes. The feel of his lips on her cheek. That last, lingering stare he gave her before she left him for good.

She feels a clench of pain in her gut. "I don't have a husband," she tells Tobo.

"*Eh?* Why not?"

"In America, some women don't get married."

Tobo is sure she's a witch now. Only women who are hexed can't get husbands. "This means you don't have children?"

"No."

Tobo considers her answer. "What man allowed you to come alone to my country? Was it your father?"

Marika doesn't know what to do with his question. "My father is dead," she says, hoping that will satisfy him.

Tobo nods. Now he understands. The white mary has no husband or father to tell her what to do. It explains why she always has the lost look in her eyes.

"Is Robert Lewis your *wantok?*" he asks.

Marika wishes Tobo's strange questions would end. She's tired and hungry, and they have absolutely no food or drinking water. She pretends not to understand him.

"Is the white man Robert Lewis your *wantok?*" he asks again, insistent.

Her *wantok*—One Talk. Which is to say, someone who speaks her language, is a member of her tribe. As there are over seven hundred tribes in Papua New Guinea, she knows Tobo must think there are just as many in the United States, if not more.

"Yes," she says at last. "Lewis is my *wantok.*"

"Does he have a wife in America?"

Marika sighs. What to say? Lewis was married once. He had girlfriends—lots of girlfriends. And a few longer relationships, nothing too serious. Some people called him a "womanizer." Others said he was "fond of the ladies."

"Lewis had women," Marika says.

It is exciting news for Tobo: a white man with more than one wife. "How many wives did he have?"

"I don't know." Marika dips her hand in the water and washes off the clay on her cheeks.

"Do you also want to be Lewis's wife?"

Marika stares at him, seeing a mysterious glint in the Anasi man's eyes. When she was younger, and idolized Lewis, she would fantasize about him sometimes. It was just the sort of harmless thing young girls do, like obsessing about rock stars or actors.

When Marika doesn't respond to Tobo's question, he laughs, knowing it must be true. The white mary would like to be Lewis's wife. Tobo is not surprised. If Lewis's wives are in America, and if Lewis is here, then he will need *puspus*. Like any man.

Marika watches Tobo's lips furl into a smile. Irritated, she throws down her water bottle and walks off.

They've been paddling for days across swamps, through mangroves. The whole time, the sun blazes in a sky without clouds. Marika finds the heat nearly unbearable. She hangs her *billum* bag over her head to try to protect her face. She slathers clay on her exposed skin, though sweat soon melts it from her body. The sunlight burns her relentlessly, cruelly, and her only means of cooling off is to continually throw water on her clothes.

But now a change: they enter a stream. Trees arc overhead, providing blessed shade as the swampland gives way to forest. Everything grows dim, the sun losing its dominion to giant fern trees and hardwoods which block out the sky. Marika still hasn't seen any people, nor any trace of human passage, since leaving Krit village. She imagines herself and Tobo as First Man and Woman. All around them is unmolested jungle, resounding with bird calls and insect wails. Cockatoos and hornbills watch her fearlessly from the trees. Flocks of green and red parrots materialize from the forest only to resettle themselves and disappear again. The world has come alive with resplendent, surreal hues: neon-colored damselflies, butterflies with giant wings of blue satin. It is a glimmering, sultry place, everything reaching tentacles out, overtaking and wrapping and fondling.

Tobo uses his bow and arrows to shoot them food—ducks, usually, or crowned pigeons. Or he goes off into the jungle to hunt, returning with tree rats and possums. At dusk, he hacks away a clearing in the jungle, builds a fire, and puts up a couple of lean-tos. Burning betel nut palm leaves to keep the mosquitoes away, he shows Marika how to cut and clean animal carcasses and fasten them to spits. He must show her how to do everything. How to construct a pallet aboveground, away from the ants. How to bring smoking cinders with her into the jungle at night to keep mosquitoes from biting her when she goes *pekpek*. Slowly, the white mary learns.

They make gradual progress upriver, though to what end Marika doesn't know. The more the river narrows, the more tedious the journey becomes, dead trees blocking their way and forcing them to stop. Usually, they can lift the canoe over the debris, but at times the route is so blocked by tangles of branches, or by the enormous trunks of ancient trees, that Tobo has to cut them a portaging route through the jungle.

At last, when their canoe butts against a high wall of logs, Tobo orders them out of the boat.

"*Yumi go long bikbus,*" he says.

They will head into the "big bush."

It is what Marika has been fearing: leaving the waterways. At least with a river they have something to follow, with a beginning and ending. The jungle appears as a dark green void, without any landmarks, seemingly without end. If she ever emerges from it, she'll be in the village where Lewis is supposed to be—or she might not ever get out.

"Are there any villages between here and Walwasi?" she asks Tobo.

"*Nogat*," he says. Nothing.

Tobo makes no ceremony about entering the jungle. He simply removes their few belongings from the canoe, fills his *billum* bag with smoked meat and water gourds, and hacks a route into the jungle. Marika watches him, immobilized, as he swiftly, expertly, disappears into the rain forest.

Here is the moment, the precise point in time, that will define who she is. The moment of irreconcilability, when she must pick up her own *billum* bag, fill her own water bottle—hopelessly reeking of kerosene—and follow Tobo into the dim greenery. There seems to be nothing left behind her and, quite possibly, nothing waiting ahead. Seb used to tell her that every foolish choice a person makes is an attempt, however misguided, to find happiness.

Marika knows she could still go back. Tobo would gladly return her to civilization. He might even take her as far as the Sepik River, if she asked. Though Seb would consider that the "sensible" thing to do, he also knew the trademark stubbornness of her character that listens to no reason, heeds no warnings. It is the part of her that, ironically, Robert Lewis would have admired.

Lewis. Does she actually believe he's alive, and that she'll find him? But it's crazy-making to think that far ahead. It's enough just to face the difficult journey in front of her, and all it will entail. Probably, she's about to risk her life for a ghost—though it has never bothered her, risking her life. Marika doesn't know if that's a defect of her character, as Seb might think. Death has never really scared her.

All she knows is that if Lewis *is* alive, and if she can find him, the hard journey will be worth it. She won't give up on him. He would have never given up on her, after all.

"*Yumi go!*" Tobo shouts from the jungle, waiting for her.

She charges into the jungle, shoving branches aside. Reaching Tobo, she asks him how far to Walwasi village.

He doesn't need to think about it. "*Longwe tumas,*" he says.

Long way too much. Marika already knows that distance isn't
given in numbers out here. Miles, kilometers—they're meaningless. In the bush, distance is measured by how long it takes a normal person, traveling at a steady clip, to get from one point to
another. She knows that Tobo's conclusion of *longwe tumas* takes
into consideration all the streams and rivers they'll have to cross,
all the mountains they'll have to climb. It takes into consideration the storms and heat and agonizing nights of no sleep,
attacked by mosquitoes. His answer is, to Marika, a sobering
assessment. Long way too much. A very long way.

Tobo glances at the white mary's face. At the changing
expression. She looks like an old woman with tired, troubled
eyes, who has seen too much, though she asked for this journey
and paid handsomely for it. Tobo will never understand the white
people. Not for as long as he lives.

"Once you start a journey," he scolds her, "you must give up
all fear. That is the man's way."

He turns from her and continues chopping them a path
through the jungle.

Marika is sure of one thing: if Robert Lewis is really alive and out
here somewhere, he doesn't want to be found. He lost himself in
the middle of this country. He cut himself a tunnel through this
incredible mass of tangled, inhospitable green. The jungle
wouldn't have expected him to return. It would have reached
out, grasped, planted its seed. It would have filled his path with
new brush, barring escape.

Tobo and Marika don't walk. They climb—over trees, under
them. They plunge—through brackish black mud up to their
waists. For a week, Tobo leads her through swampy valleys, the
heat and humidity assailing her. She worries constantly about
dehydration and heat exhaustion, her head pounding desperately.

As they reach the high mountains, the rain starts. Marika has
never been pummeled by such storms; one of Tobo's gods might

be trying to drown out the earth. The jungle quickly floods, and Tobo tells her they'll have to start climbing. She wonders if he's serious—the mountains rise sharply at near ninety-degree angles and seem almost impossible to scale—but he starts pulling himself up the nearest slope using tree roots and vines, digging his toes into the muddy slopes. Marika follows as best she can, the rain loosening the soil beneath her feet. She barely makes any progress before she falls down the muddy mountainside to where she started. Tobo climbs down to get her, helping, encouraging, though his own weariness shows in his eyes. He knows there will be weeks of this sort of travel, made all the longer by the white mary's lack of skills.

Tobo goes more slowly for her, so she can get the hang of it and learn how to place her feet properly. For a woman, at least she's not as weak as he originally feared. Her body is surprisingly strong and can get her over the mountains. It's only in her head that she's unfit, blind to what's before her, deaf to the sounds and speech of the jungle. She doesn't know what to touch yet. What to hold or eat. He must teach her as if she were a child, telling her what everything is, showing her how to master the jungle and earn its respect. Tobo finds it all tedious, and misses his Anasi village, his children, his wives. If only, he thinks, he'd never run into that humbug Baku man.

They take the mountains one at a time. It's slow going at first, until Marika finally learns what to do. She becomes adept at finding footholds and handholds. She stops moving clumsily through the brush. As she keeps up with Tobo, she grows used to the omnipresent sight of his sweaty black back and the dried *tanket* leaves covering his buttocks. It isn't long before she loses track of the days. Time doesn't matter, just the awareness of when night is coming, and so the opportunity to rest. Not even the mosquitoes bother her anymore. She sleeps like a dead person, without dreams, the rancid smoke of burning betel nut palm leaves filling her lungs, causing her to wake with phlegm in her throat, her eyes red and stinging.

They arrive at the top of one of the highest mountains they've had to climb when her body screams out with stomach pain. There is a rush and gurgling in her bowels. Nausea. Headaches. She runs frequently into the muddy, wet brush to pull down her pants and relieve herself. She suspects it is the start of dysentery. Or worse. It could be any number of things, many of which she's had on assignments around the world. She knows that giardia and dysentery have similar symptoms, though very different cures, each needing an entirely different medicine. And then there are the two types of dysentery. Amoebic, bacillary. One worse than the other. One capable of planting its seeds in her organs and stealthily disabling her over time, even if she managed to survive without medicine. On all of her trips, she always carried a regimen of the antibiotic Cipro as her panacea. How many times had those small oval pills kept her from serious illness and death? But she has nothing now, and her body is forced to face the consequences.

After running into the bushes for the umpteenth time to relieve herself, red dots fill her vision. Here it is, as expected. The battle is about to begin.

"Tobo!" she yells.

She hears no response.

"Tobo!"

Her vision blurs, and she falls, passing out.

Marika wakes to the sight of a pile of cassowary feathers spread on her stomach. Tobo sits nearby, speaking incantations in a low voice. All around her the jungle regards her pensively, its leaves barely stirring.

She tries to sit up, but a wave of stomach cramps sends her reeling and clutching her abdomen in pain. Tobo turns to her without a pause in his recitations, sprinkling more feathers onto her stomach.

"Can you give me some water?" she whispers.

He reaches for one of his gourds and hands it to her. She drinks all the water inside and lies back, wiping sweat from her forehead. She knows she has a fever, is badly dehydrated. She wonders how many people die from something like this when they have no medicine for it.

Ants climb over her arm. Something crawls up her pants leg, but she's too sick to swat at it. She keeps looking for the sun through the thick canopy, longing for open space, those midwestern plains of soybeans and 360 degrees of blue sky. She misses the most mundane things. Things she never cared about before she entered the jungle.

Tobo stops his incantations to cut brush for their camp. He cushions a makeshift pallet with leaves and drags her onto it. Getting a fire going, he builds a shelter over her with branches and digs a hole just behind the structure so she has a place to go *pispis*. Marika throws up anything Tobo tries to feed her, but he keeps feeding her anyway, stuffing smoked bush meat into her mouth. Knowing she would do better with something starchy, he descends the mountain to harvest a sago palm.

Marika turns onto her side, closing her eyes, soft moans escaping from her throat. The pain is excruciating, unrelenting. She's convinced she's going to die; there can be just so much punishment her body will take. She sees images of Seb and speaks to him. She tells him that Lewis is dead, that he's always been dead. Seb doesn't answer, just stares at her with that concerned, helpless look in his eyes that he had the day she left him.

Tobo returns, carrying a *billum* bag full of moist, white sago pith. He dries it over the fire, pressing it into white patties and forcing Marika to eat one. Again, she throws it up, but he feeds her more until her stomach surrenders and she can keep it down.

The days pass. There is only the wrenching pain in her guts, and the mad dashes to relieve her bowels. The nights are the worst, the pain and mosquito onslaughts keeping her from sleep. Tobo does what he can. Sometimes he sings to her. Often, he puts his mouth to her stomach to suck out the bad energy, spitting it over his shoulder. But there is so much dark smoke to suck out that he can't do it all himself. He will need help. Great help, as he has no experience with the formidable demons of the white people.

Tobo knows he will need to call on one of his most powerful helping spirits, but first he must prepare the white mary and himself for such a ceremony. She often opens her eyes to see red parrot feathers circling her head, as Tobo builds a protective barrier of white light around her body. He goes carefully, respectfully, so as not to anger the demons causing her illness. Three times a day, Tobo puts his most potent charms around her: his effigy of Balu, the head spirit of the jungle trees, and several cassowary feather bundles empowered with protective energy by Agane, guardian of the lower realms.

Tobo debated for days whether to summon Agane, who is very hard to please and easily offended. An ornery trickster spirit, Agane is half man, half wild-pig, and can only be contacted by burning the bark of the wild mango tree. Tobo spent an entire afternoon harvesting Agane's favorite wood, knowing that if he offers the spirit a large fire at night, Agane will come to the earth realm to warm his body from the frigid cold of the lower realms. Then, in gratitude, he will order his armies of healing spirits to do Tobo's bidding.

Tobo will go to every length to try to keep the white mary alive. She is not a bad sort of white person, after all. She may be strange and bewitched, but her soul, he has noticed, is pure. Not to mention that if the white mary *does* die, Tobo is sure his family members will be cursed because he didn't uphold his part of the payback bargain. He knows he must get Marika to the village where Lewis lives—or even all his sorcery skills won't save his family from the consequences.

On the fifth night of Marika's illness, Tobo is prepared to call Agane. The bark is collected. The fire is ready.

"Tonight, Agane will come," Tobo tells Marika solemnly.

Marika, weak and in pain, opens her eyes.

"You must be polite to Agane," Tobo explains. "And you must not be scared of him, because he doesn't like frightened women."

Marika doesn't know what Tobo is talking about, but she nods. She tries to eat the sago that he hands her, barely swallowing any before she throws it up. She finishes the water in her water bottle instead, and Tobo takes it from her and walks away with it. She assumes he's going to refill it in a nearby stream and come right back, but as dusk falls, he doesn't return.

The jungle descends into darkness, Marika's ears ringing with the bold calls of night insects. Mosquitoes engulf her, buzzing in her ears and biting the bottoms of her feet. She covers her face with her hair, and the insects bite her scalp instead. Without the smoke from a betel leaf fire, the mosquitoes will feed on her liberally, and she knows there's no way to stop them.

Marika hears a screech. Another screech. She sits up with difficulty, seeing a fire moving quickly toward her through the jungle. She assumes it's Tobo coming at last, and she lies back down, waiting for him. But as the flame approaches, there's a frantic rustling behind her, the lean-to shaking. She jumps up and peers into the darkness, unable to see anything.

The fire comes closer to her. Thankfully, she realizes that it *is* Tobo, holding a torch. Screeching madly, he thrusts the fire into a nearby pile of wood. As the bark erupts into flames, the rustling intensifies behind her. Marika huddles, terrified. Tobo runs over to her, carrying a lit piece of bark. Yelling and gesticulating, he desperately blows smoke over her body. Marika feels the patter of something mothlike striking her bare feet—the soft yet firm wings of a night creature. She kicks her legs at it, but the moth wings just flutter more urgently against her.

More moths strike her. On her arms, her face. Tobo is too busy screeching like a madman to help her. Marika slaps at the creatures, trying to drive them off, but they only return in greater numbers. She grabs a couple of them with her hand, discovering that the bodies are too large to be moths. *Bats.*

Marika flails her arms and tries to protect her face. But as suddenly as the winged creatures appeared, they vanish. Heart pounding, she searches the darkness. She doesn't know if they'll return, and she curls up on her side, hopelessly exposed to the jungle. She feels profoundly tired now. So tired she can't keep her eyes open.

She falls asleep.

When Marika wakes, the dawn is just arriving. Its light gradually defeats the darkness, giving shape to trees and brush. She sits up. A trace of betel leaf smoke curls over her body from a nearby pile of cinders. Cassowary feathers cover her clothes and the ground around her pallet. The night actually passed in its entirety without waking her once with diarrhea. The pain in her abdomen is gone, and she feels as if she's slept for centuries.

Tobo rests under his own lean-to several feet away. She looks at him—at the red paint covering his face, and the mysterious, carved statue in his hand. Marika remembers the bats from last night. Had it been a nightmare? She didn't know bats could land on a person. It was uncanny.

She gets up, excited that she can move without pain. She crouches behind the privacy of her shelter to relieve herself. Cassowary feathers litter the ground like confetti. She picks one up, seeing a trace of blood on it and on the ground. *How bizarre,* she thinks. It is her only response to Tobo and everything that happened last night: *bizarre.*

Marika returns to her pallet and sits down. Her pants are muddy and torn. She needs a bath and a change of clothes. What she wouldn't give for a bar of soap right now, and some fresh water! She sees her filled water bottle nearby and picks it up, taking a sip and running water over her face. Tentatively, she chews a piece of sago, discovering she can swallow it without nausea.

Tobo stirs and opens his eyes, staring at her.

"Mi ken kaikaim nau," she says to him happily. "I can eat now."

It takes Marika three days of rest to recoup her strength for more jungle travel. She sleeps a lot and eats as much as she can. Her stomach, deprived of food for nearly a week, takes time to adjust to normal-sized meals. Marika guesses she lost nearly ten pounds, her hip bones protruding through her skin. She knows she probably wouldn't have lived without Tobo's ministrations, but whenever she tries to thank him for his help, he looks at her curiously and shrugs. Her days of sickness seem to have already passed out of his mind, gone and long forgotten.

Tobo feels extremely pleased with Agane's work on the white mary, and his mind has been filled with plans to offer the spirit mango bark fires in the days ahead, to show his gratitude. Now, though, the woman needs to start moving as soon as possible. He's worried that her expelled demons will come back and try to make her sick again. Whenever a place has been touched by sickness or death, it is always better to move from it as soon as possible. Everyone knows that. Everyone except for the white people, who don't know anything about demons and have no idea how busily they're always trying to enter a person's body to create mischief.

With enormous reluctance, Marika returns to the grueling jungle treks each day. She starts out clumsy and stays that way, not fully recovered from her sickness and feeling more discouraged than ever. As they plunge forward into the rain forest, she imagines they're only backtracking or looping around to where they were the day before. She has already forgotten how long it's been since they left Krit village, but she figures it has to be over a month, at least. They've walked so far that she can't imagine ever returning the way they've come. If they don't keep going forward, she doesn't think she'll have any hope of making it out of the jungle alive.

Deep in the mountains, they come upon a new obstacle: raging rivers. If Marika can't easily ford them on foot, Tobo ties a vine across the water for her to cling to as a guide rope. Or he cuts down a tree to act as a makeshift bridge, and she carefully walks across the trunk, agonizing over what would happen if she fell onto the boulders below. The rivers are yet another of the jungle's tests for her to pass. Another of its torments.

Facing a new day of climbing, Marika sits next to Tobo to tell him that she can't go on much longer. Her body gets weaker by the day. Her leg muscles more and more cramped. She can never drink enough water to stave off dehydration from the heat and exertion.

"Tobo," she says to him, "I need to know—are we lost?"

"*Eh?* Lost?" He stops repairing a hole in his *billum* bag and looks at her.

"Do you really know where Walwasi village is?"

Tobo thinks the white mary is acting bewitched again and makes a protective sign over himself with his hand. "Yes, I know where Walwasi village is," he says.

"How do you know?"

Tobo is perplexed by her question. Doesn't she see the sun? The stars? How could he get "lost," as she says, when he has always known his way? It is offensive to him that she thinks he is as confused as she is, when the jungle has been his home and his friend for over forty years.

"We are not lost," he says firmly. "*Walwasi i klostu.* Walwasi is close."

It is the first time Marika has heard the word *close* coming from Tobo's lips. Always, it has been *longwe,* until she finally stopped asking him. Now, after hearing this new word, she knows she should be filled with hope, but she finds it hard to trust him. Why should she believe anything he says? Hasn't this journey been all about hardship and failed expectation? And worse: what if, by a miracle, they actually *do* arrive at Lewis's village, and he isn't even there? What if he never *was* there? Then this whole trip—all the sickness and pain of it—would just be a worthless ghost hunt.

Exasperated, Marika says nothing more to Tobo and gets up to fill her water bottle from a nearby stream. So they are "close" to Lewis. She will believe it when she sees it.

A day later, they encounter tree trunks laid across streams: marks of old hunters' trails. Though the jungle never waited for those men to return, filling their paths with new foliage, the trunks are indisputable evidence of the existence of civilization— the first such evidence Marika has seen since leaving Krit village so many weeks ago.

But with no actual villages or people, each day's disappointment continues to take its toll on her. She no longer cares about arriving anywhere. Before the unrelenting jungle, all she wants to do is curl up and retreat into sleep. She grows progressively weaker, even as she manages to hoist herself up the mountainsides, her feet and legs torn and punctured, the wounds slow to heal. Heat headaches become part of the grueling ritual, and she follows Tobo until she feels too dizzy or worn out to continue. He has to constantly scold her now, pushing her into streams to cool her off and spur her forward.

"*Lewis i dai pinis,*" she keeps telling him. Lewis is dead.

"No," Tobo insists. "He is very close."

CHAPTER ELEVEN

It was July when Marika got the letter from Pastor John Wade. She'd written to him several months earlier and, having never gotten a reply, assumed that was the end of it. But as she saw his envelope with her mail, it gave her such an unexpected rush of excitement that she might have been hearing from Lewis himself.

> Dear Ms. Vecera:
>
> My apologies for the long delay in responding to your letter. I have been in the hospital, recovering from complications after coronary bypass surgery. As you can probably imagine, it's been a difficult time for me, and I've had a lot of catch-up to do after my convalescing.
>
> I must first tell you that I did not contact the Lewis family with the intention of upsetting them, or of my information going to the press. But as the Lewis family chose to share my discovery with you, I decided I would respond to your letter. I only wanted to tell them about a man I'd met who, in my strong opinion, was Robert Lewis (i.e., Robert Lewis, the famous writer and journalist). I was an avid fan of his books, had seen him many times on television, and the man I saw in Papua New Guinea looked exactly like him.

That said, of course I cannot be 100 percent sure. As you already know, the man in question would not speak to me, though I made an effort to talk to him. Yes, his camp-site along the Tumbi River was quite remote. To answer another of your questions, I can tell you that he had an unhealthy, wasted appearance, and he didn't appear to be in his full senses. None of the people living nearby knew anything about him, not even his name. I should add that he was accompanied by two native men, who couldn't (wouldn't?) give me any information. It was all very unusual and, in my strong opinion, highly suspect.

I can understand if this all sounds very far-fetched to you. Please remember, though, that I am a Christian and a man of God, and I am accountable for the veracity of what I tell people. I would not have sent the letter to Lewis's family had I not been convinced in my heart that this man on the Tumbi was him. As you know, I strongly suggested to his family that they investigate the sighting, but they never replied to my letter. At that point, I deemed it prudent to drop the issue.

Still, I remain convinced of what I saw. As I'm sure you know, the circumstances surrounding Lewis's death in Malaysia were unusual and, as I recall, had never been fully resolved. My understanding is that his body had not been recovered. Perhaps, if you feel so inclined, you might investigate his death and decide for yourself what actually happened.

I wish I could help you further, but this is all I know. It's not much to go on, of course, so I can understand if his family dismissed my letter. However, I should tell you that the rare appearance of a white man in those very remote areas of the country was always cause for interest. The man I saw was obviously not a missionary. I knew all the missionaries in that region; due to the difficult nature of evangelizing in such a challenging environment (no roads and a harsh tropical climate), we maintained a close network, chartering each other's planes, et cetera. Granted, one might come across some unusual foreigners once in a while, mostly Australian gold hunters and other such disreputable individuals, but the man I saw didn't fit that sort of description. For one thing, there were no other Westerners accompanying him; in addition, he had few supplies and obviously wasn't provisioned for exploratory work in the jungle.

I hope my letter has been of assistance to you. If that unusual man whom I saw *was* Lewis, one can only wonder what he was doing in such an unlikely place. I suppose it is a question for God.

I wish you Godspeed in your endeavors.

Yours respectfully,
Pastor John Wade

Marika put the letter down. A subway train was just passing, and her windowpanes rattled in protest. She felt a chill going through her. An inkling she couldn't quite shake. Wade's claim seemed completely unlikely. Implausible. Lewis was dead. Everyone agreed that he was dead. She read the letter again, her eyes running repeatedly over certain phrases. *I remain convinced of what I saw . . . the man I saw in Papua New Guinea looked exactly like him . . . I am a Christian and a man of God . . . accountable . . .*

Marika carefully folded up the letter, running a finger over the paper's sharp edges. *What if it were true?* she wondered. She had already written more than half of Lewis's biography, and she, like everyone, assumed she knew how he'd died. It was as if every action in Lewis's life—all the willful choices and mistakes, all the achievements and setbacks—had been slowly building toward his suicide, shaping and justifying it. But what if, as outrageous and as impossible as it might seem, Wade's claim was correct? What if Lewis hadn't actually died?

Marika laughed and chucked the letter onto a table. It lay there as she went to check her e-mail, and it lay there as she took a bath. By the time evening came and she sat before her computer to work on the biography, she still hadn't picked it up again. Yet, she discovered that she was unable to write a word of her book. At last, giving up, she went to see a movie instead. And then a second one. When she returned late at night and opened the door of her apartment, her eyes went immediately to Wade's letter on the table. She felt an overwhelming urge to go to it, to read it once more.

Finally, she did.

Marika took the letter to Seb to see what he thought. If there was anyone she could count on for objectivity and rationality, it would be him. And, even better, it would give her an excuse to drop in on him at his place.

She found him at work on his dissertation. He hadn't been expecting her—they'd agreed to give each other a few days apart to catch up on work—but he was pleasantly surprised. Always with Seb, she could count on an enthusiastic smile and greeting as soon as she walked in the door.

Seb saw her troubled expression. Without explanation, Marika handed him the letter and asked him to read it, to give her his honest opinion. As he unfolded it, he observed the crooked, heavy handwriting of someone very sick or old. Putting on his reading glasses, he read the letter a couple of times before setting it down and looking at her.

"So you're thinking Lewis staged his own death?" he asked.

"I don't know what to think," she said. "I mean, if he had, if it were *true*, can you imagine what a huge story that would be?"

Seb nodded. "Yeah, if it were *true*."

"What do you think of the letter?"

He stared at it. "Well, honestly, I don't know how you could take it seriously. I mean, this is obviously some well-intentioned, sick old man who thinks he saw someone who looked like Robert Lewis. That's it. There's absolutely nothing to support his claim. There's no name. No information. Nothing."

"I know. But he sounds so sure."

"Yeah, and so do all the people who think my brother looks like James Dean."

Marika laughed. "I know. I guess it's pretty unlikely, huh?"

"Well, yeah. 'Pretty' unlikely? More like really unlikely."

"But they never did find Lewis's body. There was only that suicide note in Malaysia."

Seb picked up Wade's letter again. He read it closely, studying it, before putting it down and going to the kitchen.

"I don't know what to tell you," he said from across the room. "Personally, if it were me, I'd just forget about it."

"You know, if you want to talk about unlikely," Marika said, "why would someone like Lewis kill himself in the first place? He was so tough. He wouldn't let anything stop him."

Seb sat down at the table again, handing her a glass of iced tea. "I remember you telling me he had some pretty close calls, right?"

She nodded.

"Well, that sort of thing can take its toll. Also, you said his son died."

"Yeah."

"See—there you go. The human mind is enormously unpredictable."

"Yeah. But let's just say, hypothetically, that Lewis didn't kill himself. Why would a person only pretend to commit suicide?"

Seb took a sip from his drink and sat back in his chair. "I don't know. Maybe if they had something to hide. You know—some kind of double life."

"God, it's so strange."

"If you really want an answer, why don't you just run off to New Guinea and find Lewis and ask him yourself?"

"Maybe I will," she said.

"I was *kidding*." Seb gave her a long, sober stare. Shaking his head, he turned back to his dissertation notes.

Marika knew the end of her book was near. Lewis's biography seemed to be writing itself, and she believed she was finally understanding the man. When walking through downtown Boston, she often caught herself trying to see things through his eyes. What would he have thought of the lunchtime crowds rushing along Boylston Street? Or of the gleaming gold dome of the State House catching the sun? Would he have found any beauty in the untouched snow lying on city streets, before the coming of the plows? Marika had read countless letters and e-mail messages Lewis had sent to friends, had conducted numerous interviews with his former colleagues. She'd studied, in the minutest detail, every article he'd ever written, looking for signs and patterns. Who was this man? What had compelled him?

Since Marika had started working on her book project, taking a hiatus from magazine writing, she and Seb had never been closer. He was profoundly relieved to have her home all the time. He often told her that it was the "specter" of her dangerous magazine assignments that concerned him most about their relationship. He feared that, one of these days, Marika would go to a place like Congo and never come back. For her part, she found it bizarre not to be traveling, her life seeming mundane; it took her months just to get over her restlessness.

As summer gave way to autumn, they'd both become busier than ever and couldn't see each other as often. Seb had a new internship that kept him on campus for long hours each day, and Marika had fallen behind on deadlines she'd set for her book. She worked more fastidiously than ever, collecting information and interviews while slipping out to see Seb whenever they both had free time. She liked to sneak behind him when he was working at his computer, gliding a hand up the inside of his thigh, watching him shudder.

It wasn't long before Marika spent nights at Seb's place. In the beginning, she'd found it oddly novel and exhilarating having a man sleeping beside her. Sometimes she'd feel his hand gently running up her body. Or she'd wake him in the middle of the night, climbing on top of him and guiding him into her. She became a glutton for the feel of his hands on her, for the way his lips felt against her skin.

As Marika allowed herself to revel in the feelings of unbridled tenderness—those soft, ecstatic emotions of love she'd never experienced before—it felt like she was tasting some kind of illicit happiness she'd never known nor trusted before. In November, at Seb's suggestion, she agreed to move into his condo on a "trial basis," keeping her own apartment as a backup. She would try out the two worlds simultaneously, weighing and comparing them, deciding which one would suit her.

On her first official day of living at Seb's place, Marika sat down before her computer to start a chapter about Lewis's love life—all the tumultuous romances of his midlife career and flings gone bad. Lewis hadn't been interested in deep, serious relationships; after divorcing his wife in his early twenties, he never came close to remarrying. But it would have been too easy to say (as many did) that he was just interested in "getting laid." "Sex was sustenance for him," said one live-in girlfriend, who had probably known him better than most. "He didn't have a mother when he was growing up, so I think it was the only way he could really connect with women." According to nearly every woman Marika had interviewed, Lewis had been—regardless of his incorrigible promiscuity—an exceptional lover. "Gentle," some women described him. "Take-charge." "Attentive." Yet, these same women would also complain of his emotional unavailability, how he'd move on to the next person as soon as things got too serious. Robert Lewis was, by all accounts, a heartbreaker.

Funny, Marika mused. Lewis seemed the opposite of Seb, whose desire for commitment and emotional involvement was— as far as she was concerned—downright intimidating.

She looked out the window at the Charles River passing placidly below, wondering whether Lewis and Seb would have gotten along. It seemed a completely inappropriate question, somehow, Lewis feeling like a secret lover whom she wanted to keep all to herself. Marika knew him just as intimately as Seb, having read all his published writing, journals, letters, articles. She'd watched hours of news footage, interviews, home movies. She'd spoken to nearly everyone who had known him—from his childhood best friends to his ex-wife, from his most devoted editors to his most virulent critics.

In particular, she'd paid close attention to his writing. A lot of the letters he wrote in his twenties and thirties, well before he became famous, smacked of inner uncertainty: "I realize I can't be another writer, only myself," he wrote in a letter to Beth. "Still, I catch myself trying to be all these other writers, as if there were something wrong with me. Who am I, when I'm not trying to be someone else? Yet, in those rare moments when I experience doubtlessness about myself, nothing seems beyond me. My writing awakens, and I can claim it as my own."

At times, Marika felt like she was also in a relationship with Lewis, considering all she knew about him. Interestingly, she was sure he wouldn't have liked Seb; he would have dismissed him as being too tedious and naive. And she was sure Seb would have found Lewis rude and overbearing in the extreme. Marika imagined the two men standing before her, as if she had to choose between them. Lewis or Seb?

Seb suddenly opened the front door, greeting her with an enthusiastic smile.

"How's your work coming?" he asked.

Marika guiltily shut her laptop. "Fine," she said.

Marika lived with Seb for over five months, but she never got rid of her studio apartment in Boston. She just hadn't been ready to give up her own space, as much as she loved being with him and experiencing the newfound excitement of having another person in her life. She wanted to keep the best of both worlds: her independence, hard-won over many years and precious to her, as well as the novelty—for that was how it always felt—of being dependent on another human being.

Seb inevitably found out that she'd kept her apartment. It happened at the worst of times—when they'd been on the verge of throwing themselves a big celebratory dinner one Friday night in early March, in honor of their recent accomplishments. He had finally finished his dissertation, and she was a chapter away from the end of her Lewis biography. As she walked into his condo with groceries for their meal, she immediately registered Seb's hurt, angry expression.

"You got a call," he said from the living room.

"I did?" She put her grocery bags on the countertop, staring at him.

"It was your landlord."

She didn't move.

"I'm supposed to tell you that they're doing some kind of remodeling work on your apartment, and so the gas has to be disconnected on Monday."

"Oh."

Seb looked pointedly at her. "So you still have your old place?"

Marika slowly hung her purse on the back of the chair. "Yeah."

"Were you ever planning on telling me?"

She shrugged. "It didn't seem to matter."

"Well, it does matter. You told me you got rid of it in January."

"Yeah, I was going to get rid of it—but then at the last minute I decided to renew the lease."

Seb cleared his throat. "Can I ask why?"

"Well, we'd decided I'd keep it until I got used to being here. Remember?"

"Yeah, you said you were keeping it for a month. But that was almost *half* a year ago. How long is it going to take you to get used to being here?"

She abruptly pulled off her jacket. "I don't know," she said.

"Can we be frank with each other?" Seb asked.

"Sure."

"I just need you to come here and be frank with me."

"Fine." She walked over and sat beside him on the sofa.

Seb took her hands in his. "Marika, while we've been living together, you've been paying a lot of money to keep an apartment that you're not even using." His eyes were fixed on hers. "What's going on?"

"I already told you. I figured it'd be safer hanging on to it, just in case—"

"In case it didn't work out between us?"

She looked down, shrugging. "I just didn't know if we'd always get along."

"So let me make sure I understand this: for the past several months, my live-in girlfriend—whom, I should add, I love with all my heart and am completely devoted to—has been expecting things not to work out between us?"

"You make it sound so awful. It's just, after I got back from Congo—after how hard you took it—I figured you wouldn't want me to do any more stories like that. I was scared there might be problems between us."

"And you know what? You're right. I don't want you to do any more stories like that. You know why? Because I love you. I care about you, and it would tear me up if something bad happened to you. But I know what your job is, and I've always known. And I may not like it—in fact, to be totally honest with you, I *hate* it, I hate how dangerous it is, I hate that you might not come back—but I've had to deal with the fact that this is what you do. That that's the price if I want to be with you. And I've accepted it. Maybe not completely yet, but I've accepted it."

"Well, I'm sorry you hate my job so much," she said acidly, pulling her hands from his.

"I hate how *dangerous* it is, Marika," Seb said, "but we've gotten away from the entire point."

"Which is?"

Sighing, frustrated, he ran his hands through his hair. "Can we just talk about the truth for a minute?" he said.

"What truth?" She glared at him. "I thought that's what we were doing."

"I'd like us to talk about the *truth*." There was a rare flash of anger in his eyes.

She sat back, crossing her arms. "Seb, you're making too big a deal out of this whole thing."

"Marika," he said, speaking slowly, trying hard to control his voice, "you know as well as I do that for the past five months, as you've been keeping that apartment, you haven't been doing any magazine work. So all this business about me getting upset about your magazine assignments—it's ludicrous."

She looked away.

"You know what I think?" he said. "I think this whole time you've wanted an escape outlet, so you've been secretly keeping that apartment. From day one, you haven't wanted to commit to a relationship with me."

"I *have* wanted to," she said immediately. She said it so plaintively, so genuinely, that for a moment Seb was taken aback.

"You know, I've always been up-front with you," Seb added. "From the beginning I told you exactly what I was looking for, and that I wanted a commitment. I mean, Christ"—he pointed to his desk, to the bottom drawer that held a small safe—"I even got a ring, just in case, you know, I was going to propose to you one of these days."

"Seb—" Her voice cracked.

"Am I an idiot or what?"

"*No*." She took his hand in hers and held it. "Oh, God. I'm sorry. I don't know why I kept the apartment. It doesn't even have to do with you."

Seb sat in silence. When he looked at her again, she saw that the anger had vanished from his eyes.

"Can I ask you something?" he whispered.

"I guess."

"Is that a yes?"

"Okay."

"I'm going to ask this, and I hope you don't take it the wrong way." He cleared his throat. "Marika, are you happy?"

She studied his face, trying to see what he was getting at. "I'm *fine*. I'm happy to have you in my life, if that's what you're asking."

"I'm not asking that." His eyes met hers. Using the tip of his finger, he brushed some hair from her cheek. "What I'm asking is if you ever feel really happy, you know? If you ever feel . . . you know . . . full of joy that you're alive? I've just been wondering about this for a long time."

"Are you saying I'm supposed to feel that way?" she demanded.

"You tell me."

She sighed. She didn't want to be psychoanalyzed. "I don't really get . . . *ecstatically* happy, you know? I don't get in some mood where I want to run through daisy fields singing hallelujah, if that's what you mean. I'm not like you. I don't get like that."

"Look—I'm not trying to judge you." He squeezed her hand.

"Well, it seems like you think I have a problem or something."

"I'm just asking, that's all."

"What, do I need to find God? Is that what you're saying?"

"That's not what I'm saying."

She looked out the window, seeing the city descending into dusk. She didn't know if she'd ever felt the sort of joy he was talking about, but then again who really did? And anyway, what difference did it make? She was fine. She didn't need to be like Seb, with his perfect, charmed life.

"So what *are* you trying to say?" she asked him at last.

He took her hands in his. "I'll tell you, but do you want to know?"

"*Yes*, I want to know."

"Marika, I think . . ." He stopped, needing to focus his thoughts. "I think you've been . . . *traumatized* by what you've seen in the world. I think your job has traumatized you."

She chuckled. "Seb—"

"Do you really want to hear what I have to say?" There was an edge of anger in his voice again.

"Fine," she said curtly. "Go ahead."

"I think your job has traumatized you. I think it's numbed some of your emotional responses to things. I think . . ." He sighed. "How do I put this? I think you're *suspicious* of happiness. I think you're suspicious of anything that actually feels good. Like us—like what we have."

Marika felt a surge of irritation. Seb, with his doctorlike arrogance, was presuming to know everything about her. Yet—she felt the sting of truth in what he said. The sting of pain.

She sat silently beside him, and Seb gave her a sidelong glance.

"Well?" he asked gently. "Does any of that feel accurate?"

She swiped at a tear. "Do you know the things I've seen?" she said. "How are you supposed to feel *joyful* when you know all these people are being killed, all these kids are getting their arms chopped off? All these people are starving to death? Right this minute, people are losing their homes. People are having to watch their children die. How can you just pretend none of that is happening?"

"Marika"—he put his hand on her cheek—"I'm not saying

that anyone should 'pretend' none of that's happening. But you don't need to let it sweep you into the whirlwind, you know?"

"I haven't let it 'sweep me into the whirlwind.'"

"Look," Seb said, "you don't have to prove your love or compassion for people by being miserable for them."

"I'm not *miserable*," she said, shaking his hand from her. "Who said I was *miserable*?"

"All right. Maybe the term is too strong." He paused, collecting his thoughts. "It's like what you told me about your mother. How she has this tunnel vision for tragedy. I think it's possible you might have the same thing—which isn't a criticism. I mean, it makes complete sense, given what you've experienced. It's a coping mechanism, you know? You learn not to expect anything good out of life, so you won't be disappointed when something bad happens."

"Oh," she spat, "so now we're back to this whole theory about me being 'miserable,' just because I didn't get rid of my apartment. You know, you can be so goddamn arrogant sometimes."

Marika rose, walking angrily to the window. The darkening skyline of Boston lay before her, so benign, so indifferent.

"You don't see me on antidepressants," she told Seb over her shoulder. "You don't see me slitting my wrists. *Je*-sus. Just because I'm not like you, with your smug, joyous outlook on everything. If you even experienced one iota of what I have."

"You know, I *have* experienced a few things," Seb said quietly.

"Yeah? Like what?" She looked back at him, her eyes blazing. "You, with your silver spoon in your mouth and your trust funds. Your whole life, everything's been handed to you. Even the money for your coke addiction. So then your parents stick you in rehab at twenty grand a month—what a fucking joke! And you try to tell me you know what I'm feeling? You know what your whole 'life experience' has *really* been? Sophomoric, rich-kid bullshit."

Seb's face turned bright red. He was about to reply—but stopped himself. "This isn't where I was hoping this conversation would go," he said at last.

"Well, sorry to botch your plans!"

She was about to say more, but tears came instead, flooding down her cheeks. She leaned close to the window and covered her face with her hands, not wanting Seb to have the victory of seeing her cry.

"Marika—" He got up quickly and grabbed a box of Kleenex, handing her a tissue. "Hey . . ."

She felt his lips on the back of her neck. His arms encircled her, drawing her against him. She shut her eyes, absorbing the warmth of his body next to hers. Here it was, she realized: an offering of that elusive joy, that rapture. If she would take it.

"You know, you never did tell me what happened to you in Congo," Seb said softly, smoothing back her hair. "I've noticed you don't really talk about any of the bad stuff that's happened to you. You can't just hold it in and expect it to go away. It builds up. It clouds everything."

She jerked away from his touch.

"Marika, it's true," he said. "It builds up. If you don't allow yourself to grieve what you've been through, how can you ever expect to feel joy? How can you ever believe anything good can come to you? Like us, and what we have. I don't know that you really believe it or *want* it yet."

"Are we done with the psychoanalysis?" she asked coldly. "Because I'm getting really sick of it."

"Have you heard anything I've said?"

"Yes, Doctor. Message received."

Seb sighed, stepping back from her.

Marika turned around to look at him now, and he could see defiance in her stare. And a kind of strength he'd never witnessed before, which seemed to be begging for a fight—just so she could win. It was a rare look, he would later realize, that she only got when she felt deeply wounded.

"So what do you want to hear?" she asked acidly. "That the first time I ever went to a war zone was when I was twenty? I was a kid, and I went to Angola—I snuck across the border from Namibia because I wanted to see what it was like. And I almost got killed. I almost never made it out of there alive."

"Marika—"

She was still looking at him, challenging him with her stare. "It was a kid's naïveté and stupidity. I shouldn't have gone there by myself. But I had to go. I had to see it. The first article I ever wrote was about that experience. I sold it to this rinky-dink literary journal, and no one ever read it. It was the most dangerous thing I'd ever done, but nobody knew. Nobody cared. I mean, I almost *died*, and I got twenty-five dollars and a free year's subscription."

Seb didn't know what she was getting at, and he waited.

"If you knew half of what's happened to me since then, you'd cringe," Marika said. "You'd lie awake at night." She twisted the Kleenex in her hands. "And you know what? Talking doesn't free you from any of it. It's just another way of pretending you can control things. Something bad happens, and you talk about it— you 'debrief' me—because that's what you're always trying to do, right? And then we all go on with our lives and everything's fine again. But it's a sham. It's bullshit."

She chucked the mangled Kleenex onto the floor.

"Look," Seb said, "it's not about talking. It's about *feeling*. These things build up. They do damage, you know? And then, when something good comes into your life, you won't allow it. You won't believe in it. You'll keep waiting for it to be pulled out from under your feet."

Her eyes settled on his. "I don't think you have any idea what I'm talking about, do you? You haven't seen any of it."

"Seen what, Marika?"

She pointed out the window. "*That*. Out there. The very worst that people are capable of doing to each other. You haven't seen it, so you can't know."

To her, Seb was only a voyeur of that world. A dabbler. He

would hear about it from his patients, perhaps. He might even recall glimmers of it in that moment of his greatest disgrace— that moment when he woke up in an alley, beaten, near death, his world of self-indulgence shattered. But yet, even that wasn't what she meant. And he knew it. He *had* to know it. She was talking about something entirely beyond his realm of experience.

She didn't say anything more, just studied the dark skyline beyond the river.

"If it's all so awful," Seb said quietly, "if it's all so dark, why do you do it?"

"Because it's my duty." She stared angrily at his reflection in the windowpane. "I can't be a voice for someone if I don't know what their suffering is. How am I supposed to empathize when I'm hiding behind a microphone or camera, or watching stuff on TV? If I'm to speak for these people, I've got to know it myself. I've got to be in it with them. I've got to live it."

"Even if it could kill you?"

"*Especially* if it could kill me." She turned around and glared at him.

"You know, the only way you can really help people is by valuing yourself first."

"That's a bullshit platitude." She was still staring him down, enticing him to take her on.

"Listen—getting yourself killed doesn't do anyone any good. It doesn't help the world. It's a waste."

"Then I'm willing to waste myself, I guess."

She saw that Seb was getting worked up now. His cheeks were turning red; the volume of his voice was increasing. Just as she started to smile at the victory, Seb caught himself and took a few deep breaths.

"Okay, I see this conversation is going nowhere," he said.

She didn't respond.

"Can I at least ask you where this leaves us?"

"I don't know where it leaves us," she said.

"I'm assuming you're still going to keep that apartment?"

"Yeah. I am."

As she walked away, Seb grabbed her arm. "Marika, do you even want to be living with me?"

"I don't know what I want. I don't know anything anymore."

"Have I just been wasting my time for the past two years? Is that what's been going on?"

She looked at him, at the pain in his expression.

"I don't know," she said. "Maybe you have."

She went to the kitchen, trying desperately to hold back her tears.

"Marika," Seb said, "I wasn't trying to hurt you by saying what I did. You know that, don't you?"

She shrugged, putting on her jacket. "I've got to go. I've got to get out of here."

He was watching her intently, worry filling his expression. "Let me come with you," he said at last.

"No. I need to be alone."

"Where are you going?"

"I don't know."

"Marika—"

But she left, slamming the door.

Marika ended up taking a taxi downtown, to Beacon Hill, where some of her colleagues were throwing a party. She hadn't planned on going, but now she welcomed the distraction. When she walked in, she knew most of the people there: fellow journalists, editors, writers. They kept asking her why she'd been "out of commission" for a year, and wanted to know when she'd be back doing magazine stories. There was a passing of business cards. Offers of possible assignments in Liberia, Afghanistan, southern Sudan. Marika realized that the niche she'd established for herself, that niche of dangerous overseas reporting, had, in the wake of her absence, been busy defining her.

She couldn't agree to anything, though. She was too distracted, her thoughts constantly returning to Seb, to how he was always so determined to open the lockbox of her mind. In the future, when she did take more assignments, she knew she'd have to face his questions. His hyperconcern. His unspoken disapproval of what she chose to do with her life. Probably, things would only get worse between them.

She was well into her fifth drink of the evening when Max Sanders showed up. He lived just a couple of blocks away and had already made his rounds of other parties.

"Vecera!" he yelled, noticing her across the room.

He had that same boyish smirk, the same unruly, graying brown hair swept behind his ears. Marika hadn't seen him since that night shortly after she'd returned from Congo—a night that had, ironically, marked the beginning of her official fidelity to Seb. As Sanders came up to her, kissing her on both cheeks and hugging her, she felt the odd liberation of being held by arms that expected nothing in return.

"So what gives us the pleasure of your presence tonight?" he asked her.

"I was in the area," she said, "and I thought I'd stop by."

"Well, it's definitely been a while." He checked out what she was wearing. The new pants and silk shirt that she'd bought to celebrate her evening with Seb. "You look good, as always."

"Thanks."

"I heard a rumor that you got married or something."

"No." She thought again about Seb. "It never reached that point."

"I was going to say, I couldn't picture Marika Vecera married. Not *you*."

She looked away, taking a sip from her drink.

"So have you been gone on assignment or what?" he asked. "I haven't seen you around."

"I've been writing a book," she told him.

"Oh, yeah. Someone told me about that. A Lewis biography, right?"

She nodded.

"You know, I met him once." Sanders fished for the olive in his martini glass. "He was at this restaurant in the Hamptons. He wouldn't say more than *two* words to me the whole time—a real highbrow prick." He sucked the olive hard into his mouth.

Marika shrugged. People either loved or hated Lewis. Never anything in between. She could have predicted Sanders's judgment, though she didn't challenge it, her world rolling and tilting too pleasantly. His arrival would save her from having to do more socializing, which was no small favor. And maybe, if she were lucky, it would save her from all the thoughts about Seb.

As she sat with Sanders in a dim corner of the patio, and as he put his hand on her knee, Seb's words started forcing themselves into her mind. All the talk about how she needed to face her past experiences and "grieve." How she was "suspicious" of happiness. Seb was always determined to pull the lid off her memories and make her look at things that weren't worth revisiting. He didn't seem to understand that nothing was accomplished by dredging up the past.

A rare tear came to her eye, and she snatched at it in the darkness.

"I want to ask you something," she said to Sanders, taking a long drink from her gin and tonic before putting it back on the table.

"What's that?"

"Do I seem . . . miserable to you?"

Sanders laughed, looking at the people nearby as if they were in on the same joke. "Miserable? Who says you're miserable?"

"No one. Am I?"

"I would not say miserable." He leaned up against her, looking into her eyes. "But maybe a little sad. What's up with you tonight?"

She shrugged.

"Vecera, I will say this: you're a dark forest, and you always have been. It's the reason why you're such a good fucking journalist, and I'm not." He toasted her.

As Marika reached for her own drink on a nearby table, she nearly fell from her chair.

Sanders laughed hysterically, helping her up. "You've had a few tonight, haven't you?"

"Yeah. So what?"

"I don't think I've ever seen you this juiced before."

"Take a picture then."

"A little testy, huh?" He scooted his chair closer to her. "So how long have you been here, swigging 'em down?"

"I don't know. For hours. For *days*."

He leaned toward her and put his hand on her thigh, speaking conspiratorially in her ear: "Then why don't we get out of here? What do you think?"

"I don't know." She didn't move.

"What?" Sanders said. "You don't have a boyfriend, do you?" When she didn't say anything, he laughed. "So who is he?"

"I'm not going to talk about it."

"You two have a bad day?"

She felt his hand squeeze her leg. He was leaning closely against her—too close. His lips were against her neck. She should have moved away, and she knew it. She should have gotten up and left. But, instead, she sat there and finished her drink. If she returned to Seb, he'd want to start talking about their relationship the minute she got in. Then all hell would break loose. At least with Sanders they could pretend to have closeness and intimacy, without all the goddamn pain.

"All right," she said. "Let's go to your place."

It was a short walk there, but she'd had so much to drink that it took enormous effort just to make her legs work properly. When they finally arrived and stepped inside, Sanders ran his hand around her waist.

"Can I get you anything?" he asked. "A liter of vodka? A gallon of Jackie D?"

"Funny," she said.

He unbuttoned his shirt. "Come here." He pulled her against him, reaching his hand between her legs. How well she remembered those aggressive yet disinterested hands that would take whatever they could get from her. They were so different from Seb's. So completely without investment in her.

Sanders didn't waste any time, taking Marika's arm and guiding her into his bedroom. She tried vainly to steady herself, leaning against the wall as she watched him pull off his pants and boxers. Sanders hadn't the slightest bit of self-consciousness, and he soon stood naked in front of her, smiling unabashedly. Opening a dresser drawer, he took out a condom packet and ripped it open, perfunctorily tossing the wrapper on the floor. As he came up to her, he was business-as-usual. And knew it. And wasn't ashamed of it. He removed her shirt and pants as a surgeon might cast off cumbersome dressings, and, without the slightest pause, unsnapped her bra and dropped it, summarily shoving it aside with his foot. Marika glanced at the bra—it was the new, black lace one she'd picked out just for Seb.

Sanders took hold of her breasts.

"It's been a while," he said, running his eyes over her body. He placed her hand on his penis. "You sure your boyfriend's not going to mind?"

Marika froze.

"What?" he asked.

She didn't reply.

"I hit a touchy subject?" He groped beneath her panties.

"I wish you'd shut the fuck up," she said quietly.

He paused. Stared at her. "Say what?"

She stared at him coolly, belligerently. "I don't think anything has ever mattered to you."

"Vecera—"

"Are you going to shut up and fuck me or what?"

"Whoa!" Sanders gazed at her—with fear, then with fury.

He whipped her around and yanked her panties down, pushing her onto the bed. He entered her hard from behind, into her ass.

"There!" he yelled at her. "How's that? Is that hard enough for you?!"

When there was no sound from her, he pounded even harder. And harder. Climaxing, he pulled himself out and collapsed onto the bed.

"God . . . ," he gasped.

He closed his eyes, melting into the lingering sensations of orgasm. It took him a while to finally move, and when he did, and turned to Marika, he noticed red on the bedspread. On her body. *Blood*.

Sanders stared at her, mesmerized. Terrified.

"Jesus . . . ," he whispered. He shook her shoulder. "Marika . . ."

There was no answer.

"Marika?" He shook her more forcefully. "Are you okay?"

He reached for the Kleenex box on his nightstand and pushed it toward her, but she ignored him. Slowly, she got up and put her clothes back on.

"Marika . . ." He held out his hand, entreating her. "Look, I'm sorry."

She just glared at him. "Fuck off."

She left his apartment, walking quickly through Beacon Hill toward Charles Street and downtown Boston. Her apartment was nearby. The very thing that had, somehow, been the cause of everything that had gone wrong that night. She didn't want to go there. She didn't live there anymore. She lived in Cambridge. With Seb.

At least, she used to live with him.

Marika reached Charles Street and stopped to stare at its old brownstone buildings. She was relieved to be back in the heart of the city again; part of her had always mistrusted the elite

self-righteousness of Cambridge. In Boston, there was only glori-
ous indifference. The city's cobblestone streets still seemed to
echo with the hoofbeats of a bygone time that had no use for her.
In the salt air, in the passing glances from crowds, in the voices that
rose above the roar of subway trains—such blessed indifference.

Marika wished she could start the evening over and repair the
damage. Her failures—of which Sanders was the latest—massed
like an army around her.

"No one ever tells you how to forgive yourself," she whispered. Blood was soaking her pants. Pain cut through her body.
She remembered how in the morning at Seb's place, sleeping
beside him, the rising sun would sometimes reflect on his mirror
and wake her with its light. Only in those first fragile moments of
day—and at no other time—did self-forgiveness seem not only
plausible but easy.

Tears trailed down her cheeks as she walked the dark, familiar
streets, her mistakes seeming to follow relentlessly. Part of her
wanted to keep moving forever, having no address, no safety, no
ties. There was rare freedom in that kind of life, where she could
die tomorrow and no one would know, or care.

Marika stopped. Her heart wrenched. *Seb*. He would care.
She hailed a taxi. She needed to go back.

It was nearly four in the morning when Marika stealthily put her
key in the lock and let herself into Seb's place. She'd assumed he
would be asleep. She'd hoped to sneak in, curl up on the sofa,
and get a few hours of rest before the inevitable eruption. But
when she opened the door, she saw that the lights were on. Seb
was up, sitting at the kitchen table. In a single instant, she took in
the sight of him: the drained look on his face, the day's worth of
dark stubble, the pain in his eyes.

"Marika," he said, standing quickly. "I've been so worried
about you—are you okay?"

"Yeah," she mumbled.

"When you didn't come back, I thought you might have gone to your place. So I stopped by and knocked on your door, but no one answered."

She flushed with shame. "I was at a party." She put her hand against the wall to steady herself.

"Oh."

"I'm all right. You don't have to stay up any longer."

He stared at her. "You know, I've been thinking about the conversation we had, and I was hoping we could talk about it."

"Not now." She flung her purse down and put her hand to her head. "I've had too much to drink. I can't even think straight."

She went to the bathroom, and as Seb followed her, he saw blood all over the back of her pants.

"What happened?" he said, alarmed. "There's blood—"

"Don't worry about it." She opened the bathroom door and turned on the shower.

"Marika—"

"It's *nothing*," she said.

He took hold of her arm and turned her around. "Are you hurt?"

She leaned against the sink, avoiding his stare. She knew she couldn't keep the truth from him. "I was with someone," she said quietly.

"You mean . . . you were having *sex* with someone?"

She suddenly caught in Seb's eyes the collapse of everything they had together.

"It . . . it wasn't like you think." Her words were slurring too much. She was too drunk to explain.

"What—were you raped or something?"

She shook her head.

Seb let go of her arm and stepped back. "So, when I was all worried about you, you were fucking some other guy?"

She glanced at him, long enough to see the tears in his eyes.

"Who were you with?" he asked, barely containing his rage.

"Just some guy at the party."

"Anyone I know?"

She clutched herself. "No. You've never met him."

"So I guess our relationship doesn't mean anything to you."

"Seb—"

He sighed, his breath ragged. "Have you been seeing this person a lot?"

"*No,*" she said. "It was just this stupid thing I did tonight . . . it shouldn't have happened. It was just this, stupid, awful thing."

He reeled around and struck the heel of his hand against the shower stall. "Son of a bitch!" he said. Without another word, he left the bathroom, slamming the door behind him.

Marika stepped into the shower. Quivering, unable to think, she just turned on the water, let it cover her like an ablution. She was sure it was over between her and Seb, and she wondered how her life had gotten to such a point. How it could have spiraled out of control so quickly, unless, somehow, she had wanted it that way. Leaning down, she vomited until nothing more would come up.

When she finally got out of the shower, she found that Seb had gone to bed, locking the bedroom door behind him. She went into the living room and stood before the window. Leaning close to it, holding her palm against it, she felt the glass's resistance as if the night itself were pushing back at her. It wouldn't be long until the dark cityscape turned gray with the coming dawn.

She knew she should move out as soon as possible. There would be no other solution. Seb wouldn't forgive her—rightfully so—and her own guilt would be too huge. She realized how easy it would be to leave. Many of her things had remained in a half-packed state in his place. There were her boxes in his closet that she'd never opened. There were clothes she hadn't bothered removing from bags. She'd brought over so little, and they'd never gotten around to buying anything new for themselves. It astounded her now: there was absolutely nothing to show for whatever it was they'd had for the past two years. Marika cringed. Maybe it *was* true, what Seb had told her—how she'd been "suspicious of happiness," waiting for everything good to be pulled out from under her?

And maybe, sick of waiting, she finally just ended it herself that night.

Marika curled up on the sofa, a tight, nauseous feeling in her gut—a feeling she got only when she knew she'd done something that could never be taken back. Her thoughts were a maelstrom. With no hope of relief, she got up and sat at the desk by the window, waiting for the last effects of the alcohol to wear off. She looked at her computer, the Lewis research strewn around it. She had one chapter left to write—the chapter about his death— though for weeks she hadn't been able to start it, and now, in her current mood, it all seemed futile. She noticed Pastor Wade's letter in a pile and picked it up, skimming it. There was such certainty in his words. Such conviction. He'd included a business card with his telephone number so Marika could call him, but when she'd gotten around to doing so, she'd found out from his wife that he'd died. Marika would never know just how trustworthy Wade might have been.

For months, Marika had toyed with the idea of going to Papua New Guinea to investigate his claims. Even the mere idea of Lewis being alive had riveted her with its implications and seemed worth the trouble of such a trip. At the very least, she'd figured she could bring back some interesting material for an epilogue—traveling to a jungle halfway around the world to see if a crazy missionary's story was true—though it would have taken her weeks, if not months, to search around a country so remote and abandoned by modernity. Ultimately, the main reason Marika hadn't gone had been because of Seb. She'd feared it would have put a serious rift in their relationship to be away for so long, on another dangerous assignment. She hadn't been abroad since Congo, after all, and he wouldn't have been used to it. He would have worried himself sick about her.

Now, though, there didn't seem to be anything holding her back from going. In fact, there seemed no better time to do it. All she had to do was move from Seb's place as soon as possible, get out of his life.

Marika gazed down at the Charles River, its dark waters curving toward the west. She wondered if Robert Lewis had ever found the peace he was looking for—or if anyone ever does. She slid her fingers along the window glass, making her decision final.

She would leave Boston to find Lewis's ghost.

Seb had just gotten up and was making coffee in the kitchen when she came to tell him that she was moving out.

"I think it's best if I leave right away, this weekend," she added.

He turned to her. The expression on his face revealed utter resignation, exhaustion, but no surprise.

"All right" was all he said.

She hadn't really expected such a response. Secretly, part of her had been hoping he'd try to discourage her and hold on to her. The fact that he hadn't—it ignited a sorrow so deep, so overwhelming, that for a moment she couldn't speak.

Seb was standing there, watching her with tired, sad eyes.

"I want you to know," she said uncomfortably, "you were right about my old apartment and why I hung on to it."

He just looked at her.

"I *was* scared of losing everything," she said. "And then"—she smiled wryly, tears coming to her eyes—"I threw it all away, anyway."

"Marika—"

"I'm going to New Guinea. I don't know how long I'll be gone, but I'm going to follow that lead about Lewis."

"You know, there's no running from stuff," Seb said. "It follows you."

"I'm not running. I'm just going to follow that lead."

He shut his eyes for a long moment. "Okay," he said.

She felt a stab of heartbreak so strong that she had to steady herself. "Seb . . ."

He glanced at her.

"I want you to know how sorry I am about everything. If I could somehow take it back, I would."

He waved away what she said. "I'm going to campus today. I'll be back late. Unless you need me for something this weekend, I'm going to be staying at my brother's."

He turned his back to her and poured himself a cup of coffee. Then, on second thought, he poured her one as well. Walking over to her, he put her mug soundly on the countertop.

Marika saw that his hand was shaking, and she took hold of it. "Seb—I mean it. I'm so sorry."

"Okay," he said.

Slowly, he slid his hand from hers. He walked to the kitchen table and sat down, opening a newspaper. It was a couple of days old, and he'd already read it, but he scanned the headlines again.

Marika wiped at her eyes. "What I did last night, I didn't mean to do it. I was just—"

"Oh, please," he said, giving her his full attention. "Don't insult my intelligence, all right? You chose to do that. At least own what you did. I think you were trying to hurt yourself—and *me*, in the process. And you know what? You succeeded on both counts."

She ran her fingers across the countertop. "What I'm trying to say is that it was a huge mistake. I was upset and drunk, and I let some man . . ." She looked down. "I let something happen that shouldn't have. I know there's no excuse, but I just want you to know how sorry I am."

Seb stared at her, not saying anything.

A tear ran down her cheek, and she swiped at it. "When we were talking yesterday, and everything got out of control, I just didn't know what to think, you know? That'd never happened to us before."

Seb sighed.

"I was *scared,* all right? I was *scared.*"

"Well, there's a start," he said. "You were scared. So you ran off and let some jerk hurt you like that." She saw tears of anger in Seb's eyes. "Jesus, you could have come back and talked to me."

"I just wanted to get rid of what I was feeling, you know? I didn't want to talk about it; I just wanted to get rid of it."

Seb threw down the paper and walked over to his desk. Opening his safe, he took out the engagement ring he'd bought for her.

"*This*"—he held it out toward her—"*this* is what I've been wanting to offer you, and all it represents. But you know what? You don't want it, Marika. You don't want any of it." He tossed the ring down, and it bounced loudly against the floor. "Can I ask, did you ever love me?"

"*Yes.* And I still do. Last night . . . it was just this awful mistake."

"Do you know, not once have you ever come to me and shared what you're feeling? Not once. When are you going to put the sword down? How can people ever love you if you won't let them in? Last night during our conversation, you just completely shut down."

"Well, it's hard for me," she said, feeling a rush of anger. "Can you understand that?"

"Look—I want you to see something."

He went into his bedroom and brought back an object in a paper bag.

"Do you know what this is?" He pulled out a small bottle of Jack Daniels. "I've kept this bottle for *ten* years, ever since I got sober, to remind me of what I overcame, to remind me that I'm stronger than any addiction. But do you know how long I looked at this bottle last night? Do you know how long I considered taking a drink?"

She bit her lip, saying nothing.

"*All night,*" Seb said, glaring at her. "I looked at this goddamn bottle all night long." He slammed it onto the table. "But I didn't drink. You know why? Because I'm stronger than it. And you're stronger than whatever it is that's been trying to sabotage what we have together."

"I told you I'm sorry," she said. "What else can I say?"

"Are you even hearing me? You don't solve problems by avoiding them—by drinking or running off with some guy. You need to face what's hurting you, and acknowledge it, or you'll never have the life you want. Not with me or with anyone else, Marika. The only way out of your pain is through it. And I wish it were easier, but it's not. As long as you resist what hurts, you're going to resist life—can you get that?"

"I'm trying."

He grabbed the paper bag that had been holding the whiskey, crumpling it in his hands. "You know, I don't have the energy to try to deal with this anymore. I mean, you obviously don't want help—at least, not my help. You're not ready to look. It's still too scary. Which is *okay*. It's okay to be scared. But my wish for you, Marika, is that one day you'll have the courage to look, and to do the work. You know, you're probably the bravest person I've ever known, but that's the one journey you still haven't made."

She looked at him—at all his frustration, love, despair—and turned away.

"You can dismiss what I've been saying," Seb said. "I can already see that you have. But I just hope one day you'll have the courage to look—but I can't force you there. That's what I've finally realized: I can't force you. And I just don't have anything left to give anymore."

He rubbed his face and sighed.

"Look," he said, "I'm done. I'm going to go get dressed."

Part Two

LEWIS

CHAPTER TWELVE

The jungle breaks overhead:

Walwasi village.

Marika and Tobo step into blinding sunlight. They stand on the edge of cultivated fields of broad-leafed taro and yams, which descend in terraces down a steep mountainside. Marika studies the valley far below and can see faint curls of smoke rising from a collection of huts. It is the first sign of any human presence that she's seen after more than a month of grueling travel over these mountains, and she drops to the ground in gratitude and relief.

Tobo surveys the small village. Just behind it, a single peak rises sharply like a green needle, its top obscured by a thick spread of clouds.

"Walwasi Mountain," he says to Marika. He points down below. "*Ples bilong Lewis.*"

Lewis's village.

Marika can hardly believe it. For her, it's enough just to arrive somewhere and have human contact again. Those huts mean rest and shelter from the interminable jungle. The heat exhaustion has been getting worse each day, and she knows her body is about to give out. Her legs already look like battlegrounds, the infected cuts and scratches visible through great tears in her pants.

Tobo stares at the huts. He traveled this same valley when he was young and under the tutelage of his Anasi uncle, a powerful sorcerer. Though he recognizes Walwasi village, he doesn't know if the white man is down below. Two rainy seasons have come and gone since he spoke with the guide who brought Lewis here, and anything could have happened to the white man in that time.

It is all downhill now to Walwasi. Marika follows Tobo through a maze of adobe walls that surround small plots of crops, the clay barriers topped with wooden barbs to keep pigs out. The midday sun scalds her face and burns the top of her head. She holds up a hand to shade her eyes, feeling her tangled mass of hair. She glances at her tanned, scratched-up arms. At her filthy, shredded khaki pants and the gray, sweat-stained tank top she wears. She must be a sight, and for a brief moment she imagines Lewis in the village below. What would he think of her, seeing her for the first time like this?

They reach the end of the fields and enter the shaded valley, following a well-trodden path that leads to the village. Marika looks for people but sees no one. Which seems strange to her; she assumes someone must have seen them coming. As she walks, her feet let out their usual cries of pain. Now, without the cover of brush, she sees how swollen and bruised they are, how covered with punctures and mosquito bites scratched raw during sleep.

A river surges before them, a narrow, thirty-foot-long log spanning its width and acting as a bridge. Marika finds this a cruel yet appropriate joke to mark the end of her travel through the jungle. If she fails this last test and falls into the rocky whitewater, she'll surely be sucked under and drown. But Tobo, probably never even considering such a possibility, walks blithely across the log, his large, flat feet clinging expertly to it. Only once he crosses does Marika follow, taking each step cautiously, with full concentration. The log wobbles and bows as she goes, and she imagines Lewis watching her from a secret place, seeing how she handles this test. She doesn't want to disappoint him. She stretches her arms out for balance like a disheveled ballerina, sliding and inching her way to the opposite shore until she can leap to safety.

Tobo smiles at her. "We are here," he says, making a protective sign over himself.

She gazes into a nearby clearing and finally sees it. Walwasi.

To Marika, the village appears shoddy at first glance. There are a few dozen huts built several feet above the ground, all slumping and in need of repair, their palm bark slats loose, their thatch roofs showing rot. Baskets filled with dusty white sago palm pith hang from the rafters under the huts, while black pigs wander about and snuff at the dirt. People—if there are any—do not arrive. The once familiar whining of jungle insects is replaced by a weighty, disconcerting silence.

Tobo lets out a shout. When no one appears, he calls again, impatient. He would like to trade a couple of his betel nuts for lunch. He has a great appetite for pig meat, after so many weeks without it.

Marika sees movement from a nearby hut. An ancient woman climbs down a notched log ladder and ever so slowly makes her way over to them. She wears only a grass skirt. Her breasts hang flat against her chest, and her wrinkled black skin looks gray and dusty.

Tobo makes another protective sign over himself as the woman reaches him. "Walwasi?" he asks her.

She nods and stares at Marika with bright blue cataract eyes, chewing something or perhaps mumbling. Her hand rises, and she runs her dry, strong fingers over Marika's back, exclaiming at the unfamiliar texture of her tank top.

"I think she is blind," Tobo says. He puts the woman's hand on Marika's head, and she lets out a cry of excitement, feeling and patting Marika's hair.

"*Wait meri!*" the woman exclaims. "White woman!"

The last thing Marika expected to hear is Pidgin in such an isolated place. She looks around the village again. She thinks she sees figures peering out at her from between the slats of the palm bark huts.

"You speak Pidgin?" Tobo asks the old woman.

"*Liklik*," she says. "A little."

"Who taught you?" Marika asks.

The old woman gestures to her chin, pretending to have a beard. "*Mista Pa-ka*."

"Mr. Parker?" Marika sighs. Of course. Instead of leading her to Lewis, Tobo has brought her God knows how many miles through this endless jungle, only to find the wrong white man.

"Do you know Rob-ur Lu-ees?" she asks the old woman.

She shakes her head.

"He is a white man," Tobo explains.

"*Wait man*," she says, nodding. "*Wait man*."

The woman guides them to the edge of the village, pointing down a ridge toward the river.

"*Mista Pa-ka*," she says.

Tobo is about to take a path in that direction, when the woman lets out a sharp yell. Several dogs bark madly, and a general exclamation erupts from the village. Scores of naked children materialize from the huts and run over. Before Marika can stop them, they grab at her skin and clothes with little black hands. Older children debate whether her reddish blond hair is on fire, and only several of the bravest boys hazard a touch. *Wait meri*, they say, over and over again.

The adults are slower to appear, climbing down from the huts or emerging from the jungle and taro fields. Both men and women wear short grass skirts that barely hide their genitals, the women's breasts bared. Cassowary bone knives protrude from the men's woven bark belts, and some, perhaps the more wealthy among them, sport large mother-of-pearl *kina* shells around their necks and dog-tooth necklaces. Marika notices that one man carries a stone ax, and there is no sign of Western clothing whatsoever—which must mean this village is a very long way from anything she would find familiar.

The men call their children back, anger in their voices, and examine Marika with distrustful eyes.

She scans the crowd for the sight of a white man. "*Wait man i stap we?* Where's the white man?" she asks them. Maybe this Mr. Parker can at least tell her where she is, and suggest the easiest way out.

The murmurings and exclamations of the crowd fall silent, and a few of the men whisper to each other.

Marika asks again, "*Wait man i stap we?*"

The old, blind woman grips Marika's arm and points once more at the river. She calls to someone in the crowd, and a young girl, no older than twelve, hesitantly steps forward.

"Hello," she says. "I am Lina."

"You speak English?" Marika stares at the crowd, searching for an explanation.

"I know a little English." The girl shows Marika a tiny silver cross sitting between her naked breasts. "You look—*Jeesus Krist.*"

"Who gave that to you?" Marika asks.

"Mista Newlove."

"Is he a missionary?"

Lina nods and smiles.

"So he taught you English?"

"No." She looks down shyly. "Mista Parker teach me."

"*Mr. Parker?*"

"Yes."

Marika searches the crowd again. "Where is he?" she asks the girl.

Lina's smile vanishes, and fear fills her eyes. She looks back at her mother, and the woman speaks angrily to her in their Walwasi language.

"I can't tell you," Lina says, apologetically.

Tobo, growing impatient, heads in the direction the old woman indicated. Marika follows him, nearly everyone in the village just a few steps behind. Lina catches up with Marika and grabs her arm.

"Missus, don't go there!" she says.

But Marika follows Tobo past vegetable crops and through patches of cleared jungle, toward the noise of the river. Chickens dash into the brush; village dogs scamper away. As the noise of rushing water gets closer, Tobo stops abruptly, and Marika nearly runs into him. He looks back at her, excitement in his eyes.

"There!" he yells, pointing.

Marika's heart races. She looks to where he points, at a large breadfruit tree in a clearing by the river.

"What?" she says, squinting.

"*Yu lukim,*" he insists.

She does. She looks. And now she can make out the figure of a white man sitting against the tree trunk. She can only see the side of him—his tanned arm, his leg—and she brushes past Tobo to get a better look. The entire crowd waits at the edge of the clearing, scared to go any farther.

"Missus!" Lina calls. "Missus! You wait!"

But Marika has forgotten everything—the pain in her legs and feet, the heat exhaustion, the oppressive sunlight and scolding from the crowd. She must get a look at the man. She has to know for herself. She circles the tree, taking in the sight of him. His beard. His glasses. His long, graying brown hair. Her heart beats frantically: this is no "Mr. Parker." Just a few yards away is a man she thought she'd never see. A man the world thinks is dead. *Robert Lewis.* His sudden resurrection holds Marika in a trance. She knows every feature of his face. The stern blue eyes. The wide chin and large, expressive lips. The scar on his left cheek—a shrapnel scar, from Bosnia.

She sighs, clearing her throat. "Mr. Lewis," she says, as loudly as she can.

He hasn't seen her yet, has been carving something in his lap. But now, he looks up. He takes her in all at once, yanking off his glasses. Paralyzed with disbelief, he can only gape at her.

Marika steps closer to him, entering the shade beneath his

tree. He has been called so many things. "Maverick," "misan-thrope," "genius," "saint." And who is he, really? Marika can't begin to answer that question now, or to know what he's doing in this jungle, alive.

Lewis unlocks her from his gaze and looks down, putting his glasses back on. He picks up the mahogany-colored box he'd been carving and resumes his work with unnerving attention and preoccupation. Marika studies him. His soiled, sweat-stained clothes: a long-sleeved khaki shirt, olive camouflage pants. His crudely cut beard. His hair tied in a ponytail and curling down his back.

She watches as he carves. On the box's lid is a rough outline of a cockatoo, and Lewis works on a single feather in the bird's crown. In his hand is a tiny knife, and he holds it with the steady precision of a surgeon as he scrapes out the tip of the feather. It is slow, painstaking work; a couple of his fingers, seemingly injured, are unable to bend. Still, a finished corner of the box displays an expertly carved tangle of leaves and vines.

As Lewis works, his lips move. He speaks softly to himself, his voice having a faint sing-song quality, like a child reciting nursery rhymes. His lopsided, wire-rim glasses rest tentatively on the tip of his wide nose. His face, tan and creased from the sun, looks older than his fifty-four years, but it is unmistakably the face of the man in the photos that Marika has spent months studying back home. The face of Robert Lewis, who supposedly drowned off the coast of Malaysia more than two years ago.

Marika walks closer to him. "Mr. Lewis," she says, "I'm glad to finally meet you."

His lips stop moving. His dirty, powerful-looking fingers stop carving. He throws his box down and yells sharply. Lina comes running over and grabs Marika's arm, pulling her away from the tree, back into the sunlight.

"He want to be alone!" she says to Marika. "You come now!"

Lewis speaks quickly to Lina in the Walwasi language. He

becomes animated, gesturing furiously at Marika. Lina listens politely, a crowd of children gathering behind the girl, jockeying to see what's happening. But no one dares to move into the shade of Lewis's tree.

Lewis stops speaking to Lina and looks hard at Marika. His gaze grazes her in an angry, cursory way. He seems to want to know what her presence means. Or, knowing what it means, wants to know what to do with her, where to dispose of her.

"Get the hell out of here!" he finally yells—in English, for only Marika to understand.

She looks at him, her hands shaking. She has no idea what to say.

"Go!" he yells. "Get out of here!"

She looks desperately around her. The high, jungle-covered peaks surround her like battlements. She feels faint. A headache pounds.

Lina speaks to Lewis in the Walwasi language.

"No, you can't stay in this village," he responds—to Marika, in English.

She glances at Tobo, who merely shrugs and purses his lips. It is as he thought: the white man is sick in the head, just as Marika is, and will not even take care of his own kind. The white people do not belong in his country. They have no ability for it; their skin does not even accept the sun.

Tobo turns around and heads back to the village. He will ask for food and a place to stay. He has fulfilled his duty to the spirit of the man he killed. Surely, the gods don't expect anything else from him now. The white mary has found her One Talk, and that should be enough.

Marika swats flies from the cuts on her legs, watching Tobo leave, as Lewis picks up his box and starts carving again.

"Mr. Lewis," Marika says quietly, "are there any villages close to here?"

He doesn't respond.

"If there's another village close by, I'll go there now."

"Go back the way you came," he snaps.

"Do you have a radio? Maybe I can try to contact someone. A chopper could land here."

She waits, but he says nothing.

"I just can't do any long walks right now." She points to the pus-filled slashes and scrapes covering her legs. "I'm kind of in bad shape."

He finishes carving the tip of a feather, roughly blowing away flakes of wood.

"Mr. Lewis, do you have a radio?" she asks again.

He looks up at her, blue eyes glaring. "There's no hotel here. No complimentary soap." He spits the words out in a southern—rural Missouri—accent.

"Yeah, I know. But do you have a radio? Or a satellite phone, or something like that?" She's surprised by the volume of her voice. By the desperation in it. The village people murmur anxiously.

Lewis's strong left hand resumes carving. Left-handed. Yes, she recalls that detail. She knows so much about this man sitting before her, none of it helping her now.

"*Olgeta man mas wokabaut longwe notwes. Longwe tumas,*" Lewis announces in Pidgin as he works. *You have to travel a long way northwest. It's very far.*

She wonders whether he's talking in Pidgin to annoy her. "What's to the northwest?" she asks.

"The vampires."

"Who?"

"Or you could always use the pay phone by my hut." He pushes his glasses up. "But it only takes quarters."

"Mr. Lewis . . . please, will you tell me if you have a radio I can use?"

"For paying customers only."

"*Do* you have one?"

"The vampires have a radio. They're four weeks northwest—over those mountains behind us. You'd better start now if you want to get there anytime soon."

Lewis blows at the area he's working on and holds it closer to his face.

"Who are the vampires?" she asks, leaning forward to try to stop some oncoming dizziness.

He doesn't answer.

"Who are the—"

"*Fopela wik notwes!* Four weeks northwest!"

The village people call angrily to Marika, and she can feel a palpable tension in the crowd.

She presses her hand to her forehead.

"This is the last time I'll bother you," she mumbles to Lewis, "but do you have any medicine or antibiotics or anything? I'll get out of here as soon as I can."

He sighs, furious. "The nearest medicine is with the vampires!"

Marika watches the river streaming by. Without another word, she turns around and limps toward the village. Each painful step on her swelled, punctured feet reminds her of where she is and of her inability to get out. She now knows that Lewis was never meant to be found. And that she should have never come here.

"No continental breakfasts!" Lewis yells after her.

Lewis is assailed by voices again. They're incessant, seeing everything he does and judging him for it. They remind him that there's nowhere in the world where he can be left alone. Someone will always find him. Someone will always try to remind him about his past, speaking his real name.

Lewis scrapes away at his box, waiting for the crowd of villagers to depart. Though they've seen him under his breadfruit tree for over two years now, only in the last year have they grown weary of the show. Soon, everyone will go back to their various duties. The women, to labor in the fields. The men, to sit in their huts and make arrows and brag of old war deeds. The village will calm down again, and the storm of the white girl's arrival will pass.

He hopes.

Before she appeared, Lewis had been thinking again of that tomb in Syria. No, not a tomb, really—a sacred spot. He can't remember the name for it in Arabic, but all the local people went there to pray for miracles. It was a great rock rising from the hillside and split in half, with an odd, cold wind coming out of it. The people had built stairs going down into the chasm, and they'd sit at the bottom, and let the wind cover them, and they'd pray for whatever it was they wanted from life. When he went to pray, too—and he took such places seriously and always prayed earnestly—he had to wait until everyone left, because he was an "infidel." Whatever that really meant. Perhaps they thought his prayers were not the same. That they would contaminate the place or, worse, offend God. When all he wanted to do was pray for his son, whom he had lost.

The insanity of it all. To even tell them about Daniel's death, to try to seek empathy from strangers (a mistake he'd made far too often in the beginning), was to invite a speech about how their *own* sons had died—but in battle, against an enemy. Daniel's death, they tried to explain, was not the same. Daniel had been shot needlessly in Africa, when he never had to leave America in the first place. Whereas *their* sons hadn't had such a choice. They were sent to war. And they were "martyred."

"But the mothers' tears are the same," Lewis told them. Those had been his naive days, when he still believed he could find, deep within most people, compassion—if he only spoke the right words, tapped into the right part of the human soul.

Sweat drips from Lewis's face onto the wooden box he carves, and he pauses to mop his forehead with his shirtsleeve.

A God who can be offended. He violently rubs his whole face and takes a moment to stare at the river, its cold waters rushing by. He thinks of the girl. She was the last person he would have expected to come here. She looked like such a mess. Clearly, the jungle had almost killed her—as it nearly did him, when he first came through. But he'd asked to be taken to the most remote place that could be found. A place even the vampires hadn't discovered. Just a year after he had arrived, though, one of their choppers found Walwasi. And six months later, Jesus Christ came to town, joining the local pantheon as another god for the people to fear. At least the vampires hadn't stayed long; Lewis had seen to that, personally.

That girl. Looking like such a mess. Had she actually come through the jungle in search of him? But someone should have told her that he's already dead.

As night comes, Tobo tells Marika to sit on a log in the middle of the village and wait. He's been trying to find her a place to stay, but with no luck. He knows it would help if she were a Jesus Mary bringing gifts. At least then the local people would fear her Christ god and let her sleep in their huts. But Marika has nothing to offer, and she is injured and unwell. And, above all else, the Walwasi people are convinced that she is a witch. Tobo tried to explain to them that, while she does get bewitched at times, she has no powers whatsoever; she could not even heal herself when she was sick in the jungle.

As the sun leaves, Tobo finds the hut belonging to the white man, Lewis. He thinks it would be best if she stayed with him. Though it's not wise for a woman to share a hut with a man, as her female poisons will sicken him, Tobo also knows that white people don't believe in such things and so they're immune to the danger. Tobo had to explain this to the local people, who were concerned that the white mary would poison Lewis. Tobo must admit that these Walwasi people are rather foolish and unknowledgeable about the most basic of things. For example, they believe that white people have green-colored blood from all the demons in them, and that white people leave their bodies each night to cause mischief. Tobo nearly laughed when he heard this. Everyone knows that a white person's blood is red—unless he is about to die, in which case it turns white, like his skin. And white people's spirits are so lost and confused that, even when they do leave their bodies at night, they can't do any damage.

Tobo, increasingly dismayed by the ignorance of the Walwasi people, has already begun instructing them about the true ways of things. Fortunately, the *bigman* of the village has allowed him to teach the people and offer his sorcerer services, in exchange for all the pig meat he can eat and carry. The people have told him they've been under great attack by the Magic Fire Spirits, who, in their view, are formidable demons. Though of course Tobo knows these spirits to be nothing of the sort.

Tobo returns to Marika, ready to guide her to Lewis's hut. "You will stay with the white man," he announces.

"But Lewis didn't want me stay with him," she says.

Tobo is surprised that Lewis thinks he can decide anything for himself. "It is not his decision. The Walwasi *bigman* gives permission."

"Is there anyone else I can stay with?" Marika looks around her, at the huts with cooking fires blazing inside.

"No," Tobo says impatiently. "No one wants you."

He guides her to a small, shabby dwelling at the north end of the village. Marika is expecting to find Lewis there, and to have to deal with another harsh confrontation, but Tobo tells her the hut is empty. Exhausted and desperate for rest, she climbs up the notched log ladder to lie down inside and wait for Lewis's return. She wonders what he'll say or do when he discovers her. As much as she wants a roof over her head, and a night out of the jungle, she tries to prepare herself for the worst.

In the dimness of the hut, she can see a clay pit full of red, glowing cinders. A gauze mosquito net hangs from the rafters at the far corner of the room, over a woven grass pallet. Against the opposite wall sits a couple of metal water buckets and various items stored in handmade shelves: empty tin cans, candles, old clothes. Marika lies down on the hard floor, pulling her legs against her and closing her eyes to sleep.

She wakes after dusk. Mosquitoes cover her bare arms and feet, and she slaps at them, getting up. Lewis is still gone, and the hut is empty save for a large, tiger-striped cat sitting in a corner, studying her. Lewis's cat? But what a strange, incongruous sight in this jungle.

Marika sits in the doorway of the hut, staring into the darkness outside. A few constellations try to assert themselves between patches of clouds. The stars reign with such brightness that it's hard to believe they're light-years away. Marika thinks about Lewis being alive. She has a million questions about how he ended up in this village, yet she no longer seems to care about the answers.

Marika rests her chin on her knees, swatting away mosquitoes, listening to the deep, rhythmic chorus of the night creatures. Tears travel down her cheeks, and she wipes them away with her hand. She has never in her life felt so alone. So helpless.

In the village, Marika hears people screaming and wailing so loudly and crazily that she wonders if someone died. She reaches into the hut for a piece of dirty canvas sitting by the doorway, wrapping it around her as protection from the mosquitoes. Once again, the night overwhelms her with its stars. The Big Dipper. The vast trail of the Milky Way. The moon rises in the east, drowning the jungle with eerie light.

Sweat courses down Marika's body, soaking her clothes. It never cools off in the jungle. Always such heat. She remembers going to college in Chicago, and how cold the nights were in winter—how, when she went outside after showering, her hair froze into icicles and jingled as she walked.

"Seb," she whispers. And listens. The night insects buzz loudly and persistently. Marika tries to convince herself that there is such a thing as telepathy and calls to him again.

Nothing. No answer.

The frogs drone. The stars tremble above.

"Seb," she says, "do you still remember me?"

She is sure he's with someone new now. Someone entirely unlike her, who can give him whatever it is he really needs.

Marika sees Tobo nearby and beckons to him.

He walks over. "*Yu laik wanem samting?*" he asks in Pidgin. "What do you want?" His eyes glint in amusement at how she huddles beneath the canvas wrapping.

"Why's everyone crying in the village?" she asks.

"They think the Magic Fire Spirits are angry and causing mischief." He spits betel nut juice onto the ground. "But the Walwasi are a mountain people, and mountain people are always crazy."

Marika yanks the canvas off her head. "Why aren't *you* scared of these spirits?"

"Because I am Anasi. I know the right magic. They don't bother me."

"What do the spirits do?"

Tobo leans against the log ladder of the hut. As Marika kills a couple of mosquitoes on her scalp and pulls their mashed bodies from her hair, he gestures to her, his large bird-quill earrings rattling.

"The *natnats* will try to bite us while I tell you this story, but I will tell them to stop until I'm finished. I think they should be polite, don't you? If I tell a story, it is rude not to listen."

Marika nods. She feels mosquitoes brushing across her cheeks—but suddenly, there are none.

Tobo has begun.

After humans were created and began to make mischief, the god of the sun gathered the worst humans and cast them from the earth. These wicked ones found a home for themselves on the stars and called themselves the Magic Fire Spirits. When they wanted to cause mischief—which they always liked to do in the old days—they rode down to earth on a trail of fire and turned invisible. Then they stole the souls of the earth people, leaving the bodies stretched around tree trunks, or floating in the rivers so the giant pukpuks *could hold them in their jaws and roll around with them until they drowned.*

When the mischief of the Magic Fire Spirits became more than the earth people could stand, they got very angry and planned a big singsing. *Tribes came from every corner of the earth to dance and raise a great magic to keep the Magic Fire Spirits away. Even enemy tribes joined as friends to raise this great magic, and the noise of the* singsing *became deafening. It hurt the ears of the moon and cloud tribes, who asked what was happening on earth.*

The earth tribes told them about the Magic Fire Spirits' mischief. They said they'd stop their singing and dancing as soon as the Magic Fire Spirits left them in peace. The earth people sang louder and louder until the moon and cloud tribes could stand it no longer. Going to their neighbors, the Magic Fire Spirits, they begged them to stop their mischief.

"But the earth tribes are a mean people," the Magic Fire Spirits said, very rudely. "They deserve our mischief."

The moon and cloud tribes did not want trouble with their neighbors, because everyone knew what great warriors the Magic Fire Spirits were. So they went back to the earth people.

"We cannot tell the Magic Fire Spirits to stop troubling you," they said. "They won't listen to us. They say you are a mean people. Tell us what we can do. Our ears are hurting."

The earth tribes talked among themselves, then they said, "It's not true, what the Magic Fire Spirits say about us. Many earth people are good. If the Magic Fire Spirits must

*take some of us away, then tell them to choose only the bad
among us. Then we can all be happy."*

*And so that is how the Magic Fire Spirits came to coop-
erate with the earth tribes. Whenever someone from the
earth is bad, the Magic Fire Spirits come down from the
stars on a trail of fire, and they turn invisible. Then they
find the bad person and touch him, and he rots. That is what
they do to bad people—they cause them to rot and die. So the
earth tribes must always try to be good.*

Marika asks Tobo if he believes the story.

"Of course," he says. The moonlight causes his red face paint
to shimmer, as if he were on fire himself. "But these Walwasi
people think they have no power over the Magic Fire Spirits,
which is not true. The spirits are very weak. All you have to do is
blow at them"—Tobo demonstrates—"and they go away."

"So the people in this village are crying because they think
these fire spirits are coming after them?" The mosquitoes are
back to biting her, and she pulls the canvas over her head again.

"Yes. Tonight they saw the spirits in a cave close to here. They
say the spirits found a bad person in Walwasi."

"What did this person do?"

"He took out a woman's heart. And then the woman saw him
in her dream, eating it."

Marika doesn't understand. "So a woman was killed?"

"No." Tobo flashes her an impatient look. "I told you it was
in her dream. But now she will be sick."

"And what are they going to do with the man?"

"Give him to the Magic Fire Spirits." Tobo is getting bored
with the white mary. She doesn't understand anything he tells
her, and now he's tired and wants to go to sleep. Fortunately,
he notices Lewis coming. They watch the white man limping
toward them, his head bowed, his long hair hanging in sweaty
strands down the sides of his face. Lewis still has the same large,

formidable figure that Marika has seen in interview footage, but now it's tempered by some kind of sickness or injury.

Tobo grunts and walks away. Marika watches the Anasi man go—his slow, deliberate stride, his air of confidence. If the mosquitoes attack him, he doesn't seem aware of it. Tobo fends off nothing.

Lewis hobbles to the log ladder and slowly climbs. He doesn't see her crouching in the dark entranceway and nearly stumbles over her.

"Goddamn it!" he says. "Who's there?"

She clears her throat. "It's me," she whispers. "I didn't know where else to go. No one in the village would let me stay with them."

He steps over her, limping across the room. He tosses a few logs into the fire pit, and, as they catch flame, walks to a bag suspended from a rafter, removing some corn and several fat taro tubers. Glancing at Marika, he pulls out a few more and chucks them all perfunctorily into the fire.

"You must miss the food back home," she says, standing near the doorway.

He just looks at her.

"Mr. Lewis—"

"Just Lewis, for chrissakes. What do you think I am? A keynote speaker?"

"I want you to know that I'm going to leave here as soon as I get healed up," she says. "Tobo—the man I came with—told me there's another village about two weeks from here."

There is no acknowledgment from Lewis. A mosquito is biting his neck, and without taking his eyes off of her, he slaps it dead.

"I've read so much of your writing," she says, stepping back against the palm bark wall and pulling the canvas tightly around her. "I never thought I'd find you here, alive—"

"Who the fuck are you?"

"Well . . . I *was* a journalist." She lets loose a laugh. "I don't know what I am now, though."

Lewis uses a stick to scoop a couple of corncobs from the fire, tiny flames shrinking on the kernels.

"How'd you know I was here?" he demands.

"A missionary told me. He said he saw you on Tumbi River."

"*The vampires.*" Lewis spits into the flames. "What was his name?"

"Pastor John Wade."

He shakes his head; he doesn't know the man.

"He died about a year ago," Marika adds, "after he sent a letter to me and your sister."

"He sent my sister a letter?"

"Yeah."

Lewis considers this for a moment, sighing. "Did anyone else read that letter?"

"Well, I know Beth's husband read it, but he didn't believe it."

Lewis stares fiercely at Marika. "So my sister sent you here?"

"No." She clutches herself. "Beth has no idea I'm here. She didn't believe the letter. I saw her throw it away."

"How do you even *know* my sister?"

Marika presses harder against the palm bark wall, forcing out a smile. "I was . . . writing a biography about you."

Lewis's dark blue eyes are trained on Marika's face. "A 'biography'?"

"Yeah."

He shakes his head and hurls a log into the fire, sending up a volley of sparks. "So you must know how I died," he snarls.

Marika's hands are shaking; she doesn't say anything.

"Well?"

"Suicide," she whispers.

Lewis nods. "That's right, Little Girl. But *how*?" His body is tilted toward her, nearly touching the flames.

"You drowned," she says.

"*Yes.* I drowned."

Lewis looks away from her and clears his throat, spitting. Stoking the fire to a bright light, he opens a bag full of wooden-handled carving tools. Taking out his smallest instrument, the kind of thing a dentist might use, but more delicate, more personal, he picks up the box he was carving by the river.

"If you're planning to eat," he says absently, "then get over here."

She approaches him cautiously and sits by the fire. "I hope you don't mind that I borrowed this," she says of the canvas around her. "The mosquitoes are driving me crazy."

There is no pause in his work, no word of acknowledgment. But at least he's not kicking her out of his hut.

"I've read everything you've written," she says to him. "You were—are—my favorite writer."

Lewis flakes away only the slightest bits of wood, carefully sculpting.

"Take some corn," he snaps, not looking at her.

She reaches for an ear and brings it quickly to her lap. The kernels are shiny black from being singed by the flames, but she takes a bite, having long stopped caring what anything tastes like.

"Water's over there," Lewis says, gesturing behind him to a couple of metal buckets. "Find your own cup. I'm not running a goddamn charity."

He leans closer to the box and readjusts his glasses; he is beginning the bird's eye.

Marika gives Lewis a wide berth as she goes to one of the water buckets. Cupping her hands, she drinks her fill before returning to her place by the fire.

She watches him work. "Will you ever go back?" she asks.

He stops carving and glances up at her. His pain, whatever it is, appears now in his eyes. It peers out at her with a certain wonder and terror, like a child with grief it can't comprehend.

Outside, the wailing starts again, and a woman screams madly. Marika's head pounds, and she runs a hand across her temple. She hears the sound of rats climbing on the thatch roof, hears the persistent ringing of night insects. Lewis's cat blinks, studying her. She sees an ear of corn burning bright red in the fire. She should salvage it. Or Lewis should, at least. One of them should do something.

Lewis suddenly throws a corncob. It passes within a foot of Marika's face and lands against the far wall.

"A millisecond!" he says.

She jumps up and scrambles to the side of the hut, wondering if she should run from him—but where could she possibly go?

Lewis grabs one of the blackened taro tubers from the coals and smashes it against the floor. "Over," he says to her. "In a millisecond. That's what any of it means."

"Your hand," Marika says, shaking.

Lewis merely flicks the steaming taro off his fingers. Putting the box down, he stands up.

"Goddamn it, I wasn't tryin' to hit you," he says angrily.

He walks to his mosquito net in the corner. Swinging the muslin over him, he curls up on the mat, his back to her. He doesn't move again, and Marika realizes he's gone to sleep.

CHAPTER THIRTEEN

Marika wakes just before dawn. She sits up slowly, her body protesting the evening's sleep on the hard palm bark floor. In the village, she can still hear the deep, hollow sounds of a drum beating. It pounded all night like a communal heartbeat, insinuating itself into her thoughts and dreams, waking her repeatedly to the sight of Lewis's cooking fire growing ever dimmer. And of course, the mosquitoes were merciless. She wrapped herself in the canvas, but they found clever ways to reach her skin, sneaking beneath folds and biting through fabric. Her feet and ankles are covered with red swellings that itch and burn for her attention.

Marika remembers how Seb used to say that all suffering holds a blessing in disguise, if you can just discover it. That was a riddle Marika could never solve. There seem to be too many experiences—the ugly, the painful and base—which surely have nothing to redeem them.

Seb. A slice of shame cuts through her, for what happened just before they parted. He only wanted to help her, of course. He wanted to save her from harm. What would he say now, if he could see the state she's in, trapped in a New Guinea jungle?

Lewis cries out. Marika glances at him through the mosquito net, seeing his body lurching from imagined attacks. She can hear his heavy, panicked breathing, watches the fitful rolling of his body on the straw pallet. Sleep, for him, must be some kind of punishment.

Her eyes run over his belongings. The candles, dirty cans, piles of old clothing. No books. No signs of any writing material. A small, cracked mirror hangs on the wall. Below it rests a walking stick, its head elaborately carved in the form of an arching tree; obviously Lewis's work. But there is nothing else to inform her about him, this "Mr. Parker." Nothing else tells her what to expect on this newest day in the jungle.

Beneath the hut, roosters let loose deafening dawn calls. Marika stands. She limps to one of the water buckets, the bark planks creaking and quivering beneath her feet. Lewis, perhaps hearing her in his dreams, cries out and rolls onto his stomach. His orange cat, sitting beside the mosquito net, resettles itself farther from him and studies Marika with its sphinxlike green eyes. She picks up a wooden cup and scoops out some water, glancing at Lewis before taking a long drink. As quietly as she can, she fills her water bottle and creeps out of the hut.

She sees no one outside. Thankful for the privacy, she walks down a nearby path into the jungle, watching the dawn rising stealthily over the forest. Trees surround her like great columns in a cathedral. Birds announce the coming day with bold calls, and not even the faint drumbeats can overpower the incessant droning of insects.

It is a rare peace. Marika leans against a tree trunk, closing her eyes. Sleep is still with her, taming the usual whirlwind of her thoughts. She knows she's stuck in Walwasi village, unwell and unable to leave by herself, but for now it's enough just to lean against the tree, to breathe in the mossy, dank smells of the jungle, and to marvel at how the events of her life have unfolded. Is it an accident that she's here? A mistake? These bird calls, insect sounds, drumbeats? Lewis, turning up alive? It would give her comfort just to know, somehow, that it was all meant to be.

She hears a low humph. Opening her eyes, she sees a large black pig standing nearby, its tail swishing belligerently.

"Go away!" she yells, picking up a stick.

The animal snorts and bares black teeth at her. As it steps forward, Marika throws the stick, hitting it on the back, but this only challenges it to come closer.

She flees into the jungle, her pants catching on a broken branch and ripping across her thighs. Tripping, she looks behind her in a panic. Thankfully, though, the pig is now following some women coming down the path, who pay it no mind as they squat in the brush to relieve themselves. The instant they rise, the animal rushes forward and greedily eats their feces.

Marika looks down at her clothes. Her pants and underwear are too ripped to be wearable, and she takes them off. Wrapping the piece of canvas around her waist like a sarong, she limps back to Lewis's hut. She hears the village's *garamut* drum beating more incessantly, more fervently. Crouching behind one of the hut posts, she watches a crowd gathering in the village, several women screaming and wailing as if someone died, the village chief gesticulating wildly. Behind him, a man—naked and covered in yellow paint—is being dragged into the middle of the crowd. His hands are tied behind his back and clenched like bird claws, a pack of dogs barking madly at his feet. It looks as if the entire population of Walwasi village has come out to view the spectacle, children holding their mother's hands, women huddling against each other. Young men take turns running up and kicking the yellow-painted man, who lies helplessly, his face in the dirt.

Marika sees Tobo on the outskirts of the crowd, watching disinterestedly and chewing a betel nut. She assumes the yellow man is the person he mentioned last night: the man who supposedly entered a woman's dream and took out her heart. Marika shakes her head at the craziness of the scene. She notices that the accused man is crippled, his right leg severely atrophied, the foot twisted in. Perhaps for this reason, he can't fight back, and no one from the crowd attempts to defend him as teenagers take turns kicking at his body and head. The Walwasi chief just looks on approvingly, cheering and waving a machete in the air.

Marika watches the spectacle, tears filling her eyes. With sudden decision, she clambers up the notched log ladder into Lewis's hut.

"Lewis!" she yells.

He lies behind the muslin netting, not moving.

She limps over to his pallet. "Lewis! They're trying to kill someone!"

He doesn't respond. Only the rise and fall of his chest tells her that he's alive.

"You have to do something!" she pleads to him.

When he doesn't move, Marika climbs back down the ladder and walks straight toward the crowd. She doesn't care if her legs hurt her now. She doesn't care about the pain in her body or what these people might do to her. Tobo sees her coming—sees how she's dressed in a funny *laplap*, with her crazy reddish yellow hair tangled about her head and that bewitched look in her eyes. Intercepting her before she can reach the crowd, he asks her where she's going.

Marika points to the yellow-painted man. "I have to stop this!"

"They won't let you stop it," he says simply.

"Is that the man you were telling me about last night?" she asks. "The one who was touched by those spirits?"

Tobo nods, spitting a bloodred stream of betel nut juice onto the ground.

She watches the chief make an angry speech over the man. "Are they going to kill him?"

Red spittle runs from the corner of Tobo's mouth, and he casually wipes it away with a finger.

Marika asks him again: "Are they going to kill the man?"

Tobo takes a moment to more thoroughly chew the concoction in his mouth. "Yes, he will die."

She looks around her. "Where's the woman who saw him in her dream?"

Tobo scans the crowd. He gestures to a woman collapsed on the ground nearby, wailing. "There," he says.

"But she's still alive," Marika says. "There's nothing wrong with her."

Tobo spits more juice onto the ground, saying nothing. He isn't in the mood to explain things to the white mary. She won't be able to understand the ways of the Walwasi people. Even *he* doesn't completely understand their ways.

As a teenage boy beats the yellow man with a large stick, Marika runs forward and holds out her hands. Everyone in the crowd watches her, not knowing what to do. Even the *garamut* drum stops beating. The Walwasi chief yells and gestures. Waving his machete, he comes toward her—until Tobo grabs hold of her arm.

"Come!" Tobo says to Marika. "You are making them angry. Do not forget you are a guest in this village."

"Tell them to stop," she says.

"I cannot tell them this. I am not their One Talk. If I try to stop them, we will have big problems."

"But they're going to kill him."

"Yes. There is nothing you can do. You will make them very angry if you try to stop them."

Marika stares at the man lying on the ground, shaking and covered in blood.

"There is nothing you can do," Tobo says to her again, the Walwasi chief glaring at her. "It is that man's time to die, so you must leave him. Let's go!"

Tobo is surprised that the white mary doesn't know one of the most basic laws of life: that everyone has a time to die. The gods decide this time at birth, and it is an unchangeable law. No one can escape their time, nor prolong it for even an instant.

Which is a good thing, in Tobo's opinion, because whose spirit would want to stay in such a tiresome human body any longer than it has to?

The white mary has become even more bewitched now and is crying like an old woman. Tobo glances around him. To judge from the look of the crowd, she's making herself very unpopular. This is not good for her. She is an unwanted guest with no gifts to give, and none of the Jesus Men to help her. Tobo forcefully pulls her away from the yellow man and escorts her back to Lewis's hut.

"Don't be sad," he says as they walk. "It is that man's time to die."

But when they're nearly to Lewis's hut, Marika yanks her arm from his grasp and runs off toward the river. Tobo watches her, shaking his head. He doesn't know what will become of her in Walwasi, once he has returned home. No one wants her here. She is probably as crazy as her One Talk, Lewis, and can't be trusted to act properly. Maybe, Tobo muses, he isn't supposed to leave her here after all. Maybe the gods expect him to guide her back out.

The thought weighs heavily on the Anasi man's mind—that he still hasn't fulfilled his agreement to the gods, even after all he's done. He wanders off by himself, unhappily pondering this possibility and its implications. In the village behind him, the drums stop beating and the crowd disappears into the jungle. Dogs sniff about the hut posts. Hens lead their peeping chicks back onto the dirt paths. Tobo decides he will consult the gods about the white mary, once he has gotten more sleep.

With Tobo not coming after her, Marika limps slowly and painfully down a slope to the river. She hears a great cheer coming from the direction of the village and wonders if the crowd will come after her next. No one seems safe in this place, ruled by spirits and superstition. She studies the clear, rushing water in front of her. Checking to make sure there aren't any people around, she slips in. The water tugs strongly at her legs as she wades in deeper. Holding on to a rock, she submerges herself, her body bobbing up and down in the current, her wet clothes weighting her down. Mosquitoes hover about her face, above the few inches of her left to them.

Whenever someone from the earth is bad, the Magic Fire Spirits come down from the stars on a trail of fire, and they turn invisible. They touch you. They cause you to rot and die.

The cool water wraps itself around Marika. In her mind, she can still see the man being beaten. Willing the images away, she lets go of the rock and floats downstream. She would ride these waters to their elusive end, if she could. But she's only carried a short way before her shoulder strikes a boulder and pain tears through her body. Gasping, she bursts through the surface of the water and digs her feet into the rocky river bottom.

She pulls off her clothes and throws them onto shore. As she begins washing off the weeks of sweat and grime, a white cockatoo glides over the water. If it's true what what Tobo once told her— that lone birds are messengers sent by departed spirits—then who would this bird be from? Her father? One of the photographers she's worked with? It could have been sent by any of the countless, nameless dead she's seen around the world. As the water envelops her body, Marika wonders if the spirits of the dead keep their hates and fears when they leave the world. She would like to believe that greater clarity comes to people when they die. An ability for self-forgiveness, maybe. Or mercy. Or love. Or, if none of those, at least an ability to stand before God and say, humbled at last, and with nothing left to lose, "Yes, I did things I regret. But I was scared."

Marika finishes her washing and wades out of the river— when she sees the body. The yellow corpse is bobbing downstream, bumping against rocks. It turns, catches on branches, frees itself, sinks, and reappears. Marika nearly chokes, her heart rushing. She swims to the nearest bank and climbs into a patch of wild sugarcane. With the *pitpit* surrounding her, she peers through the stalks at the headless corpse, watching as it meanders along the surface of the water and disappears around a bend.

She pulls in her knees, shaking. Her nakedness makes her feel all the more vulnerable, but she doesn't have the courage to cross the river and retrieve her clothes. Pressing her head against her legs, she tries to imagine Seb's hand on her back. She tries to remember what his fingers felt like as they softly caressed her. For a moment, just a flash of a moment, she feels him so strongly that she turns to look for him. But there's just the green of the *pitpit* and the indifferent river streaming by, breaking before rocks and curling around sandbars.

"Seb," she whispers, and pauses to listen. "Help me."

It is the first time she has ever asked him for help. She tries to imagine him beside her again, but sees instead that excruciating last time they were together in Boston. The way his eyes had scrutinized her. The heartbreak in them. She hopes that one day he'll forgive her for what she did.

She spreads out her legs, letting her fingers explore the new topography of her skin. Mosquito bites appear as congregations of white pustules. The same insect took its time, biting here and there, inserting and reinserting until the blood flowed easily.

"You should see me now," she tells Seb. She laughs, tears trailing down her cheeks. "Would you even recognize me?"

She can't stop shaking, unable to banish the image of the beheaded yellow corpse. She hugs her legs tightly against her, mosquitoes landing at the height only a lover's hand should reach on her thigh.

Parrots call out sharply, flashing green wings as they flee from the trees overhead. Marika wonders if someone is approaching. Across the river, she can hear a soft crunching sound, and she parts the reeds to look in front of her. Lewis, in a torn black T-shirt and camouflage pants, walks out of the jungle and crouches by the water. He takes off his glasses and cleans the lenses with his shirt before putting them on a rock. Carefully, in apparent pain, he pulls off his T-shirt and throws it on the ground. His pants are next, and as he strips them off and wades naked into the water, Marika takes in the sight of his body—the scars on his arms, chest, legs. Straight scars. Round scars. Scars too even, too perfect, to be the result of accidents or recklessness.

Flies settle on the cuts on Marika's shins, feasting. She winces but refuses to move as she watches Lewis kneel down in the water and scrub his skin with sand. Suddenly, for no discernible reason, he stops and sits motionless, water surging around him and threatening to push him backward. He places a hand on the surface of the river, trying to resist the current with his palm as water shoots around his fingers. He varies the angle of his hand, watching, concentrating.

A larger fly lands in one of Marika's cuts. As she leans forward to brush it away, the *pitpit* crunches. Lewis freezes. Water drips down his body, and he looks to where she hides. Though she stays as still as possible, a parrot surges into the jungle behind her. Minutes pass. Lewis's keen eyes don't leave the spot where she's hiding. But now, seized by revelation, he looks over to her tank top and piece of canvas lying onshore.

Sighing, he glances once more in her direction and slowly finishes his wash.

Marika stays in the *pitpit* long after Lewis leaves. When she finally retrieves her clothes and returns to the village, it's nearly night, and everything seems back to normal. Men sit beneath their huts, making arrows, glancing at her disinterestedly as she passes. Women return from working in the fields, large harvests of taro and yams swelling the *billum* bags on their backs. Children busy themselves with spear games or throwing rocks at the skinny aruka palms to loosen clusters of betel nuts. Peace and order have been restored to the village. For now.

Marika wonders how Lewis fits into this picture—or if he does. She can still see him standing by the river. She can see the obvious strength of his body. The way his eyes sought her out. But most of all, she can see the scars.

When Marika enters Lewis's hut, she discovers that it's empty. As usual, he is nowhere to be found.

❧

The next morning, Marika sits against a large tree that overlooks the river below. She can see Tobo in the village, chewing betel nuts with some Walwasi men, and wonders when he'll return to Anasi. Soon, no doubt, as he's fulfilled his part of the payback by bringing her to Lewis. Marika suddenly remembers that she's still wearing his mourning necklace. The thought unsettles her; she's been carrying around the soul of Tobo's dead sister for weeks.

Marika recalls how, the previous night, Lewis never returned to the hut. She had to endure the darkness alone, without even a cooking fire to offer a refuge of light. For dinner, she'd eaten a raw yam, listening to rats crawling over the thatch roof, half expecting a crowd of villagers to come and drag her away. Only Lewis's cat seemed entirely unperturbed, curled up against her feet, purring intensely whenever she tried to nudge it away.

Overhead now, clouds block out the sun and rain looks imminent. She feels the heaviness of her body against the ground. Feels her heart pumping, sweat trailing down her forehead. Somehow she is alive, which seems a curiosity. She doesn't know what she's going to do now. She's sure it would be suicide to leave Walwasi in her present condition. Even with Tobo to help her, she'd be too weak to make it back over those mountains.

Exhaustion tugs at her and causes the world to fog before her eyes. For the first time in her life, there is nowhere to go, nothing to do.

"It must feel like this when your life is over," she says to no one, or perhaps to the naked children gathering around her. They return puzzled glances, not understanding her language. "There's nothing left to think about," she says to them. "Nothing's worth the bother of thinking."

Rain falls. Marika concentrates on it. At times the gorged clouds let loose huge drops that crash through the jungle. At other times there is only a gentle spray and silence.

And silence. She has been sitting in the same spot for hours, not moving. Mosquitoes land on her legs, and she watches them become heavy with her blood, wiggling their bodies loose from her skin and rising unsteadily like drunkards. She allows them to escape, though—like a wrathful god—she could kill them in an instant.

As she repositions herself against the tree, her sudden movement excites the small crowd of children surrounding her. They whisper to each other excitedly, sneaking glances at her.

"Boo!" she yells at them. The youngest children run off in terror, but the older ones just laugh. One boy raises a smooth black hand and slaps dead a mosquito feeding on her ankle. Smelling the blood on his palm, he squeamishly wipes it on the grass at his feet.

Lightning shoots across the sky. Thunder splits the air, rattling the ground and sending the children running for shelter. Yet, for all their hurry, there is an ease about it, an accustomed acceptance of the storm. Marika finds herself envying them.

A downpour soaks her clothes. The wind whips her hair back, great clouds surging like armies across the sky. In the distance, the sun emerges tentatively, touching certain spots of rain forest over others like a god playing favorites. By now, Marika knows every shape and movement of the jungle across the river—how it appears in wind, rain, sun. She has charted the rise of trees in the canopy, has followed the river's course as it twists and curves toward the north. Through it all, she wonders why the world has kept her—and Lewis—alive.

As the rain lets up, the children return and cluster around her, tugging at her arm.

"*Wait meri,*" they call her. White mary. Their Pidgin fits the voices in her head, English growing stale because it's familiar. She wants nothing to be familiar. She wants to be divorced from anything she's ever known. The children's hands tug at hers. They beg her to get out of the rain. She glances at each of their faces until their smiles retreat. They motion to their eyes, asking why she cries. And then it occurs to her that she *is* crying, and how to explain? How to make them understand when she can't? She shakes her head, but their own patience and curiosity are indefatigable. If their parents didn't order them away, they could sit and watch her for hours. She has been told there are always eyes on you in Papua New Guinea—yes, but only if she notices.

Lina, toting food in a *billum* bag on her back, sees Marika and waves at her.

"Hello! How-are-you?" she asks.

Marika can't summon the energy to make a reply.

"I am going to the Magic Fire Spirit cave," Lina says excitedly. "You come with me, okay? It is good luck to go."

"A cave?" Marika gazes at the girl.

"Yes. The spirits live there. I bring them food."

Marika recalls that these are the spirits Tobo told her about. The ones supposedly responsible for selecting the man who was killed yesterday. "So these spirits *eat* the food you leave?"

Lina giggles at the odd question. "Of course. There are many spirits, and they need a lot of food."

Marika sits up. "Have you seen them?"

"Yes. Everybody sees them."

"What do they look like?"

"They are very small and red." She holds out a hand, to indicate that they're only a couple of feet tall.

Marika tries to imagine them. "Do they scare you?"

Lina fingers the cross around her neck. "Yes. Sometimes, I am scared. But they hurt only bad people." Lina tugs at Marika's arm. "Come with me, okay? It is not far."

Reluctantly, Marika stands. Lina shows her the offering in her *billum* bag: taro tubers and a cooked cassowary leg wrapped in banana leaves. The bird was a large one, the heavy leg nearly filling her bag, one of its talons dangling from the netting. Lina guides Marika down a narrow path into the jungle, her bark skirt swaying with each step. Though the girl can't be older than twelve, Marika figures she must be carrying nearly fifty pounds of meat and tubers on her back.

"*Sneks*," Lina repeatedly warns, shaking a stick in the brush on either side of the path.

First the Magic Fire Spirits, Marika thinks. *Now snakes.*

The sunset barely penetrates the thick foliage, and the jungle is dim. Lina gives Marika her hand. The girl's grip is tight; her arms are muscular from the work she does in the fields. She knows the way almost instinctively, but when Marika stumbles too often, she pulls out a torch from her bag and lights it. They reach a narrow stream. Marika is ready to turn back now, having spent too many unpleasant nights in the jungle after dark, but the girl urges her forward across the water.

They haven't walked long when the jungle ends abruptly. Before them rises an immense, sheer wall of stone, colored with the red hues of the departing sun.

"Walwasi Mountain," Lina tells her.

To Marika, it is like a huge, impenetrable rampart. Surely this is the jungle's way of telling her that she doesn't belong here. That no one does.

Lina points to a nearby ridge, covered with ferns. Marika sees a vertical slit in the cliff side, half hidden by a large boulder: the spirits' cave. To her great surprise, a light appears to be faintly glowing in the entrance.

"Do people live inside?" she asks Lina.

The girl shakes her head, shocked that she would ask such a thing. "Nobody goes there. The spirits will be angry—it is their home."

"How long have they lived there?"

"A very long time. My grandparents' grandparents saw them here."

As Marika studies the cave, fear starts growing in her. She doesn't like what can't be explained. She sees water running down the side of the entrance, and decides it's that slick surface, reflecting the last rays of the sun, that causes the glowing effect.

They approach a large, smooth stone, covered with food offerings. Lina removes the bag from her back. As she puts the cassowary leg down on the altar, Marika steps over a low wall of rocks and creeps toward the cave.

"Don't!" Lina yells out. "It is forbidden!"

A shadow leaps out of the cave: a flock of bats. They ascend sharply into the night sky, headed toward the stars. Lina screams and retreats up the path, Marika quickly following. Only when they reach the safety of the jungle does Marika stop to look back.

Thunder cracks. A strong wind tugs at the flame of Lina's torch. Marika waits, wanting some of those little red spirits to show themselves. If it's true that they decide people's fates, she has questions she wants answered. Above all else, she wants to know if she and Lewis are meant to be abandoned in this jungle.

The eerie glow suddenly disappears. She hears heavy footsteps and a crunching sound—something is coming after her.

Marika flees after the flickering light of Lina's torch.

When Marika and Lina return to the village, they see Lewis picking through a woodpile beneath his hut.

"Mista Parker!" Lina exclaims. She runs over to him. "Hello, Mista Parker!"

Lewis ignores the girl and carries a handful of logs to his hut's entranceway, tossing them inside.

Lina grabs some logs from the pile to help him. "I know what *kunawai* means in English!" she announces triumphantly.

"Oh, yeah?" he says, out of breath. "And what's that?"

"Cock-a-too!"

Lewis gives her only the slightest nod of acknowledgment, but it is enough to cause a smile to break across the girl's face.

"How old are you?" he asks her, returning to the pile.

"I am twelve years old."

"Have you ever been to America?"

"No," the girl says. "I been not . . ."

"I *have not* been there," he chides.

"Oh, yes! Sorry!" She looks embarrassedly at Marika. "I *have not* been there."

Lewis comes back carrying more logs, throwing them one by one inside the hut. Lina watches him, waiting dutifully for another question. When he says nothing further she whispers good-bye to Marika and runs off.

Lewis goes inside his hut and moves the pieces of wood closer to the cooking pit. As Marika helps him, he lets her take over the work and sits down by the fire. Pulling out a large skinning knife, he begins gutting the carcass of a crowned pigeon, tossing the entrails to his cat.

"So I see you're still here," he says to her as he works. He shoves a stick through the bird and hangs it above the flames to roast. "How long will I have the pleasure?"

"I'll leave as soon as I can," she says, glancing at him uneasily.

He gets up with obvious pain and walks to a water bucket to rinse off his hands. Before he returns to the fire, he points to a sack hanging on a wooden hook from the rafters. "There's some taro and yams in that bag. If you want to eat, you'll have to feed yourself."

Marika goes to the bag and removes a single yam, pushing it into the fire's cinders. Hesitating, she sits by the flames—but only close enough for the smoke to give her some relief from mosquitoes.

"So you changed your name to Parker," she says to him.

He has no response and reaches for his box and carving knives. Carefully selecting a tool, he holds it with unwavering steadiness, as a surgeon might. Lewis the heart surgeon, whittling out a life or death before the light of his ever-blazing fire.

Marika clears her throat. "They killed a man in the village yesterday, did you hear?"

Lewis tests the tip of his blade, running it slowly down a finger.

"He didn't even do anything," she says. "He was just—"

Lewis slams his walking stick against the floor. He does it with such force that the hut shakes and the cat flees outside. "You ever try silence?" he says, eyes ablaze.

Silence. Marika watches the fire's shadows stagger and rise against the palm bark walls.

Lewis retches up phlegm and spits it near her, his eyes finding hers. "So what's your name, Little Girl?"

Her heartbeat surges. "Marika. Marika Vecera."

He nods as if he recognizes the name from someplace out of his past.

"Well, 'Marika Vecera,' killing that man yesterday is this village's justice. Is it your habit to visit a culture and interfere, just because you don't understand?"

"But the man's 'crime' was—"

Lewis points his knife at her, glaring. "You *will* be quiet now."

His arms start shaking, and he puts the box down. Reaching for his wooden cup, he takes a long drink of water, pressing his fingers against his temple.

Marika draws her legs in against her, watching him. Waiting for what he might do next. But Lewis just shakes his head. It is another one of his headaches. A headache that would like to split his skull.

"You think yesterday was so special?" He violently massages his temples. "On the outskirts of Katmandu there's this Kali temple, and on Saturday, every Saturday, thousands of people go there with their animals. They all line up on the hillside and wait in the sun, all day, so they can get their animals slaughtered there."

Lewis pants in a breath. The headache is pounding mercilessly.

"I watched it from morning to night. There was this one man who did all the killing. Chickens, goats, cows—it didn't matter. He did everything with lightning speed. It was incredible how fast he could do it. Such expertise. Chickens were the easiest: he'd just pull back the wings, wrench back a leg, yank the neck— then slice. And the head was put in a bowl to offer to the gods."

What Lewis doesn't tell her is that the slaughtering man had been a pariah. As far as the locals were concerned, the negative karma he was creating was enormous, beyond comprehension. At the very least, he would have to spend an eternity in the hell realms, tormented without end, picked apart by demons. Which is why the man kept repeating a mantra before he killed each animal. To Lewis, it had looked like a simple mouthing of words, but it was nothing less than a desperate plea for mercy, for absolution.

Lewis kneads his ankle, glancing at the girl. He would like to break her stoicism. Make her cry.

"*Goats,*" he says. "Now goats are more complicated. They're more alive somehow. They know more. They'd huddle outside the slaughtering pen, in this stream of blood. And of course they smelled it. Their eyes seemed to know everything, had the laws of the universe in them—you know?—and they had to be dragged into the place. But the moment the man hoisted them into his arms, they always stopped struggling. I could never figure out why, but every goat would just give in. And the man would hold their hind legs back under one arm." Lewis shows her the motions. "And he'd put his bloody hand over their mouths. Then he'd yank the head back and slice. The head would end up in a bowl to be offered to Kali, and he'd leave the body to bleed on the stones."

Lewis told this same story to a woman—his ex-wife's friend—who offered him her condolences right after Daniel's death. She kept trying to share stories about Daniel. The funny things he did. The brilliant things. As if Lewis had never known his own son. As if *she* had known Daniel better than he had. It had offended him to no end.

Lewis says to Marika now: "The goats stood in a *stream* of blood—I've never seen anything like it. I watched all day. I got there at about five in the morning, when it was barely light, before all the tourists came with their camcorders. It got so boring after a while. I mean, the killing would go on for hours and hours. And then the man would get tired from dragging his knife through all those necks, and he'd have to be replaced."

The girl's eyes—he notices now—see through any words he offers. She sits silently. Her legs drawn up. Her hair tangled about her shoulders. Her face intense and inscrutable, like some Egyptian goddess's painted on a tomb. Nothing he says fazes her. She is young but has seen it, herself. And knows.

Lewis's back aches. He puts his box down and sits against one of the hut posts, smacking a mosquito on his hand.

"About eight in the morning," he tells her, "the tourists showed up in their buses with their hair-sprayed pompadours and—what would you call them?—*leisure-wear* suits, matching color ones, and they'd stand there videotaping the slaughter."

Lewis runs a finger along the edge of his beard. He has the same look on his face that Marika recognizes from photos of him. That troubled, disdainful look.

"One guy was standing too close with his camcorder, like he was at fucking Disneyland, and goat blood sprayed all over his polo shirt." Lewis massages his ankle, finally stretching out his legs before him. "Of course, the other tourists were all laughing and taking photos of him with his bloody shirt."

Lewis waits, but the girl remains unfazed. He looks at her in her dirty gray tank top, her nipples asserting themselves through the fabric. Sighing, he throws a log onto the fire, the sounds of the night creatures filling the silence between them.

"You know," Marika says at last, "I've been to Jicin. When I was little."

Lewis stares at her. "You read my letter?"

"Beth showed it to me."

For a long moment, Lewis doesn't move. At last, he uses his walking stick to pull himself to his feet. He limps over to one of the water buckets, refilling his cup.

"I've thought a lot about that letter," Marika says. "I keep trying to imagine having to write something like that. You know—saying good-bye to everyone. It must have been really hard to do."

She watches as Lewis returns with his cup, painfully reseating himself. He pushes the roasting pigeon closer to the flames, piling more cinders beneath it.

"Your sister has been in a lot of pain, thinking you're dead," she tells him.

"I *am* dead," Lewis says.

Marika moves closer to the fire. Close enough to feel its heat touch her bare shins. She watches as he picks up his box again. And his carving knife. He can almost disappear before her, his lips mouthing those silent syllables.

"What happened?" she asks him. "Why did you do it? Was it Daniel?"

Lewis yanks off his glasses. He looks at her completely now—sees her truly for the first time—and her heart leaps.

"Is that what everyone thinks?"

"That's what a lot of people thought," she says. "That you . . . killed yourself because of Daniel."

"So you must know about my son, too?" Lewis says. "Or maybe you think you know about him. What don't you know about me, Little Girl? Do you know I've slept with three women at once? Do you know I kept a prostitute in Istanbul?" His eyes stare at her almost violently. "Her name was Fatima. She was a tiny little thing. There was something about me that always scared the shit out of her."

Marika looks down at her hands.

"So what do *you* think of me?" Lewis demands. "What did you put in that book of yours—your 'definitive guide' to Robert S. Lewis?"

"Just impressions," she whispers.

"Bullshit." Lewis kicks at the flames. "You can judge me however you like, but you still don't know a damn thing about me. Not by a long shot."

Marika just watches him.

"Look at you," he says. "You're just a lamb. How old are you?"

"I just turned thirty-four."

"Thirty-four," he spits.

He puts his glasses back on and stabs a taro tuber with a sharpened stick, pulling it from the flames. He peels off the charred outer skin with a cassowary bone knife, picking out the soft white flesh inside and eating it. Marika feels like a voyeur as she watches him. His glasses hanging lopsided on his nose. His unevenly cut beard and dirt-smeared pants. Yet all about him is the look of a kind of orderly dishevelment. Dishevelment worn like a uniform, strangely dignified.

Lewis uses his stick to scoop out more taro and corn from the cinders. Seeing that they're burned beyond being edible, he kicks them away with his foot, grabbing his box instead. That beautiful little box.

"Do you think angels weep?" Lewis asks her.

Marika doesn't know how to reply and leans closer to the fire, waiting. With Lewis, she realizes, you must always wait.

"I will tell you a story about my son that you haven't heard," he says. "You might as well know what the truth is." She sees the pain in his eyes now—stark, fathomless pain—and remembers the line from his Jicin letter: *That I could tell you, or anyone, about the loneliness.*

Lewis has told this story hundreds of times to himself. He has told it to the children who gathered around him in the village when he first arrived, and to the jungle, and to the passing river. But he has never told it to someone who could hear his words and actually understand them. Marika, he sees, wants only to listen.

He tells her that Daniel was working for a relief agency in war-torn Mozambique. He was an ambitious boy, but with none of Lewis's vanity or arrogance. Daniel often said he didn't want to live the "good life" so long as others were denied it. He was smart—could have been a lawyer, a scientist, a surgeon—but he chose to go to Africa instead, traveling along the dusty roads and through the poverty-stricken towns, trying to "be of use," to make a difference.

Then Lewis got word that his son was missing. He flew to Mozambique immediately, and for days drove his Land Cruiser over the hot, dry spreads of earth, pursuing leads. He combed the charred villages. Searched refugee camps and bullet-pitted towns. No pain was as great as the pain of not knowing whether his son was alive or dead. No pain in the world could compare. It was an anguish that kept him up each night, that wrenched his guts and sent him into the war zone without concern for his life. Only his son mattered. He would find the men who took Daniel. He would get him back. No matter what, Lewis would find him alive and take him home.

The insomnia, stress, and dehydration brought Lewis close to death himself, but then he got a call on his satellite phone: his son's truck had been discovered by the side of a road, nearly two hundred miles beyond its intended destination. Daniel had been found nearby. Dead.

Lewis sped over the red dirt roads. Past burned huts and towns turned to rubble. He needed to believe that Daniel's colleagues had made a mistake, that it wasn't Daniel they had found. He sped over the Zambezi River, back to the refugee camp run by Daniel's NGO. He found the tent that doubled as a makeshift morgue. The temperature was deadly hot, and there was no way to cool the tent that held his son's body. Lewis could already smell how the remains were preserved: the sickening, pungent scent of decaying flesh was barely masked by the stench of formaldehyde.

An American embassy man was called in from the Mozambican capital, Maputo, to officially witness the body so a death certificate could be issued. He was a youngster, barely twenty-three—nearly Daniel's age. He had red hair and pale white skin, sweating profusely in his cheap, blue polyester suit. He maintained an unwavering expression of solemnity, not knowing anything about death yet. He was newly stationed in Maputo—surely an undesirable appointment in a God-forsaken place—and if he could endure it and prove himself, he would climb up the diplomatic ladder to a better locale. Maybe Peru. Or, dare he dream, a place like Spain. He'd never had to identify an American citizen's body, and though he'd been given the protocol for it, and had been told what to say and briefed on what to expect, his eyes jumped around from the sheer fear of such a responsibility.

But the boy completed his duty, telling Lewis that he needn't view the remains of his son if it would be too painful—that he, himself, could view them instead, which would be enough to issue the death certificate. He would then make arrangements for transportation of the body back to the States. In this regard, there were decisions that Lewis would have to make—and soon. Would he cremate the body (which could be arranged in neighboring Tanzania, at a reasonable cost) and then take the ashes home? Or would he prefer embalming, instead? At any rate, a special coffin would have to be made, lined with lead, to safely transport the body by plane: official regulations for anything deemed a "biohazard."

Of course Lewis wanted to see his son. A white Zimbabwean pathologist had been flown in with the embassy man, as it was official Mozambican government policy that an autopsy be conducted on foreigners killed in-country. This man, who would be cutting Daniel open, emerged from the reeking tent and introduced himself. He wore a long, blue surgical gown and was accompanied by an assistant—a young black Zimbabwean—who still wore gloves smeared with a red liquid. The assistant asked the pathologist, "When will we perform postmortem on the corpse?"

It was the language used—*corpse* in reference to Daniel, to his only son—that caused something to break in Lewis. That caused something to go wrong deep within him, in a place he knew no one could ever reach or fix. The word *corpse* had become his son, and those two clowns were going to cut open Daniel? Defile him with their knives? Reduce all that he was—all that he could have been—to nothing?

Nothing mattered now except seeing his boy. Lewis shoved past the embassy man and strode toward the tent. The two clowns tried to stop him, telling him the body wasn't ready. But as they grabbed at his arm, he pushed them into the dirt. He would enter the tent and see his son. As he burst inside, he saw the corpse of a black African man on a table. *Not Daniel!* Someone had made a mistake. A deep, inexcusable mistake. But he would forgive that person, because it meant that his son was still alive, and he would find him.

The pathologist entered the tent just as Lewis was about to leave.

"My son isn't dead," Lewis told him, furious.

The pathologist said nothing, pointed to the black man.

And then Lewis saw the Carnegie-Mellon T-shirt on the body. The short-cropped hair. The white tube socks. It *was* his boy, only a different, grotesque version. His son's skin had turned black. His body had swelled to twice its normal size—had swelled up so much, in fact, that the clothes were taut, the seams near to bursting. Yes—Lewis should have known. This is what happens to the human body when it lies decomposing in the sun for days. The bloating. The unbearable stench. The flesh eaten away by insects and vermin. He had seen it innumerable times in war zones—the unbearable ugliness of death when it wasn't cleaned up, covered up, sanitized. It was far more appalling than any movie or photograph or article could hope to convey. To look upon it was to experience nothing less than a rending of the soul.

Lewis walked up to the bloated monster and took out his pocketknife. The pathologist looked mortified and urged him to stop, but Lewis cut off some locks of hair. Then he took a second to stare at what his son had become. At the black face, swelled to twice its normal size, the tongue thrusting through obscenely puckered lips. The dull, glazed eye, for the other was gone. The marks around his son's neck—someone had choked the life out of him. Or perhaps the killer had done it after shooting him; there were two obvious bullet holes in his torso, over his heart and shoulder. And then there were the stab marks, slicing and sullying his T-shirt, cutting across his groin.

Oh Jesus, God. Oh, Jesus, God. Lewis grabbed the corpse's black arm and collapsed. *Oh, dear God. Oh, Daniel. Oh, my son, my son.*

The embassy man walked into the tent and stood politely by the entranceway. The pathologist wiped at his sweaty forehead. His Zimbabwean assistant watched the spectacle curiously, wholly hardened to death, incapable of sympathy, wanting nothing more than to do the postmortem already and leave before dark, before their plane to Maputo left without them. Lewis gripped the arm of his son and cried and raged at God. God had killed his son, and he wanted God to know that he would never forgive him for this. Not ever. Not for the rest of his life.

Lewis stood at last. He silently inspected the body one more time. Ignoring the pathologist's fervent protests, he kissed the forehead of the black monster, saturated with formaldehyde. He remembered a couple of lines from the Bible and repeated them: "You are the resurrection and the life. He who believes in me, though he die, yet shall he live."

Ignoring the watching crowd—four men now, as a Mozambican lieutenant had crept in for the show—Lewis left the tent. There was the taste of death on his tongue. The smell of formaldehyde in his beard.

The boy from the American embassy chased after him. "Mr. Lewis . . ."

"I want Daniel cremated in Tanzania," he said simply. He unzipped his backpack and took out several thousand dollars in cash. Placing the bills in the boy's hands, he walked in the direction of the airstrip. Toward the plane that would carry him away from Africa and forever away from his son.

CHAPTER FOURTEEN

Lewis wakes. The sun is reaching beyond the tops of the mountains to the east, and clear white light strikes his skin. The ferns drip from the wetness of night, and perhaps it is the cold limestone of the promontory, or the rain that fell as he slept, but he feels—for the first time in a long time—profound relief from the heat. The mosquito net around him quivers slightly in the breeze. The birds offer their morning calls. Everything feels, if not completely at rest, then full of the potential for it.

When he experiences such respites of peace, the trick is to not acknowledge them. To ignore them entirely. Then they may stay for a short while until the voices force them away.

This is his favorite spot to sleep—this crude little shelter built on an outcropping of rock on the mountainside. The men of the village helped construct it for him. It is a simple platform beneath a roof of palm leaves, with a view of the valley. There is the silver trail of Walwasi River, cutting through the mountains. There are the terraces of taro and yam crops, and the tall rows of corn near the river. Spirals of smoke leave the huts of the village, and he sees his own hut just outside the community, on the edge of the jungle. Which is where the girl must be sleeping. Marika Vecera. Her name rises out of his past, seeking recognition.

It's been three days since he told her about his son's death. He told her every detail—something he couldn't have done back home. Most people back home would have found it cruel to hear such a story—all the ugliness, the messiness of it. But that girl, Marika, listened to the whole thing. She even had tears in her eyes.

Lewis hasn't been back to Walwasi village since that night. He prefers it on his promontory but knows he can't stay long. The voices won't allow him to like any one thing or place too much. They will force him to relinquish anything he enjoys, reminding him that he doesn't deserve it by showing him the usual episodes from his past. All the things he said or did wrong, and the reckoning that surely awaits him. It is not enough for them just to remind him about Daniel—for that would be too kind, would be showing too much mercy. They prefer the things that led him to Malaysia, to his own death. It's no use trying to ignore or fend off the voices; they're much stronger than he and will punish him worse if he does.

At which time, his last recourse is sleep. It's the only thing he's still allowed to have. But if the voices decide to be cruel, they'll wake him and show him—over and over, in minute detail—the images of his sins. Or, if they're feeling especially vindictive, they'll fill his sleep with nightmares. He can never predict when they will decide to punish him, or why. He has learned to take his rest furtively, with no expectations.

The peace lingers longer than usual this morning, but only because Lewis has ignored it. He hears the bird calls but doesn't listen. He smells the sweetness of the jungle and reminds himself instead of the stench of rot. He remembers Marika bringing up Jicin the other night, saying she'd been there. He recalls how, between those browning wheat fields and the high green hills, there had been a taste of peace so profound that he wishes he'd never known about it. Life can be like a torturer who grants his prisoner sleep—makes him believe there will be blessed reprieve—only to wake him the instant he nods off. *Jicin.*

Tears come to Lewis's eyes.

Jicin.

The voices are protesting now, shaming him. But Lewis is already getting up and leaving. He has his walking stick in his hand and his wooden box and carving tools in a bark bag over his shoulder. He parts the mosquito net, leaving behind the white sunlight and soft patterns it weaves through the thin gauze. He feels the coldness of the limestone beneath his bare feet and begins his painful climb to the jungle below. Sweat beads on the sides of his nose. It won't be long before the heat comes. The kind of heat that burrows into the skin and gives him crushing headaches. He has never experienced heat as merciless as Papua New Guinea's.

Lewis leaves the rocky trail and enters the jungle. The great trees hide the sunlight and send shadows shooting across his path. It is this jungle that nearly killed him as he spent weeks reaching Walwasi village, his two guides helping him over mountain after mountain. Lewis never told the men who he really was, and he paid them fortunes to discreetly take him inland and not to talk to villagers. The journey had been exhausting beyond description. His feet had hurt him considerably at that time, and his damaged body made him feel like half a man. But they finally made it.

That was two years ago. It could even be three. He easily loses track of time in this purgatorial world, without seasons or transitions. His two guides didn't stay long, once he gave them the last of their wages: fifteen thousand dollars in cash apiece. One was a smuggler from the Solomon Islands—a worthless man, unhelpful, greedy. But the other, a Papua New Guinea national and expert jungle guide, had been honorable and fulfilled his duties. Though a requirement of their getting paid was that they had to keep their mouths shut about taking him here, one of the men must have spoken because the girl and her guide knew where to find him.

And if *she* could find him, then who else?

Lewis remembers when he first arrived in Walwasi. No one in the village had seen a white person before—which was what he'd wanted and had asked for. He needed to find a place where he would be completely beyond explanation. For days, the women of the village hid with their children in the jungle, and the men stayed armed and mobilized, waiting for Lewis to show them what he was.

He'd considered several other places in the world before New Guinea. Spots deep in the African rain forest. Even remote parts of the Amazon. But Papua New Guinea was unique, full of people who would know absolutely nothing about the world he'd left behind. It was a country with several hundred tribes, many so isolated from each other by the inhospitable terrain that they'd formed their own languages and customs, and knew of no history but their own.

It was to this world that Lewis came. And when he used the last of his antibiotics to cure two small Walwasi boys dying of dysentery, the villagers made their decision about him: he was a white spirit sent by the gods to bless them. He didn't heal anyone else—he had no more medicine—but they built him a hut and welcomed him, and the girl Lina (whose little brother had been cured) was assigned to bring him water and tend to him. The entire village took responsibility for his welfare. Robert Lewis, patron saint of Walwasi. If only they knew the truth about him.

Marika lies in a corner of Lewis's hut, the sickness sweeping across her body again. Malaria. It impresses her with its punctuality. Each day, she can count on it arriving at the same time in the late morning and staying till nightfall. It always starts as uncontrollable shivers and a crushing headache. Then, when the fevers take the place of the shaking, she grows confused and delirious. The world stops making connections in the same way. Lina, taking care of her, seems to return just moments after she left, and Marika finds it hard to place the source of sounds. They'll come from far away, only to suddenly speak in her ear with terrifying directness. She thinks Tobo may be right—that malevolent spirits are trying to torment her.

She rolls around in the corner of Lewis's empty hut, her

bones digging painfully into the palm bark floor. Nausea and aching joints make sleep difficult, and most of the time she lies half-awake waiting for the jerking of her body to subside to fever. Hours later, this too will break with a rush of sweating. Sweating means she's made it through another day, that the high fevers haven't killed her. She keeps wondering why her body refuses to surrender like her mind, why it keeps coming back for more.

It's the start of her fourth day of being sick, when she hears someone walking heavily across the floor of the hut. She opens her eyes to the sight of Lewis limping past her. The last time she saw him, he'd been telling her about Daniel. It had been an odd sort of communion between them; he'd told her the most private details of his life, then, the moment he was done, he simply left the hut and never returned. Marika could only wonder if she'd offended him somehow. Or if she'd failed to meet an expectation or hope. She can't read Lewis—and that's the unsettling part. She'd never known the traumatic details behind his son's death, yet despite them, Lewis had gone on for years, produced his best, most celebrated work. He hadn't let the tragedy stop him.

But now, inexplicably, he was here in PNG. Stopped altogether.

"I think I have malaria," she tells him now.

Lewis takes one look at her—at her shivering and jerking—and knows she's right. No other tropical illness has such an elaborate battle plan to kill the human body. Right now the disease is causing her to violently jerk, as if to shake the life from her. And in a few hours, the shaking will stop only to be replaced with fevers as high as 106°F. But it's hard for him to know which type of malaria she has. One type, the deadliest type, destroys brain cells and kills within a few days. He has had the less dangerous kind three times since he arrived in Papua New Guinea, each instance an awful trial. Malaria, regardless of type, doesn't like to take prisoners. He had to fight the disease without medicine, and with every victory— after enduring excruciating weeks of shaking and fevers and chills—he was rewarded with a buildup in immunity. It's been at least half a year now since he last got it: a new record.

"Do you have any malaria medicine?" Marika asks weakly.

"No," he says immediately. "This isn't a goddamn pharmacy." But his voice, she notices, sounds less fierce than usual. Lewis examines her as she lies on her side, her legs drawn against her body, the incredible jerking and shaking seizing her every few seconds. He doesn't want to watch it. He'll have to leave soon. He sighs and sits by the cooking pit, lighting a fire to boil some yams for breakfast.

"With malaria," she asks him, "are you supposed to get fevers every couple of days?"

"Usually," he mumbles.

"But I get a fever *every* day. Is that bad?"

He clears his throat and spits. "It's bad."

"And I can't really eat," she whispers. "I'm too nauseous all the time."

He gets the fire going and feeds it some logs. "You're gonna have to eat, if you ever want to walk out of here alive. But the most important thing with malaria is to drink lots of water. If you're lucky, you'll get better in a couple of weeks."

"Or I could die instead," she says, matter-of-factly. She's never had malaria before, but she's known people who have. Refugees, mostly, who came down with the cerebral variety and died in a couple of days. This is her fourth day, and so at least in that respect, there's hope.

She reaches for the bucket of water beside her, dipping the wooden cup inside. Taking Lewis's advice, she drinks as much as she can, and only when her stomach feels full to bursting does she stop. What is it about being seriously ill, she wonders, that makes her yearn for someone, anyone, to be by her side? But Lewis stays by his fire, of course, and Seb is half a world away. If she died here, no one would ever know. Or care.

She remembers how she used to want that. The not-caring. She closes her eyes to the world.

The jerking ends at the same time it did on previous days—at the hottest point of the late afternoon. Now the fever arrives, settling on top of her head and prompting a piercing headache as it creeps down her body. Lewis, who had been sleeping inside his mosquito net since morning, wakes abruptly. He rubs his face, staring at Marika through the film of netting.

"It's so hot," she tells him.

He says nothing. The voices have woken him up and are now berating him about her, but he doesn't know what they expect him to do. If she's going to die, she's going to die. He can't save anyone. Never could. He couldn't even save his own son.

"It's like being in a cauldron," she tells him.

"Keep drinking the water," he says, climbing out of the mosquito net.

He puts his wooden box and carving tools inside his bark bag and limps to the entranceway of the hut. Before he climbs down the notched log ladder, he stops to look at her again. Her sweat-covered body. The tangle of her hair. He doesn't know if she'll make it. She arrived weak to begin with, and of course there's no medicine in the village, no miracle cures of Western science. If you get malaria here, you either live or die. Life doesn't play favorites in Walwasi.

He goes to the fire and picks up what's left of his boiled yams, dropping them at her feet.

"Try to eat these," he says.

Lewis leaves without further word, and Marika feels the fever descend upon her. She sees a long, grassy field. She's back in Congo, in the war zone. She's standing on an island of green grass, surrounded by flames. The fire crawls toward her, incinerating the grass, engulfing her in black smoke. It's about to reach her, but someone shoves her and slaps her cheeks.

"*Ma-ree-ka!*" a voice calls out.

The field of flames disappears. She feels the ball of heat over her chest and opens her eyes. Tobo and Lina are kneeling beside her.

"*Ma-ree-ka,*" Tobo says to her, "don't let your spirit leave your body when you are sick! If you do this, you may not come back!"

Lina swabs Marika's forehead with a wet rag. "My great-grandmother, Batu, will stay here with you," she says, pointing to the ancient woman Marika met when she first arrived in Walwasi.

The old woman seems to examine Marika with her blind eyes. Lina hands her the wet rag, and slowly her gnarled fingers use it to gently pet Marika's hair.

Tobo reseats himself on the floor and examines the white mary. Even a beginning sorcerer could see that only the strongest, most dangerous healing spirits would have any chance of removing her demons and saving her. But she isn't strong enough to handle such spirits, who often want a person's soul as payment for their work. And what is the use of healing someone, if their soul is taken?

Probably, Tobo reasons, only the soul of his dead sister has kept the woman alive this long.

Tobo smears a green paste made from jungle roots and leaves onto Marika's neck and arms, to prevent more dark spirits from entering her body and causing mischief. He blows mango bark smoke over her and entreats Agane—the spirit who healed her in the jungle—to protect her from the invasion of further dark spirits. It is the best he can do.

Tobo knows that the white men have their own special spells and medicine for such illnesses, and so he figures they must have their own spirit helpers, as well. He has seen the Jesus Men on Green River swallow special medicine when they were sick, which attracted healing spirits powerful enough to rid their bodies of demons in a short time. It is the white mary's best hope: getting some of her One Talk's medicine.

Tobo has heard the Walwasi people talking about a Jesus Man who is staying in the nearest village, seven days north along the river. He will send the fastest boy in Walwasi to go get him and bring him back, so he can remove the white mary's demons with his medicine.

"I will bring a Jesus sorcerer to help you," Tobo tells Marika, as he gets up to leave.

It's easy to tell when the missionary arrives. Marika hears a communal exclamation in the village, and the excited barking of dogs. While she's much too feverish to climb down from the hut to greet him, she strains to listen for the sound of his footsteps approaching the hut. She hopes he's brought medicine. It will end the torture of this illness, which has held her close to death for nearly two weeks.

The hut shakes—but it is Lewis who enters. He's been absent during most of her illness, and she's surprised, and relieved, to see him now. As he gets his cooking fire going, she hears an energetic greeting outside in English. American English, with an obvious southern accent. Moments later, the hut quivers again, and a small, redheaded man appears. Lewis looks up to examine the visitor; Marika has never seen him take such an interest in anyone.

"Well, hello, Mr. Parker," the man says to Lewis, laughing uncomfortably. "Always such a pleasure."

"Newlove," Lewis spits out.

The man comes forward to offer his hand, but Lewis doesn't move.

"Now Mr. Parker," Newlove says, nervously scratching his elbow, "I hope I didn't go offending you during my previous visit. We do find ourselves alone in the midst of a barbaric land, and it'd be unfortunate if we were enemies."

Newlove waits. When Lewis has no reply, he turns to Marika. "Well, hello there. You must be our damsel in distress." He leans down to shake her hand. "I am Winston Newlove, of Alabaster, Alabama, originally. But now I live at June River Mission, Papua New Guinea."

She shakes his hand, feeling his sweaty, sticky palm. His light blue eyes skitter to the right or left, refusing to make eye contact with her, as if her stare contained something contagious. Marika feels herself instinctively constricting from him—as she does from anyone gone mad.

"So how did y'all get here?" Newlove asks the space just to the right of her.

"It took weeks—more than a month." She knows she hasn't really answered his question.

"You must have climbed over the mountains, I suspect. Jungle trekking of any kind is not for the fainthearted. Isn't that right, Mr. Parker?"

Lewis hacks some phlegm onto the floor, and it settles in the crack between two planks of palm bark. He puts his glasses on, reaching for his box and carving tools.

Newlove lingers before Marika. She thinks he must be in his early forties, and as he removes his pigskin bush hat, she sees that he's almost completely bald, a few long strands of reddish hair circling his lower scalp and reaching to his shoulders. He wears a sweat-stained white T-shirt, along with muddy khaki pants and a safari hunting vest full of empty ammunition pockets. He appears strikingly short—barely over five feet—and is so wiry and muscular that he might have been an athlete when he was younger. Crude, snakelike tattoos cover his arms and climb up the back of his neck. His face, while maintaining the ingratiating smile of a court jester, has sharply intelligent eyes that closely inspect the inside of Lewis's hut as if looking for contraband. Marika gets the impression, staring at Winston Newlove, that the man is in search of nothing less than a glorified version of the holy grail. That it might be found in Lewis's hut, among the moldy clothes and rotting taro tubers, seems unlikely at best. Still, his eyes don't stop scanning. They miss nothing.

Newlove notices the ancient woman, Batu, who has been keeping Marika company during her sickness and is busily knotting a *billum* bag.

"Well, hello, Grandmother," he says to her, walking over. "Bless your heart! *Mi gat samting long yu.* I have something for you."

He removes his backpack and pulls out a stalk of sugarcane, handing it to her. As Batu blinks her eyes and mumbles, Newlove takes out his knife and strips off the smooth outer stalk, cutting out the pith. Resting his hand on Batu's head, exactly as a pope might touch a minion, he places the pith between her lips.

"You got real pretty blue eyes," he says to her in a cooing voice. "Like my eyes. *Olpela i stap laik ais bilong mi.*"

"She's blind," Lewis bellows out. "Leave her alone."

At the sound of Lewis's angry voice, the woman berates Newlove in the high, unintelligible syllables of her Walwasi language.

"As soon as these missionaries hear of a new village," Lewis tells Marika, "they run out to sink their teeth into the place. They're like vampires, always looking for fresh blood." A half turn and dismissive wave toward Newlove catches his attention. "Isn't that right—you're all just vampires?"

Newlove blinks several times.

"Vampires!" Lewis says impatiently.

"We share the word of the Lord, our Father, through the teachings of his son, Jesus Christ. 'We must all appear before the judgment seat of Christ, that each one may receive according to what he has done.' Corinthians 5:10. Are you and your local . . . consorts . . . prepared for judgment, Mr. Parker?" He smiles benignly at Lewis. "I suspect not. There's a whole lot of work to be done here, that's for sure."

But Lewis has already forgotten Newlove and busily carves his box.

Newlove turns again to Marika. "So what's your name, Ma'am? We haven't been officially introduced."

"Marika," she whispers.

"Oh? That sure is an unusual name. What brings you to this village? Are you with a ministry?"

"No." She offers him nothing else.

"Well, maybe you're a scientist, then? We had one of those types visiting us at June River. He was studying 'pygmy parrots,' of all things. Bless his heart. Those scientist types must find something to study, mustn't they? He wasn't what I'd call an unpleasant sort, but now"—Newlove leans closer to her, whispering—"he was an *atheist* to the core. That's right. Truth be told, most of those scientist types are. But now, the atheist believes life is a *ticking time bomb*, and all he is, and all he has ever done, will turn to dust in the end. It must be . . ." Newlove searches for the word, rubbing his chin aggressively. "Disheartening."

Across the room, Lewis spits again.

"Are you a religious man, Mr. Parker?" Newlove takes a step closer to him. "I don't think we ever managed to broach that subject."

As Newlove waits, rubbing his elbow, Lewis's cat bumps against his legs and purrs. He regards the animal absently, remembering how things were like this the last time he came to Walwasi, about a year ago. Mr. Parker—the mysterious, unfriendly Mr. Parker—didn't seem to have a profession then, either. Newlove decides he must be a drifter, gone native, no doubt fornicating with the young ladies of the village and fathering illegitimate children as testament to a life of laziness and debauchery.

When Newlove's judgment of Lewis satisfies, and he feels sufficiently vindicated of all slights, he smiles pleasantly again.

"Well, evangelism has always been a hard job," Newlove says to no one in particular. "Why is it that the teachings of Jesus Christ come hardest to those most in darkness? Mr. Parker, I've asked you this when I visited before, but perhaps y'all would allow me to share some of the Lord's teachings in the evenings to come? You can invite your . . . daughter, here." Newlove blinks lightly, waiting for his host to show acknowledgment.

Lewis finishes giving his box a rounded corner, ever so gently smoothing it with an oilcloth. Newlove stares at him. Stares at the floor. He closely inspects an infected mosquito bite on his arm, wondering if Lewis is indeed his host. He turns to Marika in retreat.

"It sure is peculiar seeing a white woman here," he says to her.

She wrestles with this for a moment, the words seeping into her mind.

"I'm sick," she replies. It sounds reasonable, so she says it again. "I'm sick."

"Yes, Ma'am, I know. But the good news is that I have just enough mefloquine pills that I can spare some for your malaria. My Lord, it sure *is* peculiar seeing a white woman here—but I must admit it's a very pleasant surprise. And what a blessing to speak the English language! I've been in the bush for going on several months now—if you can believe it—speaking all manner of native tongues. Ten months of evangelizing takes its toll on a person, I can tell you. But now, I don't mean to complain. Of course I've submitted myself to this life 'that all the peoples of the earth may know that the Lord is God; there is no other.' Kings 8:60. Amen."

Newlove walks to the doorway and calls to several boys outside. They run over, but none wants to enter the hut.

"Well, come on up here!" Newlove says to them. "No one's gonna bite you! *Yu kam!*"

They climb up the log ladder but linger in painful indecision at the entrance of the hut, eyeing Lewis.

"Come on! *Yu kam!*" Newlove says, smiling broadly.

One by one, the boys creep inside, standing as close as possible to the door. From their nervous yet excited stares, Marika can tell they've seen Newlove before and know to expect special gifts.

Lewis looks up as Newlove opens a large backpack, pulling out what seems to be a roll of plastic—bubble wrap. He rips off several small sections, handing each boy a piece. Immediately, the popping of bubbles begins.

"Spreading the Lord's word?" Lewis asks over the noise. Before Newlove can answer, Lewis cuts him off. "I want you out of here *now*. Just give her the medicine first."

"Well, I've got the medicine down in the village. In my other pack. If you would just allow me some time to locate it."

"Go 'locate it' now!" Lewis says, glaring at him.

Newlove leaves—or perhaps flees—the hut.

As Lewis slams his walking stick against the floor, the boys dash after Newlove with their new booty. Lewis sighs heavily, resignedly. He gathers his things and swings the strap of his bark bag over a shoulder. Slowly, he limps across the hut and climbs down the ladder, heading off into the jungle.

Daylight seems to depart with him, the intense fever smothering Marika, draining all energy. She feels her body sinking, giving up—even her mind seems to be getting blotted out by darkness. She thinks she hears a storm erupting outside. Yes. Lightning and thunder. Wind. The hut's structure violently creaks and protests, rain tearing against the thatch roof, shocking her skin.

Someone small enters the hut, barely causing the floorboards to shake. For a terrified instant, Marika is sure it's one of the Magic Fire Spirits. But she hears a man's voice. Newlove's.

"Does that feel good?" she hears Newlove say.

Marika is about to respond, to ask him what he means, when she hears Lina reply, "I don't know."

"You don't know, honey?"

"No."

"I want you to say 'yes.'"

"Yes."

"They're just popping out, aren't they? They look just like two little rosebuds."

"What's 'rosebud'?"

"Those are rosebuds, honey."

Marika opens her eyes. She can make out the shapes of Newlove lying beside Lina inside Lewis's mosquito net.

"Lina!" Marika's voice cuts across the hut so loudly, despite the noise of the storm, that it surprises the girl. Lina scrambles from the netting and runs to Marika's side.

"Yes, Missus?"

"I want you to go home now," she says. "You go home *now*."

"But Mista Newlove ask me to stay here tonight."

"You go home now," Marika says again, loudly.

The girl looks at her, tears in her eyes. "Why do I make you angry, *Missus?*"

Marika feels the darkness pressing at her, wanting to pull her back into sleep. "Just *go home.*"

Marika drifts into the blackness again and wakes to the sound of Newlove's voice. "I was so lost then"—he is close to her, his voice is near her ear—"so far from God that I kept wakin' each night. It was always at the same time, right around three in the morning."

Marika forces her eyes open. She sees a tattooed arm. A fire serpent trying to eat a yin-yang symbol. Newlove is sitting beside her, nearly touching her.

"The first time the Lord spoke to me was in March of 1998," he tells her. "He woke me in the middle of the night and told me to go on a special mission to save the lost and sinful of this world. He said he wanted me in the Philippines, and I said, 'Lord, I am thy servant.' I didn't have a real job at that time, so I was grateful for the guidance. I spent three years in the Philippines, doing the Lord's work in the very worst slums and brothels you ever did see— just unimaginable sinning, right before my eyes." Newlove clears his throat. "Makes you wonder if hell ain't right here on earth."

Marika jerks, feeling Newlove's hand on her arm.

"Then the Lord went and woke me again and told me he wanted me in Papua New Guinea, of all places. So I packed my bags and joined the June River Mission as part of Operation Tribal Evangelism. In fact, and I don't mean to brag now, I was the *engineer* of that particular program. And I am happy to say that just last year, that program was successfully launched in Ghana and the Brazilian Amazon. In fact, to tell the truth, I've become something of a celebrity in my ministry, even though I was such a late convert. I made my conversion testimony when I was thirty-seven, after—I must confess—a great deal of sin-ning and worldly indulgences of various kinds. But like the prodi-gal son, I returned to my Father, and he saved me through his righteousness, that I may offer redemption to the sinners of this world. Amen."

Marika turns on her side, grabbing her stomach, longing for the fever and pain in her body to end. A flitting, hopeful thought reminds her that Newlove is supposed to have malaria medicine. It takes almost more energy than she has left, but she opens her eyes and focuses her mind enough to ask, "Can I have the medicine now?"

"Well, yes. It's in my bag. Let's just wait a little longer, all right? You just close your eyes and rest."

"I'm really sick," she says.

"Yes. I know. Let's just wait a little longer. You know, if you had proper faith, the Lord would heal you and you wouldn't need any medicine. That very thing has happened to me on several occasions. I can tell you that the body is the vessel of our sins, and sickness is the Lord's judgment brought upon us. 'Tribulation and anguish on every soul of man who does evil.' Romans 2:9. But if we ask for the Lord's forgiveness, he heals us. Have you thought of asking for his forgiveness?"

Marika closes her eyes and shuts out a chunk of time. As the fever wakes her and tries to smother her, she cries out.

"Shush! Shush!" Newlove chides.

She opens her eyes. Newlove is running his finger over her thigh, and she stares at a crude tattoo on his wrist of a grinning, spitting mouth. She realizes she's biting her lower lip, but can't stop.

The ball of heat lingers in her chest, and her heart beats frantically. She finds herself fighting for her life, urging the heat to descend. *Keep going down, keep going, don't stop there.* She closes her eyes. Time stretches out, rearranges itself.

A wet rag travels up her leg. Her face is being swabbed.

"You have some pretty bad symptoms, you know. Your fever sure is hot. You must have done *some*thing to be so sick. The Lord doesn't punish the innocent. Well, whatever happens, he has a plan for you."

Newlove runs the damp rag down her neck and beneath her tank top, over her breasts. He rewets it and runs it down to the end of her belly, stopping abruptly. Sighing, he returns it to her face again.

She wants to call out to Seb but finds herself shouting to Lewis instead.

"Shh, shh, girl! Don't do that. Quiet now. 'All things are lawful for me, but I will not be mastered by anything.' Corinthians 6:12. I have a feeling you do *not* read the Bible. Am I right? Nor, I suspect, does your friend Mr. Parker. A very unfriendly man."

Newlove stops the rag at the bottom of her stomach and lets it linger there. "A bit dirty," he mumbles. The rag creeps beneath her canvas sarong, searching between her legs.

Marika convulses, the ball of heat pressing against her chest. She tells Seb that she can't forget him. He must teach her how to forget.

They sit on a bench by the Charles River, with Harvard across the waters. The sun is setting in bright red hues, sailboats drifting past. It must be summer. It's hot. Incredibly hot. They watch a crew team pass, a slick machine of bodies.

"I've missed you," she tells Seb.

He turns to her. Focuses his bright eyes on her. "Have you?"

"I've thought about you every day."

Another crew team passes. They look like human pistons gliding across the water, their slim boat shooting toward the sun.

"Do you ever remember me?" she asks Seb.

He laughs and squeezes her hand. "Of course. I was in love with you, you know."

"What do you remember about me?"

"I remember how you saved that mangled penny I gave to you on our first date, like I'd handed you a good luck charm. And the mushrooms! When we went hiking in the spring, you were always pulling leaves off of them, trying to 'save' them."

"What else?" she asks.

Seb is wearing his overcoat in the intense heat, and now he wraps it around her. "How you always fit so comfortably next to me."

She tells him she can't breathe, it's too hot.

"I know it is, honey."

Newlove is climbing on top of her.

"He'll see you," she says to him.

"Who will?"

"God."

Newlove's hand withdraws from between her legs. "But he always forgives us."

The ball of heat is over her stomach now. She swallows hard, trying not to throw up. Time lurches.

"He forgives us," Newlove is saying.

The floorboards shake as if from a heavy wind. Newlove's body is suddenly gone, and Marika fears he's going to leave her without giving her the mefloquine.

"Please," she begs, "can I have the medicine now?"

There's the sound of a scuffle, and she hears Newlove squeal and cry out.

A voice booms out: "Why is she still sick?!" It's Lewis's voice.

"I was just about to give her the medicine."

"Where is it?!"

"In my backpack."

"Get it!"

Marika tries to open her eyes but can't. Or, rather, she doesn't want to anymore. She just wants to stay asleep for good.

She hears Newlove rifling through his bag. "Here," he says.

"That's not enough!"

There's more scuffling, and Newlove cries out again.

"It *is* enough!" Newlove exclaims, squealing in pain.

The floor of the hut shakes violently, followed by a long silence. And now Marika feels a palm resting gently on her forehead and a warm breath hitting her ear.

"I'm sorry," a voice whispers. A soft, slightly southern drawl.
"God, am I sorry."

Her mouth is opened, and a couple of pills are dropped down
her throat. Cool water follows, washing them down.

"Look at me!" the voice demands now, hands shaking her.
"Can you look at me? Come on!"

When she does, two dark blue eyes stare back at her. It's
Lewis. He looks scared.

"I told myself I wasn't going to care about anyone again," he
tells her.

She falls into blackness.

The mefloquine worked quickly. It wasn't long before Marika's
fever broke, and she was able to sleep through the night. When
she woke the next morning, she found herself inside Lewis's mosquito net, on his pallet, the piece of canvas wrapped snugly
around her waist, his shirt draped over her like a blanket. Though
Lewis was gone, she could vaguely remember his voice encouraging her through the night.

It would take a week for Marika to recover. Her stomach,
unused to food, only accepted small helpings at first. She was
skinny and weak, and so Lina came by to feed her the fattiest
pieces of meat she could find—the Walwasi way of overcoming
malaria—with plenty of starchy taro tubers. Lina fed her several
times a day, until, after a short while, Marika could walk around
and manage by herself. She was gaining weight, and her energy
was returning. Staying inside a mosquito net, on Lewis's grass
mattress, became the biggest luxury of all. It meant a sound
night's sleep and a quicker return to health, though she kept
wondering when Lewis would finally return to claim his bed.

Marika now sits with Lina beneath Lewis's hut, helping to pull
the husks off ears of corn. She hears someone call to her, and sees
Tobo approaching from the village. Newlove is with him, as well

as the missionary's two Papua New Guinean guides, who carry
large backpacks full of Bibles and bubble wrap. The group stops
near Lewis's hut, and Tobo gestures for Marika to come over.

She notices that he has his trademark red paint on his chest
and face. Cassowary talons jut from the tops of his nostrils, and
his mother-of-pearl *kina* shell gleams in the bright morning sunlight. Strapped across each shoulder is a *billum* bag, full to bursting with smoked pork and yams.

"Are you going somewhere?" Marika asks, alarmed.

"Yes," he tells her in Pidgin. "*Bai mi go tude.* I'm leaving
today."

She doesn't know what to say. She wasn't expecting him to
leave so abruptly, without warning.

Tobo looks at the clothes she wears: a white man's shirt that
nearly reaches her knees, a canvas *laplap* around her waist. She
was always a very odd white mary, whom he won't soon forget.
He will have many good stories to tell about her.

"I spoke to the gods last night," Tobo says, "and they told
me I must go home, and you must come with me. They told me
that if you don't come, you'll die here."

"But I'm not ready to go," she says.

"Listen—you must come."

"I can't get over those mountains again. I'm not strong
enough yet."

"We are going a different way, to the northwest, where there
are not as many mountains. We will go to Mister Newlove's
home on June River."

"But your village is in the other direction."

"Yes." Tobo smiles. "I will travel on the Sepik River back to
my village. It is always better to travel on water."

Newlove approaches Marika, his eyes skittish for signs of
Lewis. "So are we feeling better today?" he asks her.

She looks at the sinewy little man. A tattoo of a crude,
asymmetrical cross stands out prominently on his wrist, haloed

with beams of light, JESUS written above it in rough script. Marika sees a bruise above Newlove's left eye—and remembers how he'd been lying next to Lina. And then her. She realizes what Lewis must have done to him.

"I'm better," she says to him coolly, trying to contain her rage.

"Praise the Lord," he says. "You were on the brink of death, but God saved you. You may not be so blessed in the future, though. I really think you ought to leave this place and return with us to civilization. I don't know why you're here, but this is no place for a white woman."

Tobo shakes his head. The Jesus Man talks too much. It is unfortunate that he will have to spend many days in the jungle with such a man, but at least his two guides don't make a lot of noise.

"I will wait for you to get your things," Tobo says to Marika. "Be fast."

She stares off at the village, the needlelike mountains surrounding it on all sides. Part of her desperately wants to go with Tobo, her only lifeline out of this jungle—but she can't imagine leaving Lewis behind.

"I can't go yet," she says to him.

He stares at her, wondering if she's bewitched again. "You must go," he says, "or you will die."

"I don't want to leave Lewis here."

"Who's Lewis?" Newlove asks, stepping forward.

Marika walks to the edge of the jungle and motions for Tobo to follow. In private now, she says to him again, "I don't want to leave Lewis."

"Then find him and tell him to come with us," Tobo says. "But be fast. We are leaving now."

Marika knows in her heart that even if she could find Lewis, and ask him, he wouldn't go. For whatever reason, he chose this place, and she can't imagine leaving him behind. How would she ever live with herself if she did? Thoughts of Lewis would chase her, torment her. The world needs him too much.

She needs him too much—there is the truth of it, finally. Lewis is, and has always been, her hope.

She will stay in Walwasi and do everything possible to convince him to leave. And if she fails, she is prepared to share his death.

"I'm staying," she tells Tobo.

The Anasi man shrugs, sure the white mary is bewitched. Only a bewitched person would do something that invites death. "I will ask the gods to guard you," he says, making a sign of protection over her.

"Thank you for everything," she says to him. "Thank you for helping me when I was sick in the jungle. And for getting medicine for me." There are tears in her eyes.

Tobo purses his lips and shrugs.

Marika knows she'll miss Tobo. She never did understand him, and he certainly didn't seem to understand her. But in the usual aloofness of his expression, in the tough warrior's countenance, a softness now rests in his eyes. A subtle, wistful light. Tobo takes her hand and shakes it as he has seen the white people do. It's barely a handshake, more like a touching of fingers, but Marika knows it for what it is: a proof of friendship. Without another word, the Anasi man readjusts the straps of the *billum* bags around his shoulders and walks off toward the jungle.

Marika watches him go: the familiar black back, the swishing of *tanket* leaves over his buttocks. Tobo, her lifeline to the outside world, strides assertively into the jungle, machete in hand, Newlove and his assistants jogging behind. In mere seconds the jungle swallows them.

CHAPTER FIFTEEN

It's been barely a day since Tobo left.
Marika walks through the village toward the cool
waters of the river, wondering if she should have
gone with him, or if she could have ever made it
back to civilization. She doesn't know why Lewis
came to Walwasi, nor why he stays, but she understands that here, at least, is a place that demands
nothing from a person.

It must seem like a blessing until the malaria
gets you. Or the dysentery. Or something worse.

She feels the scratchy fibers of Tobo's mourning necklace against her neck—she forgot all
about that little piece of wood. Apparently Tobo
forgot about it too, leaving her with his sister's
soul. Well, she intends to fulfill her part of the bargain: she'll wear the necklace until it falls off and
the spirit passes on.

Marika sees Lina's mother sitting beneath a
hut and cradling a piglet in her arms, the animal
suckling from the woman's breast.

"Marika!" the woman yells. "Hello-how-are-
you!"

Marika takes a moment to digest the sight
before her. This world—Lewis's world—constantly
bewilders her.

Lina, on her way back from the taro fields, sees
Marika and comes running over.

"Where are you going?" she asks.

"To the river."

"Can I come?"

Marika nods, and the girl follows alongside her, carrying on her back a *billum* bag loaded with large white taro tubers. When they reach the rushing waters, they sit down together, and Lina dumps her load onto the ground. Together, they wash them.

"Do you remember when Lew—Mr. Parker first came here?" Marika asks Lina as she works.

"Yes, I remember. He looked sick."

"He was sick?"

Lina gets up and pretends to drag a leg. "Like this."

"Was he injured?"

She shakes her head, not understanding the word.

"Did he fall down? Get hurt?"

"I don't know. Maybe."

She tells Marika that she was frightened of Lewis at first, like many of the people in the village who had never seen a white man. But her great-grandmother Batu assured everyone that Lewis was a good man, even though he came to Walwasi on a yellow day. Because Batu was—and still is—the oldest person in the village, everyone trusted her wisdom.

"What's a 'yellow day'?" Marika asks her.

Lina looks up at the sky. Once, she explains, or maybe twice a year, they have a yellow day. The sky, the trees, the jungle—everything—turns yellow. Then a big storm comes. It rains as if to drown the world. This happens, Lina insists, because people make the world angry by not respecting it, so it punishes everyone. No one can go out in the rain on one of these days because it can kill a person. The Magic Fire Spirits make the rain, and it's poisonous. But when the rain stops, the entire village rejoices. They gather up a week's worth of food and put it in the river, offering thanks for being allowed to live.

Lina fingers the cross around her neck. "But Mista Parker was here on a yellow day. He walked in the rain, and he was not poisoned. Many people think he can't be touched by bad things. They think he is a good luck spirit."

Marika considers the irony of what Lina just said. "Do *you* think he's good luck?" she asks.

"Yes. It is true. When he came, my little brother was very sick. But Mista Parker healed him."

Marika helps Lina chop up the taro with a pig bone knife. The starchy roots slip constantly from her fingers, and she's so busy trying to steady them that she doesn't notice Lewis walking to his breadfruit tree until he sits beneath it, several yards away. Marika hasn't seen him since the day he gave her the malaria medicine, and his sudden appearance causes her to catch her breath.

"Look," she says to Lina, pointing.

Lina peers over her shoulder and sees Lewis. "Mista Parker is back." Her face lights up. "Hello, Mista Parker!" she yells. "How are you?"

He eyes them both.

"Do you like him?" Marika asks her in a whisper.

Lina looks shyly at Lewis and smiles. "Yes. I went to Mista Parker's hut every day, and he teach me English and a little Pidgin. He also teach Pidgin to other children in the village. But he do not teach now. He do not talk to people now. I think his spirit is sick."

Marika watches Lewis working diligently on his wooden box, a spread of carving tools on the ground beside him.

"Are you ever scared of him?" she asks Lina.

"Scared? No! He is a good man."

Lewis runs the back of his hand across his brow. As if feeling Marika's stare, he glances over at her. She doesn't look away, and there must be a certain solicitude in her expression, because Lewis seems to freeze up, on the verge of speaking. At last he turns back to his work.

Lina makes a noise under her breath. "Look!" she whispers to Marika. "Now, I am sure."

"Sure about what?"

Lina speaks so softly that Marika can barely hear. "He is scared of *you!*" Her finger pokes Marika's chest.

✥

Marika leaves Lina at the river. As she walks through the village toward Lewis's hut, she notices several men following her. They stay several yards behind her, in a single group, whispering. When one of the men calls out to her, Marika stops, frightened, and glances back at him. The man points furiously at the piece of canvas she wears around her waist, yelling in Walwasi. Marika looks down. She scans her clothes, trying to discern what the problem is.

Seeing nothing, she starts walking again, but more quickly. The man continues yelling at her loudly, incessantly. The faster she strides toward Lewis's hut, the faster the men come after her—but always with that cautious distance between them, as if they were scared of her. When their yells get especially vehement, Marika stops again and faces them. Soon, more people come down from their huts to join the men and stare at her. Marika looks around the village for a familiar face—Lina, perhaps, or Batu. Or even Lewis, returning from his breadfruit tree. Someone who could explain to her what she's done wrong.

But she recognizes no one.

Some women scold her now, and they point to the canvas around her waist—to the back of it. Marika shakes her head helplessly, not understanding. At last, she looks over her hip and pulls the material into view, seeing that it has blood on it. Her blood. She's having her period, finally, after assuming her sick, tired body was too worn out to function properly.

The women cluck their tongues in alarm.

"Go to the *meri haus!*" one woman tells her in crude Pidgin. "Hurry!"

Marika knows the words literally mean "mary house"—woman's house—but she doesn't know what it is, or where to go. A couple of women come forward to show her the way, escorting her toward a raised platform of palm bark planks, built in isolation from the rest of the village. It hasn't any walls and just a simple thatch roof, the jungle imposing from all sides. It looks like no one has maintained the building for years, vines climbing up the wooden frame, tree limbs reaching within. A large wooden bowl full of fetid water sits in a corner—for cleaning and, quite probably, for drinking. At the far end, just beyond the platform, lies a pile of raw sewage, its contents baking in the sun. The entire structure, crawling with insects and flies, reeks so strongly of human waste that Marika gags.

It is here where the women will leave her, as if to punish her for the crime of being female. The crime of having the power to create life, to give birth. The women wait until Marika climbs dutifully onto the platform before they return to the village.

Another couple of women are already there. They squat in a corner and observe Marika fearfully, winding pieces of bark into cord for *billum* bags. Marika tries to speak to them in Pidgin, to ask why menstruating women are isolated like this, but the women shake their heads, knowing only Walwasi. It isn't long before the heat and stench of the hut become more than Marika is willing to tolerate, and she climbs down from the platform to sneak back to the river, hoping Lina will be around to explain things and to help.

She purposely takes a path that cuts through the jungle, away from the village. Great trees block out the sun and give her a rare feeling of privacy in a world in which she almost never goes unnoticed. When the muddy path finally emerges at the river, she sees Lewis's breadfruit tree in the distance, but he's no longer beneath it. She searches up and down the shore but doesn't see Lina, either.

Marika sits down in the cool waters to wash herself and her clothing, wondering what she'll do. Maybe, if she can get to Lewis's hut undetected, she won't have to go back to the mary house. His hut is on the opposite end of the village, though, and she doesn't know how she could reach it without being discovered.

As she pulls herself out of the water, a woman sees her from a distance and calls out. Marika sprints back up the path toward the mary house, only to be cut off by the same group of men who stopped her in the village. They look angrier now and speak sharply to her, making bizarre signs of protection with their hands. Marika is relieved, at least, to see Lina among them. The girl steps forward, out of breath from having been summoned from the taro fields.

"Missus Marika," she says, her face grave, "did you walk through the village during your blood time?"

"Why?" Marika asks. "Is that bad?"

Lina looks especially distressed now. "Woman blood make men sick! Don't you know this?"

Marika rolls her eyes. She never learned that in her sex education class.

"They think you want to poison them," Lina says. "One man say he catch no animals because you have blood today. You must go back to the woman house. You can't leave it."

Marika realizes there's no way to reason with anyone on this subject. She tells Lina that the woman's house, entirely unprotected from mosquitoes, could make her get malaria again. And worse: there's nothing to eat or drink.

"I'll bring you food and water," Lina says. "Don't worry."

She takes Marika by the arm.

"How long do I have to stay there?" Marika asks.

"For eight or ten days."

"*Eight to ten days?*"

"The chief, he decide when you are safe. Then you go back to the village."

Marika stares at the crowd of men, who watch her from a safe distance away. Some of them look at her accusatorily, and for a split second she wants to charge them, make them run in fear.

Instead, she submits—for now. She lets Lina escort her back to the mary house. When they get there, a woman from the village uses bark cord to tie Marika's wrist to a pole of the hut. It's humiliating, but Marika knows she won't spend a week in the place. Not even a day. She won't become food for mosquitoes, getting sick with malaria again, or—she looks at the sewage pit—worse.

As soon as Marika is left alone, she works for several minutes to undo the cord around her wrist. The women inside the hut cluck their tongues in disapproval, but Marika ignores them completely. Freeing herself, she decides she'll wait till dusk for her escape. She lies down, watching the sun set behind the mountains. As the highest yam fields become burnished with departing light, she knows the night has begun its descent over the valley.

When darkness has taken over completely, Marika sits up. Mosquitoes cover her body, hardly discouraged by the weak smoke of a palm leaf fire beneath the hut. She slaps at them and stands. Cautiously, she climbs down from the platform, the other women offering a chorus of whispered protests. Creeping to the edge of the nearby jungle, she waits, trying to discern human sounds from those of the night creatures. When she doesn't hear anything, she sprints from shadow to shadow along the outskirts of the village. Only a dog notices her as she finally reaches the opposite end of Walwasi and climbs up the notched log ladder of Lewis's hut.

Lewis is sitting by his fire when she enters, and as the palm bark floor creaks beneath her steps, he looks up in a panic. He sees that it's her—and must know it—yet he jumps back and scrambles to the far side of the hut. Marika stands before him, anxious, unmoving, not knowing what she's done.

Lewis huddles in the shadows, his eyes terrified and searching. His chest heaves. His breaths strain and grasp for air.

"I didn't mean to startle you," she says at last.

Her voice might have broken a magic spell. Lewis stares at her, and his body relaxes. After a long moment, the fear in his eyes vanishes. He presses himself against the hut's wall and steadies his breathing.

"It's you," he says. "I wasn't expecting you."

"I was put in the woman's hut," she explains.

He evaluates her words, taking long, deep breaths. "You need to go back there," he says at last.

She hazards a few more steps into the hut. "It's awful there. I don't want to go back."

"What? Do you think you're in the American embassy now? It's their village, not mine. They make the rules."

"Well, this rule about women—this whole mary house thing—is ridiculous."

"Not to them." Lewis's eyes evaluate her in silence, his breathing calming. "They take it very seriously. They think even a single drop of menstrual blood can kill a man. In fact, if they saw you here with me now, they'd view it as attempted murder."

"Well, that's crazy," she says, letting loose a nervous smile.

"Not to them, it's not."

Lewis limps back to the fire. He tosses another log into the flames, sparks shooting into the air and nearly reaching her across the room.

"Well, at least get away from the goddamn door," he says. "People could see you."

She walks tentatively forward and kneels before his fire. He sits opposite her, vigorously massaging his temples. Overhead, the feverish sound of rats climbing across the thatch roof breaks the silence between them. Lewis picks up a stick and flings it above him, sending the animals fleeing.

"This isn't the American embassy," he says again, more to himself. "There's no safety here. There are absolutely no guarantees. *None.*"

He sits back, taking off his glasses. He looks at her now, truly sees her for the first time since she came tonight, and he can't stop shaking his head.

"You have to go back there," he says. "If you don't, they'll get suspicious. They'll think you're trying to poison their food or something. They have really strict taboos about menstruating women. You don't want them to think you're a witch—"

"Well, maybe I am a witch," Marika says defiantly.

She sits with her arms crossed, her expression undaunted. There is, Lewis sees, a kind of power and attraction about her that he hadn't been willing to notice before. He used to be drawn to strong women like her. He enjoyed the way they always stood up to him, never offering him easy smiles. Strong women were enigmas, though. Beneath their shows of toughness, they usually had the softest cores, as if all their strength were a grand charade.

It is the story of everyone, Lewis supposes. The grand charade. No one is ever as strong as they appear. Even the toughest men can be broken down to nothing, can be made to cry and piss themselves.

"Go back to the hut," Lewis says to her. "I'll make sure you get food." He leans forward impatiently, trying to hand her some cassowary meat, but she won't take it.

"I want to stay."

"Go back! If you're not there tomorrow, there'll be hell to pay. Trust me on this one." Lewis sighs in frustration. "I heard your guide, What's-His-Name, left the village yesterday."

"Tobo."

"Yeah. Well, you should have gone with him."

"I wasn't ready yet."

"Well, why the hell not?"

She doesn't say anything.

"You know, it's suicide for you to stay here," he says. "You're going to get malaria again. That's inevitable. And probably dysentery, too. And when that happens, I can guarantee that vampire, Newlove, won't be around again to give you any more medicine."

"Does that mean it's suicide for *you* to be here, too?" she asks.

Lewis looks down at the cassowary meat in his hand, squeezing it hard between his fingers. "Look—I don't want your death on my hands. I didn't ask for that. You should have gone with your guide." He glares at her.

She looks away, wiping sweat from her face and listening to the night insects calling to each other. He's probably right. She should have gone with Tobo. But it's too late now.

"So what was your plan supposed to be?" Lewis asks. "You were going to come here and find me and do what?"

Marika realizes that she doesn't have an answer for him. "I don't know," she says finally.

"Bullshit!" he declares. "I'm sure you were all ready to run home with your scoop about me and sell it to *People* magazine."

She fervently shakes her head.

"I can see the headline now: 'Robert Lewis—found alive in New Guinea.' Breaking news on CNN."

"No," she says. "When I left Boston . . . I didn't really think I'd find you alive."

"Well, surprise, surprise," he says.

"I never imagined this sort of outcome, not even when I had reason to, back in Krit village. I still"—she looks at the hut around her—"I still have trouble believing it. I didn't know if I'd ever make it here."

"So you're trying to tell me you had no plan?"

She nervously smoothes her hair behind her ears. "Not really. I didn't think I'd get here." She laughs awkwardly. "Or if I *did* get here, I didn't think I'd actually find you."

Lewis's eyes are trained on her. Such intelligent, astute eyes. "Who sent you here? A magazine?"

"No. No one."

"Was it your book editor?"

"*No.*" She hears frustration in her voice. "I came on my own."

"All on your own?"

"Yeah." She looks at him warily, fearing what he might ask her next.

"So no one knows you came here, looking for me?"

Marika pauses. Thinks of Seb.

"No one knows," she lies.

He looks relieved. "So you're the only one who thought I might be alive?"

"As far as I know."

He chucks the meat into the fire. "And now you've got one hell of a scoop to take home with you, don't you? And yet, you didn't leave with What's-His-Name."

Marika doesn't say anything.

Lewis fixes his eyes on her. "Tell me what it is you *want*." He said it to her like a plea. "Why are you still here?"

She smoothes back her hair again, not answering.

"Tell me what you want!"

Marika can see his eyes filling with fury, and he looks ready to jump to his feet. She notices the size of him, the strength, even with his apparent injuries. He's well over six feet tall, a formidable man.

She moves away from the fire, hugging her legs against her.

"Is someone else going to be coming here?" Lewis demands. "Are you waiting for someone?"

"No," she says.

"Then why didn't you leave with your guide? Or am I supposed to be some sort of freak show for you? For your little book?"

"*No.*"

"Then tell me why you're still here!" He stands up, towering over her. Eyes ablaze, he points at her. "Goddamn it, you're going to tell me why!"

"Because I didn't want to leave you here," she whispers, meeting his gaze.

He stares at her, his face twitching. The rage vanishes from his eyes, and he sinks back to the floor, furiously rubbing his temples.

"Well, I'm not going anywhere," he mumbles.

"You did so much good. People need you—"

"Bullshit!" he yells, with such unexpected violence that she finds herself backing away from him.

She waits until her heartbeat calms, until she can get the courage to speak to him again. "Do you actually . . . like it here?" she whispers.

Lewis watches a blue flame curl around one of the logs. Just when she thinks he isn't going to answer her, he says, "It suffices."

"But why do you stay?"

He massages his knee, wincing. "'For with much wisdom comes much sorrow; the more knowledge, the more grief.' That's from Ecclesiastes. I can quote the Bible like the best Bible-thumper there is. Pop used to pay me a dime for every Bible verse I memorized—do you know that? Did you put that in your book?"

Marika shakes her head, embarrassed. "No."

"Well, my sister probably forgot to tell you."

"You know, she misses you," Marika says.

"Is that right?"

"A lot of people miss you."

"Well, Little Girl, people are always missing somebody, aren't they?" He gazes sternly at her. "You ever lost anyone?"

Marika says nothing.

"Probably all you know about loss," Lewis spits out, "is some boyfriend dumping you to go fuck someone else."

"Actually," she says, "I lost my father."

Lewis seems to consider her anew.

"He was shot," she says coolly. "He was a dissident writer in Czechoslovakia, and he spied against the Communists. My mother . . ." Marika studies her fingers. "My mother never got over it."

Lewis watches her more closely, more intensely. He seems on the verge of speaking when a rat sprints across the room. Cursing, he throws a stick after it.

When his eyes fall on Marika again, he motions to a wooden

bowl near his feet full of baked yams. "Come get something," he says. "Eat."

She takes a wary look at him before getting up and walking around the fire. As she reaches for the bowl, Lewis notices her hand shaking. It always used to surprise him whenever he scared women—he'd never laid a hand on a woman in his life. Never would. He watches Marika. Ponders her as she reaches within inches of his leg to take the bowl.

When she sits down again, he says, "Tell me about your father."

"My father?"

"I want to hear about him." Lewis picks up his wooden box and selects a knife for carving. Putting his glasses back on, he looks at her. "Go on. It'll be good for me. It'll keep away my thoughts."

"You want me to just—"

"*Talk,* for chrissakes. Tell me about your father." He waves his knife at her. "Go on."

But for a long moment, Marika can only look at him. When she was younger—and going to college to study journalism—she used to imagine a time like this: meeting Robert Lewis and having the chance to tell him about her life. It had just been a silly, girlish fantasy. Marika watches Lewis now as he carefully scrapes away at his box. He's not the same man of her imaginings. Not the elated journalist receiving his Pulitzer. Not the vociferous debater on TV news shows. She wonders if he knows—in that smart, uncanny way of his—that she once had a picture of him on the wall beside her bed. She'd wanted to be just like him, have his kind of life.

And then she did.

Lewis glances up at her impatiently, pushing his glasses higher on his nose. "Well, go on. Talk."

She tells Lewis what little she knows about her father, returning in memory to the Prague of her childhood—the Charles

Bridge, the black swans. That golden city of Baroque spires, frozen by Communist rule. She describes her father, a writer and idealist who would try to make a difference in the world, and who would fail. Who would give up his life.

The words come out easily, and it never occurred to Marika until now that she might have felt sorry for herself for not having a father. That she might have missed having that kind of love and stability in her life. It is, perhaps, another of those things that Seb had been talking about—another of the things she always pushed away, never allowing herself to grieve. She continues her story to its end, expecting no sympathy from Lewis. No acknowledgment. No reaction. She tells him simply because she can, because he asked. And how few people have ever asked.

At some point—she can't recall when—Lewis must have put down his carving work. Now he listens silently, his eyes on her. Unlike Seb, he makes no interruptions. There is nothing she needs to clarify for him. He has no questions or remarks. Lewis just watches her vigilantly, and, once or twice—when she tells him what happened to her mother—she sees his lips mouthing their unintelligible verse.

When she's finally done, she clears her throat, retreating into silence.

Lewis doesn't move. He has the same intense expression on his face that used to be his trademark. "'For with much wisdom, comes much sorrow,'" he says slowly, enunciating each word. "'The more knowledge, the more grief.'"

Lewis clicks his tongue, and his cat leaves the mosquito net, trotting across the room and sitting in his lap. She watches as his hand strokes the soft fur ever so gently. Outside, the sounds of night insects drone loudly.

"It's time you went back to that pleasant mary house," he says, not looking up.

"I can't stay here?"

"Look, don't be stubborn about this, all right? You have to

go back." His Missouri drawl suddenly sounds more prominent. "Take some food and deal with it. That's an order. You'll piss everyone off if you don't."

When she doesn't move, he looks up at her.

"Hello!"

She gets up. "Okay," she says. "Fine."

"And grab some meat before you go. You need protein if you want to keep getting better. That's *if* you want to get better." His eyes meet hers.

She leans toward the fire to take some meat. The tough cassowary has trouble coming off the bone, and as she twists and tears at it, she glances at Lewis. He seems to have dismissed her and is back to carving his box, his hair shading his face.

But as she turns to leave the hut, he calls out to her.

"If you do find yourself coming back here in the days ahead," he says, his voice softer, kinder, "don't come so early, for chrissakes. You have to be careful, you know. Someone might see you."

Marika wonders when she'll be allowed to return to the village. She's stayed in the women's hut for five days now, finding it next to impossible to get back to Lewis's hut—there have been too many people wandering around after dark. And now, though her period is over, she can't return to the village until the chief decides she's "safe." She remembers Lina saying that it's usually eight to ten days before that permission is granted, and Marika's impatience and irritation have been growing. A confinement of eight to ten days is longer than she's able to stand in such a stinking, miserable place.

The other women largely ignore Marika, talking and passing their time making *billum* bags—the only permitted activities, as any sort of cooking or farming isn't permitted for fear they'll poison the men's food. No one can leave the hut, as walking around the village would create hazardous "poison trails" that men could pass through, and which a witch doctor would then have to remove with complicated spells. Marika spends her days napping or lying listlessly in the heat, gazing into the nearby jungle. Often, her thoughts try to draw her back to the past. To Seb. To what they had together. She has to be like a gatekeeper before the door of her mind, turning away any memories that might create anguish, regret. At least when she was sick and injured, the pain in her body kept her from thinking about anything else.

She does let herself think about Lewis, though. She keeps wondering what made him fake his death and exile himself in such a place. Why not just go all the way and kill himself for real? He'd never been scared of death, had spent his life confronting its worst manifestations. Most likely—though Marika doesn't like to admit it—Lewis has lost his mind. But not completely. Or, at least, not without the hope of recovery. Back in Boston when she was working on her book, she'd watched all the old TV footage of Lewis. He'd never been especially cordial. He was never known for being diplomatic or well behaved. Still, he'd been a presence. He'd claimed a place in the world.

Now, Lewis exists as a phantom. A mere shadow or suggestion of his former self. When Marika is with him, she always finds herself searching for that other self, as if missing someone she never knew.

Marika watches a half moon rise over the village, drawing long shadows from the huts. She slaps at mosquitoes, anticipating another evening of discomfort and little sleep—unless she can sneak back to Lewis's hut. It won't be easy to get there undetected, though. She'll have to stay up late until the very last voices in Walwasi fall silent.

Overhead, the constellations make slow progress across the night sky. Marika watches, waits. As the hours pass, the noises in the village don't seem to be lessening. Finally, desperate for the comfort of Lewis's fire—for him, she realizes—she steps lightly across the palm bark floor, trying not to wake the women sleeping at the other end of the hut. Climbing carefully down the ladder, Marika sneaks into the shadows. She might be playing a childhood game of tag, only with higher stakes, as she creeps from bush to bush, listening and searching the darkness for sight of someone. As Lewis's hut appears in the distance, she sprints through the village to reach it. A dog hears and lets out raucous barking, but by the time it starts to come after her, she's already climbing up the notched log ladder into the hut.

Lewis, lying on his pallet behind the mosquito net, appears to be asleep. His fire is burning so brightly that the entire hut is lit up, the flame's shadows flickering against the walls.

Marika walks in slowly, uncertainly.

"You're back," Lewis says from across the room.

She stops. Looks at him. "I didn't think you were up."

"I can't sleep." He runs his finger along the inside of the net, watching the material quiver.

"That woman's house is pretty awful," she says. "I couldn't get any sleep."

He doesn't respond, his finger still traveling along the inside of the net. "Have you eaten?" he says at last.

"No. Not recently."

"There's some roasted pigeon there, if the cat hasn't taken it all. It's actually pretty good."

"Thanks."

She sits down by the hot fire, taking off Lewis's long-sleeved shirt. She sees the meat in a wooden bowl and picks up a drumstick, glancing at him. He lies inside the mosquito net, his back to her. She hears him talking, very softly. It almost sounds like poetry, lost between breaths.

Marika eats the pigeon meat greedily, listening to Lewis, trying to make out the words. His orange cat squeezes between the folds of the mosquito net and runs to her side, purring intensely.

"Did you bring the cat in?" she asks him.

Lewis sits up, looking over his shoulder at her. "What's that?"

"Your cat," she says, "did you bring him to this village?"

"One of my guides did. He found him in Wewak, as a kitten, and put him in his backpack. It was his idea of a joke. We didn't expect him to make it here."

"What's his name?"

"He doesn't have one."

Lewis swings his legs around and climbs out of the mosquito net. He limps across the hut to pick up a bucket of water, bringing it back to his bed and putting it on the floor beside his mattress.

"Is that where you first entered Papua New Guinea, in Wewak?" she asks him.

Lewis stops and fixes his eyes on her.

"You must have traveled straight from Malaysia to New Guinea," she adds. "Right?"

It makes sense to her. Wewak, a city on PNG's northern coast, would be closest to Malaysia, where he staged his death.

Lewis doesn't say anything. He stands over the fire, stoking it until it's blazing even brighter.

"Did you go by boat?" she asks him.

He puts on his glasses and rubs his beard, staring at her. "Why do you want to know?"

"Just curious."

"Uh-huh. Curious."

"So was it by boat?"

Lewis considers her sternly. "I put that water in there in case you feel like having a wash," he says, motioning to the bucket inside his mosquito net. "You can go in there for privacy."

"Now?"

"Here"—he tosses her a torn T-shirt—"you can use this as a towel. It's pretty clean."

"Right now?"

"Or you can wait till Christmas, if you want." He sits down

and clicks his tongue, the cat leaving her side and trotting over to him, climbing into his lap.

She listens to the crackle of the fire. Does she want a "wash"? She's been in the woman's house for days, unable to bathe. She looks at Lewis, but he already seems to have forgotten her and is beginning his carving. She gets up and goes to the mosquito net, entering the thin muslin. She picks up the wooden cup in the bucket and kneels down, running cool water over her hair and neck. It feels good. Too good. She glances at Lewis now, but he's turned away from her, his lips mouthing that same unintelligible verse.

She pulls off her tank top and puts it aside. Pouring water over her body, she watches it fall to the palm bark floor and drip through the cracks to the ground below. She trickles more onto her shoulders, feeling it rolling down her breasts to her feet. She takes another look at Lewis, seeing that he's shifted away from her. The fire's shadows slice across his shoulder, across his long, tied-back hair. He's wearing a torn black T-shirt and olive army fatigue pants, and the skin of his strong arms reveals a crisscrossing of pale pink scars, shiny in the light.

Marika takes off the piece of canvas knotted around her waist and stands above the bucket. As she washes her legs, her foot slips on the slick floor, and she falls to a knee, cursing. Lewis glances over, and she quickly pulls herself up. She wipes water from her face with the back of her hand, dipping the cup back into the bucket. It's the first time in days that she's had any relief from the heat, and she shuts her eyes, savoring the coolness of the water as it runs over her face and body. But as she opens her eyes, she catches sight of Lewis. He's watching her, is looking straight at her. He has his glasses off and holds them in his hands.

"Just tell me to stop looking," he says. "One word."

"I . . ." But she can't tell him to stop. This is Robert Lewis. And Robert Lewis is looking at her.

He stares at her through the gauze of the netting. Her thighs.

The smooth rise of her breasts. He just wants to touch her. It's been years since he's touched a woman.

"I used to picture someone like you appearing here somehow," he says.

She stares back at him, unable to speak. His eyes drink her in slowly. She watches as they run up her legs, linger on her breasts.

At last, he sighs and looks down. "I'm sorry. I'm sure I've offended you."

She picks up her clothes and puts them on. Covering herself with Lewis's long-sleeved shirt, she leaves the mosquito net.

Lewis sighs again. "It's just . . . it's been a while." He puts another log into the flames. "Will you forgive an old man?"

"You're not that old," she says.

"Old enough."

"Fifty-four," she states, "as of June tenth of last year."

He looks at her and lets loose a laugh. It's the first time she's seen him smile, however briefly, and it fills her with a vague sense of hope. With Lewis, she realizes, she is always walking a tightrope of fear—and longing. A longing to connect with him, somehow, as if she were still that teenage girl staring at his picture beside her bed.

She takes a seat by the fire, and Lewis drops taro tubers into the cinders.

"So did you leave someone behind?" he asks. "A husband or boyfriend?"

"Well, I had a boyfriend. But we broke up."

Lewis nods. She notices that he's purposely averting his eyes from her now.

"What was his name?"

"His name? Seb." It seems odd to her, uncouth, to mention Seb's name. She wonders what he's doing right now, more than four months after she left him. Probably working in his internship on the other side of the world, far from the heat and mosquitoes and acrid smoke of cooking fires.

"How about you?" she asks Lewis. "Did you leave a girlfriend or someone behind?"

"Me? You already know everything about me."

"Not everything," she says.

He uses a stick to push one of the tubers farther into the flames. "No. I didn't leave anyone behind—not at that time."

"You mean, the time when you—"

Lewis looks up at her. "That's right." His eyes are fixed on hers. "When I left everything."

"Your last assignment was in East Timor, right?"

He freezes. She sees she's taken him by surprise.

"That's what your sister told me," Marika says. "That before you went to Malaysia, you were on assignment in East Timor."

"Yeah," he says. "I was there. But it wasn't an official assignment."

"You never did write about it, huh? I never saw an article."

"No." His eyes won't leave hers. "I never wrote about it."

"Why not?"

"Because I couldn't write anymore." His stare seems to be challenging her.

"Why? What happened?"

"What happened?" He looks at the rafters of the hut, his eyes following the flickering shadows of the fire.

"*Did* something happen?" she asks.

Lewis smoothes a hand over his face. Over and over, his fingers follow the curve of his brow, the cut of his chin. "You have this way about you, don't you?" he says, smiling wryly. "You can get people to tell you things. But you don't want to know this story, Little Girl." His eyes lock on hers. "Not this story."

"I do want to know."

"You'll regret it." His voice is low. "It will sully your mind."

"I want to know," she says.

"And I can guarantee you won't like me much after I tell you—that is, if you don't already despise me."

"I want to know."

Lewis shuts his eyes, collecting his thoughts. "She wants to know," he whispers. "All right, then." He looks at her again. "I'll tell you a story."

Lewis had wanted to write about the resurrection of East Timor. It was a tiny island country most Americans had never heard of. A place illegally invaded in 1976 by the Indonesian military, who launched a campaign of genocide that left one-third of the population dead by the time they pulled out in 1999. East Timor could hold its rightful place with the Rwandas and Bosnias of the world, its people subjected to violence and devastation so vast, and committed with such impunity, that it taxed one's capacity to believe.

Lewis arrived in the capital, Dili, in September 1999, right after the country had received official independence from the Indonesians. The fleeing Indonesian army had plundered the city as a final way of punishing the East Timorese for their years of defiance. Homes were set ablaze. Garbage and corpses littered the streets. Dili was left with no rule of law or protection. UN-appointed British and Australian troops had been brought in to guard key areas like the airport, but most of the city remained barren and hostile, patrolled by roving gangs of pro-Indonesian and pro–East Timorese forces, battling each other. Lewis took to the streets each day beneath the city's gigantic statue of Jesus, its arms outspread in supplication. He wandered through gutted, bullet-pocked neighborhoods, finding witnesses, listening to accounts of violence.

Lewis couldn't have done his reporting if it weren't for his good friend Manuel da Silva, a local man whom he'd met during an earlier trip to East Timor. Manuel lived with his daughter, Anamaria, in a tiny fishing community outside of Dili. It was one of the safer places in the country for Lewis to stay and make contacts, and it was there where Manuel introduced him to Paulo Ozorio, a member of Falintil, the East Timorese resistance army. Paulo had information about a massacre that had just occurred in Becora, a hamlet outside of Dili. Indonesian atrocities were as commonplace as they were brutal, but here was a report so gruesome that it overshadowed all others: at least thirty women and girls had been rounded up, gang-raped, and hung on meat hooks, their limbs hacked off while they were still alive. The bodies, according to Paulo's report, had been dumped in a nearby ditch, and Paulo urged Lewis to go there and document it.

Lewis mobilized instantly. Manuel urged him to be careful, to try to keep a low profile. Though it was dangerous to travel outside of Dili, the hundreds of newly arrived Australian soldiers gave Lewis a greater sense of security. A local man, Jorge, was willing to drive him to Becora on the back of his motorbike, and within an hour they left.

Lewis made it to Becora without incident, and found the bodies. The report from Paulo had, if anything, been an understatement. The victims were mostly girls, forty-two in all. They had obviously been beaten, raped, mutilated in the most ingenious ways. Lewis thought he'd seen everything already—in places like Liberia, Chechnya, Congo—but there in Becora was something beyond comprehension or description. Something that was wholly unspeakable.

Lewis documented it. He took photos. He jotted down quotes from grieving parents and listened to descriptions from locals. Armed with ample evidence, he got back on the motorbike with Jorge, and they sped to Dili so he could write up his report at the UN headquarters and get it to media outlets in New York.

They were nearly to Dili when five men, armed with rifles and wearing Indonesian army uniforms, appeared in the road. Jorge stopped immediately, but as he struggled to turn the bike around, he was shot in the head. Another bullet tore through

Lewis's calf, immobilizing him so he couldn't run. As he tried to limp into the nearby bushes, the soldiers caught up with him and pressed their rifle barrels against his head. Lewis thought they would kill him right there—assumed it and waited for it—but instead, they threw him into the back of a truck and drove him to some kind of detention center.

Soldiers put him into a hot, windowless cell, its cement walls smeared with the blood and excrement of previous prisoners. They stripped him naked, tying his legs behind him, ankles to wrists, and putting a hood over his head. They left him like that for an entire day, without food or water, his back screaming in pain. Every hour or two someone would come in to beat him, telling him in minute detail what they planned to do to him. When they finally untied him, he couldn't walk. One of his shoulders had dislocated, and his legs collapsed beneath him.

They dragged him to an interrogation room—a room with chipped, sea-foam green walls, empty save for a chair, a car battery, and a metal bed frame to which they tied him with nylon ropes. They wanted to know who in the Falintil resistance army had told him about the massacre. When he wouldn't answer, they took off the hood so he could see where they were going to attach the wires. They put them around his testicles. Up his rectum. Into his mouth. "We're going to make you impotent," they told him. The same grim-faced man always operated the generator, and Lewis could tell how bad it would be by how hard his little hands cranked the handle. The pain—how to describe it? Like having an electric drill driven into his flesh. It was excruciating, mind-altering pain that tore cries and screams from his throat and drove him into convulsions. If he was lucky he would faint, but he would always wake up minutes later, covered with his own shit and piss.

It went on like this for days. Without respite. He shouldn't have lived, but they were masters at their work, knowing how to hold a person on the very edge of death while inflicting maximum pain. Part of their skill lay in keeping him in constant suspense; he never knew when they were coming for him. He'd have a few hours' rest in his cell before being dragged back to the interrogation room and tied to the bed frame again. Soon, they did more to him. They tied him upside down and poured urine into his nostrils. They drove objects into his anus. They beat the soles of his feet with pipes. Who was his contact from the Falintil resistance? They covered his head with a bag dipped in gasoline. They cut his arms and legs. "Why do you want to die?" they'd ask him. "Tell us the name of the man." But what they didn't know was that Lewis didn't care if he died. He'd just huddle in that space in his mind where they couldn't reach him. That space where he'd stored all the grief for his son. Daniel's spirit would find him there, and hold him, and guide him through the pain.

Soon, though, Daniel stopped coming. Lewis was losing control over himself, his body pissing itself at the mere sound of someone approaching his cell. Voices in his head shouted and accosted him, reminding him that human beings are inherently cruel—that he needed to *know* this finally and accept it. They pointed out how his son had died, forcing him to see the body again. They showed him a gruesome slideshow of all the horror he'd seen in the world—all the torture, rape, mutilation, destruction. They wouldn't give him any peace until he accepted what they were teaching, acknowledged its truth. At the same time, the men kept coming for him, dragging him to the room with the chipped green walls, tying him to the bed frame, asking him for the name of his Falintil contact. But to tell them about Paulo would have meant arrest and death for the man and his family. Lying was Lewis's only hope. He didn't expect to live, but at least Paulo wouldn't die.

Finally, though, it all became too much. They broke him, and he gave them a name—a false one. But they knew he'd lied. They said they'd found out the real name of his contact and were just waiting for him to reveal it. They wanted to hear him say it, or there would be severe consequences. Which is when Manuel da Silva's eleven-year-old girl was brought in. Little Anamaria. They pulled the hood off Lewis's head so he could see what they'd already done to her. Her eyes were nearly swollen shut. She was naked, her body covered with welts. Lewis could see from the blood and wounds on her legs—from the way she could hardly walk—that they had raped her brutally. When Anamaria saw Lewis, and recognized him, she cried and pleaded to him.

The interrogator asked Lewis again for the real name of the man he had spoken to. Who had given him the information about the massacre? When he wouldn't answer, they dragged Anamaria to the middle of the floor. Lewis saw in her eyes that part of her was dying. She made no movement now. She didn't cry out, even as a soldier took out his knife and cut out her tongue.

They would do more. They wanted Lewis to know that her ears were next. Her fingers. Her breasts.

"We will kill you both and dump you in the river, and no one will ever know," one of the soldiers said.

That was the moment. That was the end of the person Robert Lewis had once been. He gave them the name. Paulo Ozorio. It escaped from his lips without hesitation, and he was surprised by how easy it was to say. So incredibly easy, and he felt ashamed and foolish that he had waited so long and had gone through so much.

Of course they took their knives to Anamaria anyway. They carved her up and made him watch. She was nearly Lina's age. Only eleven.

A couple of hours later, they brought Paulo in. They did the same things to him that they'd done to Anamaria, leaving him to die on the floor. Lewis expected to be next. He longed for it, because he knew his life was over.

But the soldiers wanted to make an example of Lewis in order to punctuate their opposition to East Timor's independence.

They let him keep his life. Early the next morning, in the near darkness of dawn, they untied him and took him out of his cell, putting him in the back of a truck. They drove him to the outskirts of Dili and dumped him on the side of a road. A local farmer found him, and Lewis ended up at the UN compound, under the care of Australian army medics, unable to move or speak for days. Though his condition was eventually reported to the press, none of the doctors ever found out who he was. He hardly even recognized himself when he looked in a mirror, his face so swollen and bruised that he had become a ghostly looking stranger. He finally arranged to be airlifted to a hospital in Singapore for more intensive care. Though it was obvious to his new doctors what had happened to him, he wouldn't utter a word about who had done it, or where or why. It was too late for that. It didn't matter anymore.

"I shouldn't have lived," Lewis tells Marika, his body shaking. "I shouldn't have lived."

He clutches himself, his eyes reflecting the fire. As he told her his story—all the excruciating details—it might have happened to someone else. Or he might have been recounting the unremarkable events of a movie. His voice rigid, without affect. His body motionless, frozen in the memories. And never any tears. Lewis's pain wasn't his, but everyone's. The world's pain. The world's anguish. And he, just the messenger.

Marika watches the shadows from the fire leap about the walls of the hut. She becomes aware for the first time of the sound of rain outside. Mosquitoes assail her, and she slaps at them futilely. Sweat runs down her legs, her chest. She looks at Lewis, seeing that he's left her, his eyes gazing blankly ahead. She studies the palm bark walls that enclose them. She runs her eyes over the bags of taro, corn, and yams hanging from the rafters, away from the rats. Sees Lewis's drinking water sitting in the dented metal buckets. His straw pallet rests behind the muslin shroud of his bed. The blackness of night waits just outside the door, crouching, fitful to get at them. This is Lewis's world now. He traveled the earth, reporting, writing, revealing—and finally stopped. Here. To forget.

She wipes her forehead. The heat and sweat never end. There is no respite from anything.

"This one mantra kept playing in my mind when those men were doing those things to me," Lewis says. "*Om asatoma sad gamaya tamasoma jyothir gamaya.* It's what I heard the Nepalese butcher say before he'd sacrifice an animal, thinking it'd lessen his karma. You know what it means? 'Guide us from illusion to truth, from darkness to light.' *Om asatoma sad gamaya tamasoma jyothir gamaya.* I'd say it over and over again, through everything that was done to me."

Marika recognizes it as the odd verse Lewis often mumbles just under his breath.

"When I was with those men," he says, "I never knew what would happen next. Each hour, each minute—I never knew. They were experts. They could keep you suspended for hours—for days—in that spot right between life and death. All the things a person can be an expert at." Lewis shuts his eyes. "Then, I realized I had a habit of asking this one question all the time, wanting to know the answer. It just hit me suddenly."

"What question?" Marika speaks so quietly that she's afraid he doesn't hear.

Lewis's eyes glance toward the sound of her voice, his body rocking. "*The* question. The only one: Why won't someone, some*thing* strike those men down? They put wires between my teeth, they put them on my . . ." He draws his head to the side, biting his lip and throwing his glasses to the floor. His eyes fill with tears, but he won't let them fall.

She tries to speak. "Lewis" is all that comes out.

"I have no one," he says.

"Lewis—"

But he doesn't seem to know she's there anymore. He covers

his face and speaks to himself, his voice barely audible above the sound of the rain.

"No one," he keeps repeating, breathing hard.

Lewis lies down on the floor, pulling his knees in against him. Marika gets up. She reaches out her hand, putting it on his shoulder, but he lurches from her touch.

"No one," he says, covering his face with his arm, his chest heaving.

"Lewis," she whispers.

She wipes tears from her eyes with the sleeve of her shirt. Again, she reaches out a hand to touch him, and this time he allows it. Her fingers run over his back. Down his arm. As she strokes his hair from his face, Lewis's own hand takes hold of hers. She lies beside him, wrapping her arms around him. His body shakes against hers, his chest heaving.

She stays with him for what seems like hours, hearing the rain fall, listening to his breathing. When at last he shifts, she sees that he's looking straight at her. He studies the contour of her lips. The way her dark blue eyes gaze back at him with a kind of fearful longing. He holds his hand tentatively in the air, moving it toward her face. He keeps looking at her, prepared to pull back in an instant, but finally touches her cheek.

She stares into his eyes.

"Is this okay?" he whispers, glancing at her.

When she nods and lies back, his fingers travel slowly across her lips. He reaches down and fumbles with the buttons of her shirt, opening it. She drops her arms to her sides, and he raises her tank top over her breasts. For a long moment, he can only gaze at her. Hesitantly, he grazes his fingertips over her nipples, pressing his lips against them. He runs his hands down her waist, her thighs. He loosens her canvas sarong and takes in the sight of her.

But nothing, he laments to himself, his body not responding. *Nothing.*

She's breathing fast—she's scared—but she's not stopping him. He glides his hand over her stomach. Her hips. Sitting up, he tugs her sarong free from her body and tosses it aside. Glancing shyly at her, he gently opens her thighs. His fingers search between them, and he feels the softness, the warmth of her.

But she is trembling now, and he stops to look at her. "Don't worry," he says awkwardly, gesturing between his legs. "Nothing happens."

She doesn't know what to say. She watches his hands travel down her thighs again. He runs his fingers between them, feeling that she's wet now.

But nothing.

Sighing, Lewis sits back. His lets his hand linger on her breast, her heart racing beneath his fingers.

"Nothing happens," he whispers.

He leans over and picks up the piece of canvas, covering her with it like a blanket.

Marika can only watch him, still feeling his hands on her.

"It's time," he says, turning away. "You need to go back now."

CHAPTER SIXTEEN

Marika wakes to the sound of a drum beating solemnly. The late afternoon sun has already passed beyond the mountains to the west, and the village takes on a dim, sullen glow. She sits up in the mary house, looking at the women nearby, wondering how many more days she'll have to stay. It has been feeling like a prison sentence.

Dark clouds approach the valley, boding rain. As she watches them block out the sky, she thinks about Lewis again. She thinks about him incessantly since their previous night together, unable to forget what he told her. She still sees his anguished stares, feels his fingers on her body. She has so many questions for him now. For the first time since Tobo left, she doesn't regret staying behind in Walwasi.

The drumbeats become louder, more earnest. Marika hears a crowd gathering in the village, and she recalls the last time this happened—when the man covered in yellow paint was soon to be killed.

She turns to the other women, who are squatting near the back of the hut. "What's happening?" she asks them in Pidgin, pointing to the village.

They gaze back at her, fear in their eyes, and don't answer.

"*Ol wokim wanem?*" she repeats, as clearly as she can.

No one understands. Marika rises to get a better look, seeing a large crowd in the village's main square. Everyone in Walwasi seems to be there, including the chief, who stands on a log, shouting and gesticulating furiously. Lightning flashes over the valley, followed by the first rumbles of thunder. Marika pulls Lewis's shirt tightly around her. She would go to him now, if she could. If he would have her.

Marika sees Lina running over. The girl looks panicked and arrives out of breath. She stares at Marika, fingering her silver cross and keeping a distance between herself and the hut.

"What's going on?" Marika asks her.

Lina takes a moment to catch her breath. "They say you left here last night. A man saw you."

Fear slices through Marika.

"That man who saw you last night," Lina says, "he have blood in his nose today. This is a very bad thing."

"Why? I don't understand."

"When a man is touch with poison, he bleed in the nose."

Marika's heart is pounding. "You mean, they think I *poisoned* him?"

"Yes."

She looks around desperately for Lewis.

"Missus Marika, is it true, what they say?" Lina asks. "Are you a witch?"

"A what? A witch?"

The girl nods.

"No, it's not true."

"But why you leave the mary house last night?"

"I was visiting Lew—Mr. Parker," Marika says, her hands shaking. "I needed to see him."

"But you poisoned him!" Lina has tears in her eyes.

Marika kneels down, looking directly at the girl. "Mr. Parker is *okay*. He's fine. He can't be poisoned, all right? And I need you to find him now and bring him here quickly. Tell him it's very important. Tell him what's happening and that I need his help *immediately*. Do you understand?"

"Yes. But already, I look in his hut. He is not there."

"I need you to look *every*where, Lina."

"He is gone, Missus! He go in the jungle. He don't like people to find him."

Marika hears the crowd getting louder. "You have to find him!" she tells Lina. "Please, go look for him!"

"Okay, I try!"

Marika watches Lina sprint away. A twelve-year-old girl— that's her only chance of negotiating with the crowd unless Lewis can be found. Suddenly, she regrets sending her away.

Marika sits in a far corner of the hut, waiting, praying that Lina will be able to find Lewis and return soon. Now a group of several women are heading her way from the village. As they reach the mary house, they stare up at her with fearful determination in their eyes.

"*Yu kam*," one woman says in rough Pidgin, motioning for Marika to climb down the ladder.

"*Mi laik lukim long Mista Parker,*" Marika says in return. "I want to see Mr. Parker."

They stare at each other, Marika refusing to move.

The woman motions more urgently. "*Yu kam!*"

"*Mista Parker i stap we?*" Marika demands. "Where's Mr. Parker?"

When Marika doesn't get up, the women look at each other. Finally, one by one, they start climbing into the hut. As Marika watches them surround her, she searches again for Lewis or Lina. But no one. The women beckon her forward. One woman grabs her wrist.

"*Yu kam!*"

"Where's Mr. Parker?" Marika pleads in English now. "I want to wait for Mr. Parker."

The women take hold of her arms and pull her toward the ladder, but Marika wrenches loose and leaps from the platform. She sees a path heading into the jungle and runs toward it, only to be caught by a couple of the women. They hold her tightly, and there are too many of them around her now. Too many people to fight off. She stops resisting.

As the women lead her to the village, Marika sees a large crowd moving back to protect itself from her arrival. She doesn't know what they're going to do with her or why she's being brought before everyone. It feels like a tribunal—one in which she has no hope of making her case. She fears the worst, fears the same fate as the yellow man. When she sees a man in the crowd holding a machete, her heart constricts; she might be one of those animals approaching Lewis's Kali temple in Nepal, waiting to die. The image of the temple becomes so vivid, so awesome, in her mind that she breaks free from the women and sprints back toward the jungle path.

People chase after her, yelling so loudly that she can hear them even above the increasing noise of the storm. She reaches the trail and runs down it blindly, rain pouring through the canopy overhead, clouds flickering and expiring in gasps of white light. She comes to a stream and plunges through it, recognizing the route as the one Lina showed her, that ends at Walwasi Mountain and the Magic Fire Spirits' cave. The crowd closes in behind her. She hears women screaming, voices shouting at her. Up ahead, where the jungle breaks, she sees the faint, eerie glow of the cave's entrance. She remembers what Lina told her: that no one goes past the small stone wall behind the altar that marks the border of the spirits' domain.

Marika emerges from the jungle. Before her, Walwasi Mountain rises sharply, its pale surface reflecting the last shades of dusk. Lightning cuts the sky overhead, streaking the land with light. She jumps over the wall and runs behind a large rock. There is nowhere else for her to go. Nowhere else to hide. Her pursuers reach the altar and stop, staring. As the men point out where Marika is hiding, women start wailing.

One of the men calls to her. "*Yu kam! Yu kam!*"

When Marika doesn't move, the men raise their bows. She

looks behind her at the cave entrance. She knows it's her last
hope. It's the very last place she can run. As she scrambles up the
rocky slope, the red light inside gets brighter, more ominous. She
stops. It must be true—those demons lurking within. She would
almost rather die than be consumed by them. But the crowd of
villagers creeps closer. The men are drawing their bows. She must
decide between those beings inside or the certainty of death.

Marika enters the cave.

She squeezes around a large boulder blocking the entranceway, forcing herself forward into the fiery glow, into the depth of
her fears. She closes her eyes, her body quivering. Here is that
moment Seb must have been talking about. The moment of surrender when, with nothing left to lose, she goes into the darkest
place possible—into death itself. Every instant, she expects to feel
the fire spirits' hands upon her. Every second, she expects their
flames to consume her.

She eases around the boulder, her eyes shut, her heart racing.
Such darkness now, this death without dying, her lungs breathing
air into her body, punishing her with life.

Her foot strikes an object. She jumps back, screaming, and
opens her eyes.

A carved wooden box sits at her feet.

Robert Lewis lies nearby, a small fire trailing smoke over his
body.

Marika drops to the ground, pressing her head against the
soft dirt floor, gasping and sobbing. She didn't burn up, as she
thought she would. She didn't die for her sins. Echoes reverber-
ate around her. From a chamber deeper in, she hears the anxious
squawking of bats. They know, somehow, that it's night outside,
her arrival seeming to herald the exodus of dark bodies. And
maybe it's the thick smoke of the fire choking her, or the bursts
of wind as the bats race past, but she releases a desperate sound
she didn't know she possessed.

Marika feels arms around her. Grabbing, holding her from

the whirling bats overhead. "Shh . . . shh . . ." is being whispered into her ear. She finds herself shaking violently, uncontrollably.

"It's okay, it's okay," the voice softly murmurs. "Shh . . ."

She clutches him. Lewis. She holds him against her. Even if the men outside came in, tried to kill her, she wouldn't let him go. More bats sweep by. And now there's a pounding. A thundering in her head. Something loud that wants to destroy her. She presses her face against Lewis's shoulder, screaming. Her mind becomes flooded with scenes from her past. All the horror. The bodies. Refugees with severed limbs. Children dying, dead. Her escapes. From Bodo. From Angola. From Sierra Leone. All the brushes with death. Chechyna. Sri Lanka. Bangladesh. The images seem ceaseless. All the pain she must go through, revisit, expunge.

"Shh, shh, shh . . ." Lewis holds her tighter. The wind from the fleeing bats beats against her face, preventing her from moving.

There's too much. She doesn't have the strength. She would tell Seb this, if only she could see him again. She would tell him there's too much pain. The pit is bottomless, vast. There's just too much. Her father's death. Her mother's insanity. All the suffering in the world. The death. And she couldn't do anything to stop it. Not a thing. She clings to Lewis, wanting to tell him that she couldn't save a single soul. No one could. But her screams won't stop. Her cries clog her throat, and she chokes and wails.

"Shh . . ." Lewis coos to her. He smoothes back her hair, cradles her in his arms. "Shh . . . darlin', darlin' . . . It's all right."

It seems to take forever for the bats to leave. At last, miraculously, they do. They take the memories with them, and it's silence.

Marika opens her eyes. She feels a lightness of body, as if she lost a weighty part of her. A deep, nameless part that, ironically, she doesn't miss or need. In its place is a great gap, an enormous, unaccountable space. Lewis's arms hold her more gently now, and she rests in them. Her pursuers aren't coming in. They won't come in, for their fear. And that's what the lightness is: the depth of certainty that, somehow, she's saved.

She looks around the cave. On the walls, she sees ancient pictographs of men with spears, pursuing boars and cassowaries. The dome of the cave is covered with the crisscrossed dashes of white-painted stars. A flaking moon peers from a shroud of clouds on the far end of the reproduced sky. And a multitude of little red men—the Magic Fire Spirits—swarm down from the heavens on streaks of white lightning, approaching the hunters below.

Marika catches sight of a yellow man painted near the horizon of the night sky. Beheaded, he is being carried aloft by two of the red men. She looks for herself in the drawings, sure she must be up there somewhere. She would be a white figure, a phantom figure like Lewis, but with hair of yellow fire. She would be resisting the spirit men as they tried to take her away.

Lewis's objects lie all around her. A canteen, a compass. Old shirts crumpled and blotched with mildew. A small drum of kerosene. Candles, a whole box of candles, used stumps dotting the ground. Propped on a stone is a card made by a refugee child. There is a crude magenta cross drawn on it, with the inscription GULU CAMP, UGANDA and WE LOVE ROBERT LEWIS.

Outside the women wail so loudly that Marika can hear them over the sound of the growing storm. They must think she's being eaten up, consumed by the Magic Fire Spirits for her sins.

Marika sighs. Now she knows where Lewis disappears to. And why. She watches the smoke from his fire wafting into a dark shaft overhead. He must sleep so quietly here, so completely. Few mosquitoes, little noise. Storms might rage outside, people might live in fear of gods and demons, but here the temperature is cool, the fire is warm, and there is nothing left to fear.

❧

The cave becomes Marika's new home. Lewis stops by every few days, bringing provisions, and water for washing and drinking. Marika never knows when he'll come. Sometimes it's in the middle of the night, and she'll wake to find food and fresh water; other times, he sneaks in right before dawn. His visits are short—just long enough to drop off what he's brought her, and to report on his efforts to find someone to take her back to civilization.

He already sent runners to neighboring villages to make inquiries about guides, pretending he would need such a person for himself. It's been complicated, though, as he must find someone for Marika who doesn't know about her difficulties in Walwasi. Each day, Marika hopes she'll receive news of a person who can lead her out; each day she's disappointed. And Lewis says nothing about going with her.

She feels like she's trapped in a purgatory. Sometimes, as she lies alone in the cave and stares at the pictographs overhead, she hears shouts and wailing outside. She figures it's because of her fire. She has kept it well fed, never allowing it to go out. And though it probably terrifies villagers, the flames reassure Marika that no one will come in after her, or that she'll never lose herself in the cave's darkness.

On her tenth day inside, Lewis stops by, carrying her torn pants. She's relieved to see him. His visits, however brief, are the only thing she has to look forward to.

"Any news yet about a guide?" she asks him.

"No. Here, I brought your pants—Lina washed them. They need to be sewn up, but I thought this might give you something to do." He puts a needle and a spool of thread in front of her, along with a *billum* bag of food. "How much water do you have left?"

"I've still got one bucket."

"I'll bring you more in a day or so." He examines her wood supply. The entire back chamber used to be full of logs and branches, but now it's significantly depleted. He'll have to pick an early morning to carry more wood into the cave, when no one from Walwasi will see him. But this can wait until she leaves; it shouldn't be much longer now.

"Do they ever talk about me in the village?" Marika asks him.

"Sometimes." Lewis pulls some branches free from the pile and hauls them over to the fire. "Lina misses you."

"She's a nice girl. I guess I can't ever go back to say good-bye."

"I wouldn't advise it." He throws a branch into the flames.

"So do they really think the spirits killed me?"

He nods.

Marika stares at the fire. It's almost like she *has* died. The feeling of lightness still remains. The emptied feeling.

"Has it ever bothered you that these fires in here terrify the people outside?" she asks Lewis.

He glances at her. "At least they're scared of something."

"But they don't know you're doing it."

"Look," he says, "they were scared of these spirits long before I ever got here."

He goes to the back of the cave to get more wood.

"Why did you come to Walwasi?" she asks.

"It sounded like the right place."

"How did you know?"

He gestures to the cave ceiling, to the painted stars. "Look at that. This place hasn't changed for a thousand years. It's the last true frontier." His eyes scan the pictographs. "This is one of the only places left where no one knows anything about the rest of the world."

"But why come here at all? Why didn't you just go home, instead of making everyone think you're—"

"Go home to *what*?" He glares at her. "Back home, they turn every tragedy into a Sunday night movie. All the things I used to report on, and most of it never even got mentioned on the evening news. People care more about the sex lives of movie stars than about a massacre halfway around the world. And you know why?" His eyes focus sharply on her.

"Why?"

"Because they're lambs."

She looks at him, not comprehending.

"*Lambs*," Lewis says. He sits near her, by the fire. "They've never had anything really bad happen to them. They've never witnessed a massacre. They've never been raped or tortured or seen family members shot. You know how you can tell when you're with one of those people? Because they're obsessed with what's pointless, thinking it matters. Try telling them about a genocide in Rwanda or East Timor. They have no . . . *mechanism* . . . to grasp what you're talking about. They've grown up in a world where everything horrible has been turned into entertainment, made into some goddamn movie. The only thing that wakes them up is if something awful suddenly lands on their doorstep, throwing them into the flames."

"But not everyone back home is like that," Marika says.

"Enough of them are." Lewis angrily kicks at the fire. "You think I could return to that? You come back from one of these assignments, from one of these wars, and you want to tell someone what you've seen. You just want to find someone who can understand."

He remembers his last days in Malaysia, on Tioman Island, before leaving for New Guinea. He went there because it was cheap and no one would recognize him. He needed to heal his body and prepare himself for what he was going to do. He had a friend he knew from Thailand. For a hefty price, the man would arrange to meet him at sea and take him to Papua New Guinea. It would be that easy. His crew would ask no questions.

On his last evening on Tioman, Lewis took a walk on the

beach while the sun was setting. It was one of those sunsets that had nothing to show. Just a bunch of gray clouds, with the sun straining through. It truly felt like the last day of his life. He had often wondered if people, knowing the exact time of their deaths, would view the world any differently. Would they find things more beautiful? Or take things more slowly? Or would they see, like a jolt to the soul, the entirety of their sins? Lewis felt only a seeping numbness, as if poison were filling his veins and overtaking what was left of his heart.

He can still remember the wet sand squeezing between his toes, the wind whipping across his face. The air was sultry and sickly-smelling with the ripeness of the tropics. He would call himself Mr. Parker. With no first name. If queries were made, he'd say he was from Duville, Iowa, a town that did not exist.

When it was nearly dark, he turned away from the sea and walked back to his bungalow. He had a letter to write to his sister, then one to write to the world, which he'd leave on his rented boat. People would look for him. They'd search the waves and shores. They'd go through his stuff for clues. A few might even lament. But they'd never find him.

"Back home, they make you think you have to learn all sorts of things," Lewis says to Marika. "You're supposed to figure everything out. But the truth is, there's nothing to figure out. It all just is. Here, they know that instinctively. They don't read Nietzsche. They don't debate string theory. They just wake up each day. They pray to their gods. They get sick. They die. They get well. They hope for good crops. They mourn their lost children. They're no different from anyone in the West. We all just shit, and feed, and fuck. And cry. And laugh. And get born. And fear death. But people in the West think they're special somehow. They think, because they have this thing called Science, they can control the universe. But the truth is, we can't control a goddamn thing. Not a *thing*. Death teaches you that better than anything."

Lewis stops, looks at her, waits for a response. But she doesn't know what to say. She doesn't know how to penetrate his grief.

His eyes hold hers. "Do you think I'm wrong?" he asks her. "Do you think there's anything you can control? The people here control nothing, and they know it. They wake up and wait to see what happens. They leave offerings of gratitude if the spirits have been kind. They leave blood if the spirits have been cruel. There are no mysteries, no debates. What more needs to be explained? What more understood?"

What troubles Marika is that there seems to be truth in Lewis's words. Truth, lost behind a patina of confusion and pain. As if, when looking over a brink into the depth of his soul, Lewis had spooked and stepped away, denying the entire view. He can't tell her what he saw, can only describe the outline of it. Marika knows she'd have to retrace his steps, find the place where he couldn't go on and look for herself—if she has the courage. What did he see, in that awful moment that broke him?

The question comes to her lips that she has wanted to ask Lewis for weeks.

"So why *didn't* you kill yourself?" she says, her voice quavering.

Lewis gapes at her and nods. She can tell he's thought about her question many times.

"I'll tell you why." He looks straight in her eyes. "Because I wasn't going to let God win."

For a quick, unsettling instant, his words make sense to her—but only in a deep, hidden place she's never dared to plumb.

Lewis gazes at her. "God wills everything, right? My son's death. Your father's death. What happened to me in Dili. You make it through one thing, and he has another trial waiting for you. And another, and another. God wills all of it. But I wanted him to know that no matter what he threw at me, I wasn't going to let him win. I wasn't going to let him destroy me. I raise my fist at God!" Lewis's eyes are ablaze. "I say to him, 'No matter what you do to me or the people I love, I won't let you destroy me!'"

"But God is supposed to be about love," she says. It's what Seb told her all the time, with his tone of unequivocal certainty.

"That's what they tell you," Lewis says quietly. "That's what they want you to believe. But look at those Indonesian soldiers who did those things to me, to Paulo, to little Anamaria—I'm sure they're living the good life, fucking their wives, sending their children to school, praying to their god." He throws a stick into the fire. "Will they ever pay for what they did? None of these people ever pay. It is your God of love who allows this. Your God of love champions these villains. But at least here in Walwasi"— Lewis gazes around him—"there's justice."

Lewis starts shaking, and she puts her hand on his arm. To her surprise, he lets her touch him.

"Don't you see why I couldn't go home?" The anger, she notices, has faded from his voice. "I just couldn't go back to live with those people anymore, wondering why God favored them over me. Why *my* son and not *theirs*? Why Daniel? Tell me—why Daniel?"

"I don't know," she says, tears in her eyes.

"I'll tell you why. And I learned this in Dili. I learned it in the exact moment when I didn't think I could stand the pain any longer. I'll tell you why—do you want to know?"

Marika wipes at her eyes.

"Because when it comes to some of us," Lewis says, "God has *abandoned* us."

"It's not true." Marika squeezes his arm, and Lewis holds her so tightly that he might crush her.

"God abandons us."

He presses his face against her shoulder. He runs his hand over her hair.

"You know what my worst fear was, during all that pain?" he whispers into her ear. "That I would lose my compassion."

She can only kiss him, cradle him.

"And you know what? I did."

"Leave with me," she says to him.

He doesn't respond. Instead, his hands travel over her body. He presses himself against her. God might try to take this moment from him, but he will fight to the death for just one more chance to touch her.

When she puts her hand on his thigh, he grabs her wrist and tries to stop her.

"Nothing happens," he says.

But she won't let him remove her hand. She moves it between his legs.

"Come back with me," she whispers.

As she undoes his pants, Lewis remains still. She must stroke him, wrap her legs around him, convince him that there's more. Finally, in a rush, he yanks off her clothes. He draws her body against his. But when he reaches down, he sees it's no use. There's no response. How he wants to, he tells her. But they hurt him. They took his manhood from him. His apologies come in soft words.

"Try," she says. She takes hold of him herself, gently guides him inside her.

He feels the old sensations. Exquisite sensations he hasn't felt in years. It is almost too much to bear. The ecstasy. As he moves around, his body gives a slight response. Not much. Just the slightest change. But it's enough.

He pushes and presses more urgently. And now he discovers himself collapsing, releasing into her. He clutches her, panting, losing himself.

"Come back with me," she whispers.

Lewis finally returns after their night together. He doesn't announce his arrival, just appears at the entrance of the cave, standing in the shadows, watching her. To Marika, he might be a spirit himself, coming as silently and stealthily as he does.

She wonders how long he's been there without her noticing. "You're back," she says.

He just stares at her without a word.

"Is there any news?" she asks. "Has a guide come?"

He walks toward the fire and puts down a pair of old hiking boots. "Tobo came this morning," he says.

"Tobo? I thought he left with Newlove."

"He did. But he decided to stay in the next village over. He said the people there were hiring him for something, but I got the impression he didn't like Newlove."

"Oh." Marika smiles to herself.

Lewis points to the hiking boots. "Those are mine, but I stuffed up the toes. I want you to have them. I don't want your feet getting ripped up in the jungle."

She runs her hands over them. "When does Tobo want to leave?"

"First thing tomorrow morning." Lewis looks at her. He watches the light from the fire reflecting on her face, her lips. "He'll meet you here just before dawn."

"That soon?"

Lewis throws a *billum* bag at her feet. "I've brought you some smoked meat. And there's a candle and an extra shirt. I don't have much, but if you think there's anything else you need, I can try to—"

"Are you coming with me?" she says.

He turns away from her. Lighting a candle, he heads into the back of the cave. "I've got to find you a backpack." He flings old camp items aside, dust particles swirling. "I know there's a small one somewhere."

"Lewis—"

"It was here just a week ago. Where could it have gone?"

"*Rob*—"

He stops and peers over his shoulder. "No," he says. "I'm not coming."

He finds the backpack and drops it beside her. "You can have this. Sorry about the bat shit, but if it's cleaned off it won't be so bad."

She reaches out and touches his leg. "Come with me."

"Don't do that anymore," he says, stepping away from her.

He shoves the food he brought into the pack.

"It'll be hard getting out of here," he says, "as I'm sure you already know. I hear the route to Newlove's mission is a lot easier than heading east, though you're going to hit a lot of swamps. But I'm assuming leeches are preferable to climbing over all these goddamn mountains."

She smiles. "I guess."

"Anyway, I told Tobo to follow the way Newlove went. You should still be able to find their trail."

Lewis wonders if he's forgotten to tell her anything, or if there's anything else he ought to do. He was never good with good-byes. They always seemed to demand special action from him—as if anything could possibly mitigate the fact that he'll never get to see her again. Or touch her. Or feel her arms around him. Good-byes are like small deaths.

"It's time I leave," he says.

"So you're just going to go now?" She stands up.

"Yeah, it's time." He searches for the right words. "I never got the chance to, you know, thank you for the other night."

"You don't have to thank me." She smiles, tears coming to her eyes.

"It . . . it was more than I could have hoped for. It was very kind of you, taking pity on—"

"It wasn't 'pity,'" she says.

"Well, whatever it was, I thank you for it." He runs a hand over his beard, staring at her. "I have a request to make," he says. "When you go back and write about this place—and you *will*, you know--please don't tell anyone you found me."

"Well, first of all," she says, "I've got to get out of this jungle—"

"You'll get out."

"And then, I don't know who could find you even if they wanted to."

"You'd be surprised. There *are* others like you."

"Other crazies out there?" She laughs. "Really?"

She sees a rush of pleasure spread across his face. Or it might have been the shifting light from the fire.

"Do we have a promise?" he asks her.

She looks down, unable to answer.

Sighing, Lewis picks up his empty *billum* bag. "I've got to go."

But he lingers before her. Tentatively, he reaches out and smoothes back her hair, kissing her on the top of her head. As she tries to take hold of his hand, he quickly steps away. Without another word, he limps out of the cave. He doesn't look back, and Marika can only watch him go, his graying brown hair tangled about his shoulders. She watches him long after he leaves. She sees him five, ten years later, curled up behind the muslin shroud in his hut. She watches him getting sick with malaria, getting well, his long hair turned gray, turned white. And always before him: the flame of his cooking fire, writhing out light.

Tears fill her eyes. She pounds at the dirt floor. "Come with me!" she yells, hoping he can still hear her.

There's a sudden rustling at the entrance.

"Lewis?" she whispers.

She thinks she sees a figure standing just inside the cave. Small, obscure, it watches her from the shadows, but the moment she gets up, it vanishes.

CHAPTER SEVENTEEN

The land gives way to civilization. The jungle hesitates, and stops altogether before verdant fields of broad-leafed taro. To Marika it is a dazzling sight, this new green. She pauses with Tobo on the outskirts of the fields. The sunlight touches her face. A breeze shifts her hair. Here, now, she feels her journey ending.

"Not long to June River Mission," Tobo says, pulling out a betel nut from his *billum* bag and cracking it between his teeth.

She nods and kneels down, clasping her hands and closing her eyes. Tobo glances at her absently. She has acted like this a lot on their long journey to June River, since her One Talk, Lewis, sent her demons away. Tobo has seen her running her hand around the trunks of trees. Or dipping her fingertips into streams. Once, when a green parrot landed on a branch in front of them, she stopped just to watch it, though she had seen many such parrots before. He thinks something strange has come over her. He is certain she is seeing the gods in things now.

Tobo uses the tip of his cassowary bone knife to remove some coral lime powder from a pouch around his waist, licking it off and adding a mustard seed pod to the cache in his mouth. Marika watches as he chews the concoction and spits his first red stream of betel nut juice onto the ground since they left Walwasi weeks ago. Chewing must be a luxury he reserved for this homecoming.

"Are you sure we're almost to the mission?" she asks him, having known too many disappointments.

Tobo points to a distant white house on the top of a high green hill. "*Klostu.*"

Close to.

She hadn't seen the house before. And now that she does see it, she feels a burden lifting. She knows it must be true—that there are happy endings. She feels the sunlight on her skin again. She hears the sound of women working in the fields nearby, their melodic voices drifting to her on the wind. Before her is open space. Distance. The jungle has succumbed to blue sky. During her journey here, there were entire days when not a glimpse of the sun revealed itself through the thick canopy. She had learned to accept this, just as she had accepted the weeks of wading through swamps, the water up to her shoulders. It hadn't been long before she found herself able to jog right behind Tobo, skirting muddy pools without slipping, emerging from swamps without a single leech attached to her skin. To her great surprise, she had mastered the jungle.

Down below, June River winds around a bend, its docile waters gleaming in the sun.

"Tobo," she says, "do we need to have some kind of special ceremony for the spirits?"

He studies her. "What kind of ceremony?"

"A thank-you ceremony. Because we're now at June River."

He looks at her, confused. "Of course, we are here." He chews vigorously, spitting out some betel nut juice. "The fish swims in the river. If it wants, it can go to the Sepik River. Or it can go as far as the ocean. It does not have a 'thank-you ceremony' for this." He chuckles.

"But I could have gotten sick in the jungle and died."

He studies her closer, unable to detect any bewitchment. "You wanted to come here."

"Yes."

"Now you are here." He shrugs.

She needs to explain it to him, get across what she means. More than ever, she wants Tobo to understand her.

"During our trip," she says, carefully choosing her words in Pidgin, "maybe something didn't want me to leave the jungle alive?"

Tobo stares gravely at her. "Do you mean a *masalai*?"

A demon. She smiles. It feels hopeless.

"Maybe a demon," Marika says. She shakes her head, astounded by her next thought. "Or God."

Incredibly, her whole life she'd felt like one of Lewis's "abandoned," as if she'd somehow fallen from grace. As if God—the Universe—had always been against her. When the opposite had been true, and she just wouldn't let anything good into her life.

Tobo is perplexed by the white mary. She has unaccountable tears in her eyes now. "Listen," he says to her sternly, "I will tell you a secret about your demons: they are never stronger than you."

What he just told her is very important—is, in his opinion, the most important thing he could tell anyone, and will most certainly help her—but he's not sure she heard. Most people don't hear—or, if they do, they don't believe him. Which isn't a completely bad thing: it means he will always have plenty of work as a sorcerer.

Tobo hands Marika his water gourd. "Finish," he says.

She looks again at the white house in the distance before drinking the last of their water.

"Does Newlove have a radio?" she asks Tobo.

"Yes. A radio and many things. Planes come here."

Planes. Could she really end her long journey that easily—by stepping on a plane and having it return her home? Ever since she left Lewis and Walwasi behind, she's been discovering that she has a choice about things and how they turn out, instead of allowing herself to be cast willy-nilly before the Universe. This shift has been new and exciting for her, though confusing. She often heard Seb speak with reverence of suffering, calling it a "great teacher"; he had a Christian background and liked to use the metaphor of Jesus bearing the cross. But what she should have asked him, and never did, is whether it's possible to learn through joy, instead.

She suspects that it is, and wonders why no one ever told her this. Or why people like her mother always wanted her to believe otherwise. Marika readjusts the straps of Lewis's backpack, confounded by all the possibilities before her. Why does it sound like blasphemy—that she needn't suffer? That God, the Universe, Whomever, Whatever, doesn't want that for her, and never did?

"*Yumi go,*" Tobo says impatiently, urging her forward.

Planes. If she can get herself one—have it actually pick her up from June River Mission—it would be more proof that kinder, easier roads are possible.

She has no money, though. No passport or possessions. She'll need to find someone who can help her.

Seb.

Many times during her trek from Walwasi village, she imagined talking to him again. She even imagined the first thing she would say to him: "I'm back from the dead." She wishes she could speak to him right now. Tell him everything she's learned.

Tobo starts walking at a near jog, and Marika quickly follows. The white house looms ever closer, the sunlight seeming to grow more intense.

They soon approach the gate of a small mission school. A girl wearing a navy uniform notices them and runs off to a nearby shed, knocking urgently on the door until a middle-aged man appears. It's not Newlove, Marika sees. This man wears shorts and a green, sweat-stained baseball cap over a sunburned face. He's an American; his shirt advertises the University of Nebraska.

The man walks over to them.

"Well, hello there," he says to Marika, shaking her hand.

"You've obviously come a long way." He gestures to the scratches covering her legs. Lewis's hiking boots, waterlogged and muddy, sit huge upon her feet.

"Yeah, a long way," she says. "A very long way."

"My name's Jack."

"Marika."

"Oh, yes." He considers her name. "Pastor Newlove spoke about you. You were with a Mr. Parker, I believe. In Walwasi village?"

Marika nods.

Jack greets Tobo: "*Gude, Tobo. Yu stap gut?*"

Tobo nods absently, chewing his betel nut.

Jack sighs and turns back to Marika. "So you sound like an American," he says.

"Yeah."

"Where you from?"

She's not sure how to answer. She doesn't feel like she's from anywhere yet. Here is another thing she'll have to decide. She's amazed by all the new choices—whereas before she felt pulled downstream by her fear, with no say in where she ended up.

"The East Coast," she says at last.

"You know, I've never been there. I've been all over Papua New Guinea, but I've never even seen the Empire State Building. God has surprising plans for us, doesn't he?"

Marika nods. Tobo cracks open another betel nut with his teeth and opens his lime powder pouch. He has often noticed that the white people waste too much time talking.

"I'm surprised you came from the jungle," Jack says. "That must have been rough. Visitors always arrive from the river."

Visitors. They only seem to explore the world's edges, its inlets. But Marika feels as if she's come from the very center of something, from the source. Reaching June River almost feels like arriving at the sea. It leads out, away from this land, toward home. She feels tears coming.

"How long have you been traveling in the bush?" Jack asks.

"It's been a while," she says. "Weeks. Probably a month or so. I don't really know."

She looks to Tobo and translates Jack's question into Pidgin, but Tobo shakes his head. He doesn't keep track of days like the white people. There is no sense in looking at what is behind.

Jack examines her. The muddy, ripped clothes she wears. Her dingy backpack. "Are those the only things you have?" he asks with concern.

It feels like such a long time since she lost everything—but funny how she no longer misses any of it. "Everything was stolen," she explains simply.

"Someone took all your things? Your money? Passport?" He shakes his head.

"Everything," she says.

"Well, my wife may have some clothes she could spare." Jack points to several bright pink patches on Marika's arm where the tanned skin has peeled off. "You've also got *grili*. You've got to nip ringworm in the bud, or else it spreads and scars. I've got some medicine you can put on it."

"Thanks." She absently glances at her arm.

"So are you an anthropologist or scientist of some kind?" Jack asks her.

"No."

He waits, expecting more of an answer.

"I'm a writer," she says at last. It sounds sufficient, for now.

"Interesting," Jack says. "Are you writing something about Papua New Guinea?"

Marika shrugs. It's too much talking for her. She puts her hand to her forehead, wiping the sweat away. "Sorry," she says, "I'm feeling a little faint."

"Well, why don't you have a seat." Jack gestures to a nearby bench, beneath a tree. "This sun's no good for fair complexions."

"Is Newlove around?" she asks. "I'd like to find some way to contact the States."

"Pastor Newlove's teaching right now. But he does have a satellite phone I could let you use—if you're *very* brief. It costs us a dollar ninety-nine a minute. Highway robbery." He takes off his baseball cap and dabs at his forehead with a handkerchief. "But do you want to wash up first? Do you want something to drink?"

"No, thanks. I'd just really like to use the phone now, if I can."

"Well, all right. The reception's good up here, so why don't you wait and I'll go get it."

She watches Jack trotting over to the white house. Flies land on the cuts on her legs, and she brushes them away. Newlove has a phone. She can make a call. Again, it seems too easy. Too benevolent.

She tries to prepare herself for calling Seb. She wonders if he still has the same phone numbers. Or address. It's been nearly half a year since she last saw him. Maybe he's living with another woman now—and what if she picks up? Marika must prepare herself for every eventuality. Another woman might pick up. Seb might not answer. The number might be disconnected. Ultimately, she may never get to talk to him at all.

But she doesn't want to talk to anyone else.

Marika tries to figure out what time it is in Boston. Now, in PNG, it's about midday or one o'clock. So it would be a day earlier there. And nighttime. Probably about 11:00 p.m. Usually, Seb goes to bed early—unless it's the weekend, though she has no idea what day of the week it is back home.

It's too much for her to figure out right now. She puts her hand to her forehead again and goes to the bench to sit down, leaving Tobo standing on the hilltop.

Jack quickly returns with the phone. He raises its antenna and turns it on. "Remember—keep it short," he says. "Do you know the number you want dialed?"

"Yeah."

"Okay. Shoot."

But for a moment, she can't speak. She doesn't know if Seb will be there, or if he'll even take her call. Maybe he hasn't forgiven her for the way they parted, and for what she did. As her hands start shaking, she recalls what Tobo just told her about demons.

Jack waits, concerned. In a gentle voice, he says, "Can I have the number?"

She takes a deep breath and gives him Seb's home number. Jack dials and hands the phone to her, stepping away. Marika hears a pause, a message about how many minutes are remaining. She waits, her heart racing, tears clouding her eyes. She hears a clicking sound. A phone rings. It rings again and again. Seb's answering machine used to pick up after six rings. It's four rings now. Five rings—but a pause. A click. The sound of a man saying hello: Seb.

"It's me," she says to him.

"*Who?*"

She pauses, her heart racing. She can barely speak. "It's Marika."

"*Marika?*"

"Yeah."

There's silence. Silence that lasts so long, she's scared he's hung up.

"Oh, God," he says finally. "Where are you?"

"I'm in Papua New Guinea."

"You're in New Guinea? Still?" There's another long pause. A haggard sigh. "God, I didn't know what happened to you. I've been so worried. Are you all right?"

She glances at her muddy, scratched-up body and smiles; she's actually talking to Seb again. "Yeah," she says. "I'm okay. I can't talk long, but I'm calling to see"—her voice cracks, and she wipes away tears—"if maybe you'd help me. I know I don't have the right to ask you for anything, but I didn't know who else to call."

He takes a deep breath. "Marika, what's happened?"

"It's a really long story, but I'll have to tell you later. I can't stay on very long."

"Look— what do you need?"

"Well, all my things—my money, my passport—it's all gone. I don't have anything, and I was wondering—"

"Oh, God. What's happened? Are you hurt?" His voice sounds desperate. "I've been so worried about you. You left some of your things at my place, and you never came back to get them. You said you were going to Papua New Guinea, but then I never heard from you again. No one did. No one knew where you were. It was like you dropped off the planet. We all just assumed the worst."

Marika puts a hand over her face. "I don't even know how to begin to apologize."

"And then as the months went by, I—"

"Seb, I'm *so* sorry."

"I thought you were dead. Everyone, we thought you were dead. Do you know how many people care about you?"

Unable to stop herself from crying, Marika turns away from Jack and walks off with the phone.

"I'm so sorry," she says to Seb. "I didn't have any way to contact you."

"What have you been *doing*?" he asks. "Where have you been?"

"I went looking for Lewis. And then it got really bad. Really hard. I was in the jungle for months."

"Jesus," he says. "You didn't actually find him, did you?"

She pauses. It will be the only lie she'll ever tell Seb—or the world.

"No," she says. "I never found him."

Seb sighs. Clears his throat.

"But so much has changed for me," she says. "I've realized so many things. If only I could explain it all." Marika watches a man slowly paddling his dugout canoe downriver. "I know there's nothing I can do to take back what I did to you before I left, but I just want to tell you how sorry I am."

"Marika . . ."

"You were right. I didn't want to let anyone help me. I didn't want to look at anything." She tries to steady her voice. "Look— I won't interfere with your life now. I'm sure you've moved on and you're with someone else, but I just didn't know who else to call. And actually, the truth is, you were the only person I *wanted* to call. I'm going to say something now, and I don't say it to mess with your mind or to cause you any more pain—but I just really need to tell you. Seb, the whole time I've been gone . . . the *whole* time . . . I never stopped loving you. I want to thank you for what we had together and for what you taught me."

There's a long pause. Marika waits, cradling the phone against her ear.

She hears Seb clearing his throat again. "Just so you know," he says quietly, "there hasn't been anyone else. I never . . . I haven't felt like looking. To be honest with you, the idea of losing you . . . thinking you were dead . . . it just hurt so bad. Marika, I don't know if you ever realized how much you meant to me—and *still* mean to me."

"Seb, I'm so sorry." She wipes her nose with the back of her hand.

"I kept kicking myself for letting you go," he says. "I just let you walk out of my life, when you were obviously in a lot of pain."

"No, Seb. Look what I did to you. You were right in letting me go."

"I could have been more patient. I could have been more understanding. I feel like I failed you."

"No, you didn't," she says. "It was my choice to leave. I didn't want to let anyone in. You were right. There was nothing you could have done."

"But I should have at least *tried*."

Marika thinks of Lewis, in his cave. "There was nothing you could have done," she tells Seb with certainty.

For a moment, neither of them can speak.

"So you have no money or anything?" Seb says at last. "Are you injured or sick? Tell me the truth."

"Well, I've been doing a lot of trekking through the jungle, so I'm kind of a mess right now." She laughs. "But the truth is, I'm okay. I feel good. I'm so happy to be talking to you again."

"So where *are* you?" he asks.

She looks around, smiling. "A place called 'June River Mission.' On the June River somewhere."

"Hold on—let me write this down. June River? Like the month?"

"Yeah."

"Look, I want you to stay where you are. I'm going to charter a helicopter to pick you up. What's the name of the nearest big town?"

"I'm not sure."

"Well, I'm going to hire a helicopter to get you out of there, at least. I may not be able to organize anything immediately, but I want you to wait there and call me back as soon as you can, all right?"

"Okay," she says.

"How are you calling me now?"

"I'm borrowing a missionary's satellite phone."

"Do you have the number?"

Jack approaches her, tapping at his watch.

"No," she says. "But I'll give it to you later. They want me to get off now."

"Wait," Seb pleads, "don't hang up yet. Marika, I don't want to lose you again. Can you give me the number?"

"I'll call you back with it. I promise."

"Look—I'm going to get you some money. Is there a bank that takes international wires?"

"I don't know. Probably."

"I'm going to book you a hotel room in the capital, and I'll meet you there."

"You're going to 'meet me' there?"

"Yeah. I'm leaving as soon as possible."

"Seb, you don't have a visa or anything. Look, I'm all right. You don't have to worry about me. I'm definitely coming home. I—"

"Marika," he says, his voice determined, "I'm going to *meet* you there and take you home, all right?"

Marika blushes. That the world could offer her someone like Seb—she's humbled, flabbergasted. "Okay," she says.

Jack stands in front of her, holding out his hand for the phone.

"Seb, I have to go now. I'll call you back. I promise."

"Don't forget," he says. "*Stay there,* and call me back, and get me the number of that phone."

"Okay. Seb—I love you."

She hands the phone to Jack, and he ends the call. She wipes at her eyes and smiles, looking out at the river. She notices the colors everywhere. The bright red of the flowers leading to Newlove's house. The blue sky, white clouds, green hills.

"Everything all right?" Jack asks her.

"Yeah."

She wipes at her nose, tears running down her cheeks. Jack glances shyly at her and reaches into a pocket, handing her a tissue.

Marika knows it'll be an adventure for Seb, trying to get here. She remembers her own flight across Papua New Guinea; probably, Seb will also have to fly over the Central Range of the country, and there will seem no end to the jungle below. It will reach to the very farthest points on the horizon, meeting the sky in a gray haze of space. There can be nothing like it in the world. Nothing could ever prepare Seb for just how big this jungle really is.

Without knowing it, he might even fly over the forgotten valley that hides Robert Lewis. The pain of that thought brings new tears to Marika's eyes. Just an hour earlier, she escaped his jungle. She may get sick with malaria again, but she escaped. And nothing seems as tragic to her now as being left behind in it. If she could be granted any wish, it would be that Lewis will someday, somehow, make the decision to leave.

But she shakes her head. She knows it's already too late for him. And worse: she might have died along with him.

Marika understands something now, and it feels like such a shock, such a blow, that she has to kneel down to catch her breath. It is this: no matter what tragedies in her life, no matter what horrors in the world—no matter, even, that Lewis is never coming back—she must choose happiness for herself. She *must*. Or else the pain was all for nothing.

Jack comes up to Marika. Not knowing what to do for her, he tries to help her to her feet, to console her with another tissue, but she only waves him away.

She doesn't want to miss any of this message. She wants to understand. Real courage isn't about visiting the world's hells and returning alive to tell about it—it's easy to risk her life, and even easier to get herself killed. What takes real courage is choosing to *live*, choosing to save herself at all costs. Which means looking into her darkness and pain, and figuring out how she got there, and how she can get out. Marika understands finally. She knows what to do. And she won't do it just for herself, but for the world. For all the ugliness in it. And for all the grace.

Marika hears a "Hallo!" and Jack looks behind him.

"Pastor Newlove," he says.

She nods. She knows the voice.

Marika gets up, walking with Tobo to the white house on the hill. Newlove stands on his porch, watching them, waiting expectantly. As soon as she reaches him, he rubs his tattooed elbow vigorously. She says nothing, just steps onto his porch and sits down on a chair in the shade. June River, curving around the bottom of the slope, catches glimpses of the sun. Children race each other in tiny dugout canoes. Women drift downstream, fishing for river catfish with hooked strings.

"I hope you all had a better journey this second time around," Newlove offers, swabbing his sweaty forehead with a bandanna. "My Lord, it looks like you've had some hard travel."

She fans her face with her hand, not looking at him. "It wasn't as bad coming out."

"I suspect that's true," he says. "I do find it easier leaving the jungle than going in. What are your plans now?"

"I'm going home."

"Well, I should tell you that we'll be taking our monthly trip to Angoram soon, for supplies. You're welcome to come along. There's a road from Angoram to Wewak, where you can catch yourself a commercial flight."

A village girl in a pink sun dress waves heartily at Newlove as she passes. He pats his hair and grins, eagerly returning her wave.

"Thanks," Marika says, "but someone from back home is going to get a chopper to pick me up."

"Well, if you don't mind a piece of advice, you'd do better chartering one of the Cessnas. We do have a halfway decent airstrip. Choppers are harder to come by. But either way, it does set you back several thousand dollars. I hope your friend can handle the expense." He rubs his elbow again. "It'd be much cheaper for you to go with us."

Marika nods but says nothing.

Newlove looks at the cassowary claws jutting from Tobo's nostrils. He scratches his own nose and sighs. "It sure is tough, getting out of that jungle. It usually takes me three or four weeks to return from the Central Range—if the Lord needs me to make such a trip. But now, I've only gone three times since I've been living here."

Marika shoos flies from the cuts on her legs.

"Could we have some water?" she asks him.

"You most certainly can," Newlove says. "I am forgetting my manners. Just a second."

He goes inside the house, a structure that looks like any typical ranch-style home back in the States. She takes a moment to study it. The white wood siding. Shingles. Glass windowpanes. A generator roars nearby, explaining the gush of air-conditioned air that assails her as Newlove walks inside. She finds it utterly surreal, having spent months living in huts or camping in the jungle.

She turns to Tobo. "Will you be returning to your village soon?"

"Yes," he says. "In a dream last night, I saw my older wife with a new child." He smiles and nods. "It is good sign."

"A boy or a girl?"

"It is a boy. He is a gift to me, because I did not leave you in the jungle to die. The gods are happy with me again."

"I want to thank you for guiding me out," she says.

He nods and shrugs, spitting a stream of red betel nut juice over the white railing. "Will you be coming back to my country?" he asks her.

"Maybe someday," she lies.

"I think you will miss my country."

She smiles and says nothing.

"I know things," he says. "I was told you will come back."

"By who?" She hears Newlove opening the door.

"The Magic Fire Spirits."

Newlove catches Tobo's words. "You mean those little spirit men who come down from the stars and drink people's blood?" He chuckles, handing Tobo a glass of water.

Tobo takes a sip, eyes narrowed and focused on the curve of June River.

"Now *those* are Mr. Parker's 'vampires,'" Newlove says, giving Marika her glass. She's surprised to actually see ice cubes inside.

"A hard one to love, that man," Newlove adds. He absorbs

their silence, clearing his throat. "I have to check on our school, but I'll be back. Take your time here. There's a bathroom inside. I've also got a shower"—Newlove's eyes run over Marika's body—"if you feel the need."

He leaves, and she watches him trot down the slope toward the river.

"Do you talk to the Magic Fire Spirits a lot?" she asks Tobo.

He picks out the ice cubes from his glass and tosses them into the dirt. "Of course."

"What do they say?"

"They say you will come back." He reaches into his *billum* bag. "I have something for you. I was told not to give it to you until we reached June River."

He takes out a rectangular object wrapped in a piece of canvas and hands it to her. She knows immediately what it is: Lewis's box.

"Did Lewis tell you I'll be coming back?" she asks.

Tobo shakes his head, smiling.

She undoes the string, pulling the material away. The box, finished and oiled, gleams at her. The carved cockatoo sits on a branch, staring off at a sun rising. Or perhaps setting. She can't tell.

"It's beautiful," she whispers.

Tobo points at it. "See, this is the moon here." He points at the sun. "*Mun,*" he says.

"Moon?"

"And these are the stars. *Yu opim dispela.*"

She does—she opens it. There's a note, written in a heavy scrawl. She picks it up, her eyes clouding with tears.

> *Marika, I'm going to a new place and will be gone when you read this. Don't look for me. Love, R*

She slowly closes the box. She keeps wrapping and rewrapping the canvas around it, wanting the creases to land perfectly. At last, she throws the material to the ground.

Suddenly, she remembers. "Tobo—I don't want to forget again. You need to get your mourning necklace back."

She starts to take it off, but he shakes his head.

"You must wear the necklace until it falls off. Then my sister's soul will go on."

"But I'll be flying back to the U.S. with it."

"Yes," he says. "She will know where to go."

1. What is at the heart of Marika's quest to find Robert Lewis? What does he represent to her? How does her image of him change throughout the novel?

2. How did your impressions of Seb shift throughout the novel? What sustains his relationship with Marika? What are their greatest challenges?

3. How does the spiritual world of the Papua New Guineans reflect their view of themselves and their place in the world? What universal fears and rites are captured in their beliefs? Do Marika's spiritual beliefs change as a result of her journey?

4. During her travels, Marika is often asked if she is an anthropologist or a missionary. What do those two vocations have in common with her work as a journalist? What motivates all three occupations to immerse themselves in worlds far removed from their comfort zones?

5. Kira Salak and her family experienced profound grief when her brother, to whom the book is dedicated, died in Africa in 2005. She has said that she wanted to explore themes of similar traumatic loss in *The White Mary*. How do the characters respond to tragedy? Does Lewis prove to be someone "who wouldn't let the darkness win," as Marika describes him at the end of chapter two?

6. What is Tobo's role in Marika's life? Does he give her guidance beyond geography?

7. How did you react to the villagers' belief that menstruating women are poisonous to men? Was Marika right to reject

their ritual or, as Lewis insisted, should she have respected it? What is the appropriate way to respond to another culture's traditions?

8. How is Marika affected by her family's past? How does she reconcile her own life to the legacy of her mother's mental illness and her father's tragic death?

9. Marika endures sexual exploitation many times, even at the hands of Newlove when she is dangerously ill. What is different about the way Seb treats her in bed? What does sex mean to her throughout the novel? What did impotency mean to Lewis?

10. Discuss the unique structural aspects of the novel, including the use of present tense incorporated with flashbacks. How does Salak evoke the way memory often works?

11. What do you predict for Marika's future? How will she be changed by her encounter with Lewis?

How does describing a place like Papua New Guinea in fiction differ for you from writing about it as a journalist, as you did in Four Corners, *your nonfiction account of your walk across the country? How much of the setting is invented, and how much based on your memories and reporting?*

I don't think you can write about something unless you've directly experienced it in some way. Also, readers are very intuitive; they feel when something smacks of truth. When I wrote *The White Mary,* I tried to rely on what I knew from personal experience. Though Marika endures some things that never actually happened to me, there is really little separation between my real-life experiences in Papua New Guinea (and elsewhere) and what I wrote about in *The White Mary.*

One of the book's strengths is its willingness to describe different cultures on their own terms. How did you go about writing an inner life for Tobo, a character whose life and consciousness are likely shaped by very different factors from those of any American or European?

I've always been fascinated by remote tribal cultures, seeking them out on my trips. In particular, I have a deep interest in shamanism. Tobo is the product of my firsthand experience with the shamans I've met around the world. In the West, there's a tendency to believe that we have the "right way of thinking" or the "right beliefs about things." We don't. We just have our own perspectives. Tobo was my attempt to convey a point of view that is wholly alien to our own—but one that deserves equal respect.

You started traveling to inhospitable places alone when you were twenty years old. Do your motivations for traveling to dangerous places for work overlap in any way with Marika's? Do you expect to continue working in those places?

Unlike Marika, I first started backpacking alone in places like Africa to empower myself. I needed to learn what I was capable of; I didn't yet have a sense of my potential as a woman. Still, like Marika, I was always pulled to the more dangerous or tragic places in the world, especially when I started writing for magazines. On one level, I wanted to tell the stories of what was happening to the people in those places; on another, much deeper level, I wanted to understand the reason for such suffering in the world. Now, though, I'm married. I've moved on to a new chapter in my life. I no longer feel compelled to visit places where my life would be seriously endangered.

How does the process of writing a novel differ from writing memoirs?

I find fiction writing much more liberating than nonfiction writing. I can reveal more of myself in fiction because, interestingly, readers seem to cut you more slack when they don't know what's true. Whereas nonfiction writing is a very naked process. You're putting yourself out there, and that can be pretty hardcore.

The book's main characters represent very different expressions of spirituality. What role do you see spirituality playing in the story?

The White Mary is very much intended to be a spiritual book. In the East, there are individuals called arhats. They are people who have transcended the egoic self and approach life from a state of pure compassion. My character Seb was meant to be a kind of Western version of an arhat—an example of the spiritual potential within us all. Lewis, on the other hand, grapples with sorrow, loss, tragedy. He is the person who believes that spirituality has failed him. When Marika cries for Lewis in the book, she is really crying for all people. She is crying for humanity's suffering.

Did the novel require any research, beyond your travels to Papua New Guinea? For example, are the various spiritual beliefs and practices of the tribes in the novel based on real tribes, or did you invent them?

I did do some research for the novel, but most of it comes from my own direct experience. For example, a large part of the Congo chapter was derived from events that I wasn't able to put into a magazine article. Also, like Marika, I almost died from malaria. Most of the details about Papua New Guinea tribal mythology were based on what people told me during my travels.

How did you decide on the structure of the novel, which moves back and forth in time to describe Marika's relationship with Seb, her research for the biography of Lewis, and her trip to the Congo, in between chapters on her travel in Papua New Guinea?

It was important that the main story take place in Papua New Guinea, in the present time, with Marika embarking into the unknown, the void. The book starts at a point where Marika has already thrown herself to fate, and she can't really turn back. Through the back-and-forth structure of the novel, I could show her wrestling with the consequences of the decisions that led to her present predicament.

Having traveled to nearly every continent and seen some of the world's extreme environments, what's it like for you to return home to America?

There's always a difficult period of adjustment when I first come home from my trips, especially if I've been somewhere that was really difficult or dangerous. More than anything, I always feel a rush of gratitude to be living in a country that has so much wealth, freedom, and opportunity.

Did you write this book abroad or at home?

I took a year off from my magazine writing and traveling to write *The White Mary* at home.

In your mind, what role should a journalist play when reporting on environments of great suffering?

As a journalist, I think it takes tremendous courage to witness a war or genocide or disaster. That's the dark side of life that people tend to turn away from. Still, there's a lot of sensationalistic news these days, with people's tragedies being turned into postmodern entertainment. I wince at that kind of thing because it's easy to forget that an actual person—who could have just as soon been you or me—went through something utterly horrendous. A good journalist does more than just sensationalize events or spit out facts. A good journalist allows us to *feel* another person's pain as if it were our own.

Like Marika, do you pay no attention to your gender when you travel, and are you surprised when other people do?

Yes, like Marika my gender is irrelevant to me when I go on my trips. It seems to be much more important to other people, though. When I kayaked solo six hundred miles to Timbuktu (the subject of my second book), it was nice to be the *first person* to have ever done it, not just the first *woman*. When did women become their own subspecies?

Do you think of the story as having a happy ending?

I leave it to the readers to decide.